THE
NIGHT
REMEMBERS

THE
NIGHT
REMEMBERS

Kathleen Eagle

AVON BOOKS NEW YORK

This is a work of fiction. Names, characters, places,
and incidents either are the product of the author's
imagination or are used fictitiously. Any resemblance
to actual events, locales, organizations, or persons,
living or dead, is entirely coincidental and beyond
the intent of either the author or the publisher.

AVON BOOKS
A division of
The Hearst Corporation
1350 Avenue of the Americas
New York, New York 10019

Copyright © 1997 by Kathleen Eagle
Interior design by Kellan Peck
Visit our website at **http://AvonBooks.com**
ISBN: 0-380-97521-1

Library of Congress Cataloging in Publication Data:

Eagle, Kathleen.
    The Night Remembers / Kathleen Eagle.
        p. cm.
    I. Title.
PS3555.A385N55 1997   96-46832
813'.54—dc21   CIP

First Avon Books Printing: June 1997

Printed in the U.S.A.

FIRST EDITION

RR   10 9 8 7 6 5 4 3 2 1

For my family—Eagles, Piersons, Garners, all—the full circle
of my life

With special thanks to Christopher and David:
artists, comic-book experts, boys reaching manhood, sons to be proud of

And in memory of Oliver

For winter's rains and ruins are over,
And all the season of snows and sins;
The days dividing lover and lover,
The light that loses, the night that wins;
And time remembered is grief forgotten,
And frosts are slain and flowers begotten,
And in green underwood and cover
Blossom by blossom the spring begins.

From *Atalanta in Calydon*
by A. C. Swinburne

Prologue

She had fled the madness in early spring, the time of double-edged winds.

Getting away was all she was thinking about then, that and the fact that there was a double edge to every choice. But getting away was the only way to end the whole sickening cycle of craziness she'd been trapped in, and she had done that. She could congratulate herself for it now. In the coldest, darkest hour of early morning she had made a desperate move. Through the darkness she had followed the signs and the arrows, followed the long, black getaway road. She'd fled through sleet and bitter chill, flying within the posted limits, for she could not afford to attract the attention of any lawman. She'd driven with little rest until she'd found an unlikely refuge, a cold, gray, unfamiliar, end-of-the-world place, and there she'd taken a room.

Minneapolis, Minnesota. Who would ever guess?

The getaway was complete. *For winter's rains and ruins are over, and all the season of snows and sins.* Swinburne, if Angela remembered correctly, and she was sure she did, for she'd become inti-

1

mately familiar with the few things she'd brought along with her. A few plants rooted in pots of soil from home, a few pieces of ordinary clothing, a few of her favorite books to help her turn off that dripping faucet of fear in her head. Her dog, Stevie, of course, sitting beside her now on the park bench they'd taken to occupying regularly on sunny mornings. She scratched the Yorkie's blond head, smiled when the dog seemed to smile, and reminded herself that springtime and sunny mornings had a way of putting dreary frost and fear on the run.

Blossom by blossom the spring begins.

She wanted to be done now with living in fear. She had to be. She had more pressing concerns, real concerns, like earning a living and finding a place to live. Angela Prescott was unemployed for the first time in her life since she graduated from college, and she was basically homeless. A room in a motel was not a home, and Angela was a homebody. A nester. Once she found work, she'd move into an apartment. Then things would be fine. She'd make them fine.

For now it seemed appropriate that she'd taken to spending at least part of her morning on a park bench, the traditional haven for the bummed-out. Sitting with her back to the nearest street corner, she'd learned to ignore the hurry-up-and-wait at the intersection, the revving of an engine, the blast of a horn. Beneath the spring-green canopy of oaks and sugar maples, she sipped her morning coffee through a hole in the plastic lid of a paper cup and applied her once imperious red pencil to narrow columns of small print. *Wanted*, she reminded herself, also meant *opportunity*.

She knew the Classified section of the Minneapolis *Star Tribune* better than she knew the city or anyone who lived in it, with the exception of one albino squirrel. Pinky, she called it, because that was the best she'd been able to come up with since she'd imposed strict restraints on her imagination. No more shying away from shadows, no more false alarms. Living in fear was no way to live. She'd called the night clerk at the Drop Inn Motel and reported strange noises for the last time. She was putting her mind to work on the important business of getting on with her life.

She knew it would help to make friends with at least one human being, but that was a tall order for Angela. Squirrels were easy. She had earned Pinky's trust with a few pounds of peanuts. Stevie still barked at other squirrels, but not the white one, and after two weeks of the same routine, Pinky knew all about the bounds of Stevie's leash.

Animals were easy. People were something else.

She'd chosen Minneapolis because she didn't know anyone here. No one in Minneapolis knew her. She had come to begin her life anew, which meant new identity, new home, new occupation. Knowing just one person might be an asset in finding the home and the job, but knowing meant being known, and she could not afford to be known by the wrong person.

She had considered Chicago. It was big, and it was a good distance from the upstate New York community she'd called home all her life, but her college roommate lived there. Chicago would be one of the first places he would check. She had absolutely no connections in Minneapolis, no connections to Minnesota whatsoever. She had taken a random shot on a dark, sleety morning, surely a move that would be hard to trace.

But the man she'd fled would certainly try. He had turned her life into a nightmare, and there was no reason to hope that her mere disappearance would deter him from persisting in his game. He would glory in the search. He would use his boundless resources, and he would tell his endless lies. He would make her out to be the irrational one, and he would convince anyone who cared that he had only her best interests at heart. Even though their two-year relationship was over—a decision he claimed to have made himself—he would profess to care about her, to worry about her still, and he would plant the notion that she was, in her present "paranoid" state, a danger to herself.

People believed him. She accepted that now. He was who he was. She had to be careful, for a while at least. By this time her sister had gotten the note that explained nothing, promised nothing, revealed nothing except her decision to leave. The surest way to blow a secret was to tell Roxanne. Now that Angela had gotten away, she had to stay away. This was a move that had to be successful the first time, the one and only time. She couldn't manage a clean getaway again. Not as long as Matt was obsessed with the idea that she could not leave him. Besides, as unbearable as his clandestine harassment had become, removing herself so completely had still been a difficult choice to make. For the time being, she was giving up everything she'd worked for, everything she knew.

Except Stevie. The dog perked its moppet ears and watched Pinky scamper up the craggy trunk of an old oak, turn, and race down again. If the squirrel was showing off, the dog gave no sign of being impressed. Pinky expected a reward, and this time he took the peanut right from Angela's hand.

"Bit-chiin," said a small voice, startling Angela from behind. Belatedly, Stevie gave a warning yap. Angela looked up just as a small boy dressed in huge clothes climbed over the back of the bench and perched on the backrest, planting tattered low-top Converses on the seat beside her. "You got a pet squirrel?"

"Not exactly a pet. More like a friend." Angela scooped her dog over a little closer, thinking the boy's clothes were baggy enough to conceal a gun or a knife. Stevie gave the boy a quick sniff test, then wagged her tail. He smelled like a dog's favorite kind of kid—sweaty, unwashed, ready to play.

The boy braced his elbows on the knobby knees peeking out beneath baggy Bermudas cut from a pair of what must have been his father's old jeans. "You done with the comics section?" With a jerk of his chin and a quick pooch of his lips, he indicated the pile of newspapers next to his foot.

"Oh, sure." Harmless enough request. Angela pulled out the full-color pages and handed them to him. "Do you have a favorite strip?"

"Not anymore, but I like to see what they got goin'." He unfolded the section and perused the first page. "All the good ones checked out. First 'Bloom County,' then 'Calvin and Hobbs.' There's nothin' left." He snapped the pages open, scanned the spread, then shook his head. "I'm canceling my subscription."

"So am I, just as soon as I find a job and . . ." She thought better of saying *a place to live.* "Well, a job."

"What kinda work you do?"

"I'm a . . ." Teacher, but she had to get used to saying something else. She couldn't apply for a teaching job. Not this year, anyway. Sending for her credentials would put Matt right on her trail. "I'm quite flexible, actually. A woman of many talents."

The boy's black eyes glittered with infectious vitality when he smiled. "Me, too. A man of many talents. For one thing, I find jobs for people."

"Really?" He looked like a ten-year-old, talked like an adult. As small and scruffy as he was, there was something about this boy that made his claim seem almost possible. "None of my talents seem to be very salable right now. I'm new in town, and I don't have any references. If you saw my résumé, you'd say, 'Don't call us; we'll call you.' "

"Can you wait tables? I know where there's a job for a waitress."

She shook her head, chuckling. "I have no experience."

"You've been to restaurants, right?" She nodded, still smiling indulgently. "So you've got some experience. How hard can it be?"

Good question. Anyone who came looking for her would not be looking for a waitress. "I do need a job."

"If they hire you, I get a finder's fee."

She admired his pluck. "How much?"

"Two bucks."

"That's fair." Waiting tables was right at the bottom of her list of desirable jobs, but what the heck? This whole situation was only temporary. "Are you going to introduce me?"

"No way. You want the job, don't you?"

"I was hoping you had an in with the management."

"I get in, they show me the way out." Quick as her squirrel, the boy hopped off the bench. "For another buck I'll watch your dog for you while you apply for the job."

From a branch above her head Pinky chattered, protesting a premature end to the handouts.

"Right now?"

"I was just by there, and I know the sign's still up. It might not be there tomorrow."

Angela gathered her papers, slipped Stevie's leash over her wrist, and dragged herself off the bench. She'd been turned down at two offices for lack of references. "Show me where this place is," she said with a sigh, thinking, Waiting tables.

Waiting tables. Her ego was in big trouble if she couldn't get hired to balance a tray and do a little arithmetic. She'd been a cashier in a grocery store for a couple of summers. Maybe that would count for something. She tossed her cup in a trash barrel, hesitated for a moment, then heaved the newspaper in after it. She had a feeling that today's best promise was dancing in her new friend's thoroughly engaging eyes.

"Is it . . . I mean, do they serve good food?"

The boy shrugged as though the question were completely irrelevant. "It's probably okay when it's hot."

From a bench not far away, Jesse Brown Wolf watched the charming, curly-haired ragamuffin lead his new friend down the garden path. The *park* path. Same thing, with fewer flowers. In another week the spindly petunias that had just been planted near the sidewalk at the far end of the path would be trampled. The kid was one hell of a good hustler. A Minnesota angler. But the woman was a pretty fish who clearly belonged in still, safe waters. Some big glass aquarium in a cool, dim-lit restaurant. He wondered why she'd be looking for a job in a downtown greasy spoon. Not that it was any of his business. He just wondered.

He knew the boy. Part black, part Sioux, all wild imagination. The boy's mother came from Jesse's reservation in South Dakota.

Just plain wild, that one. The kid was on his own too much of the time, just like too many kids were these days. Somebody ought to be trying to look out for them a little bit. Somebody who had the heart to care.

But Jesse Brown Wolf had no heart left. He wasn't sure just what was keeping him alive. The devil, maybe, or his next of kin—a thought that brought to mind a play he'd seen long ago, when he was in school. He'd thought the best part was the ghost, wandering down the aisle of the auditorium and onto the stage like the lost, tormented soul he was supposed to be, doomed to walk the earth until he'd paid for his sins. Jesse remembered feeling sorry for the poor wretch, back when he'd had a heart to feel sorry with. If he had one now, he'd use it to feel sorry for himself.

Just as well he didn't.

He watched the two cross the street together. The woman was cautious, heeding the traffic signals, watching for cars. A breeze caught her pale green skirt and made it look like a parachute afloat on a warm updraft. Walking backward in front of her, the boy was talking a mile a minute. His gestures and his animated face made Jesse smile, just a little.

The kid had heart, and plenty of it. He deserved a break, and he deserved it now, while it could still make a difference in his life.

He deserved somebody who cared.

P ain drifted over him quietly, like a veil of madness. Or maybe it was madness that claimed him, like all-over pain. It didn't matter anymore. Pain and madness were one and the same. He closed his eyes, settled back against the cool earthen wall of his underground refuge, and let the cruel clowns take him. Iktome, the spider. Old Man Coyote. His kindred spirits, foolish and unkind. Like them, he accepted the pain, thrived on it, understood it better than any other sensation that had ever tried to mess with him. Pain was a sure thing. It came and went, and that was that.

Strange night, he thought. The air aboveground was stagnant, heavy with steam from sidewalks baked earlier by the August sun. Belowground it was heavy with earth's dampness and her own piquant scent, but it was cooler.

Restless night, he thought. The kind that trudged across the sky on slow, cumbrous feet.

Hot, heavy, sensuous night. Like a lover's kiss.

In your dreams, he thought. He could hardly remember the last time he'd kissed or been kissed. Except, of course, by Mistress

Pain, smacking her nettling lips on the backs of his eyeballs.

He hung on, anticipating the critical signal, the one that always blasted him over the threshold, beyond even his cruel mistress's reach. A single gunshot, the one he dreaded, the one he was doomed to hear over and over again. Like the crash of cymbals, it reverberated beyond the crescendo of his pain. Beyond reason, beyond light and dark, beyond memory. Beyond the gunshot lay facelessness, namelessness, blessed oblivion.

"Hey."

The voice hovered somewhere above the chink in rocks that was the entrance to his subterranean asylum—his private haven or his hellhole, depending on what was going on in his head. He recognized the voice. He knew the kid it belonged to, the one who had followed him one night after he had scared the bejesus out of a couple of smart-asses who'd picked the wrong time to cross him. He couldn't remember how long ago it had happened, how he'd let his guard down on his way back to his refuge, how much the boy had seen. Couldn't remember much of anything right now. Didn't care to try.

"It's me, Tommy T. Sorry to bother you again, but you're the only one I can trust. Are you down there?"

Small voice, raised just a notch above its own fear. Respectful. Never came any closer. Never invaded the secret hole in the rocky river bluff. Smart kid.

"I haven't told nobody. I swear. Nobody knows about this place but me. And I wouldn't bother you now except . . ." Leaves rustled. Rubber soles scraped the camouflaged beam that framed the small entrance to the underground chamber. "Except you've gotta come."

He didn't have to do anything. "Not now."

"You've *gotta* come now. Somebody's gonna get killed."

The voice was too soft, too tender, and too damned desperate. Just the kind of sound he could not long endure. "Call a cop."

"Yeah, right." The cynical chuckle gave way to a boyish whine. "C'mon, man. My brother Stoner's hangin' out because

THE NIGHT REMEMBERS ~

of the dogs. He just wants to see the dogs fight. But there's this one dude, I think he's packin'. I *know* he is. He's been tellin' around that he's got a piece and that his dog don't lose, you know what I'm sayin'? All you gotta do is show up and they'll all be—"

"Not now."

"Not now, not now," the boy mimicked impatiently. "Somebody's gonna get *dead* now. Now, man, right *now*. You gotta—"

The blast tore through his head and shattered him to the marrow. It was all he could do to contain the sound of it inside the raw pipe that was his throat, echoing within the cavern he carried in his head. It took him a moment to collect the pieces of himself and reassemble them into something that walked and talked. The shock waves were still bouncing within him, making his skin tingle as he applied white clay to the lower half of his face. The mud soothed him. His tongue flicked over his lower lip, tasting his own sweat mixed with the salt of the earth.

"Please. You've really gotta come now."

He rose wearily. The desperate voice flushed him out of his hole. They'd been through this before. He knew the kid couldn't leave him be. The couldn't-be child would never give the used-to-be man any peace until he emerged and followed and scared off the threat, one beast to another.

Anything for a little peace.

He wore a low hat and a high collar. The boy had never been permitted to see his face. No one had. He'd learned the art of camouflage long ago, in another life. He hid everything but his eyes. He knew the power of his eyes. Glittering, startling, mesmerizing power. It was power derived from detachment, power that fed on pain, but it was power nonetheless.

He followed the boy, who scrambled over the rocks, occasionally claiming a handhold as he navigated the rugged embankment on short, quick legs. At his age, the boy's agility was his best defense on the city streets. That and his wit, which seemed plentiful. It wouldn't be long before he'd start looking for something else, some deadly edge, but for now the boy believed in an ally. And for now the ally obliged, just so that the boy would give him some peace. This boy and all the others who haunted him. A little peace wasn't too much to ask.

He followed, his long-legged stride easily keeping pace behind the boy's choppy jog. Up from the cliff that banked the Mississippi River, through the moon-drenched maples and oaks of a remote city park, across West River Road to the network of back streets and alleys they both knew well, dodging the cloying orange pools of sodium-vapor streetlight. As they neared the empty lot between two warehouses, Tommy T slipped into the shadows, which was exactly where he'd been instructed to stay put. Out of sight of the cluster of boys who thought it was O.K. Corral time. No dusters. No shotguns. Just boys and their dogs.

Heads turned as the stealthy gate-crasher approached. The prospective combatants, straining at the ends of their chains, stopped growling at each other. The flop-joweled pit bull bristled. The Doberman-cross with the spike collar was the smarter of the two. He pricked his ears and came to attention, sensing the score right away.

But the boys didn't. The pit bull's handler postured arrogantly. "Who the hell are you?"

One of his smaller buddies reached up and tapped the boy's shoulder with a fist. "Just some drunk, man. Look at his face, all covered with . . . Hey, what's with your dog?"

The pit bull had gotten the signal. He hung his head, tucked his butt, whimpered softly, confirming that his canine dominance had suddenly been superseded.

The Doberman boy laughed. "Chickenshit, that's—"

"Get up here, you son of a—" The pit bull wouldn't respond, no matter how his chain was rattled. The kid—tall, lean, all of maybe fourteen—reached behind his back and pulled a .22 pistol from the waistband of his ragged jeans. The cheap Saturday-night special would do the job of "getting somebody dead" as well as the finest Austrian-made semiautomatic.

"My dog don't like winos, hey. They make him—"

"Your dog likes me fine. Take him home." Ignoring the gun, Tommy T's ally stepped closer, reached down, and laid his hand on the dog's head. The animal acknowledged him with doleful eyes. "This dog won't fight. Show's over."

"Who are you? Let me see your face." The tall boy menaced the slouch hat with a wave of his gun hand, but his voice—a little too thin, a little too loud—betrayed his uncertainty. "Go back to your cardboard box, hey."

"He's right," the Doberman handler said. "That dog's chickenshit."

"He'll fight. He don't fight, I'll put a bullet in his brain." The long, thin arm stiffened as he positioned the barrel of the gun behind the pit bull's ear. The only reaction to his move was a snicker from one of the gun toter's own sidekicks. He shot a glance over his shoulder. "What're you laughin' at?"

"You, asshole. You think that dog knows—"

"Shut your mouth," the boy ordered, waving the gun as a general caution. "You better shut your damn mouth."

The pit bull ran to the end of the chain, snapping it taut as he turned a warning snarl on his armed handler.

"The hell . . ." The boy's jaw dropped. Disarmed by his own confusion, he stared at the intruder. "Wha'd you do to my dog?"

"Your dog doesn't like guns." He snatched the .22 from the bewildered boy's hand. "Neither do I."

"Jesus."

The boy was still young enough to be impressed by someone who could growl at a vicious pit bull and have the dog whimpering as it melted into prone submission.

"Ho-ly Jee-sus."

"Now go."

They stood glued to the ground, all seven of them, peering into the shadows, trying to get a good look at his face. The gun lay in one hand. He lifted the other suddenly toward the sky. "Go on home!"

It was not the weapon but his voice and his bearing that scattered them across the weedy lot, boys and dogs, stumbling over glass and metal discards as they headed for cover. He dropped to his haunches, dismantling the handgun with practiced hands. Separate, the pieces were harmless, and separate they would stay. He stared at them, lying there in his big hands—the magazine, the short barrel, the grip, the small bullets. The hard knots in the back of his neck throbbed, reminding him of the battle he'd waged with his most formidable enemy earlier. Mistress Pain, his antagonistic lover. His fingers tingled, fresh from touching her, and now this. Cold steel barrel, shapely trigger, missile made to gouge a bloodletting hole. Slam-bam.

Slam-bam. He closed his eyes and let himself feel it. Heavenly Jesus, how bad it could hurt. He squatted there for a long time, staring and throbbing, his body shielding the means to disaster.

Somebody with short legs and a good share of nerve ran up behind him and hissed in his ear. "Come quick."

He shoved the metal pieces into his pockets and tugged on the droopy brim of his hat as he rose over the boy who wouldn't be satisfied. "What am I, your—"

"You gotta help her."

"Get outta my face, kid." He backed away. "I'm all done for tonight. Find yourself a cop."

"No cops, she says. She's hurt bad, but she won't let me..." The boy's desperate lunge took him by surprise. Small hands clamped his jacket sleeve. He tried, but he couldn't shake them off. "Please, she's a nice lady."

He was in no condition to think too much. Dimly he wondered whether the boy knew that. He allowed himself to be hauled across a street corner and into a dark alley. Beside a Dumpster that reeked of greasy-spoon garbage, the nice lady lay crumpled in a heap of slender but seemingly disjointed arms and legs. She looked dead. He'd found women looking dead and lying in alleys before, and he knew how to determine whether the appearance was a reality. This time it wasn't, and he was glad only because

THE NIGHT REMEMBERS ~

he didn't want to have to deal with a dead woman just now. Not that he had time or effort to spare for a live one. Or an injured one, which was what her soft groan suggested.

"Hey, lady, you, uh . . ."

When she opened her eyes, he drew his hand away from her delicate neck, but not quite quickly enough. She gasped in terror and tried to lift her head. "It's okay," he told her as he patted her shoulder. He didn't want to touch her again, but he had to, just to reassure her. He didn't want her screaming. "I won't hurt you. I didn't do this to you."

"Don't," she moaned as she turned her face away.

"How bad is it?" he asked gently. "What happened?"

She covered her face with her arm. "He's going to kill me."

The boy spoke up. "I think she got in the way, is all. She was comin' out of the café, and they came crashing through." His arms windmilled, imitating the collision and the melee he'd witnessed. "They ran into her, and they was pissed anyways, so they just . . . they hit her just to be hittin' somebody, is all."

"Same guys?"

"I dunno. I mean, it happened real quick. I couldn't do nothin'." He clasped his hands behind his neck and cast a furtive glance toward the street. He swallowed convulsively, close to tears. "I couldn't do *nothin'*, man. That's why I ran to get you."

"You can get to a phone and call—"

"No." Now it was the woman clutching at his sleeve, her grip as desperate as the boy's. "Please. Just take me . . ." Her hand slid away, the strength of her plea quickly fading. ". . . home."

"Where's home?" In the dim light he couldn't assess the damage, but there was some blood. He slid his arm beneath her shoulders and tucked her head into the crook of his elbow. When she didn't answer, he looked up at the boy. "Where does she live?"

"I dunno, exactly." Tommy T squatted, leaned in close, and whispered, "I could find out, prob'ly, but . . ." He touched the fine hair that curled against the side of the woman's neck, then jerked his chin, indicating the back door next to the Dumpster. "She works here at this café. I sorta helped her find this job last spring, and she gives me food sometimes."

She didn't weigh much. He discovered that as he lifted her off the gravel. A sharp edge bit into the back of his hand. Glass, probably. "You need a doctor, lady."

"No doctor." She filled her fist with the front of his jacket and hung on like a cat climbing a curtain as he stood up with her. "No hospital. Please. Just a few . . . blocks to . . ." Her head flopped forward, pitching her face against his chest. Her warm breath caressed him in quick puffs.

He tried to help her find footing. "Can you walk?"

"I can."

She couldn't. He was all that kept her standing.

"Somebody sees her like this, they'll think you done it," Tommy T whispered.

The kid was right. He tried the door to the café, but it was locked. Shifting her in his arms, he eyed the back step.

The boy read his mind. "You ain't gonna leave her, are you?"

"I got no place . . ." She was clutching at him blindly again, trying to find a handhold around his middle. He tried to hoist her, prop her up, but her legs had turned to rubber. He sighed and picked her up in his arms. "She needs help."

"You can help her," the boy said. "She don't want no doctors and no cops. You gotta help her."

No doctors, no hospitals, no cops. Three of a kind.

But maybe the trio huddled in the alley were three of a kind, too.

He nodded toward the dark end of the alley. "You make sure the way is clear."

S trange night. Hot and heavy, like a lover's kiss.

In your dreams, she thought. Angela had never experienced a real lover's kiss. She was as certain of that now as she was of her own name. More so. But she knew the meaning of *strange*, and she was no stranger to hot and heavy, not where the weather was concerned. The Land of Ten Thousand Lakes was turning out to be one humid place to spend a summer.

Sultry weather brought the weirdness out of the greasy woodwork at the Hard Luck Café. It had started out weird during the dinner rush, when one apparently well-dressed diner had confided to her that he wasn't wearing underwear. She'd almost said, "So what?" or, "Welcome to the club." *Almost.* She aspired to be a wisecracking waitress, but she wasn't quite there yet. After that she'd reheated one woman's mashed potatoes three times—"just the mashed potatoes, dear, not the cole slaw"—turned down an offer to be reconceived—"not just reborn, sister, but reconceived"—and collected a twenty-dollar tip just for complimenting an old man's handlebar mustache.

At closing time it was just her and Deacon Peale, the cook. As always, Deacon asked her to go out for "a little unwinding," and as always, she declined. *Almost* always. She'd gone along with him once, and once was enough. Deacon's idea of a "happenin' place" consisted of smoke, tap beer, pool, and wrestling on TV. As usual, then, they went their separate ways, out separate doors. But on this weird night they didn't go out their usual doors because Deacon had forgotten his key, so Angela locked the front door behind him, turned out the kitchen lights, and went out the back. She locked that door, too.

She didn't see anything unusual. She didn't hear anything until it was too late to get out of their way. The first one knocked her down, but she bounced back pretty quickly. She'd barely managed to plug her whistle into her mouth when a wrecking ball crashed into her side, popped the whistle from her lips, and left it dangling uselessly from the cord around her neck.

Use the pepper spray. She fished it out of her pocket, turned, and fired. But her aim was poor. Too high.

"Damn! Bitch!"

A head rammed her in the belly, knocking the wind out of her. She fell back against the door.

"Get back here! This bitch is trying to—hey!"

Angela tried to brace herself between the wall and the Dumpster as her attacker rounded up his friends. Somebody suddenly bopped him from behind, then skipped away. A dog snarled. More shuffling, more punches thrown on the fly. Rough bricks chewed at Angela's back as she inched it down the wall.

"Yeah, you better run, you chickenshit!"

She wasn't part of this. Clutching her middle and gasping for breath, Angela tried to wedge herself behind the Dumpster, hoping she wouldn't be missed if she slipped out of sight.

But the fearsome little shadow rounded on her again. "Damn you, bitch." He was shorter than she was, but stronger, certainly quicker.

He jerked her away from the wall. He had help throwing her to the ground. "Look what you done. Fuck!"

"Did she mess with you, Chopper?"

"Hell, yes!" She was up on one arm, but he kicked that out from under her, grabbed her hair, and slammed her head against the wall. "Practically blinded me."

"You know who you're messin' with, bitch?" It was another voice, another blow to her head, her face, another kick. She tried to protect herself with her arms, but the assaults were coming from every direction, and she was seeing spots and stars.

"You want me to turn your dog on her?"

"You're one lucky bitch. That dog don't deserve no meat tonight." He kicked her again and again, grunting with satisfaction each time. "And you're gettin' off easy. Grab her shit and let's haul ass."

The light at the end of the alley blurred. Angela listened to the retreating footsteps, mostly tennis shoes. Kids. Punks. Thugs. God, *kids!* Angela tried again to pick herself up, but the alley tipped beneath her. Up was down. She was shaking badly, disoriented, head hurt, couldn't breathe, couldn't . . .

"You okay, Angela?"

"Don't!" Hurting everywhere, she recoiled at the touch of another hand. She hadn't heard anyone coming, couldn't focus, couldn't tell . . .

"It's me, Tommy T. You okay?" The voice was close, but then it drew away. "I'll call somebody."

"No!" She grabbed for the voice and got a handful of T-shirt. "No police. I'm okay, just dizzy. Help me up." He tried, but he backed off when she yelped in pain. "Oh, God. Oh, God. No hospital, Tommy T. If he's looking for me, can't . . . the police . . . can't let them find out . . ."

She asked him not to leave her alone, but he did. She thought he did. She felt alone. She felt sick and scared. She fought for consciousness, for control of her body, but she was losing the battle to bright flashes and black blobs, dancing in and out of her head. She was going to be sick. She didn't want to be sick. Sick was unattractive, and unattractiveness attracted unwanted attention. No sense.

Nonsense. *Just take me home.* No policemen. No doctors. No questions. It's not far. Just take me home.

"Can you walk?"

It wasn't the boy's voice. She groaned, protesting the intrusion. She could walk. Of course she could walk. She had to get up and get going, get out of there fast, damn her wobbly legs. He . . . they, *somebody* was going to hurt her again.

"Make sure the way is clear."

She was riding on something, in something. A cradle, the curl of a wave. She called the boy's name, and someone hushed her. A deep, demanding whisper. Not the boy's voice, not the one she trusted. She was lost; that much she knew. Like Alice, she had fallen down a deep, dark hole.

Dark place, deep, dark voice.

Her head hurt. That was from the thing that said, "Drink me." Her stomach hurt. That was from the stuff that said, "Eat me." She could smell something minty. She could feel something warm and wet on her face. She couldn't see much, couldn't get her eyes to make much sense of anything. Flickering candlelight. A painted face in the shadows, white face, clown face with eyes that trapped the flame. Jewellike eyes in a strange watercolor face.

"Can't have you dying on me," the voice said.

She'd come too far to die. Only a headache, she said, eyes heavy and hurting. She sensed compassion abiding with her in the darkness, staying beside her in the hole. Close. Close walls. Close attention, close care. Jewel Eyes comforted her. She fought her way though cobwebs and gloom, through some boundless curdling swamp. She fought for glimpses of those eyes, for their reassurance, which she returned in kind. She promised she wouldn't die. He promised he wouldn't let her die. And he didn't. Her Jewel Eyes kept her in a small, warm cocoon, and he cared for her.

In her dreams.

*　　*　　*

He'd never brought anyone into his dark refuge, and he was a fool for doing it now. But he'd been a fool over lesser things. The boy promised not to follow and not to hang around, especially during daylight, when he could easily draw unwanted attention. He offered to check in, to be a runner, to help in any way he could, which was good. The boy had gotten him into this, after all. The question of trust, at this point, was settled. The hideaway had been discovered but not violated. The boy had proved his integrity.

Just taking her through the small opening in the rocky embankment proved tricky. He lowered himself feetfirst, pulling the woman in after him with the boy managing her lower half, like two firemen handling a hose. "Wait right there," he told the boy. "I have something for you to do."

"A mission?"

"A mission."

If that's what the kid wants to call it, he told himself, why the hell not? The word fit fine with the rest of the scene they'd been building together, each in turn throwing in some hokey element. He'd spoken few words when the boy had first discovered him, and those he'd virtually growled. Since that time, he'd perfected the voice, so that it didn't leave him with a sore throat.

"There's stuff I need, and I'm not even sure . . ." Traditional stuff. Old ways. No doctors or cops. That left the old ones. "I know someone we can ask. Just wait there."

"Ain't goin' nowhere without orders."

He shook his head over the boy's fervent enthusiasm. Under other circumstances he might have allowed himself to be amused. But he was cradling a battered woman in his arms, carrying her down the dark tunnel that led to the place where he lived. Taking another step, adding another bit of folly. He ought to let the people up there take care of their own. If anyone caught him at this, they'd lock him away and throw away the key. If anything happened to her while she was in his care, he'd probably end up doing it himself, locking himself away from humanity entirely, sealing up the portal to their world and giving it up for good. He was about half a step away as it was, and his hold on that half step was tenuous at best. This was one hell of a lot to ask, but only he knew the full extent of his risk.

He needed no light to find his bed, but once he'd settled her there, he lit several tall tapers, hoping the candlelight would reassure her should she awaken.

He took quick inventory of the injuries he could see without undressing her. They'd beat her up pretty bad. When he spoke to her, she responded. Didn't make much sense, but she responded. Her skin was cool to the touch, so he wrapped her in a blanket. The boy's first errand involved a name, an address, and a message. He wrote the message in Lakota, then made his way back through the tunnel to the door.

"You still there?"

"Right where you told me to stay," the boy reported.

"What name does the woman go by?"

"Angela."

"Angela," he repeated, testing the name out quietly and half smiling, thinking he'd gone out to break up a fight and ended up toting an angel home. He tucked the note into a handmade envelope with some cash and handed it out through his hole in the earth, his angel-swallowing hole. "Where I'm sending you, you might know these people. Old couple, good people. They won't ask any questions, so you don't volunteer anything. I've written down everything I need them to know. Got that?"

"Got it."

"They don't know about this place. You're the only one who does, and we're gonna keep it that way. Now, can you find the address on the outside? It's on Franklin Avenue, not too far from the school."

"It'll take me ten minutes to get there, max."

"That's if you cut across the lot behind the warehouse. Better stay away from there, take your time, play it safe."

"It's after curfew," the boy reminded him. "I'll be runnin' the gauntlet. Don't worry. I'll get there and back without being seen. I know how."

"Take off, then."

He could have sworn that was exactly what the boy did, straight into the night sky. He heard a little scrambling, and then all was quiet. He went back to his patient.

His *patient*. Holy Jesus, what was he thinking? He knew CPR, some first aid, some traditional remedies his Lakota grandmother had taught him way back when, but he had no idea whether any of that would serve her needs. Who was looking for her, and how bad was the threat? Bad enough for her to risk depending on his care? He knew why *he* avoided cops. He knew why the kid did. But this woman could have stepped off a TV screen or the pages of some magazine you'd buy in a grocery store. Pure mainstream middle-class wife, mother, minivan driver material, this one.

And he was going to have to take her clothes off. Some of them, anyway. Her pink uniform was torn, and she was all cut up and bruised and God knew what else. He put a cold compress over the part of her face that was already puffed up like a bloated carcass. Then he drew warm water from the solar collector he'd rigged up in the rocks that formed part of his roof and poured some into a small pot, to which he added a handful of dried herbs. The rest of the water went into a basin with soap and a soft cloth. Cleaning her up and disinfecting her wounds with what he had on hand was a place to start.

"Angela?" he whispered close to her ear as he changed the compress.

One eyelid fluttered. The other was swollen shut. "Who are you?"

"Nobody you know. You know Tommy T, though, don't you?"

"My friend," she muttered, groaning. "My only . . ."

"He asked me to help you. Said you . . ." She whimpered when he touched her injured arm. He drew back quickly, as though he'd been singed. "If you want me to get you to a doctor, I will."

"No, please." She caught his hand. Her fingers were cold, slight, trembling. "Your face is . . . I can't see it."

"It's nothing special," he told her, wondering how he must look to her, still smeared with the clay paint he'd chosen to hide behind. Her efforts to get that one eye open almost broke his heart. "Just a face."

"Clown face," she whispered, clinging desperately to his hand. "Love the clowns. Best part of . . . Are you a clown?"

He probably was. He winced at the thought as he gently swabbed her face with soap and water. She tried to turn away, but he persisted in cleaning her face and the cuts on her arms. She sucked her breath between her teeth when he applied anti-septic.

"Sorry. That stings, I know." He leaned close and blew on her gashed skin. "Better?"

"Eyes like Baltic amber," she said, peering at him through one slit. "Jewel eyes."

"You're dreaming." He didn't know what she was talking about. Jewels were out of his league. He started unbuttoning her shirtwaist dress. "Tell me where you feel pain so I can help. I won't look at anything you don't want me to see, but you've gotta tell me—"

"Head hurts." She laid claim to his hand again and guided it to the back of her head. "Here."

She had a lump the size of a wren's egg and just as delicate. He touched it gingerly. Her hair was a little sticky, but she wasn't bleeding much. A goose egg was usually a good sign. He'd heard that somewhere. He chose not to remember who'd said it, but he'd been through the door marked EMERGENCY more times than he cared to count. He figured she had a concussion, which could be no big deal, or it could be fatal. He was counting on the former.

"I feel sick," she warned.

He helped her sit up, held her head, stroked her hair, grabbed a tin basin. Not much he could do for a concussion except watch for the bad signs, give her something to soothe her stomach. The vomiting left her shaken and clinging to him. He took a deep breath and held her until the retching stopped and the trembling subsided. Then he coaxed his tea down her throat, stroking her with careful hands and soft words.

The effort left him shaken when he sat back and looked at her, really looked at her lying there in his bed. He hadn't been this close to anyone in a long time, and his visceral quaking was merely the proof. He sat on a straw cushion and leaned back against the woven willow backrest as he drank what was left of the tea. He didn't need any of this. Not the kid, not the woman, not the intrusion into his life, such as it was. It *was* a life, and he'd built it from scratch, pebble by pebble. He had his obscurity. And when the pain came he had his dark, silent refuge. It was a strange way to live, but it was a life.

A peppering of loose pebbles echoed in the air shaft, warning him that something was stirring overhead. He climbed to the entrance and waited until the boy announced himself.

"I had a hard time gettin' the old grandpa to come to the door," Tommy T reported as he handed the canvas bag down blindly, as though he made regular deliveries to a hole in the ground. "Some of this is just, like, bandages and food, right?"

"Right."

"How's Angela?"

"She's resting. I think she'll be okay."

"You sure?"

He wasn't about to repeat himself. Nothing was ever for sure.

"You were right," the boy went on. "I said I was just a runner and didn't know nothin' about what was in the message, and nobody asked no questions, nothin' about you. You know what? I know that old guy from school."

"A lot of people know him. He practices traditional medicine."

"Cool." Then, diverting to a little skepticism, "So what I brought is just roots and herbs and stuff."

"It's medicine."

"She might be worried about her dog," the boy said, hovering in the world above. "If she says anything, tell her I'm on the case."

"You don't know where she lives."

"I'll know by morning. I'll check in later, man." The voice was withdrawing. "Not when it's daytime, though. I won't hang around when it's light out."

On the note of that promise, the boy left.

The night was nearly over. The air smelled like daybreak, laden with dew, and the river sounded more cheerful as it rushed toward morning. Normally he would ascend to greet the break of day. The one good thing about the pain was the relief he felt when it lifted. Relief and weariness. He returned to the deepest chamber of his refuge, where his guest lay in his bed, her fragile face bathed in soft candlelight. She would feel the same relief, the same weariness, when she awoke in her own bed. She'd be sore, but he could ease the soreness. He could lessen the swelling. He touched a twist of sweet grass to a flame and breathed deeply of its perfume. The scent of serenity, he thought, rendering the city and its hazards utterly remote.

He made an infusion from the mixture of herbs the old man had prepared and applied it to the tattered angel's broken skin. He made a paste from ground roots and applied it to her swollen bumps and bruises, singing softly as he did so. Grandmother songs, remembered through the scent of sweet grass and the heavy dampness of the still night. The angel moaned, as though she would add her keening to his lullaby, but another tea soon tranquilized her fitful sleep.

Finally he doused the light, lay down beside her, closed his eyes, and drifted on dewy-sweet morning air.

3

Sunlight stabbed through the curtains. It was a rude awakening if ever she'd had one, as rude as the dull ache in the back of her head.

"Angela?"

She recognized the boy's voice, the unwashed-kid smell of his clothes, and she smiled when she saw his face hovering over her.

"You feeling any better?" he asked shyly.

"Tommy T." She whispered his name in gratitude. She didn't know why he was there, but somehow she knew it was a good thing. She could still see his face when she closed her eyes. Anxiety glowed in his coal-black eyes. He was her friend. She wanted to grab his little head and plant a big smacking kiss on his smooth brown cheek.

But that would surely embarrass her twelve-year-old guardian angel. She opened her eyes again and took a look around. "What happened? How did I end up here? This is—"

"Your own bed." He plopped a pile of straw-colored fur on

the bed beside her. "See, bitty bitch?" he said to the dog. "I told you she'd open her eyes soon."

The terrier smothered Angela's face with its own brand of big smacking kisses. "Oh, Stevie, you rascal. You just want somebody to fill your supper dish." She glanced up as she ruffled the dog's silky coat. "Betty Bitch? Shame on you, Tommy T."

"*Bitty*," he corrected as he dropped down, draping his upper body over the side of the bed. He reached over to pet the dog, too. "She's just a little bitty bitch, huh?" he crooned. "I been taking her outside, and I found the dog food. She didn't want me in the house, but she stopped trying to bite me after I fed her. A bitch is a female dog, right?" He cupped both hands around the Yorkie's head and held its face close to his. "Stevie, huh?" The dog growled. Tommy T shrugged and let the dog proceed to welcome Angela back among the living. "You never told me her name. Don't look like no Stevie to me."

"Stevie Nicks, the singer," Angela explained, then smiled at the blank look he gave her. "Fleetwood Mac. Before your time. Did you bring me here, Tommy T? How did you know where to . . ." The boy had never been to her apartment, which occupied the second floor of an old house. She remembered locking doors— the door to her apartment, the back door to the café. But the keys . . .

"How did we get in? Did you find my . . ." Purse. Somebody had hit her and taken her purse, but that was only the beginning, and in the end, she didn't know whom to trust, or whom she had already trusted, by default or otherwise.

"I got my ways." He watched her explore her face with careful fingertips, wincing with her when she found the bruises, one by one. "You got in the way of some punks that had a big fight going on, chasing each other all over. You just got in their way. Good thing they didn't have no guns or nothin'. They was really gettin' into it, and if they'da had guns . . ." He braced himself on his arms, drew his knees up, dragged them over the edge of the bed, and sat on his calves, grinning. "'Course, one of them did have a gun at first, but he got it took away, so that was a damn good thing."

"Who took it away? Did you?"

He laughed.

"Did I?"

"Yeah, like you and me are gonna take some punk's piece away." Still grinning, he shook his head. "No, see, they was gettin' ready for a dogfight, but I knew that wasn't all because they had some bets down, and there's this one guy couldn't keep his mouth shut for nothin', and I got good ears." He reached over to pet Stevie again. His voice dropped, his enthusiasm falling away. "I also got this really stupid brother. He's been hangin' with these punks. They tell him to drink out of the sewer, he'd do it."

Angela nodded, not that she truly understood gang loyalty, but she knew about intimidation. "And one of them had a gun."

"One for sure." He looked up, mouth set in a grim line, eyes too somber for a boy of twelve. "Brain-dead punks. But anyway, somebody came along and broke it up. He took the gun." His face brightened, and suddenly he was a typical boy again, wide-eyed and breathless with excitement. "You shoulda seen him. Man-oh-man, he wasn't scared of the dogs or the gun, nothin'. Walked right over and just . . ." He demonstrated a sudden snatch, coming up with a fistful of air.

"A policeman?"

"Hell, no, he ain't no cop. Just a guy." He glanced away as though he'd caught himself on the verge of betraying a secret. "Just this guy I know."

"I'm having a hard time remembering just what . . ."

"That's because you got hit. It happened real fast, and they roughed you up pretty good."

"But how did I get here?"

"Well, I . . ." He shrugged and faked a smile. "I helped you."

"You had help with that part, too," she assumed.

"A little." He concentrated on picking at a tufted flower in the chenille bedspread, savoring his secret. "He keeps to himself, mostly. This guy I know."

"The same guy who stopped the fight?"

"Yeah. I never bother him unless it's somethin' real heavy goin' down, but if it is, and if I can find him . . ." Tommy T flipped two thumbs up.

"He's your man, huh?" His enthusiastic nod was gratifying. The boy deserved a hero. "So he helped you bring me here?"

"Uh . . . yeah." He looked up and smiled, all sparkling innocence.

But those weren't the eyes she recalled. Glittering, yes, but not innocent. Not boyish. Not even completely human, the screwy way she remembered it, but surely humane. Watching over her in some foggy dream place, the eyes she remembered belonged to someone who, like this boy, would not harm her. Were they eyes remembered or eyes conceived in a dream? Maybe she was resorting to conjuring up heroes, too.

"Ohhh." She shook off her ridiculous daydreams and grappled with the reality of her throbbing head. "This must be what a hangover's like."

Tommy T looked skeptical. "You never had no hangover?"

"Not a serious one. Not like you read about." She eyed him speculatively. "You?"

He was scratching Stevie behind the ears. "Sure, lotsa times."

"Hmm. The twelve-year-old voice of experience."

"Twelve years is plenty of time to get experienced. How old are *you*?" He challenged her with a knowing look. "You got some experience on you, too, but if you say you never had no hangover, I'll believe you. Whatever you say. You told me no doctors and no cops, so I didn't get any. I did just what you said."

"I appreciate that, Tommy T." Twelve years was long enough to grow up, it would seem, even though he still looked like a boy. Wild, curly hair that defied control, fingers stained with something purple, chewed fingernails, small hands, and knobby elbows.

But that knowing, man-child look in his eyes bothered her, and she couldn't stop herself from adding, "Not that you shouldn't go to a policeman or a doctor for help, you understand. You really should, whenever you need to. It's just that, for me . . ." She fell to petting Stevie, too, avoiding the boy's canny eyes. "Well, doctors are expensive, and if you call a cop, he has to call a doctor. And as you can see, I'm fine." She forced an unconvincing smile. "Just a little shaky. I'm going to have to get someone to take my shift today."

"You don't work today. It's your day off. Wednesday."

"What happened to Tuesday?" She glanced at the clock on the bureau as if she thought it could explain. "Oh, gosh. You mean I've been . . . ?" She'd lost a whole day and a half, not to mention the nights in between. "Oh, my gosh. I've had the craziest dreams, too. They had to be dreams, because these things just don't happen. I was . . . I mean, it seemed like I'd fallen into a hole, and there was someone . . ." This was beginning to look more like a complete blackout than a hangover, and it scared her. There were whole days and nights missing, and she had no idea where she'd been or with whom. "Was it you, Tommy T?"

"I don't know what you were dreaming about," he said quickly, a little too innocently. "But we—I mean, I figured you'd come out of it sooner or later because you weren't, like . . ." He gestured helplessly, and she wondered if the word he was struggling with was "dying." He sighed and gave in. "I got someone to help me take care of you, too."

"A neighbor?" She didn't know her neighbors. He was suddenly given to boyish shrugs. "Who knows about this?"

Another shrug. "Hardly nobody. Just . . . just this guy I know." He scooted closer, once again wide-eyed and eager. "But I can look after you myself now, Angela. I mean . . . well, you done me a favor or two. I gave all your plants some water. Little bit, not too much. And I . . . are you hungry?"

She shook her head once, then closed her eyes and lay back

against the pillows. "There's some extra-strength headache stuff in the bathroom. That and maybe some milk."

He sprang from her bed and hustled off to do her bidding. Within moments he was back with milk and medicine.

"I'd better call the café and see if I still have a job," she mused as she accepted the pills from Tommy T's warm hand.

He stuck his hands behind his back, even though it was too late to hide the purple fingers. "I found a box of Jello in the cabinet, and I sorta . . ."

"That's okay. Pickings are probably pretty slim—" He was hanging his head, and she realized she'd chosen her words poorly. She touched the back of his purple-stained hand. "Out there in the kitchen, I mean, and we both need something to eat. Real food, huh?"

"You do have a job," he assured her. "You called in sick."

"I did?"

"Kinda like this," he said, doing a woman's voice. Then he added laryngitis. " 'My throat's killing me, Deacon. I might get germs on the food.' "

"As if germs wouldn't find themselves in like company on Deacon's food." Her smile would have been a hearty laugh if her head hadn't been pounding. "Thanks, Tommy T. Now I owe you again."

"Yeah?" He looked pleased. "Well, I won't ask for nothin' too big."

She patted the bed, offering him a seat, which he claimed with a bold bounce. "I'm curious about this mysterious guy you've been talking about," she said cautiously. "The one you went to for help. Does he have a name?"

Tommy T shrugged, avoiding her eyes.

"I'd like to thank him, too."

"I'll tell him. He's real shy about stuff like that."

"Did you . . ." She reached for his hand again, thinking she had to be careful with this. "Did you leave me . . . I mean, was I alone with him at all?"

The boy's eyes widened as her meaning became clear to him. He shook his head vigorously. "He wouldn't hurt you. Never. He's not like that. I don't really know his name, but what I do know is . . ." He paused, choosing his words carefully. "I know he doesn't want people gettin' hurt. I mean, that's just how he is."

"Where does he live?" she wondered. Tommy T's dark eyes offered a pointedly noncommittal look. "You don't know that either?"

"I just know I shouldn't be talkin' about him. He's like my ace in the hole, and if I go talkin' about him"—he lowered his voice, as if his hero might be omnipresent—"maybe next time he won't be there."

"Where?"

The boy shrugged and glanced away. "Places."

"What does he look like? Tall man? Short?"

"Tall enough. I've never gotten a good look at his face. Like I said, he's kinda shy, and he disguises his face pretty good." He used his thumb like a blade, dragging it across his cheek. "I think he might have a big scar or something."

"Really? Sounds like one of your comic-book characters."

"He's real," Tommy T insisted. "I don't think he likes cops much, either."

"It isn't that I don't like them, Tommy T. I just . . ."

"Don't want 'em messin' with you, right? Me neither. And neither does this guy. So you can understand that."

She could. Whether her reasons were in any way similar to Tommy T's or his mysterious friend's didn't matter. She understood perfectly now. She could hardly remember the time when she had no reason to fear, when she would have called a cop without a second thought. There had been such a time for her, though, a trusting time when she was Tommy T's age, even older. The time before her life had swerved off-kilter.

She sighed. "I'm glad your friend came along when he did. You knew these punks, huh?"

"Oh, yeah," the boy admitted with a sigh as he stretched out, propping his head in his hand. "I mean . . . well, you see them around a lot."

Angela nodded. "So I was just in the wrong place at the wrong time."

Tommy T nodded, shrugged, then nodded again.

"Just my luck. But it could have been worse." She gave a dry chuckle as she plowed her fingers through her hair, feeling for the goose egg on the back of her head, wincing when she found it. "I thought maybe somebody might be out to get me or something."

"You? Why would you think that?"

"No reason." She could tell he wasn't satisfied, so she added, "I'm a woman. That's reason enough."

"You mean, like that creep goin' around climbing in windows and doin' stuff to women?"

It was as good an example as any, so she nodded, half surprised that the boy was aware that a serial rapist had been stalking the Twin Cities. But then, this man in boy's skin was no typical twelve-year-old.

"I worry about my mom sometimes, 'cause I can't tell her nothin' and, you know, sometimes she stays out, like . . ." He dismissed those worries with a bony shrug. "But you need somebody to look after you, too," he said, and she smiled because his voice was still that of a boy. "Doncha got a boyfriend or something?"

"I have Stevie." She cocked a brow as she regarded the sleeping pup, and they struck a "yeah, right" chord in unison. "I'm pretty independent," she assured him. "Normally I can take care of myself."

"Me, too. Don't need nobody else."

"You have a brother, and you mentioned your mother. You must have . . ." The look in his eyes cautioned against supposing anything beyond what he'd told her. A year ago she would have pressed for more information. A year ago she wouldn't have known any better. "You must have better things to do today than look after Stevie and me."

"Not really. Found some paper in that trash can by the desk, so I been drawing on it." He hopped off the bed, ambled the few steps to the desk, and held up a handful of papers. "This was stuff you didn't want, right? Only used on one side, but it was in the trash."

"No, that's fine." They were mostly flyers advertising things she couldn't afford anymore, like dry cleaning and Chinese take-out. "In fact, there's paper—"

"This is good enough." He dragged his feet on his return to the bedside, folding the clutch of pastel and white papers in half. "Just something to do while I waited around to make sure you were still kickin'."

"I will be, soon as I get rid of this nasty headache." She eyed the papers, wondering whether she'd be intruding if she asked to see them. "You're starting back to school pretty soon, aren't you?"

"I guess so. I'm signed up." He ran the fold in his papers between his thumb and forefinger with exaggerated care. "I was wondering . . ." He risked a glance, making sure he had her full attention, then went back to pressing the fold in his papers. "I mean, if you really wanted to do me something, maybe you could let me keep some of my stuff here." His small shoulders bobbed quickly. "You know, so nobody wouldn't be messin' with it."

"Like your brother?"

"Yeah." He offered a fleeting, hopeful smile. "Just a little bit of stuff that I don't use very much because, you know, I wanna keep it nice."

"As long as you'll let me know just what it is I'm keeping. It's not that I don't trust you. It's just that I'm not . . ."

He grinned. "Stupid."

She shrugged, then smiled. He looked so cute with that impish sparkle in his eyes, that ready smile. The second time they'd met, after she'd started working at the café, he'd showed up in the alley after closing one night and offered to help her toss garbage bags into the Dumpster. It had been good to see him again, and she'd asked him if he wanted to see what the café food tasted like hot.

35

Since Deacon had left for the night, she'd let Tommy T into the kitchen, grateful for the company. He put away three hamburgers, explaining between bites that he'd inherited the curly hair she'd complimented from his father, who was black. Then he'd informed her that he was Sioux Indian, too, on his mother's side, in case she was wondering. She'd told him she was wondering if he was saving room for pie and ice cream.

"So that's why I wouldn't mind leaving some of my stuff here for safekeeping," he continued.

"I think that can be arranged."

An unexpected knock at the door sent Stevie into a yapping tailspin. Angela tucked the dog under one arm and threw back the covers with the other. "Would you see who that is? I don't want to deal with anyone right now." She plucked at the bodice of the pink uniform she'd hated since the first day she'd put it on. She wasn't wild about uniforms. "I feel like I've been wearing these clothes for a week, and I'm—"

Tommy T dashed out the door on the second knock. Stevie yapped again as Angela hobbled to the bureau and peeked in the mirror. The two bruises on her face looked pretty bad. Her back hurt. She took rueful account of her bare legs. It had been a while since she'd had a skinned knee.

Tommy T stuck his head in the door. "He says the landlord sent him to do some repairs."

"Now?" She scowled. "I've been screaming about that hole in the wall since I moved in, and the toilet and the windows, and nothing's been done and all of a sudden now, today of all days . . ."

"He says he's got a work order."

"Ask him if he can come back."

"He says if you want the work done, it's gotta be today." The boy stepped into the room and closed the door behind him for a quick conference. "This guy's okay, Angela. I've seen him doin' stuff other places."

"What kind of stuff?"

"Building stuff. Fixing stuff. I seen him at school a few times. He's a for-real repair guy."

She sighed, nodding reluctantly. She didn't want to make any decisions right now or give any answers, yes, no, or even maybe. Let the boy take over and lead the way, she thought, just for to-day.

Tommy T led the way to the door, where a tall man dressed in jeans, a white T-shirt, and brown work boots stood waiting. He looked her directly in the eye, as though he expected something from her—recognition, maybe. He was attractive. He had an an-gular face, strong jaw, black hair, dark skin, intriguing eyes. Very attractive. But she didn't know him. She was glad Tommy T did.

"Name's Jesse Brown Wolf." Still looking her directly in the eye, he produced a piece of paper. "Here's the work order from Morrison."

She dipped her chin and tugged on her hair, trying to use it to curtain the worst side of her face. Don Morrison was the prop-erty manager, not the landlord. She'd about given up on both of them, and the paper in her hand explained why. Outrage pushed embarrassment aside. "This is two weeks old."

Stevie sniffed at the bulbous, scuffed toe of the man's boot and wagged her tail. The man spoke into his shirtfront as he squatted to set his red toolbox down and reward the dog's unusually friendly overture with an ear-scratching. "I've been busy. Busy season." He rubbed his thumb between the dog's eyes, paused, then stood abruptly. The dog's nose bobbed after his hand as though magnetized. "Look, if you'd rather wait for—"

"Actually, I've been waiting long enough. Not that I'm point-ing any fingers, but I just—"

He waggled a cocked thumb. "In or out?"

He'd already gotten an eyeful of her humilation. If she sent him away now, he'd probably never come back. "Please come in. I didn't mean to be—" She handed him the work order and stepped aside to admit him. Stevie was satisfied, and the dog had good instincts about people. "It's just that the day hasn't started out well for me, and I'm pretty sure yesterday was a waste after a total disaster the night before."

"Must have been one hell of a night before," he muttered absently, perusing the paper.

"It was neither picnic nor party," she said as she wrapped her arms tightly around her rib cage. It hurt when she squeezed. "Although I was served up quite a little surprise."

Tommy T spoke up. "Angela got worked over by some creeps."

"Just kids," she mused. Realizing the number of unaccountable hours that had passed, she hadn't gotten around to recalling the details of the attack itself. It all seemed so unreal. Dark, quiet, then a sudden commotion and, pow! "Kids' games aren't what they used to be."

"I don't know much about kids and their games." He picked up his toolbox. "Not too smart for a woman to be out alone at night."

"Unfortunately, even smart women sometimes find themselves in exactly that predicament." Eyes closed, she pressed the heels of her hands against her temples and rubbed. "I'm a waitress. I work at night."

His voice dipped to a low, intimate level. "You seen a doctor yet?"

"No." She opened her eyes and found herself looking into his. Dark eyes, but not quite brown or black. Eyes that were troubled and troubling, vitreous with too much knowing. It was as though she'd caught him peering into her bedroom window. She glanced quickly at the paper in his hand. "What I do see is a whole list of things that need to be repaired."

"Yes, ma'am," he drawled, and with a soft chuckle he turned away. "If you wanna get your business done in the bathroom, I'll start with the hole in the wall."

"It's—"

"I can see it."

"Can you stay for a while, then?" she asked Tommy T, brushing aside her earlier supposition that he had better things to do. He nodded eagerly. "You must be hungry. Help yourself to anything you see in the refrigerator while I take a shower."

"I'll wait for you," the boy promised, and he made himself at home on her overstuffed thrift-store sofa.

Angela headed for the shower. She needed a good hot-water pounding, despite the stinging it caused where her skin had been scraped away. The needle-sharp spray helped her berate herself for being careless. Caution, or *pre*caution, had become her middle name. Why had she allowed herself to get in the way of a gang of adolescent punks in a dark alley? She'd made a study of keeping to herself in the past few months, of getting away, staying away, and avoiding trouble. That was her goal in life right now. And here she was, battered and bruised, standing naked in the shower with a strange man with a toolbox working inside her apartment, just on the other side of the door.

Of course, she wasn't alone. She had a scruffy little street urchin out there keeping an eye on him for her. Oh, yes, this was smart. This was super. She'd already been thoroughly tenderized. Now she was clean and stripped. Perfect. The tall, dark stranger was probably selecting a sharp tool from his big red box. She could just see her own blood swirling down the drain any minute now. There would be no epitaph, of course, no one to mourn her. The upside was that no one would be there to gloat, either. No one to point out where she'd landed when she'd finally jumped out of the frying pan.

She was almost surprised when she stepped on the mat and wrapped a towel around her living, breathing body. It was awfully quiet out there. No hammering. No power drilling. She dressed in comfortable shorts and a top, took the time to dry her hair and apply a little cover-up to the bruises on her face. If she lived through the repairman's visit, she decided she was going to take her headache back to bed.

She found him working on the pipes under the kitchen sink. That leak wasn't on the work order. She'd learned to empty the

five-quart pail every third day and decided she could live with
that. She'd requested only essential repairs, and her definition of
essential was becoming narrower every day. She wondered
whether a handyman's ears were sensitive to drips, or had he just
gone looking?

Silly to look a gift horse in the mouth, she told herself. On the
other hand, she did like the way his jeans fit him. She liked the
way his T-shirt actually disappeared into the waistband, the way
his shoulders dwarfed the opening in the cabinet he was trying
to work in, the way the muscles in his long, lean back flexed as
he plied the big red-handled wrench on some unyielding part of
the pipe. His black hair was tied back in a neat queue, and she
could see just ahead of his ear some small muscle fighting with
the set of his jaw. She liked the idea of all that strength coming
to her aid. She liked it a lot.

"Would you—"

Startled by her voice, he bobbed suddenly and bumped his
head inside the cabinet. He pivoted, rubbing his head and greeting
her with a scowl.

"I'm sorry," she said quickly. "I was just wondering . . . would
you care for a sandwich? We're going to be making some."

"You and the kid?"

She shrugged, smiling a little. "He tells me I have to eat something."

"You don't have to feed me."

"I know. It's no trouble. Just ham and cheese. Interested?"

"Yeah." He nodded briefly. "Thanks."

The three gathered quietly, knees nearly touching under the
tiny kitchen table. Angela nibbled at her sandwich. She felt a little
nauseated, much the way she had when she'd been diagnosed
with a slight concussion after an ice-skating fall when she was
about ten. Roxanne had told everyone at school that she'd been
trying to do a double axle, which was a lie. She'd only been trying
for a single. And she'd recovered from the fall without any difficulty, no thanks to Roxanne's and her friends' teasing. She would

bounce back from this, too, even though the dull ache in her temples made chewing a chore.

Furtively, she noted that her guests had no such problem. They devoured two sandwiches each in the time it took her to make a small dent in hers. The boy gobbled as though he were eating on the run. But the man somehow made his food disappear without the appearance of haste.

"I saw you around school last year." Tommy T talked around a cheek full of food. "You worked there sometimes, didn't you?"

Jesse Brown Wolf nodded once.

"I'm going back this year," the boy reported eagerly. "Same school."

Another nod.

Angela nibbled at her sandwich.

"You think you'll be working there again?"

"Got some more work lined up there. New playground."

"You mean like swings and slides? That's kid stuff," Tommy T said officiously.

The man scowled. "Yeah, well, what's goin' on right across the street from the school *shouldn't* be kid stuff. New playground might keep some of the little ones busy with some good, ol'-fashioned, *genuine* kid stuff."

"Good luck," Tommy said. "Once those dealers move in, you can't move 'em off no way. They pack some pretty heavy artillery. If they wanna play on the swings and deal drugs at the same time . . ." He gestured with a fist. "What they need at the school is somebody who ain't afraid of nothin' or nobody. Somebody who can just walk in, and all the snarling just stops"—he snapped his fingers—"cold."

"Who did you have in mind?" Angela asked. She knew about the drug dealing going on in the park near Tommy T's school, and she suspected the boy had a solution to the problem somewhere in the drawings he'd tucked under his chair. He kept his childhood alive and well in his artwork. "Show me what you've been working on."

He glanced from her face to the repairman's. He wasn't too sure about displaying his special drawings right now, here, for these two pairs of eyes.

"Tommy T loves to draw, and from the few glimpses I've seen, he's very good at it," Angela explained. "Not only that, but he's an expert on comic-book heroes. Were you ever a comic-book fan, Mr. Brown Wolf?"

No more forthcoming on the subject than the boy was, the man sipped his coffee, took his time about setting the mug down just so, then said quietly, "Guess I read one or two in my time."

"Who's your favorite?" Tommy T challenged. "Superman or Batman?"

"Goofy." Jesse Brown Wolf shrugged off Tommy T's horrified look. "My brother got all the Superman comics. He was older. I ended up with Goofy."

"Superman's too, like, fifties. Batman rules." The boy snatched his papers up quickly, snapped them open, slapped them on the table between the two adults, then eyed each one cautiously. "This is just some stuff I thought up."

Angela took the top page in hand. While she made appreciative noises, Jesse gave the next page a sober, distant perusal. "Isn't that something?" she crooned, inviting the repairman to join in her chorus anytime. "Just look at the detail, the expressive . . ." She pointed to the pencil drawing that lay on the table. "Boy, this guy looks mean."

"That's Dark Dog." Tommy T's youthful pride was in full bloom now. "He's not mean inside, but he don't take no crap offa nobody."

"Neither does Goofy," Jesse muttered.

"Goofy," Tommy T echoed disgustedly. "I'm not talkin' about some kinda cuddly stuffed animal. This is like . . ." He reached for the papers on the table. "It's just a hobby. You wouldn't get it if you're not into real comics."

"I know a good drawing when I see one." With a gesture Angela asked him to let her look at the rest of his work. He gave a tight smile, drew his hand back, and tucked it under his thigh.

"What do you think of Road Runner?" Jesse asked.

The question surprised Angela. It was the first bit of interest the man had offered unsolicited.

Tommy T screwed up his face. "*Road* Runner?"

"You don't know who Road Runner is?"

"Sure, I know who he is. That's not the same."

"I used to like the coyote," Jesse recalled. He pulled a sketch of a butterball-shaped character with a spear from the pile.

"Wile E. Coyote?" Tommy T sneered. "How could you like Wile E. Coyote? He's too stupid for words, the way he's always blowing himself up."

Jesse shrugged. "I used to think maybe sometime he'd figure things out, finally get it right once."

"And catch Road Runner?" The boy whacked his hands together. "Bam! End of story."

"Yeah, I know. But Superman has it easy. He knows who his enemies are. That coyote only has himself to blame."

"Kid stuff," Tommy T reminded him.

"Maybe." Jesse looked up at the boy and nodded solemnly. "The lady's right. You've got real talent."

"Thanks." Tommy T tried unsuccessfully to suppress a pleasured smile. "Is it okay to use the toilet now?"

"It works," the repairman reported. "It oughta be replaced, like a lot of other stuff in this building."

"He may well have saved my life," Angela confided after she heard the bathroom door close. "Well, *they.* Tommy and some mysterious friend of his."

"What were they after?"

She questioned him with a look.

"The attackers," he clarified. "Your money? Your body? What?"

"They took my purse, but they sure didn't get much money. I didn't have a chance to ask whether there'd be anything else." She signaled an offer of more coffee, but he shook it off. She sighed and permitted herself to recall the incident from a safe distance, focusing on *them,* the attackers, not on herself. "They were just kids. A bunch of boys with a dog." She shrugged. "I guess the image of 'Our Gang' just ain't what it used to be."

With a quick chin jerk he directed her attention to the situation close to home. "You need a better lock on that door. It wouldn't take much of a gang to bust through that."

"A new lock?" Her gaze followed his to one of the few mechanisms in the apartment that seemed to work. She'd assumed the security chain was a good backup.

"A butter knife is all it would take. That flimsy chain is worthless. You need a longer strike plate and a damn good double bolt, but don't hold your breath if you're gonna ask your landlord."

"I'll do it myself. What kind of tools would it . . ." She looked at him, then laughed self-consciously. "Tools I don't have, so I'd be better off to hire someone. Interested?"

He lifted one shoulder. "Sure."

"And the windows. Can you fix the windows?" She waved a hand toward the one that stood open above the sofa, affording her hanging spider plants some fresh air. She'd started them from shoots from her sister's plants, and she'd hung them up thinking they might protect her somehow, serve as a barrier or a screen. The pointed leaves reminded her of Roxanne's long fingernails. She laughed. "That one's stuck. I can't budge it. Somebody could come right in."

"You're on the second floor."

"But still."

"Somebody could come right in," he echoed with a nod. "But I can't get to it today."

She sighed. He wouldn't be back. She was lucky to have a functional toilet.

"I'll pick up a good lock and bill your landlord for it," he decided as he pushed his chair back and stood. "He'll pay me eventually, one way or another."

"I couldn't ask you to do that."

"You didn't." He drained the rest of his coffee. "Hickey and me, we've got this little game going. It's called 'chase the buck.' Sooner or later I get what's coming to me," he assured her as he set the mug back on the table. "He's a slippery one, your landlord."

Tommy T emerged from the bathroom. Angela smiled when the toilet actually stopped running automatically. Jesse set about packing up his tools.

"So what do you say about keeping my stuff, Angela?"

She smiled and reached out to tussle the mop of curly hair, but the boy ducked away. She nodded anyway. "I've got room for a few special treasures."

He grabbed a fistful of air. "Yes!"

"Comic books and trading cards, right? I don't have a place to keep anything like a bicycle or—"

"Nothin' big," Tommy T promised. "I don't got a bike or nothin'. Got rid of all my toys a long time ago. Just some little stuff. Be right back."

"Wait a minute." She took a tin cookie canister down from the cupboard, pried off the lid, and produced a twenty-dollar bill. "We have frozen pizza and the makings of a salad. If you'd stop at the store for me and pick up a quart of milk, I'd make us some supper."

"Just milk?" He stared at the money as though it were foreign currency. "Just a quart of milk? Jeez."

"Is there something special you'd like? I've got more Jello."

"No, just . . ." He looked up, all big-eyed sincerity. "I'll be back real quick, and I'll bring back all your change," he promised solemnly before he scurried out the door.

"You're pretty trusting," Jesse observed quietly.

She put the lid back on the canister and carefully pressed it into place as she eyed the repairman, who had taken the liberty of seating himself on the arm of her sofa. His hand absently strayed over the head of her "watchdog," who was curled up on the cushion looking up at him, tongue lolling, eyes full of puppy love.

"He'll bring me the change," she said, but money wasn't uppermost on her mind right now. She was trusting Jesse Brown Wolf, too, and now that they were alone, there he sat, suddenly in no hurry to leave. "Cub Foods is right across the street. He'll be right back."

The man nodded, returning her stare. "You just showed both of us where you stash your cash." Still staring, he shook his head slowly as he braced his hands on his thighs. "The cookie jar. Damn."

"Tommy saved my life. And you . . . you just offered to . . ."

"A new lock ain't gonna do you much good, lady." He slid his hands over worn denim, inching toward his knees. "Not one damn bit of good. You been livin' here, what? A few months?"

She swallowed hard. "How did you know?"

"It's written all over your trusting face."

"I don't trust anybody," she insisted. "Not anymore."

"But you forget sometimes, don't you?" He nodded for her. "It's a hard habit to break, and you're still workin' on it. But you're right about the kid. He'll be back with every penny of your change."

She nodded, too, and told herself that if he'd wanted to harm her, a twelve-year-old boy could not have stopped him. "Where does Tommy T live? Do you know?"

"That's for him to say." He levered himself off the sofa. "But do him a favor. Don't ask."

"I met him shortly after I moved to the Cities. I haven't had time . . . haven't taken the time to get to know too many people, but Tommy T's absolutely irrepressible. I really like him. I just wonder . . ." He was listening with eyes as well as ears, and it made her uneasy. "I've seen him out really late at night sometimes. He's so young, and it's so dangerous to be out . . ." She shrugged, glancing away as she gave a little laugh. "I'm living proof, right? I don't know what would have happened to me if Tommy T hadn't found me, but if he'd been there any earlier, he might've gotten hurt, too. Those kids were older, but not by much.

46

THE NIGHT REMEMBERS 〜

Just *kids*." She sighed. "He seems to have a lot of freedom for a twelve-year-old. I should probably find out if his mother minds him spending—" She caught the hint in his slight frown. "Bad idea?"

"Why are you asking me? He ain't my kid." He looked her in the eye. "Or one of my people, if that's your way of thinking. Looks like he's latched onto you, so it's your call."

"He couldn't be a runaway, could he? He goes to school. I know he has a brother. But he's not . . ." She glanced away, echoing distantly, "So much freedom for a twelve-year-old."

They could hear him bounding up the stairs. He knocked twice, then burst in with a mission-accomplished grin, a bag in one arm, and a cardboard box in the other. "Here's the milk. Here's your change." He plopped first one, then the other in Angela's hands, then dropped the box at her feet. "And here . . . you got room for all this? I kinda had it waitin' down the hall, 'cause I was hopin' you'd say okay. Look at this." Down on one knee, he offered up a comic book for her inspection. " 'Batman.' This is the one where Batman gets the new Batmobile. The one he's got now isn't the same one he started with, you know. Almost perfect condition, and somebody just threw it away. Can you believe that?" He glanced over his shoulder. "Sorry. No Goofy or Road Runner. But if I find any . . ."

"You ever heard of Old Man Coyote?" Jesse asked. Tommy T shook his head. "Most Indian tribes have some kind of Trickster in their stories," Jesse offered almost incidentally, but noting the boy's interest, he ventured on. "I remember my grandmother used to tell about Iktome, the spider, and about Old Man Coyote. Tricky guys, both of them. Usually ended up tricking themselves, just like Wile E. Coyote. Somebody oughta come up with a comic book about those guys."

"Indian heroes?" The boy puzzled briefly over that one. "What kind of powers do they have?"

"Cunning," Jesse replied quickly and with unexpected conviction. "Strong medicine if you use it right. But it can backfire, too."

47

He snapped his fingers within inches of the boy's nose. "Like that."

"I don't know," Tommy T averred. "Sounds wimpy. You gotta have power. Some kinda bitchin' weapon. I haven't figured out what to give Dark Dog yet."

"Try the double-edged sword." He turned to Angela. "I'll have your lock—"

"Tomorrow?" She attempted to smile, maybe even charm, but then she remembered how bad her face looked, and she felt silly.

"Tomorrow."

She was on the outside of her dream looking in, and someone was standing beside her. "I'm sleeping," she mumbled.

"I won't wake you up."

"Good." It was okay. She'd dreamed of the same soothing voice before. Deep, fluid, and so soft she had to still every other sound in her head before she could hear it. "Hard time . . . getting to sleep."

"Did you take something?"

"Yes . . . to help me sleep." She ought to pry her eyes open and have a look, she thought. "You won't hurt me, will you?"

"You know I won't."

Yes, she did; she knew. Warm fingers grazed her cheek. She recognized their rare gentleness. "You're the one who watched over me before."

"Yes."

"Jewel Eyes," she recalled, and she smiled in the dark. Flesh or phantom, he was exactly what she needed. A banisher of nightmares. "Were you a dream then, too?"

"If that's what you want me to be." She heard the crack of a knee joint, and the next whisper came from farther away. "You're okay now?"

"Sort of. Still scared. Scared of dark places, except . . ." She shifted to her side, following his sounds like a blind woman. "You took me to a dark place, didn't you?"

"My place is dark. That's where I took you."

"But you didn't hurt me. You wouldn't."

"No."

"Tommy T said you didn't hurt people. He trusts you." She angled her arm beneath her pillow and pulled it down for something to hug. "Can I trust you?"

"That's up to you."

"Do you have a name?"

"No."

"Then how can I call you?"

"You can't."

Her heart sank.

"You don't have to," he whispered. "I'm here if you need me."

"You're a dream, then." And that was better. She was free to be foolish with a dream. "Stay in my dream for a while, okay?"

"Okay." She didn't hear him move, but she felt him touch her hair. "Rest easy, Angela. You're safe with me."

"Beautiful dream," she murmured, drifting.

"Beautiful dreamer," he whispered, fading away.

"Want a hit, Tommy T?"

It was the kind of invitation a guy couldn't be quick to refuse unless he wanted to be taken for a dweeb. Or worse, a narc. Tommy T wanted to be part of the circle of Stoner's friends, part of his brother's brotherhood, at least when they were just hanging out. He peeled himself off the brick wall he'd been trying hard to blend in with, dropped his knees on the crumbling asphalt next to Ajax, the undisputed leader of the pack, and waited his turn for the marijuana about to be shared.

"Don't waste good weed on him," Stoner objected from the far side of the huddle. "Half the time he's got his head hung up in his—" His brown arm shot out, bisecting the circle. "Hey! I said don't—"

But Ajax would not be crossed. He glared at his minion. "Hey? What're you talkin', *hey*." The challenge went unanswered as Ajax beckoned with the hand-rolled smoke. "Take a hit, kid."

Tommy T glanced at his brother, whose attention was now focused on his own forearm, where he'd tattooed his nickname in perfectly square capital letters. Tommy T shrugged. "It's okay. I don't care."

"Take it. Your brother's being a shithead." Ajax paused, but there were no more objections. "We're havin' ourselves a ceremony here. You want a piece of the ceremony, right, Tommy T?"

"Sure."

He didn't, not really, but he did want a piece of Stoner, who lately belonged wholly to his friends. Tommy T was basically a loner and proud of it, but Stoner was his brother. Besides, a guy had to be cool if he wanted to stay alive on the streets. He couldn't cross dudes like Ajax. So he joined the small circle, spared his sullen brother a quick glance, then sucked on the joint and gave his head over to a slow spin.

"You shoulda been with us the other night when that big dude in the black hat came down on us," Ajax told Tommy T. "That was some weird shit, man, like they show in those comic books of yours. Did you tell him about it, Stoner? You talk about *wicked*. My dog ain't afraid of nothin'. You know that."

"Sure." The black-and-tan mutt, T-Rex, was tied to the chain-link fence, supposedly keeping watch on the street beyond. But Tommy T could tell by its sad eyes that all the dog was really interested in was getting back with the boys. T-Rex knew Tommy T had been there, lurking in the shadows. Stoner had banished him from the circle that night, told him to go play with his pencils, but T-Rex had a good nose on him.

"This guy comes out of nowhere," Ajax recalled, amplifying

his story with his free hand as he reclaimed the joint. "And it's real dark out, you know? Dude's got his hat pulled down, big collar. Besides a little bit of skin that looks like some dried-up white alligator hide, you can't see nothin' on him but teeth and eyes. I figure T-Rex is gonna tear him to shreds, right?" Tommy T nodded on cue. "Damn dog almost pisses down his own leg."

"Not as bad as Chopper's dog, though," the boy they all called Wood Tick put in.

"That pit bull ain't such hot shit," someone else added.

"Maybe they smelled something on him," Tommy T suggested. "Another dog, maybe."

"T-Rex eats other dogs. What it is . . ." Ajax huffed on the joint, then let the smoke drift from his lips as he regaled them with his considered opinion. "It's evil. Pure evil. Dogs smell evil right off."

"Bit-chin'," Wood Tick rhapsodized. "You really believe that, Ajax?"

"I know it."

"Get out," Stoner said. "It was just some drunk on the prowl after he run outta booze."

"We roll drunks, Stoner. We don't . . ." Ajax couldn't quite bring himself to admit to running. "That was no drunk. That was a real badass for one of Tommy T's stories."

One nice thing about Ajax was that he honestly liked Tommy T's drawings. He was always willing to look at them, so Tommy T always brought a few along. He never offered, but he whipped them out of his back pocket whenever the opportunity arose. "I got some new characters."

"Let a real art expert have a look." Ajax offered to trade the shrinking joint for Tommy T's folded papers.

"Give it here," Stoner demanded. Ajax questioned the interference with a sharp look, but Stoner persisted, admonishing his brother with a glare of his own. "It was my score, and I haven't even had any yet."

Tommy T was content to pull back and let Stoner take over on what was left of the joint while Ajax perused his drawings.

The other three boys lost interest in the whole proceedings and started playing two-on-one keep-away with the hackey sack one of them had in his pocket.

Tommy T edged closer to his brother. "Where are you staying tonight, Stoner?"

"Places." Stoner pulverized the fragmentary remains of the joint with the sole of his tennis shoe, then sat close to the wall, closed his eyes, and rested his head back against the bricks. "You go back to the shelter and stay with the ol' lady."

"I ain't sure where she is."

Stoner lifted his head and scowled. "You think she took off again?"

"Nah, she'll be back. She always comes back." He banished all worry with a quick shrug as he followed Stoner's lead, hunkering down next to the wall. "Just can't be sure when."

"You're going back to school, right?" Stoner lowered his head and eyed him anxiously. "Because you should, you know. I mean, you're still a kid. You should be in school."

Tommy T didn't need to be coaxed. He'd been counting the days until school started, thinking maybe things would be different this year because their mom had really been looking, seriously filling out the papers. If she got a job, found them a place to live, this year maybe things would be different.

He sighed. "I hate going to school from a shelter. I wish she'd find us a place."

"Just don't tell nobody."

"They always find out." He laid a tentative hand on his brother's shoulder. "I could hang out with you, Stoner. Hell, I'm hangin' out most of the time anyways."

"I can't have you following me around."

Ajax joined them like a rude bomb suddenly dropping out of the sky. "He could be useful, Stoner."

"No, he couldn't." Stoner jerked his shoulder out from under Tommy T's hand, as though his brother's gesture disgusted him.

"He's soft and he's slow, and I don't want him following me around."

"I'm just sayin' whenever Tommy T needs a place—"

"You ain't got nothin' to say about this, Ajax." His voice softened a little when he looked at Tommy T. "She'll be back before anybody knows she's been gone."

"She better be." He took the papers Ajax handed him and singled one out. "See, this one here, this is Dark Dog."

"He's pretty cool-lookin'," Ajax said. "What kind of weapons does he use?"

"Weapons? This guy don't need no weapons, man. This guy has so much power. He's like—"

"You see what I'm sayin'?" Stoner harassed his brother's earlobe with the flick of a finger, then laughed as Tommy T ducked away. "You don't have to waste no weed on this kid. He's always got some kinda magic shit going in that head of his."

"I like it. Dark Dog, huh?" With a friendly hand, Ajax claimed the thin shoulder Stoner had rejected. "Your brother don't treat you right, you come see Ajax."

Tommy T smiled, nodding agreeably as he pocketed his drawings. But he was thinking he didn't need Stoner, and he sure as hell didn't need Ajax. All he needed was an address. Maybe even a phone number. The kind of information it took to convince people that you were really a somebody from somewhere. Unless his mother showed up right away, which wasn't likely, he figured he had about twenty-four hours to disappear from the shelter or end up in foster care.

He was too damn old for foster care. Technically he was twelve, but really he was much older than that. He'd lived a lot in twelve years. He'd seen things, heard things, done things probably not too many twelve-year-olds knew anything about. He'd had his share of temporary placements in foster homes, and he knew what it was like to be the extra kid. If something turned up missing, he was the prime suspect. If one of the real kids cussed, he was the one who had set the bad example. If he didn't have the right kind of "personal habits," his poor background and lack of a good upbringing always came up for discussion, and they always wagged their heads, eyes frosted with pity, and said that was all behind him now. Or would be if he'd just learn to be more like them.

He'd given it a shot once or twice. He'd cut his hair real dweeb-o, worn his clothes the way they showed in store windows, and really tried to watch his mouth. But Tommy T didn't need that crap anymore. He wasn't going to make nice for somebody who wanted a kid around to do their bidding or take the heat whenever things weren't going just right. He wanted to go to school—he *liked* school—and he wanted to hang out, look out for his mother when she came back, and try to keep Stoner from getting himself iced.

And there was his secret friend. He didn't know who the man was, didn't really want to know. Maybe he wasn't even really a man. Some people might have a little trouble with a notion like that, but not Tommy T. His secret friend could've come from any-where. Heaven, hell, outer space, Atlantis—heroes were born in a lot of strange places and under all kinds of circumstances. All that mattered was that he was Tommy T's friend, and friends looked out for each other.

The other friend he had to look out for was back at work, and he didn't like the idea of her facing the night streets alone after the café closed. Ordinarily he'd just wait outside for her, but he'd seen Chopper and that damn pit bull of his hanging out at the park a couple of blocks away, so he decided to step inside, just to let Angela know he was there when she was ready to go.

"You got money, you can sit down and eat, kid. Otherwise—"

Tommy T's angular shoulders squared up nicely inside his vo-luminous white T-shirt as he offered Deacon Peale a cool stare. He saw only two diners left in the place. It wasn't like he was going to offend too many paying customers with his presence. "I'm here for Angela."

"That's very touching." The cook claimed his coffee cup as he rounded the end of the lunch counter and headed for the swinging door to the kitchen. "He's here for you, Angela. Ain't he a little young to be usin' that line?"

"What's really nice is that he's still young enough to mean exactly what he says," Angela countered from the booth she was clearing. Her smile was for her caller. "It's early yet, Tommy T."

"I wanted to make sure I was here when you got ready to leave. Gonna walk you home."

"Thanks." She dragged a tub of dirty dishes off the table. With a nod, she indicated the crumpled paper bag he was carrying. "What's all this?"

"Some more of my stuff, if you can find a little more space. You can check it over. There's no drugs, nothin' hot. It's just . . ." He peeked into the bag as if to check it over himself, then looked up at her and shrugged. "I got no place to keep it."

"I understand. I had a sister, older than me, so you'd think she wouldn't be that interested, but she was always into everything of mine. They can really be nosy, can't they?" She shoved the load of dishes through the pass-through window, then turned to him with a motherly smile. "You hungry?"

He shook his head. He hadn't come for a handout, and he wasn't in the market for any mothering. He was way past that stage. He was there to look out for her. "I'll wait outside."

Deacon didn't invite him back in when he locked the door, but Tommy T waited anyway. It was a nice enough night, warm and hazy. He liked the way the city felt at night when a guy knew he had a friend close by. Sort of insulated from the rest of the world, like one big house with lots of lights left on. But the friend was important. Without a friend, the house felt more like a cold pit crawling with bugs.

The image made Tommy T shiver, but when Angela walked out, the shivers went away. "I got a deal for you," he proposed as they walked down the sidewalk side by side. "I'm thinkin' you could use a bodyguard."

"A bodyguard?" They stopped beneath a corner streetlight, and she smiled at him. Her light brown hair turned golden right before his eyes, and he wished he were taller, looking down on her hair instead of up. "An escort, maybe?"

"Bodyguard," he insisted. "I maybe don't look that tough, but looks ain't that important. I'm a scrapper. Plus, I'm smart."

"Which qualifies you for a lot of jobs." She laid her hand on his shoulder as she stepped off the curb.

Walking next to her, sticking close, he suddenly found himself wishing for a lot of things, like a little more meat on his bony frame, right there where her hand warmed him through his shirt. He wished he'd been born a few years earlier. He'd never felt this way before, but all of a sudden he wanted to be old enough to ask her to go somewhere really cool. Like the top of the IDS Building, which towered over the heart of the city. He'd gotten kicked out of there a few times, but the place had stuck in his mind. Clean floors, lights everywhere and they all worked, glass stretching up to the clouds and not a crack in sight.

Someday he was going to dress up in some really cool gear, and he was going to take a woman up to the top of the IDS Building, and they'd both order the fanciest meal on the menu, with wine and dessert, the whole works. Then he'd pull out a big ol' fifty dollar bill and tell the waitress to keep the change, and it would be so cool to see the look on her face, like he was Santa Claus or something.

"So what's the deal?" Angela asked. "You'll be my bodyguard iiif . . ."

"Well, school starts pretty soon, and, see, they have this open house, where the parents and kids go to the school and meet the teacher and get all signed up for everything. I got all my papers all filled out and stuff, but my mom's—" He paused to choose the sort of words he thought somebody like Angela might use. "Out of town. I just need somebody to go over there and kinda tell them that she's, like, lookin' after me, fillin' in for my mom." He laughed as he skipped out in front of her, clutching his paper sack under one arm and gesturing expansively with the other. "Some bullshit like that, you know? Just so I don't have to answer a lot of stupid questions. All it takes is an adult, somebody like you."

"When do you expect your mother to get back?"

"Real soon," he said quickly, but feigning assurance about such things went against the grain, as if he had to pretend because he was counting on it being true. He shrugged. "I don't know, exactly."

"Who are you staying with?"

"People." This was the part he didn't mind inventing. He'd been through it enough, so he figured he could borrow on past experiences. "But they got their own kids. I just need somebody to . . ." *Damn.* He'd let that word slip out. It wasn't a for-real *need.* It would make things easier, was all.

Just say yes, woman.

"You wouldn't have to be there long or say much," he assured her quietly. "Just be there."

"Just be there," Angela echoed. The simplicity of the boy's request was exquisitely appealing. All she had to do was be there, and it would mean something to him. So uncomplicated. So painless. "When is it?"

"Wednesday. Your day off, right? And we can go any time. It's, like—"

"Open house." Angela nodded, smiling, trying not to recall open houses past with too much regret. There would be more open houses in her future. "I'm familiar with the concept." A noise, or maybe an absence of noise, or just a creepy feeling made her glance over her shoulder as she added absently, "I guess I could do that for you, Tommy T."

"What's wrong?"

"Do you get the feeling we're being followed?" She wasn't sure whether it was a ghost from the past or something more substantial that was causing a strong urge to look over her shoulder. Maybe it was both. She'd felt it often enough lately. And, of course, she had every reason to be a little gun-shy.

"Followed?" Tommy T spun around on one heel, then back again. "Nope. Don't see nobody."

"Of course you don't see them. They're not going to let you see them."

"I been listening, too." He did a little skip step to keep up with her accelerating pace. "Hey, I'm doin' my job."

"Just a feeling." She lowered her voice as they approached her residence. The big wraparound porch that must have been grand fifty years ago looked dark and forbidding now under the pale moonlight, but on the step, the trailing white geranium she'd cultivated from a plant she'd wintered over year after year fairly glowed in its pot, like a spilling of pearls. Irresistible treasures, she thought. Pieces of her, part of her life, shouting out her name like a sign on a mailbox. The nice man who had offered her a new lock hadn't shown up when he'd promised to. Somebody could be following; somebody could be lurking in the hallway; somebody could even be waiting for her inside the apartment. "Let's walk right past the house, around the corner, then double back."

"Yeah." It took a moment for the intrigue to catch the boy's fancy. "Yeah! Just casual."

Around the corner they went, through a chain-link gate and into the backyard. But the minute they'd ensconced themselves behind the lilac bushes, Angela began to feel a little silly. No one walked past.

"You think we lost 'em?"

"I think I might be a little paranoid." *In her present paranoid state.* She sighed. He'd sworn she'd never be rid of him, and the last thing she wanted to do was let the bastard be right. She climbed out of the bushes, trying to sound "just casual" as she brushed off her foolishness by proposing, "Let's go find a shelf for your treasures, take Stevie out, then make ourselves some popcorn and see what's on TV. If you have time."

"I got time."

"There's one thing I wanted to ask you about," she said as she unlocked the back door. Taking her keys out of her purse had brought the question to mind. "Where did you find my purse?"

"Your purse?" His voice shriveled up instantly into a small, injured thing. "I never touched your purse, Angela."

"You weren't the one who . . ." She reached for his shoulder to reassure him, but he shrugged away from her. "I'm not accusing you of taking it, Tommy T. Those boys who attacked me took it. Aren't you the one who brought it back?"

"I said I never touched it."

"But somebody brought it back and left it by the door."

He looked genuinely baffled. "Just left it there? Didn't knock on the door or nothin'?"

"Just left it there . . . by the door." *Inside* the door to her apartment. And the door had been locked. Now she really *was* worried.

"Anything missing?"

"Not much. Just the cash that was in it, a few dollars." She had no credit cards, and she didn't carry her driver's license. She'd hidden that, and every other piece of identification, safely away.

"I don't know nothin' about it. If I'da found it, I'da just given it to you straight out."

"I just thought it had to be you." She pushed the back door open and gestured for him to go on in, explaining, "You're my only friend here so far."

"You gotta get you some more friends, Angela."

"Mmm. I should just replace that lock myself," she said as she flipped a switch to light the top of the back stairs. Jesse Brown Wolf had obviously been right about that lock being useless, but then, so was his promise to fix it the next day. Not that he owed her anything.

As she turned to close the door she noticed someone standing just beyond the fence. A man. She gripped the doorknob. She wasn't paranoid. Someone *had* been following them.

But when he turned and she glimpsed his eyes, glistening in the moonlight, she knew he meant no harm.

Jewel Eyes had seen them safely to the door.

H e could not hide himself fast enough.

He had recognized their voices and felt curiously compelled to follow, just to see that no harm came to them. Then he'd lingered too long. She'd seen him, and he'd half hoped she knew him, almost wanted her to step back out and call to him and ask him to come inside with them. But, of course, she neither knew nor called, which was a good thing. A damn good thing.

Because now he was hurting. He was sickened by the lights that buttressed the skyline, outlining the clutch of skyscrapers in the heart of the city. Sky-spearing blue streaks announcing some event at the Metrodome terrorized him from above like divine searchlights. Damning, damnable light. God-awful light. *God-awful.* He jammed his battered hat down on his head—his shelter, his night shade—drew the brim down as far as it would go, and ducked into a dark alley.

Go away now, God. Awful God. Keep the light away. Leave me the hell alone.

Back against the graffiti-trimmed wall in some alley, just some place to get out of the way, he slid into a crouch, closed his eyes, and concentrated on the sounds of the city at night. Those sounds were real. Bellowing motors, malfunctioning mufflers, bass amplifiers resonating with hip-hop music. Genuine city-street sounds. The surf pounding inside his head was not a real sound. It was pain, and pain was soundless. And he was drowning in it.

"Hey."

Shit.

"Somebody's here. Some drunk."

He opened his eyes, looked at the feet first. Nikes with racing stripes. Two pairs, big shoes, big baggy pants. Clown pants, maybe. He was in no mood for clowns.

One of them spoke. "Get your ass outta my office, man. I'm doin' business."

He stood up slowly, eyes on the funny pants.

"Move," said a voice too youthful to be giving serious orders. "Now."

"Do 'im. Look at him. He's so shitfaced, he don't even know what's up. *Do 'im.*"

One pair of clown shoes shifted restlessly.

"Go ahead." The other shoes shifted, scraping gravel. "Go ahead. Make his day. Go on."

These clowns needed a new joke writer.

"You got about two seconds," the mouthy one warned.

He raised his head, sought their eyes, and when he knew he had them utterly, he snatched the gun. "Now you've got none. You missed your chance."

The two stared, momentarily dumbfounded, and he thought, *Damn, this pair's too young to be funny.*

"Fuck!" The big mouth turned on the one with the suddenly empty hand. "Wha'd you let him do that for? What the hell's the matter with you?"

"Nothing!" The scrawny arms flapped, like flightless bird wings. "I don't know, man. I don't know what happened. Some kinda trick. I couldn't . . ."

"Ain't no goddamn trick, you little chickenshit. You *let* him take it."

"Go home!" His bark was enough to make the big, brave name-caller back off. "You got no business here. Not tonight."

The boy he'd disarmed drew himself up, inflating what chest he had under his tablecloth of a T-shirt as he eyed the gun now pointed at the ground. "You give me back what's mine."

"Go home."

"That's my piece. I ain't goin' nowhere without my—"

"I'm letting you go with your head still attached. *Use it.*" But they didn't move. Too damn stubborn to move. "It's late," he told them through clenched teeth. "Go home."

"You think you're talkin' to some kid?"

"I think..." They couldn't know how badly their youth hurt his eyes. "I *wish*," he amended, his jaw aching. He made a conscious effort to relax the muscles in his face before adding quietly, "I wish you'd both get away from me. Right now." He stepped away from the wall. "*Right now.*"

No Gun grabbed Big Mouth by the arm. "Let's get outta here."

"Ma-a-a-n, we are gonna be in some deep shit."

"We just tell him—"

"*You* tell him. You lost the gun."

"We still got the stuff. We'll say nobody showed."

"Shee-it, man. The Man don't want the stuff back. All The Man wants is the cash. He's gonna..."

The voices faded. Whoever *he* was, whatever he was going to do was someone else's problem now that the voices were gone. Kids' voices. Children. They could pack a man's weapon and do a man's dirty work, but there was no way to acquire a man's voice except to take some time to let it happen. Grab some time, take it, and live with it a while.

Take it and *live.*

With practiced hands he disabled the gun. It was a fitting part of his curse that night after night he should face a kid with a gun in his hand. Night after night he had managed to face them down

63

and disarm them. He didn't think about it, didn't plan it, didn't even know how he was going to do it from one time to the next. Didn't care.

That was it; he really didn't care. His head was about to bust wide open anyway, so what difference did it make? A kid with a gun in his hand. If the kid pulled the trigger on him, so be it. If not, it was one less gun in the hand of a kid. At least for one night. It wasn't much, but it was something, and it brought some small relief. Too small sometimes. He ought to think about going back to the medication. He ought to give in and take something, anything, whatever he could beg, borrow, or steal. Not that it would do him any good now, this minute. He was too far into it now.

Just wait, he told himself. It's coming. The break point is coming.

"Hey."

More shit.

"Listen here. I'm looking for two boys."

"You just missed them." He was tired, and he was hurting. If he looked up now, he was going to be tempted to let go. "I sent them home," he mumbled between the points of his collar.

"Who am I dealing with now?"

"Take your business someplace else." He lifted his head, found himself looking at a black man, just about his height, his build. An even match, if that was what it came down to. "I ain't buyin'. I ain't sellin'."

"You sent them home, simple as that."

"They're just kids. Whatever your business is, you oughta leave them out of it."

"I like to see a man's face when I'm—"

The man was about to make the mistake of touching his hat. The response was reflexive. "Don't."

"Put it down." The man dismissed the pistol with a gesture. "I'm a cop. All I'm reaching for is proof." He opened his jacket, deliberately revealing his shoulder holster as he flashed a shield.

"So let's you and me stay cool. I've seen you around before, haven't I?"

"Do something with this." It was a relief to hand over the gun. "There's no clip. I took it out."

"You took their gun and sent them home?" The cop chuckled. "That's a pretty smooth trick."

"Just kids."

"I'm beginning to think there's no such thing anymore. Not on these streets."

"Yeah, there is. They go to school, they draw pictures, they do the things kids do." He had to get away now. Let the man do his job. "They need you to look after them," he said as he turned, seeking the far end of the alley. The dark end. "Gotta watch out for them."

"Yeah, well, you, uh . . ."

"Gotta get down . . . get down . . ."

Down deep, down under. Down where the light couldn't touch him.

It was several days before Jesse Brown Wolf finally showed up to change the lock on Angela's door. He offered neither explanation nor apology, but she remembered that he owed her none. Still, she was curious about the man, because he was willing to help her out, because there was just something about him. Eyes, voice . . . striking good looks, maybe? Striking in the easy, fluid way he moved his body, the way he handled his tools, the way he drove a screw. Striking . . .

He was replacing the strike plate in the doorjamb. Strike plate. So that was what it was called. "Do you do quite a bit of work on my landlord's property?" she wondered casually. "From what you said last time you were here, it sounded as though he gives you a fair amount of runaround, too."

"You could say that, I guess." He started a screw by tapping the tip into a hole with a hammer. "But a job's a job."

"That's what I keep telling myself." She sighed, folded her

arms, tipped her head to one side as she watched the forceful turning of the screw. "Have you worked in this building before?"

"Once or twice." He stopped screwing long enough to question her motive for asking with a pointed look.

"I just wondered. I thought if you might be coming by anyway, for regular maintenance or whatever, that maybe you wouldn't mind working on the windows when you have a chance. This place is so"—her gesture described "falling apart"—"and it's been almost impossible to get anything done about it."

"You haven't been staying here long."

"Four months. I just moved to the Cities, actually."

"And you're not a city girl," he concluded as he tossed the screwdriver into the top tray of his open toolbox.

"Not exactly." She watched him test the door. "Not at all. Maybe I should take a course in self-defense or something."

"One good self-defense is to get to know your neighbors. Are you afraid of your neighbors?"

"No," she said, too quickly. The woman who lived downstairs had a lot of kids living with her, and some of them didn't appear to be hers. That much she'd noticed. One of the younger ones had knocked her geranium off the step that very morning. Angela wasn't going to say anything, just wait, repair the damage when no one was looking, but the woman had done that herself. Angela had overheard the woman's patient admonishment to be more careful, and later she'd found most of the dirt scraped off the step and put back into the pot, along with a few chips of peeling porch paint. "Not . . . not afraid," she decided. "Just cautious."

"Cautious is good." He flipped the new double bolt, turned to her, and looked her in the eye. "But you don't seem to be very good at being cautious. You've got one good friend who's pretty concerned about that."

"Tommy T." She nodded and smiled, sparing the new bolted lock a quick glance. "He's a doll, isn't he? Do you know anything about his family?"

He shrugged. "I've seen the kid around, is all."

"His mother's out of town, and he wants me to go to his school's open house with him, which"—she shrugged, too—"might be a little awkward."

"Awkward?"

"Well, I don't know his mother, don't know how she'd feel about me butting in. It seems important to him to have an adult there."

"Well, you're the one he asked."

"I'm not sure why. It's just an open house. People skip those all the time."

"Maybe Tommy T wants to start out like the people who don't skip those all the time, just to see what it feels like."

"I wish I knew more about his family situation. I just want to be sure I'm not—" He turned away from her. Her voice dropped, almost apologetically. "As I said, butting in."

"He strikes me as a pretty independent kid. I wouldn't worry about butting in." He upended a small brown paper bag and poured its chinking contents into his palm, then showed her a handful of screws and knobby fixtures. "You wanna try these on your windows?"

"You remembered," she said, smiling.

He shrugged again. "I'm what you might call *ir*regular maintenance. I'll have to put some metal strips in the casings so you can slide them up and down better, and then these things can block the windows from going up more than a couple of inches." He showed her how the mechanism worked with his thumb.

"Do you have time to install them?"

"I can start with that one over there." With a nod he indicated the window above the sofa.

"I mean, it's after—" She checked her watch.

"I got nobody waitin' for me."

"Oh." His eyes challenged hers to ask him to elaborate. She wanted to, but she backed away instead. "Well, I think Tommy T's coming over to visit his comic books tonight. He'll probably be here very soon."

"Your bodyguard, huh?" He chuckled as he dropped the window fixtures into the paper bag. "I'll keep that in mind. Darlene's home, too. The woman who lives downstairs. She'd hear you if you screamed real loud. She'd probably bang on the ceiling and tell you to pipe down. Now, if you got to know her a little bit . . ."

"I wasn't suggesting . . ."

"It's okay. Caution is good." With a simple, direct look he had her cornered. At least she *felt* cornered. His smile was more feral than friendly. "Caution is very good. In or out?"

"What?"

The metal fixtures rattled in the bag as he bounced it in his hand. "This stuff. In or out?"

"In," she said quickly. "If you have time."

"I got time."

"And if you'll let me pay you. Without a work order, you might not—"

"Suit yourself. I don't haggle over money. Maybe I'll get paid twice." Amusement lingered briefly in his eyes. Then he turned away and left her speculating.

It was not named for a president or a place on the map, but for the people it served. Many Nations Elementary looked like a school, but it had a special character, a unique aura that Angela felt the minute she walked in, following on the heels of a broadly grinning Tommy T. It was like stepping off the desert into an oasis in the city, a cool blue sanctuary. The rooms were embellished with the usual WELCOME BACK TO SCHOOL signs, the requisite maps and charts, and the smiling tagboard cutouts, but it was the American Indian theme—carried out in strong colors, in geometric and floral patterns, and in a nod to a timeless natural world existing somewhere beyond the surrounding streets—that gave the place its character.

The artwork in the glass showcases and the books on display near the library boasted of the same influence. American Indian children attended school here. Some had been brought to the city by families looking for opportunities that were unavailable on their remote reservations. Others—the children of earlier generations pushed into the city by the intrusive prod of federal policies—had never known reservation life. But here in this new magnet school, their identity was proudly acknowledged.

Angela was captivated immediately. She could almost smell fresh dittos, even though she knew the ditto machine had gone the way of the dinosaur. Some schools still had them in the closet or the teachers' lounge. Small schools, like Roosevelt Elementary back home. But a new school like this would have a neat, fast, efficient copier, which the teachers probably wouldn't be allowed to touch. Teachers were notoriously hard on the hardware. The more sophisticated the machine, the more of a pain . . .

Tommy T didn't realize he was doing her a favor by dragging her out of her retrospection and into his new classroom. Angela dutifully put on a smile and introduced herself to Mrs. Garrett, Tommy T's new teacher. "We're sort of looking after each other while his mom's out of town," Angela explained as she shook the stout woman's hand.

"Are you good friends?"

"Oh, yes," Angela said, favoring Tommy T with a genuine smile. Except for a faint stain on the sleeve, his T-shirt was clean and hardly wrinkled, his brown face scrubbed almost as bright as his coffee-bean eyes, his hair nearly tamed by his obvious efforts with a comb. He'd taken pains to get ready for their date tonight. She felt a strong urge to hug him for it, right then and there. "We're buddies, aren't we?"

"I mean, you and Ricki." Mrs. Garrett adjusted her glasses as she glanced at the registration form lying on her desk. "Ricki Little Warrior. Thomas's mother."

"Well, yeah, we think Angela's way cool," Tommy T reported exuberantly. "The way she lets me hang out at her place. She puts in a lotta hours waiting tables at the Hard Luck Café, people ordering her around and complaining about their food and stuff, but she still lets me come over and watch TV, play with her little dog, stuff like that." He surveyed the teacher's desk. A book about the weather caught his eye, but he went on talking as he flipped the red cover open. "So my mom, well, she hadda go back to the rez, take care of some stuff, like, you know, family stuff." He turned a couple of pages, checked out a few pictures as he explained offhandedly, "Somebody's always gettin' sick. They're real old, some of them."

"Your mother's family lives in . . ." Mrs. Garrett consulted her records. "Let's see, where were you born?"

"I was born here, but she's from South Dakota." He glanced up. "Long ways out there. She probably wouldn't get back before school starts, so that's why . . ." He looked to Angela for backup.

She nodded and laid a hand on his shoulder. "That's why I'm here."

"It's nice of you to offer Thomas a place to stay so that he can get started in school on time. That's important. Gets us off on the right foot, doesn't it, Thomas?"

"Yeah." He turned to the study carrel in the corner of the room, where a cursor winked on a blue screen. "Did they get any new programs for the computers? I heard about this one for animation that sounds bitch—*way* cool."

"Tommy T's a fantastic artist," Angela said.

"Some of his work is on display out in the showcases right now." The teacher's voice trailed after Tommy T. "Did you show her?"

"No, not yet." He looked up at Angela and shrugged modestly. "Just some funny little stuff the art teacher kinda liked. You wanna see?"

"Definitely." She surveyed the front of the room, feeling a little gut-level envy. August nights had always been the time for back-to-school dreams, and this year had been no exception. She'd dreamed that she'd had the wrong day written down on the calendar, that they'd run out of classrooms and she'd ended up in the boiler room, that she'd forgotten about the guppies one of the kids had brought in last spring . . . that she had her old job back. "That's a nice set of maps," she told Mrs. Garrett. "Will you be covering map skills this year?"

"Oh, yes, thoroughly. Of course, we highlight American In-

dian culture and history, particularly Chippewa, or, more properly, Ojibwa, and, of course, Sioux—that is, Dakota—in our social
studies program. That's what we're all about here. I mean, besides
the standard requirements." The woman, who appeared to be
every bit the Anglo-Saxon that Angela was, gave her a quick
glance to make sure she was following all this. Angela nodded.
"But we certainly cover all the skills, all the . . ." The teacher slid
a stapled document across the desktop. "Well, here's a sample of
topics."

"What about language arts?"

"Again, we integrate Dakota and Ojibwa language, but we
teach reading, writing, and oral language skills in English."

"Do you have a scope and sequence for grade six? I'd just like
to"—she was perusing the list of familiar sixth-grade topics of
study—"look at it if you happen to have something worked out."

"That's still in committee," Mrs. Garrett said wistfully.

"I know how that goes." Angela looked up as she flipped a
page, sparing a quick smile. "I mean, life is full of committees,
isn't it?"

"A teacher's life certainly is." The woman paused for a moment, studying Angela as though she'd been asked to propose a
new hairstyle for her. "Would you be interested in volunteering
for our after-school tutoring program? We're just getting it set up,
and we really do need tutors."

"I go to work before . . ." But not every day, she thought. She
didn't have to wait on those damn tables *every* day. "I might be
able to work something out a couple of days a week." Just saying
it gave her a quick, palpable, electric shiver. She brightened.
"You'll be getting sick of me pretty soon, Tommy T. Everywhere
you go, there I'll be."

"Nah," he said, returning to Angela's side. "I know plenty of
places you'd never go. If I wanna get lost, nobody's gonna find
me."

"That's a pretty scary thought," Mrs. Garrett said.

"Why don't you show me your artwork that's on display?"

Angela suggested. "It was very nice meeting you, Mrs.—"

"Ginny. Tell Ricki to be sure and stop by any time. And please
. . . we really do need volunteers. There's a sign-up list in the reception area." She smiled at her new pupil. "Be sure to introduce
Angela to Mr. Bird, Thomas."

"I will," he promised. On the way out he confided, "I like the
way you tested her about what she's gonna be teaching us. That
was cool."

"Just plain cool, or was it *way* cool?"

"Well . . ." The boy gave a teetering gesture. "Pretty cool."

Angela laughed as she followed him down the hall, nodding
at the occasional adult with whom she made eye contact. "So
who's Mr. Bird?"

"He's one of the elders the school gets to come in and be . . .
elders. I call him Grandpa because that's what he said for me to
call him. He's from South Dakota, too, the same place where my
mom's from."

Where his mom was from. Mention of the woman, of her very
existence, disturbed Angela more all the time, and it shouldn't,
she told herself. She had no business feeling disturbed, or worse,
begrudging. She didn't even know the woman, knew nothing of
her situation. All she knew was her son. Ricki's son. The woman
had a name now. Ricki Little Warrior. Tommy T's mom.

Her friend and would-be protector, Tommy T, seemed more
properly the child now, tonight, reveling in a child's rightful environment as he led her to the display case containing his hand-
icraft. He described the way he'd fashioned the two pieces of
pottery and the beautifully simple leather sculpture of a horse.
Angela was genuinely impressed with his work, and she praised
it lavishly before they moved on to the student artwork displayed
on the walls in the long hallway.

"Hey, there's the guy that fixed the toilet." Tommy T tugged
on Angela's arm. She looked up, and her eyes met Jesse Brown
Wolf's. Framed in an open doorway, caught getting up off his
knees as he reeled in a tape measure, he'd obviously heard the

announcement, to which the boy blithely added, "The Goofy guy."

"Tommy T..." With her maternal instincts already in gear, the warning tone was automatic.

"I mean the guy that likes Goofy," he amended with an impish grin as he approached the man, who looked bemused by the interruption. "Right? Goofy and Road Runner."

"Not Road Runner. The coyote." The repairman slipped the tape measure into place on the leather tool belt that was loosely strapped around his slim hips. He was dressed in a T-shirt and jeans, his dark hair neatly anchored at his nape. "I'm a coyote man myself."

"How's the playground equipment coming?" Angela asked. The man glanced over his shoulder, as though he wondered what she was looking at. "Finished already?"

"It's on hold." Screwdriver in hand, he indicated the project under construction beyond the open double doors. "They need these partitions in here first. They call this the media center, but it looks like a library to me." He looked at Tommy T. "How 'bout you?" The boy nodded. "Ready for school to start?"

"Yeah, I guess." Deep, dramatic sigh. "Only six more days of freedom."

"You have to see the beautiful horse our friend here made," Angela said, motioning Jesse to follow as she retraced her steps. "The little pots are great, too, but this horse..." She gestured proudly. "Right over here. I think we have the makings of a real Michelangelo in our midst."

Jesse peered into the case, studied for a moment. "You did that yourself?"

"No problem," Tommy T said.

"Damn fine piece of work." He looked at the boy. "Michelangelo, hell, you could be another Oscar Howe. Famous Sioux artist," Jesse explained as his gaze strayed down the hall. With a purse-lipped nod, he called Angela's attention to an attractive black woman surrounded by a bevy of children. "There's your downstairs neighbor."

"Those are all her kids?" Angela counted seven, ranging in age from toddler to young teen, boys and girls, light- and dark-skinned. She'd never seen them all together in one spot, but she recognized the familiar faces and felt more than a little embarrassed about the fact that she barely knew the woman's name.

"They're all staying with her. She takes care of all of them." Jesse shrugged. "I guess they're all hers, huh? At least for now."

"For now," Angela allowed. The phrase sounded hollow somehow.

The woman's ears might have been burning, but she turned with a smile. "Hey, Wolf! What're you up to? Don't you never quit workin'?"

"When the work runs out," he said as she approached them. "I gotta be gettin' back to it. You guys know each other?"

"We *are* neighbors," Angela said, her smile sheepish. "I'm probably not the most neighborly of neighbors, but I do know who—"

"She's shy," Tommy T injected, ever the rescuer. "Angela's kinda shy. Kinda new in town, too."

"I thought maybe she was scared of us or something," Darlene said. "Me and my wild bunch."

"Not at all. I didn't even realize—" Angela glanced down the hall, where two of the boys were wrestling as an older girl made a halfhearted attempt to break them up. "I knew there were kids downstairs, of course, but I didn't know you had this many."

"I don't always. I've got my sister's boy right now, plus my daughter's friend, plus . . ." She lifted the smallest youngster, a boy in bib overalls, into her arms, and he promptly laid his head on her shoulder. "Just kids who need a place to stay. If they give you any trouble, let me know."

"As I said, I hardly know they're there."

"Jesse's been fixing your place up, huh? Bless that Wolf and his clever paws." She glanced past a pair of open doors at the man who had brought them together. He'd returned to his work on a panel of shelving. "You ever seen our landlord's house? That man lives in a palace. You think it would hurt him to jar loose with a little upkeep in our so-called low-rent district? I don't think his pockets would feel one ounce lighter."

Bored with the woman talk, Tommy T wandered into the media center for a closer look at Jesse's project.

Darlene suddenly fixed eyes on Angela. "Now, I *know* you ain't got no kids. I make it my business to know who's comin' and goin' through those front doors. So what brings you here tonight?" She glanced quickly past the doors again. "Besides that little con artist."

"Tommy T? He's certainly an *artist*." Angela looked his way, too, smiling fondly. "We're good friends. He wanted me to see his school."

"I've seen him around, him and his brother. They're in with one of the gangs."

"Not Tommy T. I don't know about his brother, but Tommy T is . . ." *Is who? Is what?* She was uneasy with the suggestion of some gang connection, wanted to deny it straight out, to defend her young friend by laying out the facts. But the facts were in short supply. "Well, he's still in grade school, obviously, which makes him a child. Too young to be in any serious trouble."

"What do you call serious?"

"Hanging offenses," Angela said lightly, but then she remembered the size of her recent attackers. She'd tried not to think about how old they might have been. Her smile tightened. "Irreversible," she amended.

"Mmm, that's bad." Darlene lowered her voice and glanced down the hall at the pretty blond girl who was still minding the two wrestlers. "I've got one staying with me now, junior high. She's pregnant. Her mother kicked her out. How serious is that?"

"Kicked her out because she's pregnant?" The girl's clothing was voluminous, her face pale, her willowy arms those of a child. "Can a mother just . . . *do* that?"

"Gayla's did."

"But . . ." The girl looked so young, so innocent, so . . . *inno-cent*. "What's she going to do?"

"What would you do?"

"If I were, what, fourteen? Fifteen?" Darlene's nod indicated that she'd hit the mark. Angela sighed. "I don't know. Give the baby up for adoption, I guess."

"You're guessing with an adult woman's head. Little Miss Gayla, she's got her a woman-child's head. She can't think past next Saturday. My girl, Poppy, brought her home because she was talking about taking off for California. You know who she knows in California? Not a blessed soul." Darlene adjusted her drowsy burden as she shifted her weight from one hip to the other. "What you think, Angela, is getting pregnant at that age a hangin' offense?"

Angela shook her head slowly. "And it's not hopeless, either, but I guess it *is* irreversible. Not even an abortion can reverse a pregnancy. Just ends it." She scowled. "It can't be legal to throw a fifteen-year-old out just for getting pregnant."

"I wouldn't know. You ask me, the law works in mysterious ways. All I know is, I can't stand to see them put out on the street. Not that young."

"No," Angela said, her attention drifting back to the children playing down the hall. "Everyone needs a safe place." She caught herself getting too somber, and she quickly recovered her smile. "So you have children in school here, too."

"Too?" The implied claim clearly amused Darlene. "Yeah, I've got three goin' to school here. They really like it."

"I was asked to help out with some after-school tutoring. I almost said I didn't have time, but the truth is, I have nothing better to do with my time."

"You'd be good at it. I can tell just by the way you talk. You work at the café, right?" Angela nodded. "You're from out of state. I can tell—"

"Just by the way I talk." Angela smiled, but that was all she would say. Out of state covered a lot of territory.

"I'd offer to help out, but I've got kids comin' and goin', and I work at the store odd shifts sometimes, filling in when somebody don't show up."

"It sounds as though you're doing more than your share, taking care of these children."

"That man's helped me out a time or two, but don't tell him I told you," Darlene said, indicating Jesse with a subtle nod. "Look at him. Says he ain't a real carpenter, but he does a damn good imitation."

The whine of a power drill nearly drowned out Darlene's testimony. Jesse was down on one knee, his back to the door, Tommy T looking on as the big man sank a neat row of holes into a strip of oak.

"He thinks he's keeping his generous nature a big secret," Darlene said. "Like he don't want people hittin' him up. But when it comes to kids, he likes to help out. He don't say much, but somehow he knows, and he always comes through."

"I guess I did sort of hit him up," Angela admitted, mostly to herself, as she stood watching the boy hover over the man's shoulder.

Tommy T was the one who sensed her attention. Just the fact that she was looking his way pulled him to her side like a magnet. "Come on, Angela. You gotta meet Mr. Bird. He's probably workin' on something in the art room. He makes a lot of Indian stuff." He latched onto her arm, as though she belonged to him. "He had a shield goin' last time I looked. He tanned the rawhide himself, and he was stretching it onto a hoop, making it into this cool shield, like for a warrior."

"Nice meeting you, finally," Angela said as she allowed herself to be dragged away.

"Same here."

Darlene sounded a little tentative. About as tentative as Angela felt. In three months she'd done nothing about making friends with anyone. Her situation was only supposed to be temporary. Work, eat, sleep, wait. The simple life. But before she turned away, she offered her neighbor a smile. One friend couldn't complicate the simple life too much, could it? Well, one *more* friend. Her circle was still modest in size, and she was determined to keep it that way.

Mr. Bird was a small man, but he had great presence. Great-grandfatherly presence, Angela noted immediately. Self-possessed, soft-spoken, completely serene, he held court in the corner of the art room, receiving children and their parents with handshakes and some remembrances. His white hair and wizened face marked him as a repository of memories. The rawhide shield he was embellishing with horse-and-rider figures had an instant admirer in Tommy T, who was quietly invited to slip his arm through the twisted rawhide straps as long as he didn't touch the paint. He grinned, postured heroically, then entertained by dancing around the room in a mock battle with an invisible opponent.

"You know what, Grandpa Bird? I bet if you put a steel plate inside here, or maybe a Hercutanium alloy, a guy with super-power reflexes could use it like . . ." Shield aloft, he performed a defensive pose-down. "Wham! Wham! Bullets, laser blades, everything." Explosive sound effects enhanced the exhibition. "It all bounces off."

"What's Hercutanium?" Angela asked.

"Something I invented for making armor. Foolproof protection." He traced the inner rim of the wooden frame with appreciative fingertips. "*Magnetized.*" His face brightened. "Magnetized, yeah. Then he could just suck their guns right out of their hands. How bitchin' is that?"

"Way cool," Angela said, her tone pointedly correctional.

"A warrior who would go into battle carrying that shield wouldn't need a metal plate," Mr. Bird said.

"Well, yeah, because all you had comin' at you was arrows."

"You think an arrow is a small threat? The arrow from a Lakota warrior's bow could pass right through the body of a buffalo."

79

Smiling, Mr. Bird used a leathery forefinger to spear Tommy T in the ribs. "Right through."

"Eee-yow!" The boy laughed. "So what good's this little thing gonna do?"

"Maybe none." The old man's smile faded. "When men come to kill, there is no such thing as foolproof protection."

"But killing is what being a warrior is all about, right?"

"It's about being willing to kill if necessary and to die if necessary. And knowing how to do both, if . . ."

"Necessary," Tommy T finished dutifully.

The old man eyed the boy fixedly. "The trick is knowing when it's necessary. Truly understanding why. Bravery is only one of the virtues a man seeks. Wisdom is the one that's hardest to gain."

"Yeah, well, dying sure might be necessary if you don't have any Hercutanium in this thing." Tommy T withdrew his arm from the straps and took a close look at the red-and-blue painting before handing the shield back to its maker. "See, I've been thinkin' about comin' up with some Indian heroes. On paper, you know? Somebody said something to me the other day about tricky Indians. In stories they could trick their enemies, so I was thinkin', like, what kinda weapons would I give to a coyote and a spider?"

"Ah," Mr. Bird said. "You're talking about Old Man Coyote and Iktome. Haven't I told you some of those stories in class?"

"I don't know. Maybe I was gone that day," Tommy T muttered evasively. But then he found his childlike charm. "Can you tell me? Just one story."

Without preface or prelude, Mr. Bird launched into a tale about Old Man Coyote getting himself stuck in a tree and berating the bird people for making too much noise by pecking holes in the trunk while he was trying to figure out how to get out. At last Old Man Coyote had no choice but to cut himself up and push the pieces of his body through the holes. Before he could get all of himself out of the tree, Crow came along and started eating Coyote's intestines, commenting between bites that this was good food and Coyote was a fool for throwing it out.

The telling of the tale drew Mr. Bird out of his chair. His imitation of the cut-up Coyote had Angela and Tommy T in stitches as they watched the trickster hero try to shoo an imaginary Crow away and put himself back together at the same time. When that was done, he set about filling himself up with the first food he could find. A recent prairie fire had left him few choices—a charred field mouse and a few smoking grasshoppers. Mr. Bird made a production of popping them into his mouth and yelping about a burned tongue as he continued his search. Sparks flew as he kicked at logs, occasionally discovering another roasted morsel. Without intestines, Coyote heard his food fall out behind him as he walked along. Angela and Tommy T became Squirrel and Mockingbird, whose only roles were to laugh and tell him he was still "losing it."

A small crowd of parents and children had joined in by the time Mr. Bird reached his conclusion, describing a pitch-filled anus that caught on fire and sent him dancing in circles and howling. The kids loved that!

"But nothing was lost," Mr. Bird assured them. "Coyote never dwells long in his shame before he gets patched up and on to something else. All burned and crispy, that old dog ran for the creek, really smoked up the whole sky when he jumped in. And all that had passed through Coyote's body and fallen to the ground that day soon grew back as the first tobacco.

"Old Man Coyote has his moments of foolishness, but Tunkasila gave him a job to do, and one way or another he does it. He sets things right." Mr. Bird smiled at Tommy T, who was still holding his sides from laughing. "Too tricky for his own good, that old dog, but he's a hero to us."

"Why does he have to be foolish, though? You can't have a hero who's half fool."

"You can't?" Mr. Bird wagged his head as he applied finger pressure to his stiffening lower back. "Your heroes can't be human, then. People make mistakes."

"Yeah, but half fool?" Tommy T insisted. "*Half?*"

"We try to whittle it down over time. At my age, after I've tried about everything my mama told me not to mess with, my fool part is probably down to less than half. But now that I've got my head straightened around"—he eased himself back into his chair, the spry storyteller suddenly feeling his age—"my body's about ready to give out on me. Like that old man in *Star Wars*."

"You mean Obi Wan," one of the other children supplied.

"That's the one," the old man said.

"Yeah, but that light saber is about as old-fashioned now as a slingshot," Tommy T said, returning to his original concern.

"So is this shield." But the way the old man fondled the leather fittings said that he, too, fit the description.

"Yeah, but this is cool, Grandpa Bird," Tommy T assured him. "I mean, this really looks cool."

"Bring me some of your work, *cinks*." The old man punctuated the Lakota term of endearment with a fond wink. "Maybe we can do some trading."

"For reals?" Mr. Bird nodded. "Bit-chiin."

Angela and Tommy T walked home with Darlene and her flock. It was slow going when the two-year-old wanted to walk. Up ahead, Gayla seemed content to practice for imminent motherhood by keeping the other children from straying off the sidewalk as they ran ahead. Her friend Poppy, Darlene's daughter, was thoroughly bored with their antics. Tommy T exchanged occasional words with both girls, which interested Angela when she overheard his brother briefly mentioned. She wasn't going to pry. She wouldn't make a point of eavesdropping. But she wanted to know more about the boy's family. Few decipherable words actually passed between the two, however, and Angela decided that kids that age obviously communicated with each other in code.

Darlene asked whether Angela would be interested in attending the next Block Club meeting with her. Angela dutifully asked what that was, but since it didn't really matter, she only half listened as she mentally sorted through her list of ways to excuse herself from taking part in social activities. She'd had the list down pat long before she'd moved to the Cities, having turned so much of her life, so many of her decisions, over to the whims of a madman. But she hadn't had to use it much lately. She had to choose carefully. She didn't want to sound stuck-up.

"What are you girls doin' here?" Darlene barked suddenly.

Angela snapped out of her self-absorption and realized that they'd reached their own block. It was twilight, and a trio of very young women dressed in very tight clothes were, as the plump one with a profusion of red hair said, "Just hangin' out."

Darlene took a defensive, square-shouldered, high-headed posture. "I told you to go hang it out someplace else, didn't I?"

"You don't own this corner," a leggy blonde fired back. Her heavy makeup did a poor job of disguising her acne and her tender age.

Darlene turned to Angela. "Would you take these kids back to the house?"

"C'mon, Mom," Poppy countered. "We ain't leavin' you here with no backup."

"I don't need backup for this job." With a gesture she told Poppy to take the baby's hand while she turned her full furor on the three streetwalkers. "Sorry, girls, but you ain't doin' no more business here. We told you that already. If I have to stand here and scare all your customers away—"

A petite, gum-snapping black girl hooted, her eyes flashing with defiant delight. "You would, too, with a face like that."

"I got my self-respect, girl. That's something money can't buy, I don't care how much they pay you."

"You are one ugly witch woman."

"Go get me my broom, Tony," Darlene ordered her older son. "Hurry up! I got some cleanin' up to do here."

"You're gonna be sorry," the redhead warned. But she was already backing over the curb. "You're gonna be real sorry."

"I don't think so."

The three were giving up easily, knowing that a crowd of bickering women wasn't likely to attract the kind of customers they needed.

"Hey!" Darlene shouted after them. The black girl paused. "I can put you in touch with somebody who can help you find a better job."

"Hey," the blonde shouted as she grabbed her cohort by the arm and dragged her into the intersection. "I can put you in touch with a blind man who might be willing to fuck you if you pay him enough."

Car brakes squealed, and the driver stuck his head out the window to offer a backhanded compliment on the heels of an obscenity. All three girls soon piled into the backseat, and the car roared away.

"My God," Angela said, watching the car until it disappeared around the next corner. "That took guts, Darlene."

"Sorry." Darlene shrugged, grinning, hardly looking sorry. "I guess you're one of us now, whether you like it or not."

"One of . . . who?"

"Neighborhood Watch. It's one of our Block Club functions. Just a group of us who decided to stop looking the other way. We mean to take our neighborhood back." She nodded in the direction the carload of streetwalkers had taken. "They see you with me, they'll take you for one of us."

"I certainly agree with your actions, but . . . well, I only wish I had that much nerve."

"You got as much as you need," Darlene insisted as they headed for their front gate. "You're a woman, right? You'll do what you have to. That's what women do." She cast a quick glance over her shoulder. "Those girls think they're just doin' what they have to. Maybe they are. Lord only knows who's behind them and what'll happen to them if they don't come up with some cash. But not on my block."

"I'm willing to do what I can," Angela said, "but I'm afraid I'm not much of a fighter. Right, Tommy T?"

"Aw, you just got took by surprise that one time, Angela." He opened the gate. "Without a bodyguard, it could happen to any-body."

"But now I've got a bodyguard," Angela told Darlene.

"You've got a shadow, which might be just as good."

"A friend." She glanced back at Tommy T, then up at Darlene, who had mounted the well-worn wooden porch steps just ahead of her, carefully sidestepping the potted geranium. "That's the best. One really good friend."

When Tommy T said good night to Angela, he assured her that he was going right home, which was as honest as he could get with her when she asked him that question. No, it wasn't too far; yes, he knew it was late; and yes, he would be careful. Since she didn't have any kids of her own, he figured she must have learned the routine from her mother and decided to try it out on him. He didn't have the heart to point out to her that he'd probably forgotten more about watching his back in the streets than she'd ever know.

Then he hit the streets, staying mostly in the shadows, using his reliable instincts to hunt up his errant brother. Stoner was with Ajax's bunch, celebrating T-Rex's latest victory over some Frogtown dude's German shepherd. They were passing around a pint of peppermint schnapps and a couple of joints. Tommy T didn't feel like partaking, so he pulled his brother aside and told him that he'd been hanging out some with the girl Stoner had had his eye on lately, and she'd asked about him.

Stoner thought that was pretty cool. He told Tommy T that he could crash at his new squat in a deserted warehouse until after Labor Day if he needed to. "The ol' lady usually shows up after Labor Day," Stoner maintained, based on his extra few years of experience. "But if she don't show, you're gonna have to check in with social services, man."

"I can take care of myself," Tommy T contended. "You just worry about your own self until . . ." He shrugged. It used to be *Until Mom comes back to get us.* They'd waited for her, time after time, repeating the mantra faithfully. There had to be something to look forward to, and you had to believe it was coming. Tommy T looked up at his brother and tried hard to think of something to look forward to. His brother needed it more than he did. Stoner's eyes were bleary. He smelled like rotting food. He was rocking from side to side like some wasted wino. *Damn.* "Until I find us a place."

"You!" Stoner laughed. "Find yourself a place. I've got one."

"A *clean* place. Warm and dry, with no—"

"Find yourself a place," Stoner repeated, suddenly sober and dead serious. He squeezed Tommy T's shoulder, then shook it once, hard. "I mean it. I want you to stay in school, so that means you need a place to stay. If it has to be foster care—"

"I don't need that shit." Tommy T backed away. "She'll be back, Stoner. I'll find us a good place where we can wait for her."

Stoner was still swaying like some bounce-back kid's toy, still shaking his head when Tommy T turned and ran. He took to the shadows and ran, dodging pools of streetlight and busy intersections. It was after the city's ten o'clock weekday curfew, and he was, technically, a kid. But he knew how to be careful. He ducked into doorways, careful not to step on anyone who'd already taken refuge for the night. As long as you didn't touch them, they didn't notice. No one noticed. All you had to do was run and hide and stay light on your feet. The parks were supposed to be off-limits after ten, but he could take to the shadows there, too. He knew the places to avoid. He knew how to find solitude. He knew the outposts of the city well.

Just as his hero did.

"Hey." It took the boy a moment to catch his breath from the long run. He leaned back against one of the rocks in the outcropping that hid the entrance to what he'd come to think of as The Den. "You down there?"

Yeah, he was. He answered with a disgusted groan.

"Don't worry. I ain't comin' in. Just wanted to see if you're home."

No answer.

Tommy T hunkered down, held onto himself, and just listened. He could hear the river slipping softly through the night, sliding underneath the bridge that arched its light across the city skyline a mile or more away. A police siren whined on some distant street, but whatever the danger was, it couldn't touch him here. It felt like a private world here, still and nearly quiet. Besides the crickets, there were just the two of them. Tommy T and his hero. He'd been thinking about Mr. Bird's stories and about Jesse Brown Wolf's remarks, putting some ideas together in his head and on paper, and he'd come up with something that made his insides quake, something too exciting to hold back.

Time to confide. "I know who you are."

He was rewarded with a proper growl. "Take off, kid. I'm not in a good mood."

"You never are. That don't bother me. I don't ever expect you to be any different." He hugged his knees and stared at the black hole that harbored his hero's secrets. "'Cause I know who you are."

"Great." As always, the voice was gravelly and gruff, as if it had been used hard and worn out. "What good's that gonna do you?"

"It might do you some good. You need a helper."

"I don't need . . ." A belabored breath, then another. ". . . nobody. Don't much like being bothered."

"That's what you always say. But Tunkasila gave you a job to do, and you can't help doin' it."

Heavy silence. Then, grudgingly, "Tunk *who?*"

"Tunkasila. That's 'Grandfather' in Sioux. That's also 'God.' "

"God?" The dry chuckle below made the night quiver. "Me and Him parted ways a long time ago."

"That's not how I got it figured now. I talked with Grandpa Bird, and I been thinkin' about this a lot. I know who you are."

"So you've . . . told old man Bird?"

"I haven't told nobody, and I ain't gonna. Even if I did, nobody would believe me. They'd say you're just another one of my cartoon fantasies."

"Maybe I am." His laugh was more echo than sound. "Jesus, maybe that's exactly what I am."

"You're Dark Dog," Tommy T ventured, and when he heard himself say it, he knew for sure it was true.

"So you've even got a name for me."

"Yeah. You needed one. Everybody needs a name."

"Dark Dog, huh?" The black hole in the earth heaved a weary sigh. After another moment: "That's good, kid. That's really great."

He liked it! "And I'm your helper."

"You got a name?"

"Tommy T. You know that."

"You can't do any better than that?"

"That's my name."

Silence. Just when he'd about given up, the dark voice came softly again, resigned, maybe almost . . . interested. "What's the T stand for?"

He swallowed hard. "You won't tell anybody?"

"Who am I gonna tell?"

"Terrific."

No response. Dark Dog probably thought he was being a smart-ass.

"The T stands for Terrific. Nobody else knows that except . . ." Except nobody. Talking about nobody, you ran the risk of turning him into somebody, a risk Tommy T had managed to avoid for a good long time. He plucked a piece of grass. The memory was so hazy it had to be handled with kid gloves, *a kid's gloves*, the clean-handed, trusting part of him that stubbornly held onto such things as gauzy memories.

The silence belowground seemed to grow heavier. Respectful, maybe. Tolerant, at least.

"My dad started calling me Tommy T when I was just little," he continued, carefully letting the big nobody's identity leak out in the darkness, where he could contain it, suck it back in quickly at the first sign of doubt. "He told me about this one cartoon he used to watch when he was a little kid, back when they only had black-and-white TV. It was called *Tom Terrific*. There was a theme song."

Then softly, in what was still a male child's voice, he sang, "I'm Tom Terrific. Greatest hero e-ver. I can be what I want to be, and if you'd like to see, fol-low, come fol-looow . . ."

The song drifted away, carrying a boy's sketchy memories down the river. The river took over, turning the song sloshy.

Tommy T chewed on the soft tip of the grass. He felt comfortably cocooned as the moments drifted. "You know what his power was?"

"Singing." A hint of amusement lifted the voice from its hole this time. "He sang his enemies to their knees."

"No way. Jeez. What he could do, see, he could turn himself into anything. Metamorphosis. Perfect disguise."

"I guess."

"And you know what else about that show? You could send away for a piece of plastic to cover the TV screen and some special crayons, and then they'd have this part where you could transform Tom yourself. My dad always wanted to send away for the stuff, but he said it was like everything else. It costed money he never had." He pitched the weed into the night like a small spear. "Anyway, he called me Tommy T for Tom Terrific."

"It fits you good."

"Think so?"

"Yeah, I think so. Now take off, Tommy T, before this dog decides to chew on your bones."

"I ain't scared of you." He smiled when the yawning hole groaned. And then he stared off into the night, watching the distant headlights etch a trail across the bridge, and he said, remarkably, whatever came to his mind. "My dad used to come and see me sometimes, even though my mom . . . Well, they weren't married or nothin'. She didn't seem to care for him much, so he didn't like to stay around long. He died when I was about six, I think. For a long time I didn't believe my mom, that he was dead, but I ain't seen him since she told me, so I guess it's true."

There was a long silence, but it felt good. Good and empty.

Tommy T didn't want to talk about himself anymore. But he still wanted to talk. "You know that lady you helped?"'

No answer.

"You know, the one Chopper and his posse came down on in the alley. Remember, you brought—" A testy grunt signaled him to make his point. "She's still scared."

"She has a right to be. They hurt her bad."

"It's not just that. She worries about being followed. She's scared of something else."

More silence.

"I don't know if it's just the city or what, 'cause I know she ain't used to it yet. But it's like she thinks somebody might be coming after her." No response. "Did you fall asleep on me, or what?"

"I don't sleep much." And then, more patiently, "I'm listening."

"Yeah, you always do, even if you make out like you don't wanna. And whenever there's trouble, you always come through."

"It's the only way to get you off my back, which is where you're sittin' right now."

The boy laughed.

"I'm no hero, Tommy T. You're not gonna make me into one even if you've got the magic screen."

"I don't have it, and I don't need it. I know who you are." He stared at the black hole so hard he could have sworn he saw two amber lights. He smiled. "You're Dark Dog."

J esse Brown Wolf wasn't stupid. He knew when he was being watched, especially when the watcher was a cop.

There were two other guys working on the school playground project with him, but the man sitting in the squad car wasn't interested in them. They took a lot of breaks, those two, but the man just sat there, watching Jesse. He showed no interest in what was going on across the street. Neither did Jesse, but it wasn't his job to be interested. He wasn't getting paid to check out the two characters who'd been sitting over there in the park all morning, waiting, also watching. Jesse was getting paid to build a playground.

A *playground*, for God's sake. Sunk right down in the middle of a treacherous traffic pattern without the kind of stoplights that might keep kids from getting run over. None that Jesse could see, anyway. One lazy-ass cop sitting in a squad car wasn't going to stop the kind of trade that had been going down so regularly that they could easily just go ahead and put up a sign.

Jesse was blocking cement footings. The rest of the crew had gone off to use the can. He didn't much care what they did, as long as they didn't mess with his work. They weren't *his* crew. They'd all been hired under a city program that was supposed to put people to work, and he was working, which was all he cared about. The less the other two did, the longer the job would take. He knew the part he was doing was getting done right, which was good for the kids. It felt good to be making something for kids to use. Finally, after feeling bad about kids for so damn long, he realized this work felt good.

"Got a light?"

"I don't smoke." Jesse went right on smoothing the wet cement. Didn't even look up. Didn't have to. "If you're looking for ID, I got nothin' on me. I'm here doing a job."

"I can see that."

The man stood there watching him. One thing Jesse found hard to ignore was being stared at. Not just being watched. Being stared at. He knew it was the same black cop he'd run into in the alley when he'd been half blind with pain. He'd turned a gun over to the guy. What more did he want?

Without looking up from his work, Jesse finally gave in. "What can I do for you, Sergeant?"

"You don't drive?"

Jesse almost laughed. "You need a ride?"

"You said you had no ID. No driver's license?"

"I said no ID. I got nothin' to drive."

"How do you get to work with all your equipment?"

"I walk or I take the bus, and I travel light." Jesse looked up, squinting into the morning sun. "Am I doing something in violation of some ordinance?"

"Not that I've noticed."

Jesse slid his work gloves off as he stood. "You want me to rub two sticks together for you, or what?"

"I'm sorry." With a chuckle, the man stuck out his hand. "Mike Richards. I work this neighborhood."

"Tough beat." Jesse reciprocated on the handshake but not the introduction.

"Tell me about it." Richards folded his arms across his chest and took a wide stance. "You're the guy I ran into in the alley. You took a twenty-two off some kids."

"You got the wrong guy."

"I don't think so. I know who you are." The cop paused for effect before adding, "And I know who you used to be."

"What business is it of yours who I am?" Unruffled, Jesse met the man's stare with one of his own. "Or even who I used to be."

"You're working around kids. Can't be too careful these days."

"Far as I know, the school never bothered with a background check. All I'm doin' is—"

"You're not working *with* kids. This is what we call close proximity."

"Yeah, well, you've got all kinds of lowlifes hangin' out in *close proximity*." Jesse glanced across the street at the pair of loiterers in the park, one lying on the metal-frame bench, the other sitting on the ground. The only movement they'd made was to switch places. "You're wasting your time on me."

"Maybe." Richards glanced, too, following Jesse's lead. "You're right. This park's been crawling with vermin for a long time. First it was just drunks. Drunks are a nuisance, but they're usually not hurting anybody but themselves. So they tear down the liquor store, cut down on the drunks, now it's drug dealers. *Real* vermin. The kind you wish you could just..." The cop scraped out a small hole in the ground with the heel of his boot. "But if you do, they slap the city with a lawsuit. Meanwhile, they put a nice new school here, and the vermin find fresh prey. Tender meat to sink their parasitic teeth into."

"Look, I got a job to do here. I ain't bothering nobody, ain't putting the bite on nobody. I don't even..." Jesse looked down at the ground between them. Rocks and red dirt. Kids needed a place to play. He didn't want to hear anything about tender meat. "What do you want with me, Sergeant?"

"I want your help."

"Help with what?"

"Ridding this place of vermin."

Jesse tipped his head back, took a deep breath, watched the sun duck under a wispy cloud. Finally he permitted the other man's gaze to touch his with its elemental challenge. He hardly felt a thing.

"I'm just a handyman. You need to find yourself an exterminator."

"I'm looking for somebody who isn't a cop"—Richards gave him one of those you-and-me looks—"anymore."

"You can keep right on lookin'." Jesse turned away, looking—*groping, really*—for something to hang onto. He found a piece of pipe and tried to remember how it was supposed to fit into the scheme of his project. "I'm not your man, Sergeant."

"They use children nowadays," Richards said, determined to drop more words into deaf ears. "Drug-dealing always was a shitty business, but there was a time when we were busting mostly adults for it. Now they've got kids fronting for them, and they get younger every day. But hell, I'm not telling you anything you don't already know."

He was waiting for Jesse to look up so he could drill him with another one of those looks, but Jesse was busy keeping busy. "Or anything *everyone* doesn't already know," he muttered as he leaned the pipe against the steel frame he'd erected earlier.

"They don't know it like we know it," the cop claimed. "It feels different, arresting a child. It feels like your own personal failure. Like everything's going to hell and you're the one standing at the gate, just passin' 'em all through."

"Maybe you need to think about gettin' yourself a new job, Sergeant." Jesse spared him a glance. "And I need to get back to mine."

The man sighed. "Look here, you see anything you don't like to see goin' down in this park, you let me know. You hear what I'm sayin'?"

"I've got ears."

"And eyes, trained to spot trouble."

"Wrong tree." Jesse pointed across the street with a jerk of his chin. The two men were still there, still waiting. "Try barkin' up one of those. They hang around here so much you'd think they'd put down roots."

"Question is . . ."

"Ask *them*," Jesse said, taking care to connect with an icy look. "Ask them your questions, Sergeant. I got work to do."

The cop finally walked away. Jesse eyed the back of that blue uniform furtively until it disappeared into the white squad car. He refused to think about how it felt to arrest a child, cuff him, manhandle him into the back of a car. Thinking about those things was only the beginning. Next he'd remember how it felt to drag the kid back out of the car.

Or lift him out of the car.

He closed his left hand around the pipe and pounded it against the steel crosspiece, carelessly mashing his fingers and shattering the encroaching memories into glittering, unrecognizable shards of pain. He didn't flinch. He knew the pain would be temporary, as pain always was. Death was the only thing that lasted forever.

The squad car finally moved on, taking the damn blue uniform with it.

Jesse hadn't worn a uniform in a very long time. Police Sergeant Mike Richards would have had to do some particular snooping to dig up that shade of blue from his past. He'd managed to become so completely colorless, he wondered why the man had bothered. He had spent much of that very long time perfecting the art of blending into the urban scenery. He said nothing, did nothing to attract attention. He lived one day at a time, took all the work he could get, and he kept to himself, mostly. Tried to, anyway. He'd taken the kid's gun only because it had been pointed in his face. If a kid was in trouble, Jesse would do what he could to help out. A kid or a woman. A man owed the world that much if he wanted to be able to call himself a man.

And Jesse still wanted at least that much. To be human again.

To be able to call himself a man. He wasn't sure what else he was, what else he'd been. Some other animal, at least partly. He wasn't sure why he hadn't managed to transform himself completely, unless maybe it was because he didn't have enough heart. Not much heart at all, which was why he was ill-suited to be anything else but a man. Even a heartless man had his hands, and it couldn't hurt to lend one on occasion, Jesse had decided. He could join the human race again by lending a hand once in a while. He could do that much for a kid.

Or for a woman.

He'd also decided he was going to have supper at the Hard Luck Café that night. Darlene offered him supper when he stopped in after work to clean up, which was part of a bargain he'd struck with her. If he kept the plumbing and other troublesome old fixtures in working order, he could use the shower, no questions asked. Darlene was always good about offering him a share of whatever she had going on the stove. He was always diplomatic about declining. The shower was the only favor he was looking for. She had enough mouths to feed.

Besides, he'd sat down at a real supper table only once in recent memory, and he wasn't sure what had made him do it then. He was even less sure why he'd made up his mind to do it again, and this time to order off a menu. He didn't like restaurants, but he had a wild urge to be served by someone in a uniform.

"Hello, Jesse."

A female someone in a pink uniform. He'd forgotten how pretty she was. He nodded, unexpectedly tongue-tied.

"Would you like coffee?" He nodded again. She turned the brown mug over and filled it. "We're known for our coffee here."

He tasted it and grimaced.

"Not for the taste as much as the strength." She slid a menu in front of him. "I've never seen you in here before."

"I'm not one for . . ." He cleared his throat as he flipped the plastic-coated menu open and scanned it without making sense of a single word. "I usually just grab something in a bag, especially when it's nice out."

"What can I get you on a plate?"

"What's good?"

"What do you like?"

He bit back *The color of your eyes*, which came to him out of the blue, maybe because that was their color. It was something he might have said in another life, one he rarely even remembered. He might have felt this way back then, awkward and dumbfounded. Caught off guard by an extraordinary impulse and suddenly wondering what the hell he was doing here, he might have tried some lame line rather than sit there acting like he didn't know what to eat.

"The special's usually pretty good. Tonight's is sort of a 'down home' dish, I guess. Hamburger in some kind of gravy over mashed potatoes." She smiled when he looked up at her, his face expressing what he hoped was a cool response. "I'm sure it's at least filling."

"How 'bout a plain hamburger?"

"That we can do." She wrote it down on her pad. "The playground is shaping up nicely."

Speaking of shape, he was admiring hers, which was nice. Her shape and the fact that he was admiring it. He'd pretty much gotten out of the habit.

"The one you're building," she reminded him.

"At the school, yeah." He wrapped both hands around the warm, shapely coffee mug. "We'da been done by now, except guys keep quitting. I was working solo two days this week."

"I was there, over there at the school..." She gestured in a vaguely down-the-street direction. "I went to a workshop for tutoring. If you volunteer, you have to attend—"

"Hey, Angela." The stocky, rubicund cook stuck his head out the kitchen pass-through. "We got other customers here."

"That's his way of reminding me that the sooner I put your

order in, the sooner you get to eat." She leaned over to pick up the menu, adding quietly, "Message: We care."

"It shows." So did the hint of a hollow between her breasts, somehow turning up the heat in his hands. "I can finish up those windows tonight."

"Tonight?" She brightened. "Tonight would be fine. I didn't realize you were planning to do any more. I mean . . . well, I was mainly concerned about the one you already fixed in the front room, because I couldn't even get that one . . ." She motioned with her pad, up and down. She seemed a little nervous, too.

He nodded. "How's it working?"

"Great. It works great. I feel much safer."

"You're *a little* safer."

"And I still owe you for the last job. You said you'd get Hickey or Morrison or whoever to pay you one way or another, but knowing how they operate . . ."

"Morrison hires me by the job. We'll settle up sooner or later, him and me. Meanwhile, I got some time I can spare."

"No way," she said, and he liked the way her smile came easily. "I told you, I'll pay you myself. I'm not a charity case."

"Did I say you were?" He hoped he wasn't blushing. If he was, he hoped she couldn't tell. "I like to finish a job right."

"And I like to—"

"Angela! You got an order for me?"

"Yes, I do. I'm sorry." She was backing away from the table, brandishing the green pad, her smile turning her eyes to glittering crystal. "Finish a job right. Good credo to live by."

She delivered his order with the requisite "Is there anything else you'd like?"

Sit with me, he wanted to say, then mentally drop-kicked his own head for hatching the thought. Because food wasn't what he wanted, he took his time eating it, which was a new experience in itself. He didn't want the coffee, either, but he forced down several cups because when he emptied it, she was right there on the spot with a refill. Each time, they exchanged a few words about nothing either of them would remember. He knew exactly what he was doing, felt more than a little foolish about it, and hoped to God she couldn't tell. He ordered a piece of apple pie, figuring at the rate he was going it would take until closing to finish that, at which time he might as well walk home with her and get at those windows.

Tommy T dropped by just as Jesse emerged from the men's room. "Come on in and take a number, kid," the cook said as he flipped the card on the door from OPEN to CLOSED. "I might have to get a bench to put by the door for all the guys waiting for Angela to get off work." He slipped Jesse a cock-of-the-walk look on his way back to the kitchen.

Jesse returned the look in kind.

"So how come you're here?" Tommy T demanded.

"Came to eat," Jesse said, thinking the walk was getting a little crowded. "This is a restaurant."

"Yeah, but how come you're here waiting for Angela? It's pretty late. She don't like to be out late."

Jesse folded his arms. "Maybe I'm going over to her place."

"So am I. She already said."

"I've got some more work to do on the windows." He couldn't help smiling. The boy was standing his ground, looking decidedly doubtful about his intentions. "You staying with Angela now?"

"No."

"Your mom get back yet?"

"What's it to ya?"

"Just wondered." Jesse glanced over the top of the boy's head. Angela was busy behind the lunch counter, and the cook was rattling stuff around in the kitchen. "It's gonna be gettin' cold pretty soon."

"So? My mom's gonna be back before then. Before you finish that playground. You don't wanna be workin' on that when it gets cold."

Jesse lifted one shoulder, matching Tommy T's nonchalance. "Don't matter to me, long as I'm gettin' paid."

"You shouldn't be hustling jobs from Angela. Waitresses don't make a lot of money, you know."

"She's no charity case. She set me straight on that." The boy was unimpressed. "It's work the landlord ought to be doing on the place anyway. He'll pay me for it."

"It's good for her to be gettin' those windows fixed," Tommy T said. After a moment he allowed, "I guess it's good you're doin' it for her."

"As long as you approve."

It felt good to walk home with a man on either side. It was a beautiful late-summer night, and the city felt friendly for a change. No sirens. No cars screeching around the corner just as she was about to step off the curb. No footsteps, real or imagined, dogging her from behind. For once, she wasn't intimidated by the rattletrap with souped-up sound equipment that lingered at the stoplight to flex the muscle of its pounding bass. For once, the angry rap lyrics didn't scare her. There was little conversation on the way home, but the companionship felt fine.

Jesse stopped at Darlene's door. "I'll be up in a minute," he told Angela. "Just need to pick up some tools."

She and Tommy T headed up the steps. She wasn't paying much attention to ten-year-old Tony's "Hey, Jesse, you back already?" And she really wasn't listening for his answer. She was fairly religious about minding her own business.

Stevie greeted Jesse enthusiastically when he came upstairs, which was an unusual response for the terrier. Even more remarkable was the way Jesse stopped her from jumping on him with a subtle hand signal. "Stevie isn't usually such a pushover," Angela assured him.

"I like dogs," he said, and then, as if it explained something, "I'm Sioux."

Out in the kitchen, Tommy T giggled.

"So I need to keep an eye on my dog for some reason?"

Jesse shook his head, but his answer was for Tommy T. "This

one's too skinny. Wouldn't even make a decent snack."

She did a little *Go on* gesture and offered him a choice of cold drinks, but he wanted coffee. Strong coffee. "Don't skimp on the caffeine," he told her, and he went to work on the bathroom window.

She doubled up on the coffee grounds and perked half a pot. By the time she brought it to him, he had the window out and was working on the casing. He took the cup with a slightly unsteady hand.

"Are you sure this is what you want?" she asked. "You drank a whole pot with your supper."

"This is what I need." He sipped so eagerly she was afraid he'd burn himself, and when he looked up at her, there was something different about his eyes. "I'm a little tired. A strong dose of caffeine is just what the doctor . . . just what I need."

"You don't have to do this now."

"I said I would."

"But it isn't—"

"I *said* I *would*." He grabbed at the windowsill, as though he were dizzy, and for a moment he seemed disoriented. Then he drank the coffee much faster than he should have been able to, given how hot it was, and he handed her the cup. "And I will. I'm okay. I just . . ." He glanced past her. "You and Tommy T watch some TV or something, okay? I don't do windows when somebody's watching. I'll try not to leave a mess."

"Don't worry about . . ." She touched his arm. "You're sure you're okay?"

He lowered his gaze to the hand on his arm, and for a moment neither of them moved. Then he nodded and gave a tight smile.

Somebody at their feet whined.

"The pup can stay," he said. "Is the cup bottomless here, too?"

She kept him in coffee until he emerged announcing, "You won't have anyone climbing through the window to use the john."

"That's good news," she said, taking the empty cup from his hand.

With a gesture he told her that he'd drunk his fill. "And I located the source of the water problem downstairs. You've got some loose tiles in the shower. I'll have to get to those."

"You should be the owner of this building, or the manager at least."

"The American dream?" Smiling wistfully, he shook his head. "I see a leak, I want to fix it, that's all. Any excuse to break out the tools."

"Must be a man thing." She was studying his face, and she knew there was something seriously wrong. "Would you like something else to—"

"I gotta be goin'."

"Jesse—" She welcomed the excuse to touch his arm again. Neither the weather nor the close quarters could account for the intense warmth of his skin. She wasn't ready to see him go. "You look a little . . ."

"I'm fighting a headache. It's no big deal."

"Do you need some aspirin or something?"

He made a sound that might have passed for a laugh, and he shook his head. "The coffee helped."

"You don't have too far to go, I hope. I mean—" She glanced away easily enough, but her hand lingered lightly on his arm, fingers tingling. "I hope you don't have to walk too far with . . . and carrying those . . ."

"Darlene lets me keep some of my stuff in her closet."

He gave her a moment, but she found the good grace to refrain from asking him just what stuff and why. She didn't know why she was even tempted to, or why she was too embarrassed to look into his eyes. He was just a repairman, for gosh sakes. Nice enough, helpful even though she hadn't asked for help, not this time, and she hadn't asked because she didn't want anything more than . . . courtesy. Pleasantries. Nodding acquaintances. She didn't want to be curious about why he kept his belongings in Darlene's closet, and she wasn't. She truly wasn't.

"I'll get to the other windows as soon as I can. Maybe I'll . . ."

He turned the doorknob and stepped away from her, taking himself out of reach. "I gotta go."

She looked up quickly. She thought she saw her own regret reflected in his eyes. So much grief over the removal of a simple touch?

Then she reminded herself that he was fighting a headache. And she was fighting for peace of mind.

9

Tommy T had been working on something at Angela's, and he was eager to share it with Dark Dog. He was getting really good at finding his way through the park at night, covering his back trail, making sure no one followed him. His own night vision was becoming a superpower. He wouldn't try telling that to somebody like Stoner, but he knew what he knew. He settled himself into his crow's nest, facing the entrance to The Den.

He waited for a few moments, then called out in a theatrical whisper, "Hey, I've got something for you."

"Hey," the gravelly voice responded wearily. "Leave it by that rock before you make yourself too comfortable out there."

That was just Dark Dog's way of saying hello.

"It's a drawing. I been working on your character."

"My character? You going into the priesthood next?"

"You need a better outfit," Tommy T advised. "And a weapon. Nothing like these street punks use. No ordinary gun." He pulled the folded collection of designs from his back pocket and cast about for a safe crevice to tuck them into. "You need something cool. Something that takes special skill. What kinda skills you got besides the obvious?"

"What kind is obvious?"

That was just Dark Dog's way of being modest.

"Obviously you could crush your enemies with your bare hands."

"If it's so obvious, why don't you take a hint?"

"You'd never do nothin' like that to me. I'm your partner." He discovered a fist-size niche. "The dog thing is obvious, too. I ain't the only one who's seen you do that. I mean, that is *so cool.* Even Ajax was blown away. How do you do that, anyway?" He raked a little loose gravel out of the natural cubbyhole with his fingertips. "I didn't think you'd tell me. That would, like, destroy your power, wouldn't it? If you told. It's because you're one of them, right?"

"You got that right. A real son of a bitch."

"No, I mean in spirit. Because you're Dark Dog. Maybe you've got enough weapons already." He'd worked up some great ideas for hero attire, but something was still missing. "You need something in your hand. Something you can fight with, but it's also like a symbol of your power."

"You work on it."

"I am. That's what partners are for. I may be small, but I'm smart."

A deep, hollow response echoed below.

"Did you . . ." He wasn't sure what to call it. "Was that a laugh I just heard?"

"Hell, no."

The boy sat there, still and quiet for a moment, steeling himself against the stupid, prickly feeling that was creeping up on him. Hurt feelings were a waste of time. But he had to offer a comeback, anyway.

Unfortunately, it came out in a stupid, small voice. "I *am* smart."

"Never said you weren't." It was almost an apology. "But you shouldn't be coming here."

"Why? It's not safe for me to be out on the streets at night?" Tommy T hung his head for nobody's benefit but his own. They belonged together, and he wanted Dark Dog to say so. "I'm safe here."

"It's late."

"I should be in bed, huh?" He tossed off a laugh, but the truth was, he didn't want to think about where he might be sleeping tonight. He'd found a sheltered back entrance to a church, but after a couple of nights there, he'd lost it to some girls. He wasn't going to fight anybody for a squat, mostly because it might get back to Stoner, who'd been acting funny lately, making noises about getting him off the streets. All he needed was a little more time and he'd have it all worked out himself.

But the appeal of being completely on his own was wearing thin, especially when it came time to crash at night. He'd often thought about curling up in the grass near The Den, but he knew that wouldn't be right. He'd be visible in the morning, which might tip someone off. He'd never let that happen, never give Dark Dog up to his enemies. He'd take the secrets of Dark Dog to his grave.

"You need some kind of an outfit," he told his hero. "The hat's good for camouflage, but it ain't enough. I been thinkin' . . ." He'd imagined a fur mantle, but that reverie always led him back to a particular worry. "It's gonna be gettin' cold pretty soon."

"Yeah."

"So . . . will you be takin' off then?"

"Dogs don't fly south, kid."

"I know, but . . ." Particular Worry, Part Two. "Your voice always sounds kinda cracky. Maybe that's just a disguise, or maybe you're, like, dying of something. Do you smoke?"

"Been known to smoke the hide of a nosy kid, use it for a rug."

"Yeah, right. No, I mean it." Finally, Part Three. "You ain't sick, are you?"

The answer was slow in coming. "Not so I'm gonna die."

"But you *are* sick?"

"I got a terrific pain that won't leave me alone. Calls himself Tommy T."

"You need some medicine? I could ask Mr. Bird. He never said nothin' to me about that other time, so I could just—"

"It doesn't work real good for me."

Tommy T swallowed hard. "I could get you something else, maybe."

"There's nothing . . ." Pause, then softly, "I don't use anything, kid. Not what you're thinkin'. It doesn't work for me."

A long, heavy silence passed, and Tommy T began to worry even more. Maybe it was more than just a scar. Maybe it was some dreaded disease. Something totally disfiguring and ultimately fatal. He shook his head, physically banishing bad-luck thoughts. Dark Dog thrived on secrecy. "No doctors, no cops, right?"

"Right."

"I'm going now. I just came to report in. Everything's pretty quiet tonight."

"You got a place to stay?"

"It's nice out. Anyway, I got friends."

"The lady?"

"I told her my mom was back."

"You might try trusting her, Tommy T. You know she won't report anything that might bring the cops down on you."

"I know. But I don't want her thinkin' . . ." *Bad-luck thoughts.* His mom would be back, sooner or later. And he surely didn't want pity. Like Angela, he was no charity case. "Everything's cool just the way it is. I gotta go. I'm leaving this picture I drew of you and something else, right here inside these rocks. Not medicine, but maybe it'll make you feel better. Candy always makes me feel better. Kinda keep an eye on her place, okay? In case she does have somebody following her."

"Thanks . . . partner."

Partner. Grinning, Tommy T scaled the embankment. He was sure he'd developed superpower suction feet.

Angela went to bed late, hoping she was tired enough to fall asleep right away and that her dream would come to her soon afterward. She chided herself in the waking hours in the absence of an older sister to do the chiding for her. She was being silly again. Although her sister's idea of silly and her own idea of silly were two different things, she knew she was being silly by any sane standards. If she wanted to get all dreamy and romantic over a man, there were plenty of real men living in the real world, and most of them were nothing like the one she'd come to fear and despise.

Don't be silly. Matt is a great catch, Roxanne would say. Had said, in fact, many times. *Don't lose him, whatever you do.*

Lose him? That was a laugh. Had he been an average Joe, Roxanne's tune would have been, *Lose this guy, Angie. He's got no credentials.* Her sister had "lost" an average Peter in favor of a blue-blooded Paul, and she swore by the difference. It didn't matter that Paul had a habit of behaving like a jerk. He was a rich jerk. When Angela first told her that she was uncomfortable with the changes in Matt, with some of the demands he was beginning to make, Roxanne had advised her to go along with him, particularly since his public demeanor was always impeccable.

But not in private. She'd tried to tell her sister that. *Why do you always have to be so melodramatic?* had been Roxanne's response.

Melodramatic. Was that it? Was it normal for a man to enjoy twisting a woman's arm, verbally at first, but later physically, nudging the breaking point without ever quite reaching it? It was too embarrassing to tell Roxanne any specific details, but she had mentioned his temper.

He has to control it, Angie, Roxanne had said. *Use your head. It would ruin him if he didn't. Just keep him happy. Cachet is everything, and the man is loaded with it. Don't lose him.*

She'd had the devil's own time losing him. In the end, she'd given up a major piece of her life to do it, but she had to believe she'd succeeded. All she had to do was start thinking like a whole, healthy, normal woman again. A new woman.

She truly was a brand-new woman, created from scratch. Well, scratch mixed with the ashes and broken bits of a woman much too young to be all used up. It was the broken woman who had been afraid of her own shadow. The new woman worked at *night*, for gosh sakes. Roxanne would be mortified. The woman Roxanne's little sister had become lived in a rough neighborhood, and she walked everywhere she needed to go, bold as brass. The new woman was creating her own cachet. She could easily live without a man, but if she had any interest in one, it was going to be a healthy interest. It was going to be based on respect and mutual interests . . . which probably ruled out a certain strange fascination born of some shadow fantasy.

But shadow fantasies were safe. They somehow helped her out when she was in trouble, when she had nowhere else to turn. When she woke up, they would always be gone, and she would still be safe. And so she took an over-the-counter drug that promised to help her sleep and had proved to be a procurer of dreams. She shooed Stevie into her own bed in the front room, closed her bedroom door, turned out the lights, pulled down the shades, and crawled into bed. She drew up the covers, but not too high. It was hot. Besides, when she was a little girl, the covers had kept the creatures in the closet from getting into her bed. She didn't want creatures in her bed. Not hot, hairy creatures, not even her dog. But she wanted . . . someone.

She didn't exactly want him *in* her bed. Just close by. She wanted him to come close and be close. It was up to her to decide how close. But she had to go to sleep first. Like all good spirits who did their magic at night, he wouldn't come until everyone in the house was fast asleep . . .

"I'm sleeping," she muttered, she had no idea how much later. Time played no part in her dreams.

"You talk in your sleep. Did you know that?"

She smiled in her sleep, too. "I talk in my dreams. Everyone does."

"Then talk to me, Angela. Tell me what you're afraid of."

She groaned. "If I talk about *that*, then this dream will be ruined."

"I can protect you," he said, his voice coming closer, and yes, she wanted it closer still. "But it would help if you told me what to look for."

"Bad dreams." She opened her eyes to her good dream, but she could barely make out his shape. He'd gone down on one knee beside her bed. "You're just the man for the job, aren't you, Jewel Eyes? They live in your world. Takes a good dream to drive out a bad dream, huh?"

"I guess so."

"You were right. I don't have to call you." She lifted her hand, half expecting it to disappear into the hulking shadow when she reached for him. But it landed on coarse cloth. Denim, she thought. Her dream wore denim. "I needed you, and you came."

"You needed me tonight?"

"Yes."

"Why? What happened?"

"Nothing, really. I have a new lock on my door, new safety catches on the windows. It would be hard for anyone to get in now."

"I got in."

"But you won't hurt me. You won't do anything I don't want you to do." She clutched the cloth, pressing a round snap into the center of her palm. "Will you?"

"If you have to ask, maybe you ought to be conjuring up a different dream."

His hand felt rough against the back of hers. She turned hers over and met his, palm to palm. "You're warm for a dream." And thick-skinned, she decided. But gentle.

"Some dreams are like that."

"Do you have a face? If I touch your face, will you disappear?"

He drew her hand higher and pressed it against his cheek.

"Warm," she whispered. The simple gesture had her heart racing. "Smooth. It's a nice face. Not bristly." Her thumb strayed to his mouth. He stayed perfectly still, but she heard him swallow. "Smile for me." She touched the corner of his mouth and felt it move. "Nice smile, but it doesn't come easily, does it? Don't you smile much?"

"Not much."

"What does it take to make you smile?"

His hand closed over hers. "You don't worry about making me smile. I'm here to watch over you."

He sounded troubled. "And you're not happy about it?"

"I don't have any feelings. I'm a dream."

"You're *my* dream, right?"

"Right."

"Then I want you to have feelings."

"That's asking too much of a dream." He gave her hand a quick squeeze. "I don't want feelings, so don't wish them on me. I'm just here to see that you're okay."

"I'm okay." She drew his hand to her cheek. "Do I feel okay?"

"You'll have to tell me."

"To the touch. Your touch." She uncurled his incredibly long fingers and laid them against the side of her face. "Do I feel okay?"

"Yeah." The long fingers stirred, the blunt tips finding their way into her hair. "You feel very . . . sweet."

"Sweet is a taste. Do you want to taste me?"

A moment passed before he answered. "Not unless you want to be tasted."

"I think I do."

"Where? What do you want me to taste, Angela?"

"My mouth, of course."

He leaned closer. She saw nothing. She feared nothing. She smelled a newly plowed field and anticipated tasting something delicious as his deep, raspy voice abraded her everywhere. "Then you'll taste mine, and that might spoil the dream."

"Why? What have you been eating? What do dreams eat?" She touched his lips again and imagined them touching hers. They were wide and full and would cover hers completely. "I want to know all about you, Jewel Eyes."

He kissed her fingers and whispered, "Dream on, then."

"I want to know what a dream tastes like."

She let her fingers slide over the side of his neck, certain she detected a response in him, something like a shiver. She gripped his shoulder and pulled him down, and he leaned down, and there was no shadow, no shape. There was only the smell of damp, rich earth and the rustle of denim as he planted his elbow in her pillow, close to her ear, and curved his arm around her head, not touching, but guarding.

His kiss consumed her. There was nothing ghostly or tentative about it. He tasted faintly of cinnamon. Her taste seemed to please him when his tongue tested it, for then it plunged deeply and repeatedly and hungrily for more. Finally it took some shallow kissing, some leveling off, before he could leave off. His lips hovered above hers for a moment longer, his breath soft and warm and most welcome to mingle with hers.

She let her lower lip flirt with his, rubbing a little before she whispered against it, "You taste like a man."

"Is that good?" She felt his smile. "I've never tasted one myself."

"A *real* man." Her tongue flickered, lizard-style, just the tip of it snatching one last sample. "A good man. Kind of hot and spicy."

"You're confusing me with chicken wings," he said as he drew back, his whisper accented with amusement. His thumb lingered to sweep back and forth over her temple as though to clear the cobwebs from her head. But he couldn't, she thought. He was part of the cobwebs, a suspicion he confirmed when he warned, "Be careful what you eat before you go to bed. It's liable to shape-shift in your dream."

"And what is 'shape-shift'?"

"Just what it sounds like. Change shape, appear in a different form. I must have started out tonight as a hot, spicy chicken wing. You ate me, swallowed me." He laid a fingertip on her chin, then drew an illustrative line. "I slid down your throat. The taste of me went to your brain and made a lasting impression."

"And then came to me in my sleep as a good and gentle man's kiss?" *Bring on the chicken wings.*

"That's something I've never been called."

"A gentle man," she repeated, emphasizing each word separately. "So where are you now? Really?"

"Really?" Without missing a beat, his hand went to her stomach. "I must be down here."

She reached unerringly for the back of his neck and drew his head down. His lips found hers again. His fingers flexed, tentatively at first, sliding fine cotton over sensitive skin, then flexing again until he was gently kneading her belly. Her insides liquefied, pooled in her middle, and whorled beneath his hand. Cinnamon was a sexy flavor.

"Why are you letting me do this?" he whispered into her mouth.

"I'm not. I'm just—" She turned her head, closed her eyes, and tried to think of an answer. "I'm dreaming this."

"I'm here to watch over you."

"You're feeling something." She covered his hand with hers, stilling the motion but trapping him. "Why are you feeling something?" she challenged.

"I'm not." His breathing was ragged.

"I think you are. I want my dreams to have feelings. If they don't, they're likely to hurt mine."

He pulled his hand away. "Then I'd better be gettin' out of your dreams, Angela."

"Can you do that? Or is it up to me?"

"Interesting question. I'll answer yours if you'll answer mine." He drew back gradually, denim rubbing against denim, and she imagined him sitting on his heels, studying her with his extraordinary eyes. "What are you afraid of?"

"If you live inside my head, you must know."

"Dreams don't live with you. They only visit." He paused; then she could have sworn she heard a sigh. "Tell me what to look for, Angela. Is it someone you know?"

"You never know," she said. "You just fool yourself into thinking you do."

"Maybe so. But you can't fool a dream."

She had no answer for that. He'd retreated into deep shadows and deeper silence. She listened hard, but she heard nothing. There was nothing else moving in this dream, not even her dog.

"Are you still here?" she whispered.

No answer. She drifted in peaceful darkness until a sliver of gray light glimmered beneath the window shade. She'd lost the night somewhere in the narrow margin between waking and sleeping. Shadow fantasies were safe. When she woke up, they were gone, and she was safe.

But she was alone.

Angela was fishing for the hole in her earlobe with the tip of a silver hook, but without a mirror she wasn't having much luck. It had been months since she'd worn a pair of earrings. Either she'd lost her touch, or her holes had closed up. Or she was nervous.

Nothing to be nervous about, she kept telling herself. She wasn't really going back into the classroom. She was going to be a part-time tutor. No credentials required. Strictly volunteer. It was not a big deal, but she was excited about it, anyway. After pulling back-to-back shifts with Deacon Peale bawling orders at her, she was so worked up over the prospect of a change of scene that a knock at the door sent her earring flying.

"It's just me," Darlene shouted from the hallway as Angela scrambled to catch the silver teardrop before it rolled under the refrigerator.

"Hi." She managed to run the hook through as she stepped back from the door. "Come on in. I'm just getting ready to head over to the school for my tutoring orientation. I have to observe

in the classroom so I can sort of get a sense of what my students—
my *tutees*, I guess would be the right term if I'm the tu*tor*—what
they're doing in the regular—"

Darlene closed the door behind her and leaned back against
it. She was a statuesque woman, an imperious, attention-getting
presence. At the moment, that presence was all agitation. "I need
fifty, cash, real quick."

"Fifty?"

"Fifty bucks. I'll pay you back Friday."

Angela was dumbfounded. She couldn't remember the last
time anyone had asked her for a loan. Her sister, maybe, when
they were kids.

Darlene raised her chin a notch and looked Angela straight in
the eye. "I'm good for it. Jesse would vouch for me. Only don't
ask him straight out." She glanced past Angela, first the living
room side, then the kitchen, as though she thought the man might
be in the apartment somewhere. "I know he'd give it to me, but
he's done enough for us lately."

"I haven't seen Jesse since he came over to do some more
repairs."

"Me neither. You'll probably see him over at the school. He's
still working on that . . ." She folded her arms and took a deep
breath, her breasts rising like inflatable pillows. She wore her
clothes tight, like an overstuffed chair. "Listen, if you can't spare
it, just tell me. I wouldn't ask, except I need the money now."

Angela's immediate response was suspicion, but shame followed quickly. Who was she to judge? The woman worked in a
convenience store nearby, headed up the Neighborhood Watch,
and was responsible for seven children. She was also her neighbor. This was a test; true or false, yes or no.

"I'll have to see what I can dig up. Wait here just a minute."

She remembered what Jesse had said about showing people
where she kept her cash, and she'd since moved it to her bedroom.
Fifty dollars wasn't that much. One night's tips. One *good* night's.

"We're in luck," she announced as she presented Darlene with the money. "Normally I wouldn't have this much around."

"Normally I wouldn't ask." The diffidence clouding Darlene's face also weighed her hand down. "It's for my sister. It's her baby I'm keeping, just temporarily. She's trying to get herself on track, but it's hard, you know?"

"It is hard." She did know.

"Once they've got something on you, they just keep on using it." She stuffed the money into the front pocket of her jeans while Angela watched it disappear as though she were saying good-bye for good. "It's not what you think. You'll get your money back Friday," Darlene snapped. "I hate asking more than you hate being asked, but it's important. And she's still my sister."

"I understand. It's not . . ." Darlene's cool expression challenged any disclaimer Angela might make. She said simply, "I hope it works out."

Darlene gave a quick nod. "Thanks."

Classes didn't actually get started until ten in the morning, what with the complicated bus schedule, breakfast, and other morning rituals, but once the reading, writing, and arithmetic instruction got under way, Many Nations Elementary felt more like home to Angela than the apartment she lived in. The only trouble was that she wanted to stand in the front of the class rather than at the back, where she was supposed to be observing the two sixth-graders whom she would be tutoring. Tasha and Jeremy both had attention-deficit problems. They would need patient, individualized instruction. Fortunately, Angela was far better trained for delivering instruction than hamburgers and coffee.

Merely observing the school's program made her blood sizzle with excitement. She loved being surrounded by buoyant, barely contained energy. She treasured the spontaneity of small voices, the comforting, universal routine. The waxy smell of crayons, the sound of locker doors, the colors, the patterns, the shuffle of feet— everything intoxicated her. All she'd ever wanted to be was a teacher, and that was what and whom she had become.

It was who she would be again, given time. There were teachers everywhere, thousands of them, and in time she would find a way to lose herself among them just as she had lost herself in the city. It was a matter of laying claim to her credentials without giving up her emancipation. She could never go back to the kind of emotional slavery her life had become in the shadow of someone else's obsession, not even for teaching.

But here was a chance to do what she loved, if only for a few hours a week, and she resolved to embrace it. It might help her restore her sanity. She was pretty sure she wasn't quite "all there." Not yet, anyway. But it was coming. She was deciding for herself whom she liked, whom she might trust. Starting with nobody, she'd taken first one baby step, then another. No sense in *over*stepping in a situation that would be temporary.

There had been only one really bad incident. That and the one continuing bit of foolishness that made sense only at night, when illusion and fantasy held sway. She couldn't really think about it during the day. Whatever it was, it was a comfort to her in the darkness, and by daylight it was too ridiculous to contemplate.

Almost as ridiculous as the Coyote and Rabbit story she listened to Mr. Bird tell a group of students in the art room. Two dozen or more encircled him on the carpeted floor, jostling one another until their positions were established and the story was under way. The old man delighted in animating the tale with his own antics, drawing his audience into the action. They howled when Rabbit was able to trick Coyote into believing that getting into a gunny sack would protect him from a hailstorm, which turned out to be Rabbit pitching rocks. No sooner had the laughter died down than Coyote was falling for another trick—sticking gum on his eyes to protect them from the sun. When Rabbit set fire to the brush, Coyote ended up with gum melted all over his face and in his fur. It made him "so mad he was biting his tongue" as he chased the boy who'd been dubbed Rabbit by the story circle. But no sooner had Rabbit escaped the stew pot than Coyote fell for yet *another* trick. And so it went until it was time for the children to return to their classrooms.

"Look at these," Tommy T said, slipping Mr. Bird a large piece of drawing paper. Angela edged closer as the old man's appreciative gaze followed the boy's finger across the page. "This is from that last Old Man Coyote story you told me. See, this is where he's stuck inside the tree. It's a cross section, like you'd see in a science book, and you can just tell he's really cramped in there. And see? Here's all the bird people pecking on the tree. I looked up the different kinds of birds you said, and I used what they really look like, but I put it together with a little bit of human character. Like, this is Flicker. See the eyes?"

Angela was peering over Tommy T's shoulder by this time, admiring the resolute expression he had managed to capture in the woodpecker's eyes.

Tommy T turned the papers over to Mr. Bird. "I thought you could use these sometime when you tell the story. They're for you."

Mr. Bird nodded toward a bookcase, where the shield he'd been making the night of the open house was on display. "For you."

"Thanks." Wide-eyed, the boy darted toward the gift, but he stopped short, collected himself as though he'd suddenly remembered some rule of decorum, and drew back. "It should be kept on display here, though. I want people to see how nice it turned out."

"Your teacher's waiting for you." With another nod, the old man excused him to join the departing class. "There's something else he wants," Mr. Bird confided to Angela as they watched them go, the kids at the end of the line getting in a little slap and tickle when the teacher wasn't looking. "But I think he'll have to work a bit harder for it."

"What is it?"

"He has his eye on this wolf hide." He lifted a gray fur pelt off the back of his chair and draped it over one arm for display.

From muzzle to tail, the full skin was intact. The ears had been salvaged, perked up, and reinforced with stiff rawhide. But the empty eye holes gave it a ghostly aspect. "These are hard to come by. This one is older than I am. My father gave it to me."

"It's beautiful," Angela said, petting it as though it were a living thing. It once was, she thought, but she put away niggling thoughts of fur coats and pets like Stevie as Mr. Bird permitted her to touch a piece of his tradition.

His focus was still on the door. "I can tell he has some purpose in mind for it. I wonder what it is. He's a schemer, that boy."

"A description that sounds like a match for Old Man Coyote, from the stories you tell."

"Ho, not that bad! No one would want to try to match up with Coyote. He *really* does crazy things." Mr. Bird laid the wolf pelt over the back of the chair. "But we need him around for balance. In the end, he sets things right." He sat down and looked up at her through tired eyes. "Does the boy stay with you?"

"He comes and goes," she said with a shrug.

"A free spirit, but not by choice. Not him. It's his mother who can't seem to settle down."

"You know his mother?"

"I know her, yes. Little bit. Her family first came out here on relocation, back in the sixties, when they had government programs to get Indians to move to the cities. They've been locating and relocating us Indians for four hundred years, you know."

"I know." She thought better of adding, *I'm sorry.* Then she caught the twinkle in the old man's eye, and she knew he'd read her mind. "I just wonder if Tommy T's mom . . ."

He shook his head. "She can't help the way she is, any more than Coyote can. The boy sure tries to, though. Help her, I mean. He never gives up on her."

"And I don't want to interfere with his mother's role or meddle in their relationship in any way. He's been spending a lot of time with me lately, but not actually . . ." She backpedaled a bit. She and Tommy T had an unspoken pact about not asking too many questions or revealing too many specifics. Not to each other and not to anyone else. "Sometimes I do think he's conning me a little, but all he seems to want is a quiet place to light on once in a while, maybe to watch a little TV or do some drawing. All he's ever asked for is a place to store his comic books and a few other things so his brother doesn't get into them." She shrugged. "Maybe he's got a little coyote in him."

The old man nodded. "We all do."

Angela welcomed the opportunity to take a walk outdoors on her lunch break. It was a beautiful, temperate September day. The voices of the younger children playing a game in a small, grassy courtyard were music to her ears. That they were so closely supervised by teachers and instructional aides carrying two-way radios was a testament to the dangers that surrounded them in this part of the city, dangers they simply lived with. But their voices sounded no less joyous and innocent than the voices of children at play in any other school yard.

Near the front entrance to the school she noticed Jesse Brown Wolf sitting on what appeared to be a nearly complete climb-in-and-explore apparatus made of wood, rope, old tires, and concrete. He was eating alone.

"This is really coming along nicely," she said by way of a greeting. "More like sculpture than playground equipment." She hopped up on a low platform, raised her arms toward the sky, grasped a dangling knotted rope, and took a pirate-style swing, landing on her feet in the sand. She turned, smiling when she caught the surprised look on his face. "Pretty tame, but that's nice for kids. Safe."

"You'd rather live dangerously?"

"Oh, no, safe is good." She joined him on the balance beam he was using for a bench. "Caution is very good, as someone pointed out to me not long ago."

"But not much fun." He leaned over to pick up the paper sack that was sitting on the ground next to his foot. "Have you had lunch?"

"I thought about trying the cafeteria. I haven't had school food since, well . . . since my school days." As she talked, she watched him unwrap a long sub sandwich. He took half for himself and offered her the rest, waxed paper and all. She shook her head, chagrined, realizing she'd probably been watching with hunger in her eyes. "No, I didn't mean to interrupt you."

"Plenty for two." The look in his eyes was guarded, unwavering, his offer waiting in his outstretched hand. He was testing her, echoing the overture she'd made the first time he'd gone to her apartment. "It's just ham and cheese."

She smiled, nodded. Her fingers brushed his as she accepted his food. They ate together in silence, uncomfortable for Angela until she came up with something to say.

"I started tutoring today."

"Good." He nodded and went on eating.

He was, she realized, a disturbingly attractive man. Disturbingly soft-spoken, disturbingly unruffled, undemanding, unintrusive. Disturbing eyes. He permitted her only brief glimpses, perhaps because he knew how disturbing they were, how much knowing they revealed and how little explanation. So disturbing that he made her want to talk, just for some distraction.

"It's really wonderful," she said. Then she shrugged, embarrassed by her lack of restraint. "I mean, you know, so far, so good. It's only my first time, and I'm really just getting trained in. Observing, mostly."

"I hear some of these kids can be hard to handle."

"I guess they went easy on me today." She nibbled some more on the thick French bread. Not only did she want to talk, but she actually wanted to share, to say what was on her mind. "I got to sit in on some of Mr. Bird's storytelling. Remember when you suggested some Indian heroes as models for Tommy T's creations? Mr. Bird was telling some of those stories, and Tommy T made some drawings for him. Marvelous drawings. He's so . . ." She turned suddenly, looked him in the eye as if she wanted him to make something happen. "I'd like to meet his mother."

"Why?"

"Well, because I just think I *should*. I got something in the mail addressed 'To the Parents of Thomas Little Warrior.' I gave it to him, and he said that I might be getting more because I was the one who came to the open house with him, and somehow my address got recorded somewhere, and 'you know how computers are.'" Jesse was looking at her curiously now, and she gave a little laugh and shook her head, remembering. "That's what he said to me, that rascal. 'You know how computers are.' And he was dancing around like . . ." She shook her head again, her gaze dropping to her hand, her crisp cotton khaki slacks, her nibbled sandwich. "Well, you know how kids act when they're trying to pull the wool over your eyes."

"How do they act?"

"They"—she glanced up, then away—"can't look you in the eye."

"You don't say." He gave a mirthless chuckle, eyeing her over the top of a can of Coke he'd just popped open. He drank, pressed moist lips together and gave a quick headshake. Her mouth watered. "That yardstick won't work for Indian kids. That's not the way they're raised. They probably won't look a speaker in the eye, especially not an adult. To us it's rude." He offered her the can.

"Really?" She sipped from his drink as though sharing with him were second nature. "But it wasn't just that. I know Tommy T. He wasn't comfortable with what he was telling me."

"He probably ain't too comfortable with what he's *not* telling you, either." He gave her that knowing look. "You know how that is."

"Yes, I do. I do." Moreover, she knew she was confessing more than she wanted to. Not the secrets themselves, but the fact that they existed. He nodded, but there was no judgment in his eyes. She liked that. Disturbing as they were, they were nice eyes. "It wouldn't make any difference to me. Whatever he's not telling me, it wouldn't matter. I would still . . ." She smiled wistfully. "It wouldn't change the fact that he's Tommy T."

"If he needed a place to stay, would you take him in?"

"Gladly." She said it without hesitation, and she meant it. Inevitably, though, her second thought was a complication. "But I wouldn't want to get involved with, say, social services or . . . or the legal system in any way. I mean, I probably wouldn't be considered suitable for any sort of formal or . . . or *legal* . . ." Ah, those dark , disturbing eyes. Smoky mirrors, reflecting her predicament right back in her face. Her gesture was feeble. "Because of the hours I work, you know."

One corner of his mouth turned up in amusement. "You're dancin' around a little yourself, aren't you?"

"No." Abruptly she returned his Coke.

He took the can, then stared straight ahead, past the slide he'd built, past the cars rolling by on the street, deep into the park across the street. "Your new locks workin' okay?"

"Fine. I'm fine. I'm not hiding."

He turned, his eyes questioning this second lie.

She glanced away. "I mean, *avoiding*. I'm not trying to avoid anything where Tommy T's concerned. It's just that it's such a big responsibility. I couldn't assume full, complete . . . not the way Darlene has." She paused. "It's nice of you to help her."

He shrugged, contemplating the top of the Coke can. "I'm kinda like Tommy T. I help somebody out once in a while, maybe they'll let me park my stuff in the closet."

"That may be fine for you, but Tommy T is still a child. He shouldn't be quite so footloose." She wrapped the paper around her sandwich, smoothing it into place as though she might put it away, save it for later. "So the answer is, yes, if he needed a place to stay, he could stay with me anytime. As long as he wanted. As long as his mother gave her okay. I really would like to meet her."

He looked up, checking her eyes for sincerity.

Her smile was self-effacing. "I don't meet people easily. I tend to be sort of standoffish in a new situation."

He nodded, and she didn't know whether he was identifying with her problem or simply confirming it.

"I should have made an effort to get to know Darlene right away, but I was . . ." She shook her head. "I really like her. Already. I like the way she takes care of . . . handles so many . . ." She sighed. She figured she had a few things to learn from Darlene. "I think she and I may become good friends. At least I hope so."

He nodded again, then tipped his head back and finished his Coke.

"Maybe you'd like to come up for supper some night."

He swallowed. "Again? A steady diet of Hard Luck could be hard on a guy's gut."

"No, I meant . . ." She laughed, a little nervous. "Well, it could turn out to be hard luck. I haven't seriously cooked anything for quite a while. But I meant, come up to my place for supper." He was giving her a funny look, sort of shocked, so she amended her proposal quickly, her voice rising on the excitement. "We could even have a party. You and Darlene, all the kids. Tommy T, of course."

He was just about to smile—she could see it in his eyes—but he caught himself and glanced away. "I don't have much time for that kind of thing."

"What kind of thing? Supper with friends?" She watched him crush the can with one hand. He tossed it into the open lunch sack. "No repairs needed," she urged softly, because he seemed to want urging. "No apologies required. Just eat and run if that's all the time you have."

"You don't owe me anything."

"It wouldn't be much."

"You get together with Darlene and her bunch. And Tommy T, of course." He snatched the sack off the ground and balled it up as he stood. "Especially Tommy T. You don't have to do anything formal or legal. Just give him a regular place at your table."

"I can do that, too."

They stood there for a long moment, just looking at each other. She almost said, *Come fix something, then. There's so much that needs fixing.*

He almost asked, *What night? What time?* She could see the wanting in his eyes. And the apprehension. He finally muttered something about getting back to work as he turned away.

"Jesse, wait."

He stopped, turning when she laid a hand on his bare, brown arm, staring first at her hand, then at her face.

She lifted the sandwich. "Thanks."

He nodded, then stepped away.

Angela ate a few bites of the spaghetti as it was on its way into the refrigerator. She wasn't quite as hungry as she'd thought she would be when she'd made enough food for at least six people. But there weren't six people to eat it. There weren't even two. There was only Angela. Stevie's soft but persistent whine forced her to make a slight mental correction. There was only old Mother Hubbard and her tail-wagging beggar of a dog.

"This is people food." She dropped the lid back on the pan and slid it in next to the milk. "You're right, though, you've got a doggie treat coming."

The refrigerator door thumped shut. She knew darn well there was no point in allowing for more than one regular place at her table, and even that one wouldn't be occupied at anything like a regular suppertime, not the way she was living these days. Most nights she ate on the run. When she didn't, she hardly knew what to do with herself. Should she look forward to a visit from one of her elusive friends, or was it better to pretend it didn't matter?

She reached for the Milk-Bone box. "This is for hanging in

there with me, Stevie girl." The Yorkie spun around like a top, then sat for her reward. She got two. "And this is for not once telling me I'm crazy."

It had been simple at first, when she'd settled in a place where no one knew her. Any sound in the hallway was suspect. There was no one she looked forward to seeing at her door. Being alone was a wretched road to relief from the torment she'd almost learned to live with before she'd come to her senses, realizing first that she no longer loved Matt Culver.

Once those blinders were thrown off, it had dawned on her that he had never loved her. He was obsessed by her, or by the notion that she belonged to him, and that was it. They'd never lived together. He was twelve years her senior. He was settled, well established, well respected. She'd looked good on his arm. She'd felt good there, too, for a while. As police commissioner, he led an exciting public life, full of interesting social events and well-placed friends. They'd talked of marriage. He'd said she would make him the perfect wife, and she'd been flattered. Oh, yes, there had been plenty of cachet.

There had been regular attention, too, like the daily calls, which seemed sweet and thoughtful at first. *How's your day going? I miss you. I want to put my arms around you.* No one had ever been that attentive to her. He'd praised her wit, her good taste, her green thumb, and she'd enjoyed the production he'd always made of sending her flowers on the anniversary of their first meeting, first date, first kiss—events she'd neglected to mark on the calendar. But Matt had marked them. At least he'd said he had.

Angela drew the drapes behind her collection of spider plants, then curled up on the sofa beneath the trailing shoots and imagined herself in a garden on an island somewhere. She loved plants. They helped her create an exotic world for herself within safe walls. But with Matt they'd become, like everything else, a way to control her. He had showered her with African violets, cyclamen, massive Boston ferns that had taken over her apartment. She'd left them all behind, taking only her own plants, those she'd chosen herself and those she'd started from her sister's cuttings.

She'd raised the jade plant that stood on the telephone table from a three-inch gift from one of her students. She'd started several new pots of jade from the branches that had broken off in transit. With the right kind of attention, a plant could always bounce back with new vigor. It was a good thing to watch, a good model. Good connections, a little something of the old Angela for the new one to hang onto. She missed her classroom on the second floor of Roosevelt Elementary. She missed her sister. Down deep, she did.

She stared at the phone on the table and thought about calling, imagined the sound of Roxanne's voice. First the sound, which would soothe her, then the words she didn't want to hear. The questions, the inevitable belittling of her answers, the advice, the second guesses about Matt. She couldn't deal with any of that yet. She had no answers. All she knew was that there had been no other way.

In public, Matt was flawlessly courteous. In private, he'd had his quirks. That was what she'd called it at first. He was domineering. In the beginning she'd told herself she liked that in a man. But he made all the decisions, all the plans, all the requirements, *all.* And he was demanding. When he'd started telling her what to wear, whom to talk to, what to eat, what to read, and how and when she should be willing to please him, she'd realized she did not like that in a man. She didn't like it in *anyone.*

But he was Matt Culver. He might have been hard to get along with at times, but he was also bright, charming, handsome, distinguished. All she had to do was assert herself. Matt was then by turns overbearing and apologetic. When she finally told him it wasn't working, he simply laid his position on the line. The man who had once made her a thousand promises finally whittled them down to one; she would accommodate his wishes, or he would make her life a living hell. And in his world—the tidy, seemingly comfortable world she'd lived in all her life—it was a promise he had the power to keep. It was then that the nightmare had really begun. So she'd fled from hell and moved to the city, which was definitely a step up.

But a step up from hell was still a lonely place to be.

Darlene, of course, had no way of knowing that she'd found Angela anyplace but the first door at the top of the stairs when she knocked, and she probably wondered why she was immediately dragged across the threshold to the tune of an elated welcome.

"Here's your money back," Darlene said, doing a mystified double take as she handed it over. "What's going on?"

"Nothing. Less than nothing, in fact." Angela waved the folded bills. "Boy, that was quick."

"Turned out she didn't need the money, but thanks for the loan. Wonder of it is, she brought it right back when the big sting fell through. Could be there's still hope for that girl." She was following Angela into the kitchen. "But only if she lives through this crazy undercover-decoy thing."

"Decoy thing?" This sounded interesting. A welcome change from her own tail-chasing thoughts. With a gesture, Angela offered a chair.

"That's what she needed the money for. The cops are trying to use her to catch them a drug dealer." Darlene took a seat at the small table. "She's been through rehab, got herself a job, done everything they said, but they still won't let her have her boy back until she proves she's really changed. And the cops are trying to say that sticking her neck out like a fool is going to prove it. Hell, that ain't no change. She's been sticking her fool neck out ever since she met that no-good—" She dismissed the no-good with an impatient gesture. "But it's their call. The cops, you know, they get to decide what proves what.

"First she gets herself arrested. No, first she gets messed up with using." Another gesture, more impatience. "No, *first* she falls in looove," she crooned sarcastically, her neck going rubbery as she wobbled her head from side to side. Then she cocked an accusatory index finger. "First she gets messed up with a man. You know what I'm sayin'?"

Angela chuckled. "I know exactly how that works."

"Yeah, exactly. First comes love, then comes the baby carriage. Did we skip a step? Well, too late, honey. You got your heart stuck into it now, and if the man's trash, well, pretty soon you're sittin' in the trash heap right alongside him, huh?"

Not quite, Angela thought, but she nodded anyway.

"She was messed up, my sister was, but now she's clean, and they tell her she's supposed to leave the stuff alone, stay away from those kinda people. That's on Monday. On Tuesday they want her to call the people up and arrange to make a buy. Wednesday comes and it's back to the trash heap she goes, only this time she's a different kind of wired."

"Wouldn't that be pretty dangerous?"

Darlene gave her a look meaning *No-doubt.*

"If it was their idea, you'd think they'd give her the money to do the job."

"That's what I said. I checked it out, though; I ain't stupid. I talked to her probation officer myself. It was on the level." With an openhanded gesture, Darlene explained. "My sister wants her boy back. She wants a second chance to be a good mother, and she's willing to earn that chance. I just don't think they oughta be using her as bait. They didn't get what they were looking for this time, but they'll be wanting her to try again. Bait gets chewed up and swallowed."

"She'll be protected, won't she? Someone will be watching?"

"Oh, sure." Darlene laughed and shook her head. "All kinds of people watching."

"People were watching you, too, when you chased those girls off our street corner. You stuck your neck out *without* protection." Angela slid into the chair across the table. She could tell it startled Darlene, to be looked at and actually seen, maybe just because it was Angela doing the looking and admiring. "That was so . . . I was really impressed."

"Impressed? Get out, girl," she teased, gesturing effusively. " 'I don't know this woman,' you wanted to say. 'No connection at all.' "

"What can I say? I'm ninety-nine and forty-four one-hundredths percent pure coward."

Darlene looked sympathetic. "I heard about what happened to you, girl."

"What?" The smile faded from Angela's face, and she glanced away. "Oh, you mean that little scuffle in the alley. Did Jesse tell you?"

"He didn't say much. He never does. I put two and two together. You got no man. How else would you get your face messed up like that except some kind of a mugging?"

"Carelessness," she confessed. "I know better than to go out the back door at night."

"I get so tired of it all." Darlene leaned back in her chair, spraddled her legs, and searched the water-stained ceiling as though she were hoping for relief from on high. "That's why I talked to those girls the way I did. I've got kids living here, kids who could go either way, you know what I'm saying? They can't be looking at that kinda stuff every day, learning from it." She slapped a hand to her ample bosom. "I can't stand to be looking at it every day, so those girls are just gonna have to move on, 'cause I got no place else to go right now. This is where I live, and I don't have to put up with that stuff. It makes me sick, and it'll make my kids sick." She shrugged. "So I guess that means I'll have to stick my neck out."

Sounded nervy. Admirable, but nervy. Angela braced both hands on the table, preparing to rise from her chair. "Want some spaghetti?"

"You made some?" Angela nodded. "Are you having some?"

"I haven't eaten yet. I made supper, and then I didn't feel like eating." She shrugged, then offered an invitational smile. "But I will if you will."

"Sounds like a dare. Are you as bad a cook as I am?"

Angela laughed. "Sounds like a loaded question. Let's find out."

She was awakened from a sound sleep by a noise. She lay there, eyes peeled wide against the dark, listening. Stevie yapped. Thunder rumbled in the distance, but she knew that wasn't what had disturbed her. Someone was there, and it wasn't the right someone. Whenever that particular someone came, it was always in silence, and her awakening was always a soft, misty moment. But not tonight.

Again the noise, and this time she recognized it as a man's fist, insistently pounding on her door as only a man's fist pounded. A man who wanted something from her, a man who had come to make demands.

Stevie growled, then yapped again.

Please, God, not again.

She remembered the way Darlene had stood her ground the other day. *Got no place else to go. Can't live with this,* she had said.

Angela threw the covers back. *This is my place,* she told herself. *This is as far as I'm going to run. This is where I make my stand.*

"Who is it?" she demanded through the door. She was standing there in her nightgown, barefoot, hugging herself in the dark. She wasn't cold, but she was trembling.

"Lookin' for Gayla," a man's voice returned. It was not a voice she recognized. She sent up silent thanks for that.

Stevie huddled between her feet, yapping her head off. The dog's full-body trembling matched Angela's own.

"You won't find her here." She wished she had one of those peepholes so she could check this guy out. She'd have to remember to ask Jesse if he could put one in, or maybe she'd just punch a hole in the door herself. Her place, her stand, it was all up to her.

"I know she's here. I just wanna talk to her."

Yeah, right. "You've come to the wrong place. There's no one here but me, and I'm not Gayla."

"Who the hell are you, then?"

"The person who lives here. Who are you?"

"You're gonna find out soon enough, you don't tell me where Gayla is."

Angela took a deep breath. Poor little Gayla. She'd imagined her mixed up with a boy, barely old enough to shave but old enough, unfortunately, to make babies. This sounded like a man. Her father, maybe? An older brother? She could tell him to try downstairs. Darlene would take care of this.

The thunder rolled again.

"I don't know anyone by that name," Angela said in a small voice.

"The hell you say." He started banging again. "I don't like talkin' through no fuckin' door."

"Go away!" She stepped back, still trying to hold on. She was freezing with fear, her heart lodged in her throat and galloping in place. "I'm calling the police! Go away!"

"By the time they get here I'll have what I want, and you'll have a busted door, so why don't you just"—bam! bam! bam!— "open it!"

A man's fist pounding on her door. The pounding, the pounding, the terror slamming around in her head. It couldn't happen to her again. She had to stay calm. She had to be absolutely composed, no hysteria. Men scorned hysteria. Police, she thought as she backed into the phone table. Her jade plant crashed to the floor.

No police! The police wouldn't help. She'd tried, and they wouldn't believe her because he was who he was, and she had no proof. He might even have the nerve to wait until they showed up, meet them at the door. All he had to do was tell them she'd called him first and that she was hysterical. Pathetically, disgustingly hysterical. Then he'd tell them that he would take care of her, and they would be on their way. She couldn't get away from him. He had eyes everywhere; he *was* everywhere.

And now he was here. He'd changed his voice. She remembered someone saying something about a shape-shifter. Shape-shifter, voice-shifter, damn him! He'd found her.

More pounding and lock rattling sent her streaking to the bedroom. She slammed the door and dove into the closet, seeking out the darkest corner like a child hiding from some great and terrible retribution. She should have bought a gun. If she had a gun, she'd shoot him. No quarter, no hesitation, no mercy, just *bam! bam! bam!*

But she had no gun. No protection, no way to stop him. Hot and sick with fear, she curled up into a quaking, helpless fetal ball with her yapping little dog at the center and wept without sound.

The closet door squeaked when it opened. Her mouth opened, too, but not much of a sound would come out. Just some sad little cornered-mouse noise uttered into the darkness.

"It's all right, Angela. You're safe."

Stevie whimpered and wiggled out of her arms.

Safe. The voice from her dreams . . . wasn't it? Lord, she'd lost it completely.

"I'm not sleeping, am I? I know he was here. He was trying to get in."

"He's gone now." The voice moved in closer. "Are you okay?"

"Where did he—" She clamped her hand over her mouth and listened. No pounding, except her heart. No shouting, except the echo inside her head. Her hand came away hot and wet. "Where did he go? What did you do?"

"I made him leave. That's all." He was shadow on shadow. Even without touching her, he was heat banishing cold. "Is that the one you're afraid of?"

"Was he . . . was he really here? I thought . . . I was sure it was . . ." She hated the catch in her voice, the uncontrollable trembling, and the hot tears, but most of all she hated the fear. It muddled her head, turned her into something quivering and pathetic. "I don't know what's real anymore."

"He claimed he was looking for Gayla. Wrong address?" Her

squeaky sob was meant to confirm. "Or was he lying? Is that the one, Angela?"

"I . . . he almost got in."

"No, he didn't. That's a good lock. It kept him out."

"But not you," she whispered, lips trembling. "It doesn't keep you out."

"You needed me. It won't keep me out if you need me. Come on," he said, reaching for her, scooping her out of the corner. She gasped, gulping for air like a drowning woman, one deep breath, two . . .

He smelled of summer rain. Quiet, gentle rain. "It's safe for you to come out now."

She was blubbering like a sobbing child. "Where's my dog?"

"Guarding the door."

"Right." All Stevie could do was yap her head off. The perfect guard dog for a lunatic. Here was crazy Angela, crouching on the floor of her closet, knees to knees with a phantom. She tried to laugh, but it came out hiccupy.

"I promised her I'd look after you. Now come on out."

"Am I dreaming you?"

"I wouldn't know."

She grabbed the front of his jacket with both hands. "Did I dream him? I don't know anymore, either. It scares me that I can't even *tell* anymore."

"You know I won't hurt you. Come on."

The hands cupping her elbows were strong and sure, his gentleness blessedly familiar. She hung onto his denim jacket and let him draw her to her feet, both of them ducking the clothes in the closet that was less than half full. Amazing how much she'd found she could do without. All she wanted, all she needed, was a little peace.

"He would have hurt me." Her legs were rubbery, and she was shaky inside. "I think . . . he sounded like he wanted to, the way he was . . . slamming his fist on the . . ." It was all so sickeningly familiar.

"Did you call the cops?"

"No. They won't help me. They never do. It's because—"

Stevie started yapping again. The knock on the door was more polite this time. "It's the police, Miss Prescott. Are you all right?"

"I didn't call them," she whispered, hanging onto the front of his jacket for dear life. "I can't talk to them."

"I can't either." His hands covered hers as he stepped back. "Just tell them you're all right. Otherwise they'll think they have to get in and make sure." With a quick squeeze to reassure her, he loosed her hands.

"Angela?"

"It's Darlene, from downstairs," Angela whispered into the dark.

"Answer her. If she made the call, the complaint will be made in her name." His voice was barely audible. She conjured an image of him dissolving into the night.

"Don't go. I won't let anyone in," she resolved as she searched through the closet for the feel of terry cloth. She snapped her robe off the hanger and slipped it on. "I promise."

She turned on the table lamp in the front room and snatched Stevie up before she approached the door. "Darlene?"

"We heard some commotion, so we called the cops. You okay in there?"

"Yes, I'm fine." She shushed Stevie. "I heard it, too, but whoever it was, I guess something must have scared him away. Maybe . . . I knocked a plant over."

"Would you mind opening the door, Angela? I'm a cop. I just want to make sure everything's okay."

"I'm fine," she said to the doorjamb.

"Are you alone?"

"Yes, I'm . . ." In answer to that one, she opened the door wide enough to let herself be seen. "My poor dog's going crazy," she said. "It scared me, as you can probably tell, but I'm fine. I just got new locks. None too soon, huh?"

"What happened?" the portly policeman wanted to know.

"Some guy looking for—" She slid Darlene a glance. "Some girl, I don't know. He was probably either drunk or crazy. I tried to tell him he was in the wrong place."

"Looking for my girl?" Darlene demanded.

"Well, I . . . don't . . ."

"Anybody comes lookin' for my girl in the middle of the night, he better be wearing a halo and a pair of wings." Darlene folded her arms and stood shoulder to shoulder with the cop, looking just as formidable in her bathrobe as he did in his dripping blue cap and yellow slicker. "Did you see him?"

"Oh, no, I didn't open the door."

The cop had his notepad out. "He didn't say his name?"

"No. He was just raving about kicking the door down."

He clicked his black ballpoint pen. "Could I get your full name for the report?"

"There's nothing to report, really." Soothing Stevie with some heavy petting, she slipped Darlene another quick glance. "Is there? I mean, I really didn't see anyone."

Darlene took the hint. "I'm the one who called. I know damn well it was me the son of a bitch meant to harass. Darlene Gilbert. That's Gilbert, spelled just like it sounds. You got my address. You got . . ."

The cop was still looking at Angela. She cleared her throat. "Angela Prescott. No . . . no middle initial. But I don't know him, and I didn't see anything."

"You don't want him coming around you again, do you?"

"No."

"Listen here, I'm the one who called you, and I know damn well what it was all about. Remember those hookers I sent on their way the other day, Angela?"

"Yes." Thank God for Darlene.

"It had to be some pimp who don't want me shooing his girl off the corner where my babies have to catch the bus." Launching her report, Darlene led the officer toward the stairway. "There was two. I didn't hear nothin' until one of the kids come and got me. I looked out, and I thought sure I saw two."

"I don't think so," Angela said. When the cop turned, Darlene gave her an exasperated look behind his back. "There was only one voice," Angela explained. "I'm almost positive only one person came in."

Darlene shrugged, then cocked her head to one side as though she'd just noticed Angela's face. "You gonna be okay, girl?"

"Yes." She gave her friend a tight smile, a quick nod. "Thanks for . . ."

"I had the big window fan going in my bedroom. Didn't hear nothin' until one of the kids woke me up. Otherwise . . ."

"I'm okay," Angela assured her. "Thanks."

She closed the door, turned, and leaned against it, hugging Stevie as she listened to the retreating footsteps and fading voices. Her hands shook as she stuffed the jade's root ball back into the plastic pot and set it on the table, leaving a trail of dirt and broken leaves on the floor. When the house was once again dark and quiet and Stevie had settled into her basket, Angela went back to her room and tried to hold on as she let her robe slip to the floor. Standing by her bed in the dark, she actually wrapped her arms around herself, felt her own trembling, and condemned it as weakness. Darlene would have scared the creep away herself. Darlene would have roared at him and made him go flying from her doorstep.

Step? She didn't have a doorstep anymore. All she had was a landing and a front door to a crummy apartment with rickety walls and windows, and all because she'd given up and run away.

All because she couldn't win and she'd given up fighting.

All because she was a poor excuse for a fighter. She always ended up crying.

The heavy hand on her shoulder sent her skyrocketing.

"Shh. It's just me."

"You!" This was no dream, and she had to stop acting like such a fool. "Who are you, anyway? I'm going to turn on the light and find out. I'm not going to be—" Her hand bumped the lamp-shade.

"Don't." He caught her arm with his free hand, still gripping her shoulder with the other. "Just go back to bed. I'll be gone before you can—"

"No." She swallowed hard and let her arm drop to her side. "Stay a little. I trust you." The pressure in his grip lessened. "I need someone I can trust."

He slid his hand up her arm until it came to rest on her other shoulder. "Can I trust you?" he challenged.

"There was a policeman at my door a moment ago."

"If you'd told him, he wouldn't have found me. I would have disappeared. You know that."

"Am I crazy?" He'd begun to massage the tension from her shoulders. A siren wailed in the distance. Was this her passage to peace? "Are you the harbinger of my insanity?"

"Could be. I'm pretty sure I'm over the line myself."

"Oh, God. That's just great." With a sigh, she let her head drop back until it rested on his shoulder. "Your clothes are damp."

"It's raining. Listen."

The terrible echoes in her head faded, replaced by the soft patter on the roof and the gurgling in the rain gutter. Slowly the tension drained away from her. His hands were magic.

She groaned. "What kind of a dream are you, anyway? Who invented you?"

"You'll have to share the credit with Tommy T." His chuckle was a low rumble close to her ear. She could feel the heat of him through her cotton nightgown. "Or the blame."

"Is he crazy, too?"

"He's a kid. He's allowed to invent people."

"I suppose he thinks it's safe to share his inventions with two lunatics."

"I suppose he's right." His lips brushed her hair, his warm breath filling her ear with a whisper. "He has good instincts."

"Does he?" She turned to him, but somehow he read her intentions, and he caught her wrists before her hands reached their destination. "If you won't let me see you, won't you at least let me touch your face?"

"Not now."

"Why not? I've touched it before. You've touched mine."

"I've seen yours." He placed her hands on the front of his damp jacket and caressed her knuckles lightly with his fingertips to let her know that he wanted her to keep them there. Then he cupped his hands around her face, taking the liberty he'd denied her. "It's a very pretty face."

"Is it because . . ." She closed her eyes, longing to trace his cheekbones with her thumbs as he did hers. "Are you afraid it would scare me?"

"My face?" His deep chuckle reminded her of the distant thunder.

"Tommy T thinks you have a scar of some kind. That you suffer from some kind of—"

"Don't, Angela." Her hand barely moved, but he stopped it again. "There's nothing to see. I'm nobody."

"Nobody took care of me after I was beaten up in an alley? Nobody comes to check on me whenever—"

"Tommy T," he whispered, his arms surrounding her. "A boy with good instincts."

"Nobody drove an intruder away from my door?"

He drew a slow, deep breath. She could feel the pounding of his heart beneath her hand. It was a real heart, a true heartbeat. "Nobody's holding me in his arms?" Her voice dropped to a whisper. "Nobody kissed me?"

"A dream."

She lifted her chin. "Nobody's ever going to kiss me again?"

His openmouthed kiss stole her next breath, replacing it with his. She pushed the front of his jacket aside and splayed her fingers over his soft cotton T-shirt, holding his heartbeat in her hand and answering his kiss with hers. She discovered the taste of doubt mixed with desire, and she wasn't sure whose doubt, whose desire, where hers ended and his began. They were both savoring, both struggling, both thinking, *What in God's name am I doing?*

"Is that what you want?" he whispered against her lips.

"I want to know I'm not crazy." She wondered that she was able to breathe, much less speak. She closed her eyes and rested her forehead on his chin.

"I don't think you are." He lowered his head just slightly, so that she felt him smile. "Does that help you any?"

"Do you know what would help?" With a soft sound he invited her to tell him. "If you could just hold me."

After too long a pause he said, "I guess I could do that."

And he did. He sat in the chair in the corner of the room and cuddled her in his lap, and she knew he'd done this for her before. In some dark, earthen womb he'd held her like this and cared for her like this, asking nothing in return, and she could not imagine why. They'd never met. Whoever he was, whatever his secrets, she'd done him no favors by falling across his path.

"I want to know who you are."

"Nobody," he insisted. "But I'm not going to hurt you, and I'm not going to let anyone else hurt you." He brushed her hair back from her face. "Do you know someone who might try?"

"If he finds me, he will."

"Who will?"

"Somebody." She burrowed into the front of his jacket and breathed his night-rain scent. "A real somebody. If he finds me, nobody can stop him."

"That's right. Nobody *can* stop him." He kissed the crown of her hair. "And nobody will."

She pressed her small kiss over his heart, then smiled against his T-shirt. "You talk in riddles. You must be that Trickster Mr. Bird was talking about. Old Man Coyote?"

"I feel like a very old man sometimes. As old as the hills."

"You don't kiss like an old man."

His amusement was couched in a doubtful *humph.* "How do old men kiss?"

"I don't know. On the cheek, I guess."

He lifted her chin with one blunt finger and brushed her cheek with his lips, the tip of his nose, the warmth of his breath. "Go to sleep, Angela. You're safe in this old man's arms."

"So you *are* a man," she said triumphantly. "You're somebody, then."

"Sometimes, when the wind shifts and the moon fades." But it was he who shifted, getting comfortable, snuggling with her in the chair even though there was a bed only a few steps away.

"Gallant phantom," she said, drifting, content. "Stay . . ."

"Go to sleep now. I'll watch over you."

J esse was pleased with his playground. He was just putting the finishing touches on the igloo-shaped metal climber that had been a bitch to put together. But it turned out fine, he told himself. The kids were going to enjoy it. The little ones, anyway.

The older ones didn't seem to want to do much except hang out, especially on days like today. Late afternoon, quiet street, clear sky, warm breeze, leaves on the trees just beginning to turn yellow. Three boys had claimed a bench in the park across the street, perched on the backrest like cocky cardinals, restlessly flipping hands and feet around for want of flashy tails. One lit up a cigarette. The second one bummed a drag.

Tommy T was hanging out, too, but he was sticking close to Jesse's elbow, handing him screws, trying out tools. Jesse figured this sudden need to stick close had to do with the trio across the street. He didn't ask. He didn't mind being a buffer for the boy, if that was what he needed, but it hurt a little. It rocked that hollow place inside him, like somebody sloshing the dregs around in a barrel just to remind himself that it was empty. It made him light-headed with hunger.

He didn't have to ask what was on Tommy T's mind. The boy was a talker.

"So, like, what I was thinking was maybe I could work for you on weekends. I'm not old enough to get a job, but this way I could be learning about this kind of stuff, kinda like an apprentice." He was squatting next to the toolbox, arranging screwdrivers by size in the top tray. He looked up, squinting one eye against the sun. "And you wouldn't have to pay me much."

Jesse handed him a crescent wrench. "How much is not much?"

"I don't know. Where does this go?"

"Underneath."

The boy lifted the tray. "How much do apprentices usually get paid?"

"I never had an apprentice. Never could afford one."

"I'm affordable," Tommy T assured him eagerly as he fit the tray back in its place. "And I wanna learn how to do this stuff. You know, build stuff. When I have a place of my own someday, I wanna be able to fix things myself, the way you do. I don't want no holes in the walls. I want the heat to work right, the toilet, the shower. Put the best locks on the doors so my wife and kids don't have to worry about nobody breakin' in." Jesse was gathering up wood scraps, but he was listening, hiding a smile. "You're not married, are you?"

The question was a smile-killer. "Not anymore."

"Split the sheets, huh?"

"You could say that." Jesse tossed an armload of scraps into a black plastic barrel. It had been a while since he'd thought about Lila. She'd split more than sheets. Her strength had outstripped his.

"No kids?"

He cast a sharp glance over his shoulder. "You writing a book?"

"Yeah." Tommy T laced his fingers together and made a hammock of his hands for his wildly curly head. His arms looked like browned chicken wings. His grin radiated confidence. "I am, as a matter of fact. A comic book."

"Comic books are supposed to be funny. I ain't too funny." He had to turn away, though, because that grin was daring him not to grin right back.

"Goofy's funny." The boy waited, dangling that grin behind Jesse's back. Finally he sniffed and shuffled his feet, scraping some gravel. "So, do you live alone?"

"I do most everything alone, including . . ." He was looking at the bench across the street again. The players had changed. The smoker was still there, but his two buddies were gone, replaced by an older kid, early twenties, maybe.

"You know that kid?" Jesse asked. He knew the boy did. The real question was, would he say? They'd both run into the beefy kid with the cold eyes before, and he figured it was about time he got a handle on him. Especially since he recognized the guy the kid was clearly fronting for. The exchange of cash and crack was about to take place, right before his eyes. Not that his eyes mattered to them. He couldn't see the guy's face, but he didn't have to. He recognized the stringy hair and the red-and-green cap he was wearing. Too old to be messing with the girl Darlene had taken in.

"Yeah, I know him. Kinda." Tommy T shrugged, his glance cautious. "I don't know his name. Not his real name."

Jesse grasped a crossbar on the climber and gave it a test shake. He knew it wouldn't budge, not the way he'd anchored it into the ground. "What name do you know him by?"

"They call him Chopper. He's kind of a badass. Likes to think he is, anyways. He's got this thing going with my brother and the dudes he hangs with."

"What kind of a thing?"

"A war, I guess." Tommy T hung his head and mumbled, "Chopper's the one that messed with Angela that time."

Jesse nodded, his gut clenching like a fist. "How about the other one?" He laid a hand on top of the boy's head, holding it still. "Jeez, not too damn obvious."

"I don't know the other one." Tommy T looked up. "Why are you so interested? You writin' a book?"

"Gotta be careful who you turn your back to these days," Jesse said, and Tommy T nodded. "You need money for something special?"

"Not *that*." A subtle chin jerk defined *"that"* as what was going on across the street. "I'm lookin' for—*we're* lookin' for a new place."

The claim brought Jesse up short. "You and Angela?"

"I'm not livin' with Angela. I need a place for my mom, my brother, and me."

Not Angela. It was because of the wishful images that came to his own mind whenever her name was mentioned that he'd made the leap. Wishful, but uninvited. He didn't like wishing.

He gave an empathetic nod. "Rent money can be pretty hard to come up with."

"You gotta have two months' worth, plus that deposit they always keep for things that were already wrecked when you moved in, plus . . ." He stared at the toes of his battered tennis shoes. "I was thinkin' I could earn some money to help out."

The kid was good at spinning fairy tales. Jesse cleared his throat. "When do you have to move?"

"Before it gets too cold."

"I'll see what I can come up with. The thing is . . . your mom . . ." Tommy T looked up sharply, his dark eyes putting the man on notice. Jesse glanced away, chagrined. "Okay. I can't have you working on a site like this. You're too young. But maybe you could help me with . . ."

In the park, the stringy-haired guy with the red-and-green cap was in the kid's face, jabbing a finger in his chest. The boy was nodding vigorously. Jesse gripped the smooth metal crossbar. "I'll think of something."

"Soon?"

"Soon." He nodded, shifting his gaze. "You made any good pictures lately?"

"Hell, yeah, I'm making good pictures lately. Take a look at this." Tommy T whipped a wad of paper out of his back pocket and quickly unfolded it. A pocketful of dreams, Jesse thought, half smiling. The boy wanted him to take them in his hand, but he just looked. And listened. "See, I'm giving Dark Dog some fresh gear. Like in the old days, warriors used to wear this kind of stuff. Wolf pelt, buckskin leggings. This is a breastplate, but it's made of Hercutanium."

"Hercutanium?"

"Not even a laser gun can penetrate it."

"Nice touch." Jesse pointed with his lips. "What's he wearing on his feet?"

"Those are knee-high moccasins with Hercutanium shin guards and steel-reinforced toes."

"Just plain steel? Hell, I've got steel toes in these." He planted one booted foot on a low rung of the climber.

Tommy T regarded the laced boot. "You think I should put Hercutanium in the toes, too?"

"Steel works pretty good for protection. Better than your average shit-kickers."

"Do they slow you down?"

Jesse laughed. "I haven't run any marathons in them, but I didn't break any toes when I dropped a hammer on my foot the other day."

"I'd probably have to get some boots like that if I worked for you, wouldn't I?"

"Wouldn't hurt." He pointed to a smaller figure in the drawing. "Who's this guy?"

"That's Dark Dog's partner. I don't have a good name for him yet."

"How 'bout Curly Pup? Or Puppy T." Jesse ruffled the boy's curly hair. It was a spontaneous gesture that startled them both.

They exchanged a look, both withdrawing, flustered.

"No way," Tommy T said without much conviction.

"Did you know that Crazy Horse's name when he was a boy was Curly?" The boy shook his head. "They say his hair was light and kinda curly. Unusual for an Indian."

"Kinda like mine?" the boy speculated. Jesse grunted. "I'm not full-blooded Indian," Tommy T said. He looked up, shrugged, compelled to explain. "My dad was black." Jesse nodded. "Are you full-blooded Sioux?"

"I'm part rattlesnake and part—" He almost said "son of a bitch." Like Dark Dog. "I've got some other stuff mixed in. A little French, a little Cree. Most of us do. Hybrid vigor."

"What does that mean?"

"It means you cut a mixed-blood, he bleeds just as red as anybody else." He laid a hand on the boy's thin shoulder, gave a quick squeeze. The charge shot up his own arm. "It means you're fine just the way you are, Tommy T. And I just thought of a job you could do for me."

"A *paying* job?"

"You wanna work by the hour or by the job?" He took the paper from the boy's hand. "First I better ask, how long does it take you to draw a picture like this? Two people."

"An hour, tops."

"Top secret, okay? And it's gotta be good."

"It will be."

"I want you to draw those two. Try to get the older guy . . ." He sidestepped, inserting himself between the boy and the street. "Look past me. Can you see him?" The boy shifted his gaze, then nodded once. "Can you draw him?"

"What for?"

"Because I'm gonna pay you for it."

"Five bucks an hour?"

Jesse nodded appreciatively. "Those are some pretty good wages."

"You'll get yourself a good picture, too."

"Then it's a deal."

The city's glass-and-steel skyline underlined the night sky with neon and halogen, encasing Minneapolis in an eerie glow. The river bluffs were pitch-dark. Tommy T clutched his treasure in a brown paper bag stuffed inside his roomy shirt. He probably looked like a pregnant girl clutching her belly, but he was running at a faster clip than any girl could ever manage, especially in that condition. He couldn't let anyone stop him now, because if one or two people did, they'd ask him what he was carrying, and if they saw it, they'd take it off him for sure. It was beautiful.

He couldn't believe Mr. Bird had traded him the wolf skin for a few pencil drawings. He hadn't seemed too interested at first, but when Tommy T mentioned the dream he'd had, the old man's ears had perked right up. Okay, so maybe he'd dreamed up a few extra details on the spot, but he really *had* dreamed about somebody who was half man, half wolf. Or coyote. Or dog; he wasn't exactly sure. Canine, anyway. Mr. Bird had said that he was getting old, might be time to give the pelt away. And he *did*, right then and there.

Tommy T scrambled over the rocks and poured himself into his favorite niche. A breeze rattled the leaves in the topmost branches of the trees that separated the river bluff from the city. He stared hard at the hole, wishing for X-ray vision.

"Dark Dog? It's me. Are you there?"

The voice sounded labored, as though it had to push itself through gravel. "I'm here."

"Did you like the picture I brought you before?" He took the grunt to mean something positive. "Wait'll you see what I brought this time." No response. "Can I put it someplace where you can reach it?"

"What is it?"

"Something for you to wear."

"Keep it for yourself. Nights are turning cold already."

"I ain't cold." He stuck his hand into the big paper bag, soft from repeated crushing, and stroked the fur. "Are you still sick?"

"Not really," came the quiet response. "It's all in my head."

"Oh." Did that mean Dark Dog was crazy? He bit back the question. If his hero had escaped from some kind of nuthouse, he didn't want to know about it. "I think what I brought you will help. You need to keep your head warm. Neck, too. You know about the temperature receptors in your neck? Your neck's pretty important. It's got, like, your spine and your windpipe and that one big artery."

"You shouldn't be giving me stuff you might need yourself."

"No, this is for you. I got it for you. Traded for it. Can I put it . . ." He scooted close to the black hole, which was mostly camouflaged by rocks and weeds. "I'll put it just inside your door, okay? This goes with the picture I made. You'll know what to do with it if you put the two together." Squatting there like a pilgrim with an offering, he carefully folded the top of the bag around the package. "I'm giving you this because you've helped me a lot."

"You haven't given me much choice. You're like a damn mosquito."

"Mosquitoes are bloodsuckers. I ain't no bloodsucker."

"No," came the reply, quietly. "No, you're not."

"Angela says people have to make their own choices. I couldn't make you help if you didn't wanna. And Mr. Bird says when somebody gives you something, you're supposed to just shake their hand and accept the honor."

"Mr. Bird's right. But it's hard . . ." He heard some movement, and then a harsh sound, as though the hole itself were struggling to breathe. ". . . when my head's about to split open."

"You hung over?"

"I wish."

Tommy T swallowed hard, his eyes wide, trying to peer into the hole's deep, disturbing gloom. "You gonna be okay?"

"Yeah. Just don't ask me to kill any dragons for you right now, okay?"

"Dragons? That's kid stuff." He wasn't scared. He'd gotten in the way a time or two when his mother was hurting, but this was different. This was Dark Dog. "You need . . . anything?"

"I need the dark. I need . . . quiet."

"Okay," he whispered, resolving to stick around for a while. Obviously Dark Dog had one serious weakness, just like all true heroes, and he was battling that weakness right now. He needed his partner to stand by him, just in case an enemy should come along and try to take advantage.

Tommy T put the paper bag just inside the mouth of his hero's den. "Here's what I brought you. I hope you like it."

He heard the scrape of a boot. Then the big hand appeared, and Tommy T latched onto it, holding it more than shaking it, comforted by the rough texture, the strength, and the heat that enfolded him with a simple gesture. Then, at the core, he felt a slight tremor, and that startled him. Dark Dog's serious weakness was pain. The kind of pain that could make a person shake and sweat and cry. Tears suddenly burned deep in his own throat. For a moment he simply hung on tight, and he could have sworn the tremor passed from his hero's hand into his own. And then it went away.

He'd kept a silent vigil, watching the stars and listening to the river roll until a cramp in his leg drove him to abandon his watch. He made his way through the maze of alleys and back streets, thinking he might arrange to stumble across his brother. He hadn't eaten since lunch—hot lunch was another advantage to being in school—and what he really wanted to do was go to Angela's. But it was too late for that.

He'd pay her a visit in the morning, though. She'd make him take a shower first thing. He'd tell her the shower wasn't working at home, and she'd tell him to put on some clean clothes. She'd bought him some stuff a couple of times, even though he'd told her not to. He was thinking about how they'd take Stevie for a walk and he'd try not to sack out until she left for work. He was so busy figuring all the angles that he forgot to avoid Chopper's territory.

They caught him in the driveway behind Twin City Storage and pinned him to the wall. Chopper, two of his boys, and that damned pit bull of his, snarling like somebody'd just taken his T-bone away.

A gap-toothed black dude named Shank braced his forearm across Tommy T's throat, forcing his chin up so that his nose was within inches of getting stuck between Shank's front teeth. "Where you goin', you squirmin' little sucka?"

"Shit, man, that's Stoner's little brother," Chopper said. "Stoner got you runnin' stuff for him, has he? That damn chickenshit."

A shaft of light brightened the dead end beyond the corner of the building. Through the corner of one eye Tommy T could barely see Chopper's pasty, pimply face. "I ain't runnin' nothin' for nobody."

The arm beneath his chin stiffened. "You're runnin' loose in the wrong part of town, little bro."

"I ain't your 'bro.' I was just takin' a shortcut. Just lookin' for something to eat, is all."

"Lookin' for scraps?" Chopper pulled the gap-toothed dude back so he could stick his own face in. One was as ugly as the other. "You're one sorry little shit, ain't you?"

"Yeah." Tommy T hung his head and swallowed all his pride. "Sorry, Chopper. I guess I got lost."

"Lost?" Shank laughed. "This little shit knows his way around better than any of us. How 'bout we tie a bone around his neck and see if the dog wants to play with him?"

"You're sorry?" Chopper grabbed a handful of his hair and stretched his scalp a little. "How sorry? You wanna show me how sorry?"

"I said I was sorry."

"You think that's all it takes?" Shank buried his fist in Tommy T's stomach, knocking the wind out of him. Chopper grabbed the hair again and bloodied his face with a couple of punches. "You wanna tell me something about Stoner and Ajax? What did you wanna tell me?"

"Sorry, Chopper." Tommy T shook his head to clear it. There were tears in his eyes, but he wasn't crying. Tommy T didn't cry. "That's all I got to say. Sorry."

"I'm sorry, too." Shank twisted his arm behind his back. Chopper landed another punch, then hammered his head against the wall. "Did that hurt? I'm real sor—"

A high-pitched whistle paralyzed them all, like a bird of prey dropping out of the night sky on an alley full of mice. The dog lunged, hit the end of its lead, and hung there snarling until the third boy dropped the chain. With his free hand, Tommy T took a swipe at his eyes to clear them.

There stood Dark Dog, a hulking shadow at the edge of the pool of light. The head of the wolf mantle formed a headdress that draped his shoulders and hung down his back. Beneath the wolf snout, the top half of his face was painted black, the bottom white. He looked glorious. Tommy T couldn't have designed him any better.

"What the fuck . . ."

"Let him go," Dark Dog ordered.

The pit bull bristled at his feet, snarling.

"Get 'im, Hog," Chopper said.

The dog moved in, teeth bared. A deep growl rumbled in Dark Dog's throat. He snapped his fingers, and the dog tucked its tail between its legs, stretched its neck, and sniffed, then whimpered and wagged its whole butt.

Stunned, Shank eased up on Tommy T's arm. "Who is that? Who's . . ."

"Strange name for a dog," Dark Dog muttered as he laid his hand on the animal's head, claiming dominance. He spoke quietly to the dog, then ordered with a sweeping gesture, "All of you move away from the boy."

"You better . . ." The pit bull was snarling again. Chopper

glanced at his sidekicks, the dog, Tommy T. He shrugged. "That dog'll kill him if we step away. Look at him."

"He's lookin' at *you*, kid." Dark Dog's teeth glinted in a feral smile. "That's a line from a movie. You like old movies?" He spoke to the dog again, words unfamiliar to the boys, inciting more snarling.

"What kinda language is that?" Chopper stepped back. The dog went wild.

"Who the hell—" Shank shoved Tommy T away. He slumped against the cinder-block wall.

"Don't move," Dark Dog said. "Nobody move. You guys shut your eyes. Hog doesn't like the way you're looking at him."

In two strides Dark Dog had reached Tommy T, catching him to his side before the boy slid to the ground. "You okay?" His young partner nodded, steadying himself on Dark Dog's arm. The other players shifted. Dark Dog snapped his fingers, and the pit bull snarled on cue. "I said shut your eyes if you wanna keep them in your face." He lifted Tommy T in his arms and started backing into the shadows. "That's good. Now keep them shut real tight. You guys know how to Indian-dance?"

"Indian-dance? We ain't no fuckin'—"

The dog snarled.

"Guess you better just keep your mouth shut. Hog doesn't like the way you talk, either. You guys watch TV sometimes, don't you? When you're not beatin' up on people?"

Chopper opened his mouth and tried to move, but the dog was right on him.

Dark Dog's hiss turned the growling down a notch. "Just nod. You've seen Indians dancing in movies? Hog wants to see you guys dance. So I'm gonna give you guys a song, and you're gonna dance."

Chopper couldn't decide whether to bolt or stand. "You're fuckin' crazy."

Hog went wild, teeth snapping within inches of Chopper's

belly as the boy instinctively, stupidly, threw his arms above his head.

"Shut your eyes!" Dark Dog issued more strange commands, and the dog dropped back, snarling still. "Damn, this dog wants to eat your eyes, kid. Now here's the song. You start dancing, he'll stop snarling." It started low in his chest, then rose to a high pitch. At Dark Dog's signal, the pit bull yowled. "Dance!" The three boys shuffled their feet. Dark Dog sang, and Hog howled. When Chopper paused, Hog's howl turned to a vicious snarl until Chopper got his feet moving again. Hog kept right on howling as Dark Dog slipped away, carrying his partner. The last they saw of them, Chopper and his two buddies were still dancing.

"Is that you laughing, little fox?" He could feel the boy quaking in his arms as he hurried through the alley. He could barely see his face in the dark. "What are you laughing at? You're bleeding like a stuck"—he grinned, shaking his head —"hog. What a name for a dog."

"You got all the superpowers you need," Tommy T said. He was hanging on, head held up like a trooper. "You're Coyote, aren't you? I got you the wrong kind of skin."

"A skin's a skin, kid." And they were two of a kind. He had to laugh, too. "They did look pretty funny, didn't they?"

"How's your head?"

"Better. How about yours?"

Tommy T groaned.

"How bad is it?" Dark Dog asked solicitously as he approached a familiar chain-link fence. "How bad are you hurt?"

"It's nothin'." Tommy T looked up at the house they'd come to. "I can't go to Angela's. The door's locked by now."

"You think a lock stops Dark Dog?"

"They might come lookin' for me and make trouble for her."

"I won't let that happen." He set the boy down on the back porch, then shielded his sleight of hand on the lock with his body. "Don't scare her," he whispered to the boy as he ushered him

163

inside. "Let her know it's you. She'll take care of you now."

"I don't need any—"

He scooted the boy toward the back stairs. "I'll stay close by, just like you did for me. Let her look after you."

Angela was positive she'd locked the doors this time. One of the kids must have sneaked in or out again, and this time she was going to have to speak with Darlene about it. She took a deep breath, collected herself, then asked through the closed door, "Who's there?"

"It's Tommy T. I know it's too late to be bothering you, but I had—" She threw the door open and gasped when she saw all the blood. "I had a fight with some—"

"Oh, sweetie, what have they done to you?" She grabbed his shoulders and reeled him over the threshold, reaching back with one hand to lock the door behind them. "This looks bad," she fretted as she ushered him into the bathroom and sat him down on the toilet. She snatched a couple of clean washcloths out of a drawer, turned on the water, tipped his head back in the crook of her elbow, and started swabbing.

He said nothing. Their eyes kept meeting over her attempts to stop the bleeding. She let him see the worry in hers. He let her see the relief in his. And the love.

"Where's all this blood coming from?" she asked finally, because his nose wouldn't quit gushing.

"Pressure," he said, gasping for air through his mouth, and he tried to show her with hands so grimy she wouldn't let him touch his face with them.

"What's the closest hospital?" she muttered, mostly to herself, pressing two fingers against the side of his nose. "Let's . . . we'll go to the emergency room. You might have—"

"It ain't that bad. They just hit me in the face a few—ouch!"

In her swabbing she'd uncovered another scrape near the corner of his eye. "Sorry. We should get you X-rayed, Tommy T. You might have a broken nose."

"I get nosebleeds all the time." He sounded stuffy, as though he had a cold. "You might've had something broken before, too, but you said no hospitals and no cops, remember? I'm okay."

"Who did this?"

"I don't—" He tried to duck away from the antiseptic she'd started applying to the cuts on his face, but she persisted. He gave in, wincing. "Just some punks."

"The same ones?" He nodded dumbly. "What do they have against us, anyway? We haven't done anything to them. And we can't let them keep getting away with this."

Watching her rinse out the bloody cloth in the sink, he managed a lopsided smile. "Dark Dog got 'em good. Made 'em look like fools."

"Dark Dog?"

"You shoulda seen it, Angela. All of a sudden, there he was, a lone wolf stepping out of the shadows. Scared the hell out of those turkeys. And you know what he did?" She didn't. All she knew was that Tommy T needed a bath. "He turned their own dog on them."

"The dog attacked them?" She was reaching for a box of Band-Aids.

"No, it was even better than that. He talks to the dog in Indian, see, and the dog understands. Cooler'n hell! He's got this pit bull ready to jump the next guy that moves, and then comes the best part." Now that she'd stanched most of the bleeding, he seemed to have forgotten the worst part. "He makes them close their eyes and dance, just like in the movies when they shoot at the guy's feet and make him dance, you know? Only he doesn't need a gun. It's like a trick or something. He just—" He snapped his fingers, then gestured expansively. "Cooler'n hell."

"Sounds like it." She plugged the bathtub and turned the water on. "Did he bring you here?"

"He's out there somewhere, watching in case those punks tried to follow me." He let her peel off his bloody T-shirt, coming out of it beaming, almost smiling. "Bitchin', huh?"

"Way cool." She daubed at a little fresh blood. "You need a lot of soap and water, Mr. T. I guess it isn't as bad as all that blood made it look, but I'd still feel better if we had a doctor look you over."

"Angela, they'd be askin' a lot of questions. You know what I mean?"

She nodded, sighed. "Why should we be the ones who have to hide? It isn't fair."

"Anybody ever tries to hurt you again, Angela, I'm gonna . . ." He smacked his fist against his palm. "I'm gonna deal with 'em myself."

"You're going to stay here, Tommy T. For a while, okay? If . . . if your mother wouldn't mind."

"She don't mind," he said quietly, suddenly avoiding her eyes. "She can get along by herself pretty good. She don't need me."

"Well, I do." She shut the water off. "Do you mind sleeping on the sofa?"

"The sofa's great."

Tommy T spent the weekend at Angela's. She fussed over his injuries a lot, but he didn't mind. She made him chocolate pudding just because he said it was a favorite of his, and she gave him some real drawing pencils. He felt a little guilty for lying to her about where he was going when he went out looking for Stoner, but he didn't want to answer too many questions about his brother. She'd be asking who he hung with and where and like that. Stuff that was hard to explain. They were getting tight, him and Angela, but Stoner was his brother. Stoner would always be his brother.

He finally caught up to him at the basketball court in the Indian Center. Stoner had been looking for him, too. Tommy T wondered what was in the plastic grocery bag tucked under his arm.

"Jesus Christ, what happened to you?" Stoner demanded right off when he saw his brother's face.

"I got into it with Chopper."

"Chopper? What the . . ." Stoner glanced across the court, postured, shifted his feet. "I'll kill him, I swear to God."

"Killing's too good for him," Tommy T said. Stoner looked doubtful. He also looked tired, not much life in his eyes.

Useless as he knew it was going to be, Tommy T couldn't help elaborating, hoping to impress. "But I got a friend who knows how to get somebody better than dead. Shamed him out really good, man. You shoulda seen it. Turned his own dog on him, and made him dance. Practically made him piss his pants, I ain't lyin'. It was so—"

Stoner tried to laugh, but it turned into a coughing spasm, which he shook off. "You been smokin' weed with Ajax again? I told you . . ."

"Told ya, I ain't lyin'! You've seen him, Stoner. You've seen what he can do. He ain't evil, and he ain't no drunk."

"What is he, then? Some New Age Superman?"

"Hell, no. He's real. I've never gotten a good look at his face, but he's Indian. I know that for sure. And now . . ." A stray basketball bounced between them. Stoner batted it back onto the court while Tommy T went on with his story. "He looked so cool. His face was painted black and white, and he was wearing—"

Stoner tapped his shoulder with a fist, shaking his head. He

168

was really almost smiling. "The cops catch this guy, they're gonna lock him up in a padded cell."

"They won't catch him."

Stoner looked down at the floor, and Tommy T knew what was coming next. "You heard from . . ."

"No."

Which meant neither of them had heard anything. When the ol' lady was gone, it was bad luck to keep asking. It was like it scared her away if they got to thinking about her too much. They had to let her surprise them. She always liked that.

Tommy T changed the subject. "You know that foxy blonde, that Gayla? Remember I told you she asked me about you?" Stoner nodded. "I'm gonna be hangin' out right upstairs from her. Just for a while, though. This lady I know, she said I could hang out at her place. I kinda like . . ." He shrugged and glanced away, suddenly feeling too clean, too safe.

"Why was he after you?"

Tommy T shrugged again. "He thought you had me runnin' some kind of delivery."

"Shit." Stoner grabbed him by the shoulder. "You can't be runnin' all over the goddamn city by yourself, Tommy T. You're my *brother*, for crissake."

Stoner was scared. Tommy T could hear it in his voice, and that shook him. His big brother Stoner was scared of that punk Chopper.

"I was thinkin' . . . you know, this lady, Angela, she's really nice. And the place downstairs where Gayla stays, that lady's pretty cool, too. Gayla's ol' lady kicked her out, I guess, so she's hangin' out with this Darlene. Anyway, I was thinkin' maybe if we can't find no place else by the time the weather turns cold . . ."

"I got friends," Stoner said stubbornly. "I got a place where nobody tells me what to do, nobody screws me over the way some of those assholes the ol' lady always had hangin' around used to sometimes. I got my freedom, and I like it just fine."

"Yeah." Another loose basketball hit Tommy T in the thigh.

He caught it, bounced it once, and passed it to the kid who was signaling for it from the top of the key. "I'll probably only hang out at Angela's place for . . . until . . ."

"Maybe I'll come over, just to check up on you." Stoner laid a thumb on his brother's chin and turned his head to the side for a better look at the shiner Tommy T was sporting. "I oughta kill him for this."

"You know where Angela's place is?"

"Damn right," Stoner said. "You think I don't know where my little brother's been hangin' out? Maybe that Gayla might be there when I drop by."

Tommy T grinned. "We could watch TV or something. Angela wouldn't mind."

"Yeah. That might be cool." Stoner offered his brother an empty smile. "You're doin' okay in school and everything?"

"Yeah."

"Yeah. Cool." Stoner suddenly remembered the grocery bag. "Oh. Here. You need some shirts?" He pulled a black T-shirt out of the bag, followed by a bright pink one, shoving them into Tommy T's hands.

Tommy T examined the front of the pink shirt. There was a big sunburst, some women's names, and an advertising slogan. He laughed. "Where'd you get these? Jesus. 'Hot Reads For Cold Nights'?"

"What the hell, they're extra large. You can turn 'em inside out, hey. I copped 'em out of a Dumpster behind a bookstore. Figured you could use some school clothes." He dug into the bag once more. "Found these, too."

"Bit-chiin," Tommy T crooned, his eyes wide for the real prize. Two new comic books. "They threw these out?"

"I think those might have been waitin' on a truck, but nobody's gonna get as much out of them as you. You still drawing?"

"You wanna see?" Tommy T pulled his latest work out of his back pocket. His heart pounded as he watched his brother unfold the papers. Stoner rarely showed any interest in his drawings. But when the second page had Stoner scowling, Tommy T had to crane his neck and check it out.

It was the sketch he'd made for Jesse Brown Wolf. He reached for it. "Not this. This is just some—"

"This is good," Stoner allowed, snatching the drawings out of his reach. He gave him a considering look. "Good enough to recognize one of them, anyway. What's it for?"

"For school," he said too quickly. He shrugged and glanced away. "Just, like, they said to draw somebody, anybody you see. You know, for art class."

"They don't do stuff like this for sixth-grade art. You're the only sixth-grader I know can draw this good." Stoner stared at him, his eyes gone cold. "You turnin' into a narc?"

"No."

"You let us get Chopper. Me and Ajax." This time when Stoner tapped his brother's shoulder with his fist, it was more like old times, when they'd scrapped over some little piece of nothing much. And, of course, Tommy T had always lost out. "You don't narc on nobody. *Nobody.* You got that?"

"Yeah. I got it." Stoner pulled at the neck of his brother's T-shirt and stuffed his drawings down the front, all but one. He kept the sketch of Chopper. "What're you gonna do with that?"

"Burn it." He brandished the paper under his nose. "A thing like this could get you killed, Tommy T. Don't ever—"

"I ain't scared of Chopper. Dark Dog won't let him touch me."

"Dark Dog?" Stoner laughed. He shook his head and all the anger drained away. This was still his irrepressible little brother, Tommy T. "You're reading too damn many comic books, kid. But that's okay. That's what kids are supposed to do. Just don't be narcin' on nobody, and stay off the streets at night."

A utumn had staked full claim over the city. The basement of the Bread of Life Church reminded Angela of her grandmother's cellar. It was cool and damp and smelled of ripe apples. Steam puffed from the lid of the tall urn perched on the kitchen pass-through, but the scent of apples overwhelmed the brewing coffee. The front-row seats she and Darlene had claimed put the kitchen, the stairwell, and center stage right under their noses.

Darlene had not invited Angela to attend the meeting with her. She had simply stopped by to pick her up. "The Block Club meeting starts in twenty minutes, so you're gonna have to shake it, girl." Feeling oddly honored, somehow chosen, Angela had gotten dressed for work, where she was due in a couple of hours, and fallen into step without question.

Even though she'd lived in the neighborhood for nearly half a year, she still felt a little like the parakeet who'd flown through an open window and landed in a maple tree. Sitting in the comfort of Darlene's shadow, she drew herself inward and assumed the attitude of a visitor, an observer making mental notes on a foreign lifestyle as though she might give talks on the ways of city dwellers when she returned to her home. There were more women present than men, she noted, along with a bevy of young children hanging on their mothers' sleeves, and faces from a rainbow of races.

The basement buzzed with chatter until a tall Indian woman with long, gray braids rose from her chair at the front of the room and claimed the floor. "Marie LaRoche," Darlene whispered to Angela. "Block Club leader. I'll introduce you later."

Marie stepped to the side of the long table that served as the dais, leaving an officious-looking man and two equally solemn-faced women sitting at the opposite end. The table was also the repository of the flyers and handouts people had collected before they sat down. Angela glanced at the six-page newsletter, *Voice of the Village*, as Marie launched the meeting by announcing the dates for the annual neighborhood "Come On, Spring!" festival and appointed people to set up committees, for which there was no shortage of volunteers.

Next came a discussion of forming a teen council, with some disagreement over whether "kids nowadays" had any interest in such things. The consensus seemed to be that some kids might, that there was leadership out there, and the community needed to tap into it quickly. If a teen council didn't work, Marie summarized, they would have to try something else. "We have to get them involved in a good way," she said. "There are plenty of people around here ready to get them involved in *their* ways."

The report from the Neighborhood Watch was delivered by a small white woman who started out by fielding jokes about the cast on her forearm.

"Looks like Nadine tried to make another citizen's arrest," somebody said. "Was it a hooker or a meter reader, Nadine?"

"It was those damn in-line skates," Nadine quipped, laughing. "Thought I'd found a whole new way to be hell on wheels. Ten years ago I'da been adding to my speeding tickets." Somebody hooted. "All right, ten *months* ago, but who's counting? Better not be you, Darlene. I heard about you scaring them hookers off the corner."

Heads turned. Darlene raised a victory fist, and Angela joined in the scattered applause.

"It's the pimps we oughta go after," someone said. "Some of these girls, they got a lot of sass, but hell, they're just kids, a lot of 'em, doing what they're told."

"Doing what they're told?" A doubtful guffaw came from a woman sitting behind Angela. "They won't do like their mama says, but they're out there doing like some pimp says. We gotta turn this thing around."

With that particular spigot turned on, the ideas started pouring in.

"We oughta be stringing all pimps up by their tender parts."

"*What* tender parts?"

Nadine brightened. "Hey, let's string 'em up at the festival. A Maypole, kinda like."

"Listen here," the woman behind Angela said, "what we need to do is go after the johns. If the demand dries up—"

"If the demand for sex dries up?" Nadine gestured grandly with her cast. "We're talking about the so-called oldest profession here."

"We're talking about getting it off our streets," Darlene put in. "You can get them to move on one week, but they're back the next. I've been thinking." She leaned forward in her chair, offering the Watch captain a challenge. "Let's take their pictures."

"Who, the johns?"

"Then what?" came the response from a young woman in the back who was breast-feeding a baby. "Put 'em in a scrapbook?"

Darlene turned in her chair and raised her voice in response. "We get their license plate number, we get their smiling face, we send it to Mama for her scrapbook. We let the friends know, the boss. Just shame 'em out every way we can."

"What we need is a video camera," said an elderly black man as he hauled himself out of a front-row chair and headed for the coffee urn. "Who knows? Maybe we'll get a make on somebody famous."

"And sell it to *Hard Copy*," Darlene said.

"*Then* we put on one hell of a spring festival." The old man greeted the laughter with a grin as he pulled a Styrofoam cup from the upended stack.

But Nadine was serious. "Who's got time to be goin' around trying to sneak up on johns with a video camera?"

"Some of us could probably spare a couple of hours from playing bingo on Friday and Saturday night, huh?" Still grinning, the old man filled his cup from the urn. "I know I could. This could be a whole lot more fun."

"Could be a whole lot more dangerous," the young mother said.

"I'm willing to do some research on this," Nadine allowed. "It could fit in with neighborhood patrols, which is what I really wanted to bring up here. We've got our Neighborhood Watch reporting what they see, but maybe we wanna take this one more step. Maybe we wanna get right out there on our streets and let the dealers and junkies and gun-totin' gangbangers know who has the right to do what around here."

A uniformed policeman rose from the seat he'd claimed in a shadowing corner of the expansive basement room. "You ready for me yet?"

"Some of us know Sergeant Mike Richards better than others," Marie said, scanning the small crowd as she waved him over to the long table. If she'd expected a laugh, the community disappointed her. Feet shuffled and chairs creaked as people shifted restlessly, but the room was otherwise silent except for the sound of the policeman's footsteps on the cement floor.

Marie folded her arms and started in again. "The police generally look for cooperation from us on their terms, and a lot of us have learned not to trust those terms. But here we are, worrying about johns and dealers and gang violence, and that's police business. That's what they're here for, and the thing is, we're all after the same thing, basically. We want a safer neighborhood. We don't want our kids gettin' into gangs and drugs. We don't want our kids lyin' dead in the street. But sometimes it feels like the police think we're all in on it. If we live in this neighborhood, we're suspect." She exchanged looks with the cop, who simply stood at the end of the table, like a pilot waiting for clearance. "Okay," Marie said. "They got their ideas; we got some ideas, too. Mike came to listen, but he's also got a few things to say."

Mike Richards wore his neatly pressed blue uniform with pride. He stood tall in front of the group, perfectly at ease admitting that, yes, he did recognize a few faces. He'd delivered their kids into their hands after curfew. He'd investigated their bumps in the night, recovered their stolen bicycles, broken up their fights, and cited them for letting their licenses expire. "But nobody's ever ridden to Detox or anywhere else in the trunk of my squad car," he told them.

Dead silence.

"Cops loaded two Indian men into their trunk a couple years back, drunk, passed out. Took them to the hospital," Darlene whispered. Angela returned a quizzical look. Darlene recounted the explanation with a shrug. "They already had a third guy passed out in the backseat, you know, taking up all the room. Witnesses at both ends of the ride reported it as an outrage, and the city got sued."

"Good," Angela whispered.

"Yeah, like that really settles it."

"But I am a bad man," Richards said, nailing the two whisperers with a schoolmasterish stare. "I got this badge, this gun. Some dudes run and hide when they see me coming."

"Some don't," said a slouching skeptic.

"Some don't," the policeman agreed. He looked down at the table, picked up a newsletter, and ran his fingertips over the masthead as though it were written in Braille. "But I don't want to see civilians taking the law into their own hands. I don't want you confronting these guys, pitting your righteousness against their

three-fifty-seven magnum. I don't want you to risk getting your-
selves killed."

"You mean you don't want us to be walkin' out our front
doors at night?" Nadine said with a wry smile.

"What I'm saying is, you've got some good ideas. This video-
tape thing could work. Neighborhood Watch works. Neighborhood patrols, well, they can work, too, but you want teams, not
individuals. And you don't want the John Wayne type. He'll either get his head blown off or somebody else's."

"What do you mean, *he*?" Laughing, Marie deferred to the
largely female audience with a sweeping gesture. "Look around
you, Mike."

Angela unconsciously took the cue, stepping out of herself for
a moment to take stock of the whole gathering. It was surprising,
a little unsettling, but she actually saw herself as part of it. She
was a woman living in a dangerous world, one of *these* women,
living in *this* neighborhood, worried about her safety on *these*
streets. And tired of hiding. She was getting damn tired of hiding.

Richards was absently rolling the newsletter into a tube. "The
Jane Wayne type, then. What I'm saying—"

"I said look around, Mike. How many 'types' do you see
here?" Marie's gesture demanded that the man look again, and
he did. So did the people around him—the old man with the
coffee, the nursing mother, the small woman with the broken arm,
Angela, Darlene. They looked at one another, acknowledging one
another with a glance, an in-this-together nod.

Angela felt a strange surge of power. *Get to know your neighbors,*
Jesse had said, and here they were, together for a cause. Good
cause. Angela was a good cause, and so was Tommy T, *her*
Tommy T, whom she did not want getting into gangs and drugs.
She touched Darlene's arm and whispered, "Can we stay a few
minutes for coffee after?" Darlene looked at her, smiled, then nodded.

"What we're saying is, we're willing to stand up for ourselves
and our kids," Marie continued. "We need teams? We got teams.

We're not looking to get ourselves killed, Mike. We're looking to get on with living."

"Okay. I've got a few suggestions on how to make it safer for us to do that." He smiled as he slapped the newsletter against his palm. "You know, I live right over there on Lake Street, not that far from here. This is my turf, too."

"How do I get on a team?" Angela asked Darlene as they headed back from the meeting. The autumn sun warmed her back, tempting her to peel off her cardigan. She stretched her stride to match Darlene's. "How do I get on *your* team? Do we choose up sides, or what?"

"If we do, you'll be the last one picked." The hurt look in Angela's eyes made Darlene laugh. "No offense, girl, but you ain't no kinda scrapper."

"We're not going to be scrapping. We're going to be patrolling." On a power roll from the meeting, Angela refused to let herself feel wounded. "My eyes and ears are just as good as yours."

"We'll put you on the Watch. You've got a second-story window that looks right out onto the street."

"If we get those pagers like Mike suggested, all we have to do is call for backup."

"*Call for backup.* She's all ready for *NYPD Blue*, this one." Darlene looked at her sideways as they turned a corner near the Plexiglas enclosure of a metro bus stop, which at the moment housed two young girls who were sneaking a smoke. "You know what? You'd be great working with that teen council."

"You think I'm chickenshit, don't you?" Angela demanded. Darlene did a double take, laughter bubbling from her throat, and Angela scowled. "What?"

"Cuss much?" Darlene gave her a playful shoulder-to-shoulder bump. "Girlfriend, you say that like you've got a bunch of it in your mouth. But I don't care how much trash you learn to talk, I *still* ain't puttin' you on my team."

"I'm not the right *type*?" Angela returned the shoulder bump, skipped a step to catch up, then fell back into a matching gait. A few blocks down the street they would part company at the door of the Hard Luck Café. "I admit I lived a pretty sheltered life once upon a time, but that time is long past."

"Do you want your picture in the newspaper or flashed on the six o'clock news? They just might decide we're some kind of a media event." Angela's quick glance affirmed the fear she'd never had to explain to Darlene. "I didn't think so. Everybody's got something dogging them. Something they're trying to outrun."

"I've reached the end of the line with my running." Angela smacked her fist into her palm. "This is it. This is where I make my stand."

"Girl, you picked some pretty poor ground for it."

"It's as good as any." Better, she thought. She had friends here. She was getting to know her neighbors, like those she'd met today—the editor of the neighborhood newsletter, the coach of a women's volleyball team who'd asked if she played, and the old man who had just come back from visiting his grandchildren in Oregon. "I wonder . . . I haven't seen Jesse Brown Wolf much lately. Is he still . . ."

"He's around." They stopped at a crosswalk. Darlene stared hard at the red light, as though willing a change. "Days go by, sometimes a week or more, nobody sees him. It's like he just goes underground. I figure maybe he goes back to the rez or something." She turned to Angela as a Metro bus roared past. "Some things you just don't ask him about, you know? It's like a wall goes up. I think he's got some demon after him, too, but I got no clue what it might be." She shrugged, her eyes now fixed on the curb. "Depression, maybe. He gets the blues real bad sometimes."

"He says he . . . parks some of his stuff in your closet."

"He does. Tools mostly, if he's working in the neighborhood." The light had changed. The traffic was on hold, the crosswalk clear. Darlene nailed Angela to the curb with a look. "But he don't park his boots under my bed, if that's what you're asking."

"I'm not." Angela's face burned. Her voice rose an octave. "I wouldn't."

"Why not?" Darlene smiled and gave her head a quick, sassy toss as she stepped off the curb. "You ought to if you're finding yourself wondering where he's been keeping himself lately."

"I'm not looking for . . ." Angela hurried to catch up. "It's the last thing I'm looking for, really. But he's been very nice. Helpful. I really like him. I invited him over for supper, and he acted like . . ." She grabbed her friend's arm as they stepped up to the sidewalk. "I just wondered if I'd scared him off."

"Scared off the last thing you're looking for?" Darlene tipped her head back, as was her habit when she laughed. "Lord-a-mercy. You see why I don't want you on my team? If you don't know your own mind any better than that, girl, you are dangerous."

"I do know my own mind. I asked the man to come over for supper. I wanted to have supper with him. Big deal." Angela was marching now, seriously covering ground. "Is my shower still leaking into your apartment?"

"Only when you run the water for more than half an hour. What do you do in there, anyway?"

"Meditate. If you see Jesse before I do, you might mention it to him."

"I might." With a hand on her arm, Darlene slowed Angela's pace. "Have I told you how I met Jesse?" Angela looked up, shook her head. "I was getting evicted. I had five kids with me then, no place to go, no money. Jesse was doing some work for Don Morrison, saw what was going on, and told Morrison to put his next paycheck toward my rent. Can you believe that? He didn't know me from Whitney."

Angela questioned the reference with a quizzical look.

"Whitney Houston. I'm often mistaken for her."

"Oh."

The ingenuous expression on Angela's face made Darlene

laugh. "You are a piece of work, girl. Anyway, my boy Billy had given Jesse an apple when he was taking a break for lunch. That's it. That's all the man had from us." She gestured, illustrating with an open hand. "I try to pay him back, he tells me to buy whatever the kids need. So what's a little closet space?"

A shared closet was a connection, Angela thought, and she was hungry for connections. "How many of the kids are actually your own?"

"Three. I got one grown. She's in training to be an X-ray technician over at St. Catherine's."

"That's wonderful."

"It is. She's doin' real good, too." Darlene turned with a mock-haughty smile. "As good as any kid of *yours* could do."

"I don't have a kid," Angela said as she dodged an oncoming pedestrian threading his way between them. "I wish I did."

"Honey, we've all got kids. All of us. You've got one staying up there with you right now."

"Yes, but for how long?"

"As long as the good Lord sees fit. That's how long mine stay with me. My oldest, she left home, she came back, now she's doin' what she's doin', and it's workin' out." They'd slowed their pace as they neared the restaurant. Darlene turned, squinting into the afternoon sun. "Does the boy talk about his mama?"

"Not much." Angela paused, entertaining a thought that nagged her more all the time. "I should report her to somebody, shouldn't I? But if I did, it would just be a lot of legal red tape." She shrugged. "And he'd hate me for it anyway."

"He loves you now." Darlene smiled, her dusky face gleaming, sun-kissed and sagacious. "It's pretty hard to turn them away sometimes, isn't it?"

"It's going to be hard to see him go."

"It always is, when the time comes. Which it always does."

Tommy T wasn't narcing. He didn't care what Stoner said. He was making a drawing that somebody was willing to pay him for.

In fact, he'd had another look at the guy in the red-and-green cap, and he thought he'd done an even better job on him in the second sketch. He didn't know why Jesse Brown Wolf would be interested. Probably just wanted to get Tommy T off his back about working for him. But Jesse's purpose didn't much matter. What mattered was the five bucks. He'd draw cars, cats, or naked women for the repairman for five bucks a shot. When Angela told him Jesse was coming over to work on the shower, Tommy T got busy with his new pencils.

And when Jesse came to the door, he was greeted with, "Got any cash on ya?"

That quick, he had the man digging into his pocket. Must have been some picture, because Jesse didn't want change from the ten he handed over.

"You sure, man?" Tommy T said, barely controlling the childish yelp that was making his chest swell up. Yipping at his heels, Stevie seemed just as excited.

Jesse had to laugh as he leaned down to pat the dog. The kid was a hustler. "Darlene says you guys are still running your shower into her bathroom. Is that true?"

"Must be, if Darlene says." In one fluid motion the boy swept the tail-wagging terrier into his skinny arms and stepped back, grinning playfully. "What are you gonna do about it?"

"Fix the damn thing, what else?" He lifted his toolbox, flaunting it as proof of his good intentions. Then he considered the drawing again. "You got something I can put this in? I hate to crease it."

The boy's dark eyes glowed big and bright with innocent gratification. "We save big envelopes that advertising stuff comes in sometimes. I'll get you one."

We. He'd said it easily, naturally, as though his life had always been entwined with the woman who lived there. Jesse smiled as he watched the boy slide on stockinged feet over the waxed wood of the short hallway, then disappear. He drew a deep breath, savoring the aroma of a home-cooked meal, the robust smell of beef and potatoes, the sweetness of apples and pastry crust all mingling in his nose and making his mouth water. He could hear Tommy T rummaging in a drawer in the back room, Angela's room. The boy was home. This arrangement was working out just fine.

Angela came upstairs from Darlene's apartment moments later to welcome him with the news that Tommy T was staying with her, at least for the time being, and that she had been appointed "captain of the safety patrol." Her excitement was as infectious as the boy's, her smile equally contagious. Jesse caught himself wearing one of his own when he headed into the bathroom.

As he went about his work he realized that the water problem wasn't all that connected Angela's bathroom with the one below it. The two apartments were becoming one household. The stairs were like locks on a river, with kids flowing up and down as freely as the water in the system he was working on. When he turned to step out of Angela's tub, he was greeted by two big pairs of chocolaty eyes glistening in two young faces. The older one ventured the small-boy question "Whatcha doin' in Angela's bathroom?"

"Fixin' on it, Billy. Wanna see?"

The two heads nodded. No choice; Jesse had to lift the little one in his arms. There was no other way he could see the new tiles as Jesse explained how he'd just put them in, no other way the baby could mess in the grout with his stubby fingers. Seven-year-old Billy had to climb into the tub beside him and get his fingers into the gooey stuff, too.

It had been so long. He'd been so cautious, letting himself do little things to help out without getting too close.

Careful, son. Don't get too close. It could hurt you.

Some guys kept their distance from small children because they had little experience with them, but not Jesse. He missed his own, missed them so bad sometimes, he could just be watching a group of kids shooting hoops, and he'd think where he'd be if things had been different, and his eyes would burn.

But it had been a long time, maybe long enough. It almost felt good to hold the toddler in his arms. His chest ached where the warm bundle of squirming life rested against it, but it was almost a pleasant ache. The slight weight of a little one roused those damned custodial instincts in a man, made him feel like putting on some kind of armor and standing guard at the door. Or maybe a blue uniform. The thought made Jesse groan inwardly. In his head a big red *S* and a cape were added to the uniform. Then a badge. He chuckled as his cheek got smeared with grout.

Then he imagined the cape turning into a wolf pelt, and he groaned aloud this time. Coyote was no Superman, as any kid could surely tell him. And would, if he asked.

"What's the matter?" Billy peered up at him, then giggled. "Careful, Marco. You're really gettin' him messed up."

"It's okay," Jesse said. "I was plenty messed up already." He patted the little bottom that rested on his forearm. "Is it just me, or do you guys notice how this place is turning into a jungle?"

"Those are African violets," Billy said, pointing to the pots on the shelves above the toilet. He indicated the basket dripping with variegated purple-and-green vines next to the window. "That's wandering Jew. We got some of that, too. We killed the first one, but Angela gave us some more and said not to water so much. And see that?" He pointed to a pot above the sink. "That's pig- gyback plant. See how they make babies? We got one of those in our bathroom, too, and it's making babies now."

"It is, huh?" Jesse leaned over to set Marco down outside the tub. "You wanna show me? We'd better put a stop to some of this baby-makin' or you guys are gonna have to be hacking a path to the john every time you have to pee."

The boys both giggled over that prospect.

Jesse was downstairs working on Darlene's bathroom when Gayla appeared at the door. The wispy, pallid blonde was fairly new to Darlene's clan, and Jesse hadn't seen much of her. She was shy, probably a little embarrassed about being pregnant, young as she was. She reminded him of a faded little madonna statue he'd seen in a niche outside a church where he'd been hired to put up a chain-link fence. All the other niches in the wall were empty, all the statues stolen but that lonely little madonna, draped in a gown that looked as shopworn as Gayla's blue smock.

Jesse's smile came surprisingly easily. But then, it had been of late.

"Darlene wants to know if you have any little tiny nails," Gayla reported. "She wants to put the kids' school pictures up."

"On the wall?"

She measured a space between her slight forefinger and thumb. "Just little tiny nails."

"Look in the top of the toolbox." He nodded toward the red box, which stood open on the closed lid of the toilet. "Gayla, right?" The girl made a sound of assent as she availed herself of the box. "Who was that guy who was looking for you that night Darlene called the police? The one who tried to get into Angela's upstairs."

She glanced up, her pale blue eyes wide with fear, or the memory of it. "Looking for me?"

"Yeah." He glanced down at his hands, pumped the handle on the caulking gun he'd been preparing to use. He hadn't been prepared to ask questions. Suddenly they just started rolling, like an old habit kicking in. "Skinny guy. Light brown hair, probably about twenty." He glanced up at her and saw the fear growing. "He seemed a little too old for you."

The light in her eyes dimmed. She slammed the defensive shutters on her fear. "You don't know how old I am."

"I know you oughta be in school, going to ball games and dances." He wiped caulking compound off the tip of the gun with a stained rag. "I know this guy ought to be strung up."

She snorted derisively as she poked around in a compartment filled with small nails. "He's usually strung *out*."

"Has he been back since that night?"

"I don't think so. I haven't seen him." She hung her head, speaking softly into the toolbox tray. "I hardly ever go anywhere.

Don't want anyone to see me, so I just stay here and get fatter."

"You tell me his name, I'll make sure he doesn't come around anymore." She looked up at him, and he wasn't sure what to make of the surprise in her eyes. "If that's what you want."

"I don't want to see him. I don't want him bothering me."

"But you won't give up his name," he surmised. "Hey, I'm not a cop. I'm just the repairman."

"So why are you asking?"

"Right. It's none of my business." With a quick chin jerk he indicated the toolbox. "Find what you need?"

She showed him a three-quarter-inch nail. "Five of these?"

"Take whatever you can use," he said.

After he finished his chores, he stowed his toolbox in the closet and headed back upstairs. "You're staying for supper," Angela announced from the landing. "It's already decided. We've already cooked, and we've fed the kids. Right, Darlene?"

"Right," Darlene called out. She awaited them in the kitchen, ladle in one hand, blue roaster lid in the other. "I got myself a raise at the store this week. Twenty cents an hour. We're celebrating, and you're stayin', Wolf. Go wash your paws."

He wasn't about to argue, not with the meaty aroma in that kitchen and the way the ravenous creature he carried in his stomach was growling. He sat down at the tiny kitchen table and permitted himself to enjoy having the women serve him generous helpings of pot roast and potatoes, crusty bread, and some cooked green stuff that looked suspiciously leafy, but he peppered it up and ate it anyway. He watched the kids come and go, arguing over who was going to watch what on which TV. Angela settled it like a seasoned playground supervisor, sending the bigger boys downstairs.

When one woman was sitting, the other one was up. He smiled to himself, thinking this was always the way of it, at least in the world he used to know. As instructed, he went ahead and ate, but he took his time, remembering that around women, you had to take it slowly or you never got to share any part of it with them. If he remembered correctly, that was true of a lot of pleasures. He was half finished with his meal by the time they were both settled on either side of him. Darlene joked about her big raise, wondering whether she'd soon be pricing herself out of the market. She needed a bigger apartment, she said, but she knew she'd probably just fill it up with kids.

"You ought to run a group home or a safe house," Angela said, and Darlene laughed. "Not that yours isn't safe. What I mean is, somebody ought to pay you for it."

"They got plenty of group homes around," Darlene said, but she eyed Angela over the rim of her mug as she sipped her coffee, obviously willing to be persuaded.

"Not like yours. These kids come to you because—"

"They didn't have much choice," Darlene pointed out. "This world is hard on kids."

"What do you think, Jesse?" Angela asked, pulling his focus away from his fork. "We should just throw our doors open and call it Darlene's Place."

He could see the sign, the open door, the kids coming in out of the cold. The image made him smile. "I wouldn't advertise." He leaned back in his chair and watched the boys file back through the front door, Tommy T in the lead. "Not that you'd have to."

"The other tenants would run us out on a rail," Darlene said.

"We hardly ever see the Dexters," Angela said of the older couple who lived down the hall from her. "I don't know about those new people who just moved in downstairs. Do they like kids?"

"Haven't had any complaints yet," Darlene replied absently as she regarded the proceedings in the living room. After a few words with the boys, the girls were getting ready to vacate. But the boys were on their tail. "What's up, you guys?"

There was a group about-face. "We're just going out in the yard," Poppy reported to her mother.

"Yeah, we'll be right out in the yard," Tommy T said. "We're taking Stevie out, too."

"It's getting late." Darlene signaled Gayla to leave the baby with her. "Don't anybody set foot outside the yard."

"We won't, Mama."

"We won't, Mama."

Giggles tumbled after the rush of footsteps on the stairs. Angela looked at Darlene. "Gentlemen callers, perhaps?"

"That ain't exactly what we call them in this neighborhood."

"Give them a few minutes. Then I'll take out the garbage." Jesse tipped his chair back and glanced over his shoulder toward the stove. "In return for whatever that is that smells like apple pie."

Tommy T led the way out the back door with Tony close on his heels. Tony was okay, but Tommy T was glad Poppy and Gayla had managed to persuade the younger kids to watch TV downstairs. If the whole crew went piling outside, his brother would likely take off. He was surprised he'd lured Stoner this close the way he'd been acting lately, like some hermit crab, always pulling back into his shell. He'd been steering clear of people too long, all but his homeboys, his close buddies. The only thing Tommy T could think of to help pull him away, even for a few minutes, was a girl.

He shushed Stevie as he skipped down the back steps, feeling as lighthearted as a matchmaking cherub. He'd been trying to pull this off for days, and now it was happening. Gayla was coming out the door, too, right behind Tony. Poor Gayla. Another hermit crab, except she carried her shell out in front of her instead of on her back. This city was not the best environment for hermit crabs. It was up to him, Tom Terrific, to take these two for a walk on the beach. All he had to do was to get the two tender shells within reach of each other, then step back. He was pretty sure they'd at least touch pincers.

Stoner was still waiting in the alley, a tall shadow amid shadows, reluctant to venture inside the fence when Tommy T opened the gate. Stevie barked furiously, sniffed out the visitor, then concurred with Tommy T's acceptance.

"You guys, this is my brother," he announced as his new family drifted closer. He felt a strange urge to put his arms around Stoner—something neither of them had done since he couldn't remember when—and pull him into his safe zone, his own new turf. But he made do with just slapping a hand on his back. Stoner was wearing a hooded zip-front sweatshirt that smelled pretty clean and a dark baseball cap Tommy T didn't think he'd seen before. "Hey, what's up, my best and only bro?"

"Just checkin' up on you." Forgetting the onlookers, the girl he'd been asking about, forgetting even himself, Stoner took Tommy T by the shoulders and moved him closer to the house, where the light from the windows permitted him a look at his brother's face. Traces of the damage Chopper and Shank had done were almost gone. "Are you healin' up okay?"

"Doin' good," Tommy T assured him. "Stepping outside here, you know, just hangin' out in the backyard." He tried to maintain an air of unaffected cool, but he really had to smile a little for the joy of having his brother stop over to hang out a while, having a backyard to hang out in. Damn, he felt good. "We thought we'd come out and take a look at the stars."

Poppy plunked herself down on the back step.

Gayla shoved her hands in her jacket pockets and edged closer to the boys. "What do you know about stars, Tommy T's brother?"

"Stoner," Tommy T volunteered. "That's what his friends call him. And he knows plenty."

"We used to live out in the country when this guy was a baby. That's where you go if you wanna see stars." Stoner stuck out his thumb, as though he were hitching a ride. "About two, three hundred miles west of this place."

In the absence of small talk, they all dropped their heads back and searched the sky. "Hard to find the North Star here," Tommy

T said, desperate to keep everyone entertained. "That's where we'd always start, but you gotta find the Little Dipper."

"Too much city lights," Tony said.

"Yeah, too much light."

"But you can see a few."

"A few, yeah."

The hermit crabs weren't looking up. Within night's safe harbor, they'd edged a few steps away from the rest and stuck their noses out, sniffing a little, defying the darkness, each searching for something in the other's face.

"Gayla, right?"

She nodded.

He nodded and glanced away. "I saw you down at the Mall of America that time, with, uh . . ."

"Yeah, with, uh . . ." She, too, glanced away. "That was before."

"You go to school?"

"No." She risked another quick peek into his eyes. "You?"

"Nah. I quit."

"That's what I was gonna do." She looked down again, cleared her throat, and drew an arc in the grass with the toe of her tennis shoe. "I think I might go back. Darlene says I can still sign up. For a special program, you know."

He nodded. "That might be okay. It's hard to keep goin' every day when you've got—" He shoved his hands into the sagging patch pockets of his sweatshirt and shrugged. "Well, other stuff goin' on."

She nodded. "I miss it sometimes, though. It seems like, I don't know, every day gets to be the same."

"You little guys stay in school," Stoner said, smiling now, the man of experience.

"And do your homework," Gayla supplied, mirroring his smile.

"Yeah, listen to the old folks." Poppy lit a cigarette, took a drag, then started to offer it to Gayla.

Kathleen Eagle

"Hey." Stoner shot out an intervening hand, caught himself, and stepped back, frantically searching for something to look at besides Gayla's middle. "You shouldn't be smoking, should you? I mean . . ." He shoved his bold right hand back into his pocket and shrugged. "I don't think you oughta be smoking, is all."

"Stay in school and don't smoke," Poppy recited sarcastically. She glared at Stoner as she puffed on the cigarette, just to show him. He turned his face from the smoke she spat at him. "Real bitchin' advice from somebody who maybe oughta think about takin' a bath."

But Gayla was laughing, really laughing, for the first time in weeks. She gave Poppy a playful shoulder thump. "Shut up, girl."

"You shut up, girl."

"Hey, look!" Tony thrust a finger overhead. "I think that's the Little Dipper. Ain't that the North Star?"

"That's a plane." Tommy T laughed. "One good thing about having your head in the clouds. A guy learns to recognize a plane when he sees one."

When Jesse took the garbage out as promised, he saw nothing amiss. Before he stepped outside, he stood for a moment and listened for tip-offs to trouble. A word, a sound, or just loaded silence. He knew what to listen for, had the knack, and once upon a time he'd had good use for it. When he was satisfied that the backyard scene was exactly what it seemed to be—kids stargazing—he did his little chore, wordlessly reminding everybody that there were adults around. Not in their faces, but close by. He was surprised when they stopped him and asked for a piece of his stellar knowledge. All he could remember were a couple of Lakota legends, which he shared briefly, sizing up the visitor all the while. He knew who Stoner was, inside and out. Tough, calloused exterior. An outsider who carried everything he feared most around inside him. He was a risk to the kids.

But Tommy T was a caretaker, and right now there was no keeping him away from his brother.

192

Jesse understood the older boy completely. He used the darkness as a cloak to cover the raw need that brought him here, to the perimeter of safety, the periphery of warmth, within reach of a caring connection. It wasn't easy to come this close, but he couldn't help himself. The need was so strong that a guy had to give in and open himself up once in a while. Sometimes he had to tolerate the pain in return for a moment, a word, the touch of a warm hand, just to feel at least some part human.

Jesse understood all that. He also knew that Angela and Darlene had rounded up a clutch of precious sheep, and here they were in the backyard pen, safe for the moment, but always vulnerable. Save what you've got, he thought. Forget about the stray. But he couldn't quite bring himself to chase the kid away.

After all, who was the real wolf here?

Later, after the children had come inside and Darlene had taken them all downstairs, exiting with a twinkle in her eye, Jesse and Angela shared the last of the coffee and a few moments alone. He kept thinking it was time for him to go, too, but he was feeling surprisingly good, remarkably free of pain.

"Tommy T must've gotten into a pretty bad scrape," he said absently as he rinsed out his coffee mug.

"The same kids that attacked me. I . . . I guess." Angela folded her arms and leaned back against the refrigerator. "I'm thinking of getting a gun."

The statement chilled him. He upended the mug and set it in the wire dish rack with exaggerated care. "Have you ever fired a gun?"

"No, but how hard can it be?"

"It's easy. Any kid can shoot a gun." He looked up at her, smiled a little, or tried to, even though her suggestion made him feel sick inside. "They do it all the time."

"I want to be able to protect myself. Protect *us*. Now that Tommy T's staying with me, and since . . . well, since the night he got hurt, I've really been . . ." She closed her eyes and blew a long, deep sigh. "Even before that. Even before I came here. It's like

Darlene says, I'm 'no kinda scrapper.' So what do you do? You run, you hide, but you still don't feel safe." She looked at him plaintively, gesturing with an open hand, perhaps seeking his blessing. "So I was thinking, maybe I should take some kind of a class and buy a gun, just for protection."

He stared at the small hand with the pale, smooth palm. It was a hand that nurtured houseplants and helped kids with their math. He tried to imagine it wrapped around the grip of a semi-automatic pistol. "You plan on buyin' it legally, you'll have to get a license."

"That's right." She closed her hand. "Complications, huh?"

"Yeah. All kinds of complications." His eyes sought hers, candidly entreating. "You wanna protect Tommy T? Keep him away from guns."

"He ain't my kid," she recited, then softened her tone. "I think those were your words."

"Probably. Sounds familiar." He pushed away from the sink. "I gotta be goin'."

"I could make some more coffee. Stronger, if you—" She stepped in front of him, blocking his way with her body.

Sweet little body. She had half his size, twice his courage, and he desperately wanted a piece of it. Just to be able to rub his size up against that body, maybe some of her strength would rub off on him. The offer was in her eyes. Didn't she know she had the wrong man? The wrong *piece* of the man. Dark Dog would accept gallantly, respond attentively and in full measure.

He closed his eyes.

She touched his face. "Jesse . . ."

He drew back from her, his eyes aching from the sight of her. "If I don't leave now, I'll make a damn fool of myself."

"That's okay," she whispered. "God knows I already have."

"You're a kind woman, trying to do a little charity work." He shook his head, closing his hand over hers. "I'm an old dog with only one decent trick left in him."

It was that shred of decency, he told himself, that drove him to the door. Decency or cowardice. He couldn't blame it on pain this time. Where was that goddamned headache when he needed it? He saved his plaintive, self-effacing, howling dog laugh until he was safely outside.

I t was an impulsive move when Jesse walked into City Hall, home of the Minneapolis Police Department. He'd been carrying Tommy T's exceptional sketch around with him, but he hadn't seen Richards around lately. He'd circled the station from blocks away, approaching it like a predator, assessing the risks. There were many, and they were great, but he needed an ally, and he was about to settle on Sergeant Mike Richards, who was as good a bet as any. After all, Richards had picked him first. He had the instinct, the cop's nose. And Jesse had it, too, even though he knew damn well this whole thing was a harebrained idea. It might be a step toward taking two scumbags out of commission, but they'd be replaced. The best he could hope for was that the replacements wouldn't be connected to his kids.

His kids? Back off, Jesse told himself as he shoved past a pair of glass doors. He was an old dog, as he'd told Angela, with no illusions. *De*lusions, maybe, but those were grist for some other department's mill. He'd be sure and will his brain for psychiatric research.

A detective directed him down a flight of stairs, and he hit them hard, willing the momentum to carry him through this fool's errand. The rock-ribbed building was dark and dank, smelled of pine cleaner and floor wax, and made him feel queasy. He'd take earth walls over these any day. Jeans over pressed blues. There was a time when he had truly believed in law and order. He had worked for the Department of Law and Order, Bureau of Indian Affairs, but that had been another life, another Jesse Brown Wolf. The one who'd believed all his own bullshit.

"I didn't think I'd find you here," Jesse admitted when he walked into Richards's cubicle. A desk, a phone, a tackboard, a swimsuit calendar with female models—all the amenities. Jesse was impressed. He'd never had his own cubicle.

"But you came looking anyway?" Richards offered a loose-grip handshake, which showed that Jesse wasn't the first Indian he'd ever shaken hands with. He had to give the man another point. "I'm backed up on paperwork. You know how it is."

"I don't do paperwork." The cubicle was littered with it. Jesse took a quick survey, letting his contempt for this particular part of the job show as his attention finally drifted to the man behind the desk. "I don't know what you think you know about me, Richards, but I'd appreciate it if you'd let it go. Nobody's looking for me. I got nobody depending on me for anything."

The black man met the challenge in Jesse's eyes with his own personal version of it. "That's what you came here to tell me?"

"I came to give you this." He laid Tommy T's drawing ceremoniously in the middle of Richards's work space, then planted an index finger above the heads. "These two need to be stopped. That kid—they call him Chopper—he's got his little gang terrorizing the neighborhood. They play with guns. They beat on women and kids. They're fronting for this guy." He searched the policeman's face as he withdrew his finger from the paper. "I'm not telling you anything new, right?"

"Have a seat." Richards took the drawing in hand, studied it for a moment, then pushed an appreciative whistle between his teeth. "This is good. Who did it?" He looked up, eyes smiling. "Is he looking for a job? We've got a sketch artist now who can't do peanuts."

"Peanuts?" Jesse chuckled as he dragged up a chair and sat down. "This kid could draw some pretty fancy circles around Peanuts. He doesn't know why I asked for this. This is just between you and me. Are we clear on that?" Richards flipped him a thumb and went on studying the drawing. "We watched these two conduct a business meeting in the park, just like the kid had picked him up a candy bar and brought back the change."

"I know Chopper. Damn, this is good." He brandished the paper in Jesse's direction. "The other dude must be new to the neighborhood, but we shouldn't have any trouble getting a make on him. They move these guys around, thinking it keeps us guessing, but we can backtrack pretty good."

"Which should put you a step closer to the one you *really* want."

"It should, shouldn't it? Coffee?" Jesse declined with a polite gesture. "These slime bags shield themselves with kids. Not that Chopper's any choirboy, but he's still a kid. Can't do much to him until he gets this guy's job a couple years down the road. But they're both expendable. We take them in, their boss can find ten more of them before the day's over."

Jesse pointed with his lips. "Right now I wanna see those two stopped."

"You work for Don Morrison sometimes, don't you?" Jesse nodded. "What do you know about Morrison?"

"He's basically just a property manager. I think he owns a little property, but Ed Hickey's the—"

"Hickey's a damn slum lord. His crimes are something else. We're interested in Morrison."

Jesse shrugged. "All I see is what Morrison shows me. Busted windows and rotted floorboards. And all I do is fix them."

"You could be fixing more than busted windows." Richards eyed him across the desk. He had the look of a guidance counselor

Jesse remembered from his school days. Younger, slimmer, different color skin, but he had that same omnipotent look in his eyes, same kind of crap on the tip of his tongue. "You were on your way to the FBI training academy. You were—"

"That was all just talk. Somebody thought it would look good to get an Indian cop into the FBI program." Jesse glared at the man. "What's your interest in what I did or what I could be doing?"

"I like to know who my neighbors are. I live over on Lake Street, not too far from my usual beat." Richards leaned forward, hunched over his desk, making a pretense of looking Tommy T's drawing over again as he spoke. "That south-side neighborhood has major blood vessels directly connected to reservations up north, out west. I know people. I talk to people. That's how I do my job." He nailed Jesse with that almighty look again. "That's how you used to do yours."

"I got a different job now. One that lets me keep to myself."

"Something I want to show you." Richards shoved his chair back and waggled a finger under Jesse's nose. "Don't go away. I'll be right back."

Left alone, Jesse read the walls—or the partitions that served as walls. Plenty of crooks for Richards to catch. He thumbed through a stack of bulletins on the top of the file cabinet. Plenty of mysteries to solve. One has-been Indian cop shouldn't even draw a second look.

Which was exactly what the photocopy of a familiar face did to Jesse. One missing person in a four-inch stack stopped him cold. Her hair was different, shorter now. He couldn't be sure about the color from a black-and-white picture, but it looked as though her brown hair might have been lighter at one time. She couldn't change the shape of her eyes, the softness of her lips, the angle of her chin. He slipped the paper from the stack, folded it, and put it in his back pocket just as Richards rounded the corner, folded newspaper in hand.

"You know this guy?"

Jesse glanced at the picture of a cop in uniform. "Tom Hawk. I went to school with him." He gave Richards a dubious look. "Friend of yours?"

"Hell, the dude just became a U.S. marshal." Richards slapped the paper with the back of his hand. "That's a first for an Indian cop, according to this."

"Is this some kind of a pep talk? *This could be you*?" Jesse laughed. "Small potatoes. I'm holding out for first Indian astronaut."

"Fly much?"

Jesse chuckled. "I stay grounded."

"I've met Tom," Richards said, giving the newspaper the kind of appreciative once-over he might have afforded Miss September. "Pretty cool dude."

"He was always one for shootin' the shit with other cops." He'd obviously dumped a load of rez gossip on this one. Jesse pointed at the sketch Richards had left on the desk. "See what you can do about those two. They like to hurt people."

"I'm always hauling in the small fry. Like to catch me a big fish sometime." The cop sighed as he tossed the newspaper aside; then he paused, finger to lip, Lieutenant Columbo-style. "Which reminds me, those same small fry have been filling my ears with some wild stories lately. Real whoppers."

Jesse shrugged. "Take a few days off and head for one of the lakes up north, Sergeant."

"You a fisherman?"

Jesse snorted impatiently.

"Hunter? You like dogs?"

Jesse's lips tightened. He glanced away.

"I been hearing these wild stories about some phantom who walks the streets at night taking guns off kids, breaking up fights. They say he has a way with dogs." Richards returned to his chair, reaching for Tommy T's sketch as he spoke. "Just kids talkin'. Making stuff up."

"They'll do that," Jesse said quietly, backing away.

"Lookin' for heroes, I guess. Somebody besides these two."

"Get those two off the streets, you'll be the hero."

Richards nodded, dismissing Jesse with a funny little salute. "Thanks for the help."

Two days later, Jesse was back working at the school. When he'd stopped in to pick up a paycheck at the district offices, he'd been offered more work, which pleased him. From his perch on top of a ladder in the boys' bathroom he could hear kids' voices, teachers' voices, announcements coming over the intercom along with music. Powwow music on the intercom. He thought that was pretty cool. The flutes and dance bells, the steady drumbeat, and the chanting of an old honor song took him back to summer nights long past. With his head poking up through an opening in the ceiling tile and his hands busy replacing the sprinkler some kid had managed to screw up, he didn't realize he was singing softly into the ceiling joists.

"I know a drum group that's looking for another man."

Startled, Jesse smacked his head on a water pipe.

"Sorry," Arthur Bird said, wincing sympathetically. "You'd better go down there and get yourself some of that fry bread they made for lunch."

Jesse scowled, rubbing the back of his head as he stepped down a wrung. "Is it any good?"

"Not as good as my wife's, but it'll do. Especially if you haven't had any in a while." The old man folded his arms and stepped back as he watched Jesse make his descent. "The headaches letting up any?"

"They come and go. Nothing I can't live with if I don't go crashing into too many pipes."

Bird nodded. "You got a good voice, Wolf. That drum group sure could use you."

Jesse shook his head, but he did it with a smile. Arthur Bird had known his father, his uncles. He was an elder. He had the right to offer unsolicited advice, a right to the role he'd assumed in Jesse's life. There had never been any discussion of it.

The story was that Arthur had actually courted Jesse's mother at one time, but she'd chosen Vince Brown Wolf, and Arthur had married his Sarah, maker of melt-in-your-mouth fry bread and healing teas and poultices. The immediate truth—the *rest* of the story—was that the old man had dragged Jesse out of an alley one night not long after he'd wandered out to Minneapolis some years ago, patched him up from a beating he'd taken, and helped him find work. Jesse never forgot a favor, although he had long since stopped keeping track of the years. The warm green seasons of dreams, the cold black ebb and flow of nightmares. He'd hung the years up to dry inside his head, like ugly black bats in a battered belfry. And he remembered.

The old man knew how it was with Jesse. He didn't ask for more information than a guy was willing to give, which was why Jesse was able to say what was on his mind. "I'm better off if I keep to myself. You get around people, they talk. They want you to talk. Pretty soon you're mixed up in their business, they're mixed up in yours." He squatted next to his toolbox, all set to trade a wrench for a Phillips screwdriver. But his purpose drifted with his thoughts, and he smiled wistfully. "Almost forgot how easy it is to get sucked in."

"Into something you don't want to be part of," Arthur reflected.

"I don't wanna be playin' cop." Jesse braced his hands on his knees and stared into the toolbox. "Guy comes along, thinks he knows something about me, wants to recruit me for the cause."

"The cause," the old man echoed softly.

"The cause of bringing law and order to the streets of our fair city. Helluva good cause." Jesse sighed, tipped his head back, and peered up at the hole on high. "Guy needs a snitch. Thinks a lobo lurking in the shadows would fit the bill just fine."

"And that's you?" A long silence passed. The old man's knees cracked as he leaned down close behind Jesse's right ear. "The lone wolf is all mysticism and romance. A vanishing breed. Is that you, Jesse?"

"Sure." Jesse stared straight ahead, fixing an empty smile on a urinal. "Wolf, coyote. Some kind of dog who sleeps during the day and goes around scarin' up trouble at night."

"It's high noon, and you're awake."

"The man's awake. The dog's asleep."

"Ah. Shape-shifter," the old man concluded. Jesse felt a heavy hand on his shoulder, heavy words in his ear. "The two parts of you must make peace with each other, my young friend."

"They don't even wanna know each other. One feels damn stupid about the other." He sighed and hung his head as low as it would go, as low as he felt. Here he was, down on his knees in the can, getting advice from an elder. Hardly the way Tommy T would have depicted it on paper. "What is it that rules me? Coyote's a pure fool, but then there's that damned Iktomi."

There, he'd gone and said it, and the sound of it, reverberating in the bathroom, made him shiver. Iktomi, the evil trickster. The name his grandmother had taught her young grandsons to fear. He couldn't believe he was discussing all this here and now, serious as hell, listening to the echoes of ancient words he would have thought too brittle and dusty to bounce off tiled walls. Mythology in a can. He couldn't believe he was asking, "Where does Iktomi fit in? What's he done to me?"

The heavy hand tightened on Jesse's shoulder. "Iktomi has legs like a spider but they say he has the hands and feet of a man. His hands can hold a gun or a bottle or a bag of something that's gonna feed on your soul. And he can change his shape, but there are ways to tell when he's around. If he's a guest at your place and you feed him, he's the one who relieves himself on the wall or just squats and takes a dump right on the floor. That's just his nature. Sometimes he rides the wolf or the coyote, but they say he makes their hair fall out."

Jesse's hand went to his own thick hair, and the old man chuckled. "That's what they say. I never seen it myself."

A quiet time passed, and then the old man said, "Long time

ago it was Wolf who helped Iktomi lure the people from the womb of the earth, where they were happy and safe, into this world that we live in now. Iktomi told Wolf to give the people lots of promises because they were innocent, and they would believe anything. It was true. The people followed Wolf and all those promises. But once they came through the hole in the earth and it closed up and there was no way back, Wolf felt sorry for what he had done. He saw how scared the people were and how they didn't know nothing about this strange place. Iktomi, he didn't care. He just laughed at how helpless those naked, hungry people were, but Wolf knew he had done wrong, and he got help from Wazi, the rattlesnake master, and from Watanka, the old woman, and they showed the people how to get food and make shelter. So dogs have always been our friends."

"Then why did we eat puppy soup?"

The old man chuckled again. "How many stories you got time for?"

"There's always a Part Two, huh? Two parts. Two parts to every story," Jesse muttered as he slowly pushed to his feet. Back to the real world. "It's the headaches is what it is. Nobody can figure out where they come from or how to get rid of them."

"Make peace with yourself," the old man repeated. "Coyote makes mistakes. Big mistakes. But he also sets things right."

The schoolkids were having recess when Jesse walked onto the sunny playground seeking a breath of early-autumn air. The summer had been a long one, easing its way into October like a pan full of hot coals. An old-fashioned bed warmer, the Wind Spirits' occasional boon to the North Country. As far as Jesse was concerned, a day like this one had its own way of setting things right. The sun felt friendly on his face, as genial as a house full of kids and two caring women. He'd been pain-free for days, and the thought of crawling into a cave right now seemed ludicrous. Maybe he was cured.

"Hey, Jesse!" Tommy T accosted him from behind, whopping

him high on the back in the hands-on way of Indian kids. "Got any more work for me? Maybe I could draw a picture of the kids out here using your playground stuff. People would hire you to build more of those if you advertised."

"I just did what they told me to do. Nothing original. No big deal." He glanced across the yard toward the apparatus he'd built, which was crawling with kids, just the way he'd envisioned. He had to admit, the sight pleased him. "Guess I wouldn't mind having a picture of kids playing on it. You got yourself another job." He gave the boy's shoulder a quick squeeze. "People will hire you, too, Tommy T. You're a hell of an artist."

"So you'll pay me another five bucks, right?"

"I'll pay you—" A sharp *pop!* cut off his promise. "Jesus, that sounds . . ."

Another *pop!* It was coming from the park across the street.

Jesse's hand became a pile driver on the boy's shoulder. "Get down," he ordered as he swung around. Holy Christ, kids everywhere. "Everybody down on the ground! Down!"

Another shot was fired, closer still.

Jesse sprinted for the kid-draped playground equipment, a dozen or more small bodies arrayed over it like brightly colored birds in a shooting gallery. "Drop down!" He spotted a playground supervisor with a walkie-talkie strapped to his hip as he pulled two little girls off the climber. "Call in on that thing! Gunfire!"

The young man complied as the children, the proverbial deer in the headlights, picked up on the sound. Some started falling like dominoes. Others were like clutches of flightless birds, heads bobbing, eyes big as Ping-Pong balls.

"Down on the ground! Flat! Head down!" Jesse ran in a crouch, dragging kids down, bowling them over under his body, then rolling back to his feet to go after more. Another bullet popped. He motioned to a group of eight or ten older kids standing near the corner of the building. The message sank in all at once, and it was as if someone were taking a scythe to all the strings at a marionette show.

Jesse counted two handguns, a .22 and a .45, easily distinguishable by sound. But the first kid to run past was unarmed. The shooters were coming at the runner from two directions, herding him like steer hazers into the very corner he was trying to avoid. As Jesse sprang for the closest gunman, something sharp and hot jabbed him in the side, a quicksilver poke with white-hot steel. He crashed to the ground with the shooter, the small pistol clattering across the sidewalk.

"Stoner!"

"Shit . . ." Jesse pushed himself up, pressing his prisoner's face to the sidewalk as he turned and shouted Tommy T down.

"My brother!"

"If I have to knock you down, this guy gets away," Jesse shouted. Eyes shifting in terror from Jesse's stern face to the route his brother had taken, Tommy T finally sank back down.

The second shooter got another shot off, splintering a tree branch, but the blast of a siren had him wheeling back into the park.

The entire incident was over within minutes. Two squad cars screeched to a halt near the BUS LOADING sign, doors flew open, and four uniformed policemen emerged, weapons drawn. Mike Richards took care of Jesse's prisoner, a kid with purple acne scars and tangled brown hair who was sniffling and whining about his glasses. Jesse picked up the glasses—one lens was shattered—and handed them to another cop, who had already bagged the gun.

"You okay?" Richards asked Jesse as he handcuffed the kid.

"Yeah." He was holding his side, backing away. Had to get away.

"Whose blood is that?" Richards jerked his chin in the direction of a small red pool on the sidewalk. "Somebody hit? What happened here?"

"Two on one," Jesse said, trying to keep his side steady as he heaved a deep breath. He felt a little disoriented, as though he'd just flown off a merry-go-round that had spun out of control. "Shooting at another kid, unarmed. This guy's buddy headed that way." A nod toward the next building, another step back. "Kid they were after, I didn't see where he went."

Richards scowled, his full, dark lips forming a sympathetic pout, his eyes persistently prying at Jesse's side. "What about you?"

"Later," Jesse panted. "You see to these people." Richards stared, bent on questioning the way Jesse was holding himself. "It's nothing. I fell. Scraped my hand. You see to your perp there."

From one end of the playground to the other, dazed children were rising cautiously, one by one, looking at each other, then looking to the adults who were scurrying around, checking them out.

"Is everybody okay? Anyone hurt?"

"Let's go inside now. Quickly. Quickly." A round-faced Indian woman clapped her hands in the way of teachers, as though the incident had just been a fire drill. "Is everyone all right? Uh-oh, skinned your elbow, huh? We'll get you a Band-Aid," she promised a little towhead with tears streaming down his face. "What?" She leaned closer, smoothing his sun-glazed hair back with a calming hand. "I'll see if we have any blue ones."

Jesse collared Tommy T, who obviously had the same idea he had—making tracks. But the boy was headed in the direction of sure trouble. "Where do you think you're going?"

"I need to find Stoner. That was my brother they were after."

"You go inside. One of those guys is still loose." But the boy was trying to break free, yearning after his brother. Jesse slid his arm around Tommy T and drew him back, pressing the small, trembling shoulders against his own chest. "Let him go. He'll have a better chance without you tailin' him."

For a long moment the boy stood staring in the direction his brother had run. Nothing but sidewalk, bricks, and boards. Finally he tipped his head back. "Are you . . . did you . . ."

One of the teachers signaled for the boy to join the others. Jesse had to get away, before Richards could start trying to mess with him again. He gave Tommy T a determined push toward the door. "Get your ass inside now. I'm okay."

But he wasn't okay. He was bleeding and shaky, and unless he caught some kind of a ride, he was going to have one hell of a time getting *himself* inside.

16

Tommy T was late getting home from school, and Angela was furious. From the front window at Darlene's she saw him mount the porch steps, and she met him at the front door. She'd already heard about the day's events from Darlene's kids, Tony swearing a bullet had whizzed right past his head and young Billy announcing that now he knew what it meant to "bite the dust." No one knew what was keeping Tommy T, and *Just where have you been?* was on the tip of Angela's tongue when he finally came trudging up the walk.

But she couldn't quite get it out. She was too glad to see him. She was too eager to put her arms around him and wordlessly rejoice in his being there, safe and sound.

"It was Stoner they were after," Tommy T said, allowing himself to perch briefly in Angela's embrace. "My brother. I went lookin' for him, but . . ." He swallowed hard and shook his head as he drew back toward the stairs. "I can't even find Ajax or none of 'em."

"If you can't find your brother, that probably means nobody else can," Angela offered.

"Chopper got away. I'm pretty sure it was Chopper. Jesse made us get down, keep our heads down. It happened so fast . . ." He grabbed the banister and used it to haul himself up to the second step, then sat down in a weary heap. "I'm pretty sure it was Chopper."

"Did you talk to the police?" Angela asked anxiously. She'd left Darlene's door open, and now it was crowded with faces, all peering out like the innocent siblings, eager to witness any comeuppance, catch every word.

The boy wagged his head despondently, planted his elbows on his knees, let his head sag forward, and plunged his fingers into his thick thatch of curly hair. "Stoner don't want me narkin' no matter what."

"But Stoner's on the run, and it's Chopper—"

"Yeah, but if I nark, that would just make it worse. Chopper's slippery. They catch him, they never hold him very long."

"How old is this Chopper?" Angela asked. "Does he live with his parents?"

"No more than a rattlesnake lives with its parents after it's hatched," Tony piped up behind her back.

"I don't know where he stays," Tommy T reported, turning sulky on her. "I don't go payin' him no visits."

"Jesse caught one of them, though, right? That's what Tony—"

"I think he got hurt."

"Who?" Angela stiffened. "Jesse?"

"He said it wasn't nothin', but I think he was bleeding pretty bad. I mean, I know I saw some blood. Here, on his shirt and stuff." Tommy T laid his hand on his own side to demonstrate. "Didn't look like no scraped hand to me."

"You mean nobody checked him over?" Angela asked.

"All of a sudden he was just gone. I mean he . . ."

212

"He probably went over to the hospital right away," Tony suggested.

"That's probably what he did," Angela said, glancing at Darlene for confirmation. Darlene's eyes lacked reassurance, and her circumspect shrug was no help, either.

Angela took Tommy T upstairs and fed him a bowl of chocolate chip ice cream. Consolation food, as her own mother used to call it. She was mad at him for being late, but she was glad she'd been home when he'd finally walked through that door. She had traded for the early shift that day, the one she hoped to work herself into regularly, and now she had supper to fix and Jesse Brown Wolf to worry about. She was out of milk again—she was learning that kids who like cereal, shakes, and Oreos used milk by the vat—which meant she had to run to the store. She'd have to worry about Jesse on the way.

But Gayla stopped her on the stairs. "I need to ask you about something," the girl said, and the distress in her eyes gave Angela pause. "Do you know Jesse Brown Wolf very good?"

Angela pulled a quick, inquisitive frown.

Gayla pressed the small of her back against the banister and stretched her thin arms along the rail. "The reason I ask is . . . well, I asked Darlene, and she says she really doesn't know how to get in touch with him or anything. He just kinda shows up here sometimes, but . . ." She rocked her shoulders back and forth, her eyes darting everywhere but at Angela's face. "I was thinking about what Tommy T said about the blood. What if he needs help?"

"Doesn't Darlene think he'd get help if he needed it?"

Gayla shrugged. "Hard to tell. What I know is that he offered me help. Last time he was here, he was asking me about somebody I know. I mean somebody I . . ." She hunched her shoulders, glanced up at the landing, lowered her voice to secrecy level. "Remember that time that guy was banging on your door looking for me? And you never gave me up or anything, not to him, not to the cops. You just said he was looking for some girl."

Angela nodded as she took one more step down, putting her eye level even with the girl's.

Gayla leaned closer, sticking her neck out like a turtle. "I heard him up there. I didn't want him to find me, so I just kept quiet."

"Who was he?" Angela asked a little too eagerly. Gayla flinched, the turtle withdrawing.

The question echoed in Angela's own head. *Who was he?* Simple question, posed by a man in uniform, thumbs hooked in his belt, backed up by a side arm and a sidekick and looking to her to prove herself. *Either you know, or you don't. If you do, just tell us.*

If only the answers were as simple as the question. What do you say when he's their boss and your lover? Like Gayla, she had choked on the name. She'd felt foolish. She'd been scared.

"You don't have to tell me," Angela said, touching the girl's shoulder. "Whoever he is, I don't blame you for just keeping quiet. I've done the same."

"You?"

Angela nodded, offering what she hoped was a consoling smile. "A creep by any name is still a creep. Mine called himself Matt."

Gayla's eyes widened. "Was he, like, *mean?*"

There had been a time when she would have hesitated, hedged, questioned her own judgment. No more, she thought, and she nodded. "He was, but just looking at him, you'd never guess."

"Yeah, well, lookin' at Keith . . ." The girl sighed, disgusted. "Jesse asked me about him. That guy in the red-and-green hat, he said. Keith always wears that ugly cap with the stupid bulldog on it. Jesse said if I told him who the guy was that was looking for me that night, he'd make sure he didn't come around anymore."

Angela stared intently, replaying the incident in her mind. The intruder had already been chased away when the police came. *He's gone now,* her phantom had whispered. *I made him leave.* "The guy in the red-and-green cap. That's what Jesse said," Angela repeated.

Gayla nodded. "He said the guy was tall and skinny, brown hair, which is—" She shrugged. "Which is Keith for sure. I wouldn't give his name, though. You never know what kind of trouble it might cause, you give up somebody's name. Even if you never wanna see his sniveling face again."

Angela knew all too well. "We should have told the police, Gayla. I should have. You should have."

"Yeah, right," she scoffed, sinking slowly, letting her spine slide down the spindles of the stair rail as she sat on the steps. "Then I get into trouble."

It was a point Angela was in no position to argue. "But you know what? I think we could talk to that policeman who came to the Block Club meeting. Sergeant Richards." She sat down, too, her back to the wall. "I'm getting on the Neighborhood Patrol. I'm going to have a beeper."

"A beeper." Gayla's sun-deprived face brightened. "Whoa. Cool."

"Way cool." Angela nodded, smiled, then remembered her errand and started sliding her back up the wall again. "I'd better be getting Mr. T some supper."

"Angela . . ."

The look in the girl's eyes solicited a little more time, a lingering ear. Angela paused, sat back down, offered an obliging smile.

"Darlene says maybe I should think about giving this baby up for adoption." Gayla slid her hand over what, at her age, ought to have been a firm, perfectly round melon she'd swiped from somebody's garden and tucked under her baggy sweatshirt for a prank. "I feel her moving, Angela. My baby. She's right here with me, all the time. Darlene says I need to think ahead, but right now . . ." Angela was mesmerized by that slight, pale hand, lovingly caressing a dream. "She's all I've got."

"You've got Darlene and Poppy and Tony . . ."

"For now. I could have my baby forever."

"Babies aren't babies forever," Angela said gently. She caught herself trying to imagine Tommy T as a baby, wondering how much he'd weighed at birth. She gave her head a quick shake to clear it. "From what I've seen, they grow up fast."

Gayla's hand stilled. Three of her fingers were decorated with tarnished silver and cut-glass rings. Her nails were chewed to the quick. "You think I'm too young to be a mother."

"I see you looking after the little ones, Gayla. You're good with them." Angela tipped her head to one side, trying to get the girl to look at her, to see that she meant every word. "You care about them, and you want to make sure they're safe and that they have what they need. And that's what you want for this baby, which may not be the same as wanting this baby. Do you know what I'm saying?"

Gayla pouted. "You're telling me to give her away."

"No, I'm not. That's for you to decide. You're a woman who's about to have a baby. If you keep the baby, you'll have to be her mother. And if you can't be a good mother to her, if you can't keep her safe and provide what she needs because you're not ready or you're not old enough or whatever, you're going to be angry with yourself. Maybe even with your baby."

Gayla looked up, horrified. "I would never—"

"I know you wouldn't, Gayla, but you're not there yet. Just try to think about it. You'll be fifteen, and you'll have a baby to take care of twenty-four hours a day, seven days a week." She laid a hand on the girl's knobby knee and spoke quietly. "Just try to think what it'll be like."

Gayla's head was down again, lower lip quivering. "She's all I have."

"And you're all she has. You're the one who has to make the choice. Will you make it for her, or for yourself?"

"That's real easy for you to say. You're not pregnant."

"Is Keith the father?"

Gayla's mouth tightened. She turned her head abruptly, as

though the mention of the name might send her flying through the front door. Angela knew the feeling. Oh, yes, she knew it well.

She scooted a little closer, lowered her voice just above a whisper. "The guy who was pounding on my door and threatening to break it down? Is he the father, the guy you were hiding from?" Gayla turned, and the look in her eyes was all the confirmation that was necessary. "I'm not pregnant," Angela allowed, "but I have been hiding. I know what it's like to be afraid of a man you thought you loved. I know what it's like to run away from a man like that. I really do know."

Gayla looked at her, then looked away. She was ashamed.

Angela knew that, too. She knew because she felt it, deep in the softest part of her gut. Gayla was ashamed of being a victim, ashamed of being preyed upon. Angela knew because she, too, had been stunned, like a bird that had flown into a window, and the paralysis had shamed her. When she'd finally regained the use of her wings, she'd flown, all right. Flight had been easier than fight, and she was ashamed of that now, too. But she was proud of herself for finding her own direction.

"I've just told you more than I've told anyone. I do not want this man to find me," Angela ground out, then drew a deep, cleansing breath and expelled it quickly. "But you gave me a name, so I gave you a name. First names, but they're hard to say, aren't they?" Gayla nodded. "I'm trusting you because . . . because when you're alone and scared . . ." Angela searched the girl's eyes, offering understanding, looking for some for herself. "It's hard to know what to do, isn't it?" Gayla nodded again. "It's hard to take steps. The littlest step seems hard, and when you need to take a big step, boy, you just wanna hang onto whatever you've got, whatever there is in your life that still feels okay. Just hang on tight, no matter what." Another nod, more vigorously this time. "You're not alone, Gayla."

The girl's lower lip quivered as she stared at the door to her own safe haven. "I'd have to find my baby the very best mother." She looked at Angela long and hard, as though she were assessing her qualifications. "I'd have to make sure she had someone who really loved her, who would stick by her, even when she makes mistakes."

Angela nodded. "Mistakes are part of life. Not the end of the world, not if you're willing to try to make things right again." She touched the girl's shoulder. "And certainly not the end of love. Love gets us through."

"If you've got somebody to love you," Gayla said, her voice as small and thin as her willowy limbs.

Angela reached for the girl, pulled her into her arms, and hugged her close. She suddenly felt powerful, like someone who'd been lifting weights, discovering muscles in a body that was turning out to be stronger than she'd realized. "You do," she said. "We're getting it together, all of us."

Gayla clung to her. "It's hard for Darlene, with so many."

"I know. But you help out a lot, and Poppy does, even Tony." And Jesse, too, Angela added mentally. Jesse, who was more than Jesse, and Jesse, who was more than a friend. Jesse, who might be hurt and might need help and would not seek it for himself. Jesse . . .

A door opened upstairs, and Tommy T appeared on the landing. "Angela? You mind if I make some popcorn?"

"I'll mind if you don't eat a good supper tonight," she said, jumping to her feet.

He laughed. "When do I ever turn down food?"

Later, over supper, Angela tried to get Tommy T to tell her more about Jesse's injury. Had he "taken a bullet"? Tommy T laughed at her TV terminology and assured her that the man had walked away under his own steam. "If they didn't keep him at the hospital, maybe he'll come over and show us if he got stitches or something," the boy offered. "He wants me to make another drawing for him. He's gonna pay me."

But Angela knew that Jesse wouldn't be coming over tonight. She'd put the pieces together from what Gayla had told her. He'd seen her ex-boyfriend that night, the night her phantom had chased the intruder away. Angela knew that Jesse wouldn't be in any hospital tonight, either. She realized now that he would not have sought medical attention and that her enigmatic, jewel-eyed friend might well be in trouble. If he was, she was going to help him. She owed him that.

She didn't know exactly where he was, but she knew someone who did know. And even though that someone would never intentionally divulge his friend's secret, she had a feeling, given the day's events, that this predictably unpredictable someone was going to lead her to him.

Tommy T was asleep on the sofa when she went to bed. He looked like an angel, his young face relaxed, peaceful, free of common worries, and full of mythical dreams. She was certain he was asleep.

She was also certain he'd wake up. Tommy T was a light sleeper. He often got up at night. It had scared her the first time she'd heard him, and she'd gotten up to see what was wrong. "Just taking a break from sleeping," he'd told her. That particular night he'd gone back to bed, but on two other occasions she'd checked on him during the night and found an empty sofa, empty bathroom, empty apartment. Once he'd even taken the dog with him. In the morning, both dog and boy were back in the living room, looking innocent as you please.

Coward that she was, she'd said nothing. A free spirit, Mr. Bird had called him, although he'd been quick to say that it was not necessarily the boy's choice. She'd been trying to think of a way to curtail Tommy T's night-prowling without driving him away. She was going to talk to him about it, just as soon as she figured out what she could say to make him stop. She dreaded hearing him remind her that she wasn't his mother. He hadn't said it yet, but they hadn't had any real confrontations . . . *yet*. If he caught her following him, they would probably have their first showdown.

If he caught her following him, waiting for him to sneak out and then following him, stealing along in the shadows through a maze of creepy alleys and essentially deserted streets, she would be hard pressed to call herself the voice of adult reason. She carried her pepper spray in her pocket, an old-fashioned hatpin, almost as big as a fencing foil, tucked into the fabric of her sweater, and a hand weight in the bottom of the long-handled canvas bag she'd filled with the supplies she thought she might need for this errand of mercy. Still, every car was a potential threat. The sound of any voice was suspect.

She kept her distance and nearly lost her unwitting guide a couple of times. She had some vague recollections of shadowy trees, the lights on a distant bridge, the sound and smell of water. She had a sense that they were headed for the river, but she muttered a curse when he darted across the street and disappeared into a park. At night there was no such thing as a municipal park, especially not in this part of town. In the dark, it was all woods. She steadied herself and followed, telling herself that this was it. Once her mission was accomplished, there would be no more nighttime excursions for Mr. T.

She walked carefully, trying not to shuffle the dry leaves or to come down too hard on the twigs underfoot. As she moved from tree to tree, cover to cover, she began to feel a pulsation of energy, a stirring of inner strength. Every nerve in her body tingled, every cell was alert. She hadn't been caught yet. Hadn't been attacked from behind. Maybe she wasn't half bad at this prowling around.

Up ahead, she saw Tommy T emerge from a thicket into the moonlight, and she realized they'd reached the river bluffs. She crept as close as she dared, then sat with her back against the trunk of a big sugar maple.

"You okay?" Tommy T was saying. "You sound kinda funny."

The strained, husky voice seemed to emanate from an inconspicuous hole in the hillside. "I always sound . . . kinda funny."

"Yeah, but this is more . . ." Squatting on his haunches, Tommy T inched closer. "'Member you called me little fox that time? Guess what. That's who I am. I'm Fox." The announcement evoked no response, but that didn't bother Tommy T. "I was reading up on this stuff in the library, you know, for the stuff I've been workin' on. Sort of an illustrated, well, comic, but not . . . Anyway, Fox. I'm Fox. See, in the Coyote stories, Fox kinda looks after Coyote, like if Coyote gets hurt or something. 'Cause you know how he's always getting into some kind of trouble, and sometimes he gets all torn up or blown up, you know, like Wile E. Coyote. Well, what happens is, as long as there's even one piece of Coyote left, his sidekick, Fox, can make him whole again." Pause. "So I'm Fox." Another pause. "I mean, not that you're Coyote. You're Dark Dog. Because, you know, Coyote pulls some really dumb stunts sometimes."

Finally: "So does Dark Dog."

"No way." Tommy T chuckled. "No, you're, like, supercool, and I ain't lyin'. But . . . so . . . what I came to ask . . ."

Angela strained to hear, eager to hear, wishing she could help him get his question out.

"I need you to look after my brother, Stoner. I mean, look for him, find him if you can, and make sure . . ." Knees tucked under his chin, butt dragging the ground, he inched closer to the dark hole. "See, this thing went down today at school, right out on the playground. Chopper was after Stoner, and he damn near had him. And I mean he was—"

"I heard about it," the voice said abruptly. "I can't . . . I need you to do me something first, Tommy T." And then, in a tempered tone, "I need your help, Little Fox."

"What do you need?"

"Medicine. Same place as before, where you got the stuff to help Angela."

"Mr. Bird." The name was confirmed with a grunt as Tommy T reached into the cave, apparently accepting some proof of his commission. "So you don't want me to tell him anything, just . . ."

"You don't need to tell him anything. When you come back, just leave me the stuff and you take off back to Angela's. You look after her, and I'll see what I can . . ." A long pause hung heavily in the air, and Angela imagined that the weight was pain. "Try to hurry, now."

"Okay." Galvanized by the charge, the boy scrambled to his feet. "Okay, I'm on the case, Dark Dog. Round trip, forty minutes, max."

She watched, and when she could no longer see him, she listened until she could no longer hear Tommy T's retreating footsteps. Then she took his place at the mouth of what appeared to be a cave and announced that she was coming in. There was no answer. She ducked inside, flashing the small penlight she'd brought with her over the earthen interior. There was a three-foot drop to the floor, which she scanned with her light. Nothing scurried, nothing slithered. She pointed the beam upward. No beady eyes, no flapping wings. She'd been here before, she reminded herself, once upon a dream. This was where Jewel Eyes lived, and he wouldn't let her hurt herself. He would surely warn her if the place were booby-trapped.

Clutching her bag in one hand, flashlight in the other, she dropped through the opening, heels skidding over loose gravel, and landed in a crouch. She aimed the small light to the right and found wall; to the left, tunnel. Not much light, not much range, but what she saw amazed her. It was like a mine shaft she'd toured during a summer vacation when she was a child. Once again she imagined finding the seven dwarfs chipping diamonds out of the walls at the end of the tunnel. No threat there. She ventured deeper, sweeping the floor and the walls with her little beam of light, fully expecting to catch the glitter of gems.

"Turn your light off, Angela."

The low, soft whisper enveloped her. "But I can't see in the dark," she protested, cleaving to all her childlike imaginings and hoping dearly to see all the magic clearly with her own eyes.

"There's a small candle here. That's all the light you'll need, and it's all I can stand."

"Okay." She pulled the button back on her penlight. "Okay,

it's off. I'm coming in now, so . . . so here I come."

She could have sworn she heard him chuckle. She made her way carefully toward the smell of candle wax and the dim glow of a flame, thinking this was really weird, really crazy. Then she thought, Who's to say what's crazy? She? Her former Jekyll-and-Hyde boyfriend? She didn't know where she was going, but at least she knew who was waiting for her. She knew him by what he had done. The passage was a gradual descent, a conduit to the heart of the earth. *Lub-dub. Lub-dub.* The steady thumping filled her head, and she could feel its presence when the tunnel became a wide and wondrous room.

It struck her that she might have entered the master's bed-chamber in a brown stone castle, for the walls, studded with granite, were draped with colorful blanket hangings, and the floor was covered with straw. The votive candle burning in a small glass sphere on a block-and-board table cast dancing shadows on the star quilt hanging above it. The room was not cluttered, but it was furnished with shelves, large storage baskets, a willow chair, a couple of low stools, a bed. A basket of sage enhanced the com-mingled scents of earth and candle wax and dried herbs.

When her mind, whirling with incredulity, finally settled on a formed thought, it was: So this is Middle Earth. Home to creatures with tender hearts, like rabbits and hobbits and Vincent the Beast. And her gallant, jewel-eyed phantom. He stood back, as though she'd cornered him, a shadow amid shadows. His bare chest was slick with sweat, his eyes glittering with pain. Pressing a wad of cloth against his side, he stared at her, wordlessly challenging her to explain her rude intrusion into his improbable world.

She lifted her canvas bag. "I brought bandages and antiseptic and anything I thought—"

"The boy would not have brought you here," he said impas-sively. "I take it you followed him."

"Yes."

"Why?"

"I knew you were hurt," she said, rustling the straw with a single step. "I came to help you."

"I can lick my own wounds," he said quietly. "I sent the boy after some medicine. I don't need anything else."

"You were shot." She lowered her gaze to the evidence, but the way he was guarding it, she felt as though she were invading a moment of intense privacy. She caught her lip between her teeth, determined not to back away. "How bad?"

"Flesh wound," he reported with a shallow sigh. "Went in one side and out the other. Didn't hit anything vital."

"How do you know?"

"It's my body. I know." He took what might have been a menacing step toward her. "And this is my place. No one ever comes down here. Not even the boy."

"I've been here before. This time I came under my own steam. Did you actually carry me all this way? You really must be some kind of super—"

"Don't start," he warned, chafing under her scrutiny. "As you can see, I'm completely mortal."

She eyed the hand he was holding so tightly against his side. "Have you looked?"

"I know there's an entry, and I can feel an exit." He lifted the stained cloth for a perfunctory look, then glanced at her expectantly. "Can you sew?"

"I used to be pretty good at it, actually." She took his question to be an invitation to come closer. "As luck would have it, I was a veterinary assistant for a couple of summers," she said as she knelt beside him and pushed his hand aside.

"Perfect." He chuckled cheerlessly. "You're right. I'm one lucky son of a bitch."

She couldn't see much except a dark, viscous insult to his long, smooth torso. "Looks like you've done some bleeding. I suppose I should be concerned about sanitation here."

"Damn right you should." His tone hinted at amusement. "Did you bring any protective gloves?"

"Um . . . no."

"Then you should probably just let me bleed."

"Was I bleeding when you found me in the alley?" She pushed to her feet, noting the answer in his eyes. "That's what I thought. So I suspect we're blood siblings already." His dry laugh encouraged her to elaborate. "Just like in the movies, right? We've mingled our blood, so we're like . . ." He was smiling now, indulging her. "What am I going to use to stitch you up?"

"The boy will bring everything you'll need. Everything *I'll* need," he said with a sigh as he sat down on the bed, using the natural log bedpost for support.

"How do you feel? A little dizzy?" He nodded as she knelt on the floor near his wounded side. "That's not surprising. I wonder how much blood you've lost."

"All I can spare right now."

"I'm just going to shine this light right down here, okay? Not in your face, I promise." He gave his permission with a nod, and she made her inspection. The bullet had, indeed, passed through him. "Do you mind if I clean it up a little?"

"Have at it."

She grabbed a stool, arranged the first-aid supplies she'd brought with her close at hand, and set to work.

"The boy's brother is missing. He wants me to—" He caught his breath when the alcohol she was using hit the open wound. "Too many kids . . . need lookin' after."

"Is his brother a gangbanger?"

"His brother's his brother. I'll try to find him, soon as I—" He closed his eyes. Her daubing and prodding were obviously getting to him.

"You can't do anything about it now. Lie back." She held a sterile gauze pad against his side with one hand and gently urged him back with the other. "Lie down and rest while I do what I can with what I have here."

"When the boy comes back . . ."

"I'll take care of you," she promised. "Can I get you anything?"

He hid his eyes in the crook of his elbow. "When the boy comes back," he said. He rested, just as she'd told him to, and she sat beside him, watching over him, waiting. She longed to touch him, to make him aware of her, but he lay so still, she didn't want to disturb him. His long, dark hair formed a swirling pool beneath his head. She'd never seen it loose. It was as long as hers. She wanted to rub it between her fingers and learn its texture. She wanted to touch his face, his chest, test the warmth and the feel of his bare skin. She was letting her imagination do the touching when he suddenly jackknifed, bracing himself on his elbows. Startled, she almost blurted out an apology.

"He's here." He clamped a hand over the gauze pad as he sat up. "I can hear him, up above."

"My, what good ears you have."

"So the story goes," he quipped as he rose unsteadily from the bed.

She sprang to his side to help him, but he resisted it, opting for the bedpost.

"I'll go," she said reluctantly.

"And end the game?" The question put more than a boy's fantasy at risk. They both knew that. She glanced away, and he sighed. "We've got this thing goin', the boy and me. I meet him at the door. He confides, and he creates, and I start thinking maybe I could do . . . more than I thought. Be better than I've been." He shook his head, bemused. "I'll just tell him to leave the stuff."

She grabbed the candle and followed on his heels, steadying him when he swayed like a tall pine in the wind. She tucked herself under his arm, avoiding his injury. "You need my help."

"Put out the candle, then. I know the way."

They navigated the dark tunnel in symbiotic silence. He was the sextant. She was the mast. They stopped just short of the entry. There was no real light at the end of the tunnel, only less darkness.

And a familiar, deeply favored voice. "I got your stuff. Mr.

Bird says be careful how you use it." A rustling paper bag, thrust through the entry, blotted out all traces of night sky. "Dark Dog?"

"I'm here."

"Okay, what I wanna know is, what are we gonna do about Stoner? He said he was gonna get Chopper, him and Ajax, but now . . ."

"Is your brother dealing?" He took the bag and offered his thanks. "*Pilamaye lo*. But now I want the truth, Little Fox. About your brother."

"He's into weed, but that's all." There was a pause, a scraping of gravel. Angela could almost see the boy wrestling with his loyalties. "I'm pretty sure."

"Then we have to make it safe for him to return."

"From where?"

"Wherever he's gone to hide."

"How can we do that?"

Angela stiffened, certain that Tommy T had visions of being part of some kind of revenge-and-rescue mission. A quick squeeze from the strong hand resting on her shoulder reassured her.

"You . . . do nothing to attract attention. Go to school tomorrow as always."

Angela nodded.

"But if I hang out, I might hear something, see something—"

Angela held her breath and shook her head.

Again the reassuring squeeze. "Stay off the streets, Little Fox. They might try to use you to get to your brother. Or to me." He paused, and she felt him struggling for breath. It was her turn to offer the comfort of a gentle caress between his shoulder blades. She felt him catch his breath, sensed his quick nod. "Do you understand?" he pressed. "That's one of their favorite tricks."

"I understand."

"Now go, before you're missed. And be careful."

They stood together, entwined now for mutual support, and listened anxiously to Tommy T's retreating footsteps. "God go with him," she whispered, surprising herself, and he surprised her even more with a barely audible "Amen."

"I'm ready to have at it again," she said after a reverent moment had passed. "Are you still game?"

His soft chuckle echoed somewhere inside Earth's belly, which was where they were headed. Angela held him tight. "This is all so amazing," she said. "So utterly fantastic. It's like a dream."

"It *is* a dream, Angela. That's always been our . . . agreement." They had arrived in his room. In the dark he set the bag aside, and she realized they'd reached the table. He turned her in his arms. "And now that you've dreamed yourself down here and dreamed me hurt, you'll have to dream that you can mend me."

"But it isn't a dream. I know you."

"No, you don't," he whispered.

"Of course I do. You're—"

His kiss prevented her from uttering the name. His tongue removed it from her lips, from her tongue, dove into her throat for it, and swept it from her mind, leaving her breathless, tingling, totally absorbed.

"Is this who you want me to be?" he demanded impatiently. "The one who comes to you in the dark?"

She made a sound of senseless pleasure.

"Then don't confuse me with someone else." His warm, damp forehead rested heavily against hers. "I want you to stay with me tonight. Do you understand that? I need . . . I need you to care for me tonight. That's what you came to do, isn't it?"

"I came to . . ." She slid her hand down his bare back, to within inches of his wounded side.

"This is nothing. This is just a scratch." His hand closed over hers. "I want you to care for me tonight, Angela. Will you do that?" He backed away, still holding her hand like a supplicant. "Give me whatever care you have for me. Stop when you run out."

"I won't . . ."

"No?"

"I mean . . ." She clutched his hand. "I have to call you something, and I can't see in the dark, and I— Oh! Something just
brushed against my ankle."

"My occasional roommate." He chuckled. "She's a great
mouser."

It surprised her to realize how bright the flare of a match could
be. He lit the votive candle, then set a couple of tapers in small
glass holders and lit those. "This is all you get," he said stubbornly. "This and your little flashlight to do your sewing by."

But he also lit a flame under what appeared to be a fondue
pot, to which he added water and some dry herbs from a plastic
sandwich bag that he took from the package Tommy T had
brought. He touched a braid of dried grass to a flame, and when
it was smoldering, he put it in a coffee can that was rigged with
a wire handle. "Are you religious, Angela?" he asked absently.

"I . . . haven't been to church in a while," she admitted as she
watched him pull more sandwich bags from the package. One
contained a curved needle and suture thread. As if that last con-
fession might jinx her, she muttered, "Oh, God, I hope I don't
screw this up."

He put several of the packages in her hands, his eyes seeking
a connection with hers. "You've worked on my canine brothers,"
he said, smiling. "I should be easier. I have less body hair."

She swallowed hard. "I think you should probably lie down."

"I think I probably should."

He hung the coffee can over the bedpost, then laid himself
close to the edge of the bed. She pulled up a stool and set to work.
She groused about poor light, nervous hands, the infection he was
risking, the scars he would surely have. Waves of nausea threatened to undo her at first, but the occasional tremor in the hand
that held the penlight reminded her that the ordeal was really his.
He made no sound when she prodded and stabbed at his raw
flesh, but she could feel him struggling with the pain and with
the rhythm of his breathing. She found his control, like everything
else about him, to be remarkable.

And by the time she was finished patching him up, she'd decided she was pretty remarkable, too, and she declared the operation a success. "And I might as well have been working blindfolded."

"Like most two-leggeds, you depend on your eyes, and the truth is, your eyes don't care for me." He grunted as he labored to sit up, propping his back against the rails of his squeaky, hand-hewn bedstead. "But your hands care for me well."

"How many legs do you get around on?" She flashed him a pointed look as she bit a starter tear in a length of paper bandage tape. "Anyway, who says my eyes don't care for you? I've caught myself ogling you shamelessly." Even in the shadows his eyes glittered. The stool creaked as she leaned forward to apply the tape to his bandage. "Maybe you're not quite as observant as I thought," she muttered.

He tipped his head back and closed his eyes. "Let's have some of that tea."

In the part of the room she might have called the kitchen, where the table was located and the tea had been brewing, she found soap and water to wash her hands. The shelves held cups, plates, utensils, canned goods, and an orange tabby busy cleaning its splayed paw. "Does the lion coexist peacefully with the wolf?" Angela asked.

From the bed came a chuckle. "What else would you expect, my ogling angel? This is the womb of the earth."

"The womb of the earth," she muttered, smiling to herself as she reached for a mug.

The cat vacated its perch. Its leap uncovered a piece of paper. Angela apologized to the cat for the interruption, but the paper drew her eye. It was too dark to read anything other than the boldface headline.

MISSING.

There was no mistaking the face in the shadowy black-and-white picture on the bulletin. She stared for a moment. That face did not belong here. Nothing from that world, that life, that whole ugly dilemma belonged in this flame-lit, herb-scented, magical place. She set about pouring the tea, trying to drain the liquid from the leaves, fiercely trying to disregard the queasy feeling that was taking root in her stomach.

"You won't drink with me?" he said when she handed him the tea. "It won't hurt you, angel. You've had it before."

She stepped back, watching him closely as he sipped the hot tea. Friend or spy? she wondered. "Where did you get the Missing poster?" she asked pointedly.

"Police station. I slipped it out of a pile." He dropped his head back again, eyes closed, the mug cradled in his hands like treasure. "It's not a very good picture. It won't help them much."

"It's an old one." She had heard the reassurance in his voice, and she took it to heart. "Why couldn't he just let me go?"

"Your husband?"

"No." She gave a grateful laugh. "Good heavens, no. Just someone who wants to prove a point. That he has all the power, and I have none."

"You've come pretty far for someone with no power."

"Obviously not quite far enough." She sighed. "I haven't broken the law. I haven't deserted anyone. I don't owe anyone anything."

His eyes were still closed, but he spared a bit of a smile. "Sounds like you'd be a low priority."

"You'd think so, wouldn't you?" She made a loop of her hands and dropped them over her knees. "My face on a Wanted poster, for gosh sakes. And with no reward. You'd at least like to see a nice, fat reward on your head."

He was absorbed with his tea.

"What are you going to do with it?" she asked.

"With what?"

"That poster."

He shrugged. "I did what I was going to do. I stole it. You can have it for your scrapbook."

"There's really nothing he can do to me except..." Except what? He'd driven her down, driven her out, driven her nearly mad, all of which should have been sufficient to satisfy his ego. "Why would they even bother with me now?"

"They, or he?"

"*They.* The police."

"If you're as unimportant as you say, they probably won't. People disappear all the time, Angela." He turned, still suppressing the smile that touched his eyes as he offered her his empty mug. "Sometimes they even go underground."

"My hideout certainly pales in comparison." She quit his bedside long enough to refill his mug, sparing another glance at her image on a police bulletin. She liked the idea of having a reclusive ally, someone who was master of his own world. The cat, she noticed, had found new purchase on a rock ledge. "How long have you been here?"

"Always. Dark Dog was born here." He moved toward the center of the bed as she approached. "I've lost track."

"You didn't build this, did you?" She glanced at the far wall, the floor, back toward the tunnel as though she was sizing up the project. "You couldn't have. It would have taken more than one man." Or more than an ordinary man. She liked that idea, too. His eyes met hers, but they betrayed nothing as he reached for the mug. "Wouldn't it?"

His eyes, full of innocence, never wavered while he sipped from the mug, and she had a wild vision of him drilling holes with bolts of lightning and heaving boulders into the river. He laughed, as though he'd read her mind, which had surely become as inventive as Tommy T's.

"Okay, so it was all here," she decided, sitting in the space he'd made for her. "But I can't imagine what it would have been. A mine? I don't know much about the area. What would they have been digging for?" He looked at her, bemused, but he offered no clue. "A fallout shelter? A hideout for gangsters, maybe. How long has it been here, do you think?"

He shrugged, laughing silently.

"A long time," she concluded, delighted with her own myth-making. "Long enough to be completely forgotten. Then you discovered it, and you fixed it up beautifully. It's absolutely amazing."

"You said that already, even though you can't see a damn thing."

She kicked off her shoes and settled back against the headboard, stretching her legs out on the bed, which was covered with a feather tick. "How did you get a bed frame down here?"

"How do you get a ship into a glass bottle?" he challenged.

"I've wondered about that, too."

"Piece by piece." He looked quite pleased with himself. "This is an old-fashioned rope bed."

"Way cool," she quipped. Childlike enthusiasm for his ingenuity energized her smile. His eyes met hers, his smile warming to hers. "There were more candles burning when I was here before. Lots of candles." She glanced at the coffee can and its gently rising wisp of white smoke. "And I remember that smell. It's much nicer than incense."

"Sweet grass."

"Sweet, yes, and soothing. Like the way you can smell warm sunshine in a fresh peach." She heard him sip his tea, felt the heat of him, the intensity of his gaze. She glanced at the hand resting on his thigh, imagined him wielding a bolt of lightning, and smiled. Jesse Brown Wolf's power drill was just as impressive. It might take a little longer, but there was something consummately sexy about a man who could fix things.

"So you found this place, and you just moved in," she continued. "You obviously did some remodeling, made it suit your needs. Water supply?" He nodded. "Some source of fresh air?" He nodded again. "Secret escape passage?"

"Don't ask me where it is."

"Of course not. It's a secret." She glanced askance, smiling, but the gleam in her eyes was overwhelmed by the duskiness of his. "What's it like in the winter?"

"Cold. Will this be your first Minnesota winter?" She nodded. He nodded, too. "It's cold."

"So how do you stand it?"

"Dress warm." He drained his cup and handed it to her.

"More?" He shook his head. "Your brother's body hair would come in handy," she said as she reached down to nest the cup on the floor next to the bed. It made her shiver just to think of spending a December night down here.

With an affirmative sound he reached toward the foot of the bed, dragged a fur pelt forth from the shadows, and laid it across her knees.

"Ah. He gave it to you." She stroked the thick, lush fur appreciatively. "Your brother, I mean. Gave you his winter coat."

"So the legend goes."

"Are you legendary?"

His mouth twitched. He wanted to smile. "I will be, you keep on talkin'. You're almost as good as the boy."

"He's told me stories that, well, I assumed were exaggerated. But then, if I were to tell anyone about the stranger who enters my bedroom at night . . ."

"Different ghosts for different folks."

She laughed. "But, of course, you're not really a stranger."

"No stranger than you?"

"Not a bit." She shook her head, smiling. "I used to think that people were divided into two categories: normal and strange. In other words, people like me, people not like me. But it gets complicated when someone you thought was one of the normal ones, just like you, turns out to be the worst kind of strange." She looked to him for succor. "But somehow he's able to make it look like you're the one who's strange, and pretty soon he's even got you wondering."

"That does sound complicated."

"What's not complicated is . . ." She lowered her gaze, her tone becoming intimate. ". . . the way you help people. Me, Tommy T, Darlene, any number of the kids in the neighborhood. Somebody's in trouble, and you're there." She touched the back of his hand with tentative fingertips. "Maybe that is strange."

"Everything about me is strange, and we both know it. But let's just keep it to ourselves, okay?" He turned his hand slowly until her palm rested against his. "This part, anyway."

She stared at their hands resting together on his thigh and imagined a December night again, spent with him in his refuge, cradled in his warm hands. "The question is . . . why?"

"You disappoint me, Angela. I thought you knew better than to ask the ultimate question. You ask how long ago, you ask how, I can let you have magic for an answer. But why . . ." His fingers closed around her hand as he shook his head. "Ultimate questions with mundane answers serve no purpose but to spoil the mystery."

"You asked me who I was running from," she reminded him quietly.

"But not why."

"The man I ran away from operates above the law." She felt secure enough to tell him, even though he wasn't asking, simply because of the way he held her hand. "He *is* the law, which means he can put himself above the law, say what he pleases, do what he pleases."

"Above the law, huh?" He gave that notion some thought. "I guess you could say I operate *below* the law." She looked up, and he smiled. "Where it's rooted." Then, wistfully, "To protect and serve. That's supposed to be at the root of it, the sacred oath."

"Tommy T would like the sound of that. A sacred oath." She shifted, turning toward him. "You're a gallant phantom. Sometimes it's hard to believe you really exist."

"It's better if you don't believe it." He touched her hair, brushed it back from her cheek, let his fingertips trail lightly down the side of her neck. "Let me be your dream, Angela."

She looked into his eyes. Jewel eyes, gold embedded in obsidian. "But I know you exist. I know who—"

"Don't confuse me with anyone else." He touched a long forefinger to her lips. "He can't be your dream. I can."

"I don't understand."

"He does. He knows why. He *is* why." Her mystified look made him chuckle. "I don't understand, either, Angela. I don't know how you got into my life when I have no life. All I know is . . . now you've helped me."

"Jewel Eyes," she whispered, and she felt as though she were drowning in them, awash in warm and hazy memories. "You were washing my face, I think. It felt cool. You were looking at me with such devoted concern, and I remember . . ." She slipped her free arm around his back, opened her hand, and spread it over his satiny skin. "I remember the candlelight trapped in your eyes. I have to call you something. Dark Dog is Tommy T's name for you, but to me, you're Jewel Eyes."

"Call me Wolf. That's the piece of him that lives in me."

"Does Darlene know . . . you?"

He shook his head, smiled a little. "No one knows me but you. I'm your dream."

"Mine and Tommy T's."

"For him I'm Dark Dog, but for you . . ." He nuzzled her neck, then ran his teeth over it lightly until she shivered. "Dream me loving you, Angela." His warm breath caressed her just behind her ear. "Put me in your wildest dreams, and I will serve you well."

"And protect me?"

"And protect you," he promised, his voice drifting, his head resting on her shoulder. He pressed a soft kiss at the base of her neck. "The medicine is working. If I sleep now, you must stay a while."

"If Tommy T misses me . . ."

"You'll think of something." His arms went around her waist. "You're safe here."

"What about Tommy T?"

"He's safe, too. If he needed me, I would know." And he drifted, repeating, "I would know . . ."

Angela stayed a while, slept for a while, holding him in her arms, but she slipped away as soon as the first morning light leaked into the passage to his refuge. She had left him asleep in his bed, the same way he'd left her many times. Her turn to be the phantom, she thought. The gray veil of morning mist made a fitting cloak. Headlights dribbled across the distant bridge. The city's columns and pillars of glass glowed with the first hint of daylight, while the Mississippi slogged along lazily below the bluff, reflecting touches of color from its autumn mantle. It occurred to Angela that she had never seen such beauty or felt such peace since she'd come to Minneapolis.

Peace and peril, living side by side. It made Angela's spine tingle, charged her blood with unaccustomed boldness. She took a practice swing with her canvas bag, then darted through the woods toward the city streets. The new Angela was ready for anything.

She stopped at a convenience store to pick up a few items for breakfast, which would give her an excuse for being out, should anyone ask. Stevie met her at the door, but the apartment was quiet. Tommy T was sound asleep in his living room bed. Angela checked the clock and decided he could sleep for another half hour. She started some French toast, and he awakened on his own when he smelled it cooking.

"I tried to be real quiet last night," he said, padding into the kitchen wearing nothing but a brand-new pair of red boxer shorts. "Didn't wake you up, did I? I went out for just a little while and checked around, trying to find out if Stoner's okay. Nobody's seen him. The cops had just picked up a bunch of kids, so I had to be careful." He noticed the grocery bag. "You went to the store already this morning?"

"We were out of milk again." As soon as she'd said it, she realized she should have said bread or eggs, which would have been closer to the truth. She'd gotten milk last night. She couldn't look him in the eye, and she wasn't sure whether the hissing sound was coming from her sizzling face or the slice of French toast she'd just flipped over.

"I'm probably usin' up too much, huh?" He pulled a chair back from the table and deposited himself into it heavily. He probably suspected that she was harboring a secret, but he had to believe that it was separate from his, and maybe that worried him. He offered a tentative smile. "I really like cold milk."

"You drink all the milk you want. Whatever it takes to keep my bodyguard's strength up." She set a huge glass of milk in front of him, followed by a glass of orange juice and a plastic squeeze bottle of syrup. Food seemed the natural way to reassure him. The maternal way. "Today you get to guard me guarding kids walking to the bus stop. It's my turn. And then I want you to be on that bus, okay? We have someone with the Neighborhood Watch meeting the bus."

"Angela, I'm not exactly a little kid. I generally walk to school."

"I wonder if the police have caught the other boy who was doing the shooting yesterday. Chopper?" She delivered a plate of French toast to the table. "He's the reason I want you on that bus."

"You think a bus or a Neighborhood Watch is gonna stop Chopper?"

"I think it'll take witnesses to stop him."

"Narcs," Tommy T averred as he covered his toast generously with thick maple syrup.

"All right, narcs." She planted hands on hips, poised to make her point. "I'm ready to stand up and holler, Tommy T. Sing like a bird. What they did to me was bad enough, but after what they did to you . . ."

He shrugged. "It was just a fight, is all."

"One of you against how many of them, plus a dog?" She pulled out a chair, sat down, and peered across the table at him. He was busy sawing off a forkful of stacked fried toast. "I'm now a proud member of the neighborhood block patrol, Tommy T, and if I see anything that looks like a threat to our neighborhood, I'm going to nark my head off."

He glanced up as he balanced the end of his knife on the edge of his plate. "You gotta be careful, Angela."

"I know. I've got locks. I'm getting to know my neighbors. I'm your basic chicken, but you know what? I don't like it when they hurt the people I care about." Quietly she added, "And Jesse Brown Wolf did get hurt yesterday."

"You saw him?" Tommy T asked around a mouthful of French toast, his full lips glossy with syrup, his eyes wide. "Is he okay?"

"He will be. It wasn't anything real major, but it could have been. It was close. And you were close, and all those other children."

"And Stoner." He swallowed and licked his lips, almost as

239

eager to talk as he was to eat. "Stoner wasn't packin', you know. He was just runnin' for his life, and what I heard last night was . . ." He glanced away, hesitant to spill his news. But he couldn't keep it, not from Angela. "Chopper took a sketch off Stoner that I drew. Stoner let him think it was him that drew it, but it was me. Turns out the cops had another sketch just like it. They pulled Chopper in and questioned him about the other guy in the sketch."

"A copy?"

"Not exactly a copy. Stoner took the first one away from me, so I drew another one and gave it to Jesse. He paid me for it. I didn't know what it was for, except . . ." He shook his head and sighed, letting his fork dangle in his hand, all but forgotten. "I kinda figured he was gonna use it to get Chopper some way. I mean, I didn't ask no questions, just did the job and put the questions out of my mind, but I kinda figured . . ." He stared at his food, prodding at it with his fork. "Jesse almost got Stoner killed."

"Jesse almost got *himself* killed."

Tommy T peered across the table, scowling as though the unthinkable had just occurred to him. "You think Jesse's some kind of undercover agent?"

"I do not. Jesse?" She gave an incredulous hoot. "Oh, dear, Tommy T, what I really think is that you have a very active imagination, and I think you'd better be very careful about making that kind of speculation around anyone else. You know what I mean? Because I'm sure Jesse didn't know anything about the drawing Stoner took from you."

"The cops got hold of one of them. How did that happen?"

"I don't know. I do know that Jesse tackled a boy who was shooting at your brother, got him down, got the gun out of his hand. So that was a good thing." She looked at him expectantly. "Wasn't it?"

He shrugged. "That part was, yeah."

One part at a time, she thought. Learning how and where to put your trust was a lesson of many parts, as she well knew.

"Finish your breakfast, now; you've got to get ready for school."

He looked up from his plate, his eyes bright with affection, warm with trust. All for her. "You make great French toast. My mom used to make it sometimes when I was a little kid."

Angela's heart gorged itself on that loving look, but the mention of his mother echoed within the crystal confines of her conscience. Don't ask, don't tell, she tried to tell herself, but to no avail.

"Is your mom . . ." Her interest drove his attention back to his plate. "We haven't talked about her much," she reminded him gently. "I'm beginning to think of you as . . . my . . ." He looked up, watchful, maybe even hopeful. She couldn't be sure. "Is she living somewhere in the Cities?"

"I don't know." He lifted one shoulder, stabbed a piece of toast with his fork. "She'll be back. She always comes back."

"When she does . . ." She slid her hand across the table and touched his arm. "I know you miss her. But I'll miss you when . . ." They shared a look, part fear, part joy, a feeling neither could express in words. He nodded, and so did she.

Abruptly he turned back to his breakfast, eagerly sopping up syrup with a forkful of bread. "I sure love French toast. Wish I knew how to make it this good."

"Saturday morning we'll make that wish come true. We'll make enough for everybody." She rose from the table. "You and me, Darlene and the kids. Maybe by that time Jesse will be . . . up and around."

"I gotta find out what he did with that sketch," he muttered with a full mouth. "Gotta find Stoner."

"Maybe the police could help." He groaned. "I'd be willing to talk to them myself," she said. The surprise in Tommy T's face reflected her own. But why not? It was, after all, a police matter. "I'm serious. Sergeant Richards, the man who works with the Neighborhood Watch. I really think we could trust him, Tommy T."

He shook his head. "I got somebody already workin' on it. Somebody I know we can trust."

"Okay. But if you change your mind . . ." The look in his eyes said *Dream on.* "You'll come home right after school? I mean, you'll come back *here* after school?"

He shrugged. "You'll be at work."

"I'm working rush till close tonight," she confirmed with a sigh. "But that's going to change. I want to be home when you get home from school, and I hate working on weekends when you're off."

"You're not gettin' enough rest, you ask me."

She could have squeezed the stuffing out of him right about then, but instead she planted a kiss on the top of his head, nesting it in his untamed morning 'do. "Come to the café for supper, and then walk me home."

He grinned. "You're on."

18

Clutching a small hand on each side, Angela set a brisk pace as she shepherded a motley gaggle of children from her building and the neighboring houses to the bus stop. Rain pattered softly on the hood of her pea-green slicker. Tony and Billy were running ahead of the pack, jostling to be first to hit each sidewalk puddle, but Tommy T hung back. She'd gotten him a new jacket—nothing too colorful or fancy, he'd said, because he didn't want anybody "doing" him for his jacket—but he'd wanted it to cover his head and shed water. Hugging the sketch pad he'd zipped inside his jacket, he claimed the middle ground between the shepherd and the frolicking flock of kids. His slightly pigeon-toed stride, meant to be purposeful, was a bit ungainly, like the adolescent pup who had yet to grow into his paws. He deserved more childhood, Angela thought, more playtime, another season for make-believe. She wanted to give him that.

He turned suddenly, as if her thoughts had called to him, and, walking backward without a misstep, he offered his most irrepressible grin. "You got all your ducks in a row, Angela?"

She laughed, and he did another about-face, clutching his world of make-believe to his chest. He boarded the bus with the rest of the children because she had asked him to keep the ducks in line, make sure they behaved.

"Yeah, Tony was pokin' his arms out the window before," he reported on his way into the bus. With a look, he challenged the boy in front of him to call him a liar. Angela overheard the word "narc," the supreme insult, but Tommy T shot back, "Hey, you can lose an arm that way, you turkey."

She smiled as she watched the bus pull away from the curb. *Caution is good.* And looking out for each other was even better.

It was Angela's intention to stay away from the park, but she thought about the makeshift patch-up job she'd done, and she conjured up worries about all kinds of complications. She wanted to see him. Just to check on him. Just to lay eyes on him would be enough, she told herself, to assure herself that she hadn't done him more harm than good.

She packed a bag with more bandages, more tape, her uniform, and a few things she'd bought that morning. Chicken soup. She laughed when she tossed that in. Condoms. Nothing to laugh about there. The way she felt about this man, it was foolish to go to him unprepared, but her voice of wisdom had to have its go-round with her image of feminine gentility while she shoved the package to the bottom of the bag.

It was still raining. She took the bus as far as Riverside Avenue, alighted with her heart pounding wildly. She was almost there. The park looked deserted. Rain fell in dollops from the yellow-and-orange canopy and coursed in runnels through the sandy path toward the river. Brittle brown leaves, curled into the shapes of small boats, pirouetted in the puddles Angela was trying to dodge as she sprinted among the trees. Before approaching the den, she hid herself in a fading mass of red sumac and watched her back trail, just to make sure she hadn't attracted any attention. She wondered whether he'd heard her yet, whether the chamber he slept in could be right beneath her feet. She had no idea how long the tunnel was.

The gloomy daylight allowed her to appreciate the artful efficiency of the hideaway's camouflaged entry. The casual observer would never notice the opening, would detect neither the seemingly natural trough that served as a rain gutter nor the ingenious way the water was funneled through the rocks and back into the wall of the bluff.

She dropped into the entrance feetfirst, fully expecting to land ankle-deep in water despite the inventive drain system, but she didn't. She jerked at the snaps on her slicker, shook off the hood, and plowed her fingers through her damp hair. Then she directed the small beam from her penlight at the floor and followed it cautiously.

"Wolf?" she whispered. There was no answer. No sound but her own footsteps. "Jes—"

Suddenly he was there, standing behind her. The hands on her shoulders were as comforting and courteous as they were strong. She stood still, closed her eyes, inhaled deeply of the scent of sweet-grass smoke that drifted into the passage. He ran his hand down her wet sleeve, and when it reached her hand, she let the flashlight roll into his fingers. He snapped it off, pocketed it, and turned her into his arms, pushing the slicker off her shoulders.

She let it drop to the floor, along with her bag. In the dark, she turned her face up to him. He touched her first with patient fingertips, tracing the contours of her face from temple to cheek to the corner of her mouth. Her hands found his bare torso. Before she could ask him about the bandage that was no longer there, he cupped her face in his hands and kissed her so long and hard and deeply that by the time he took his mouth away, she couldn't remember her question.

But he had one. "What are you doing here?"

"I had to be sure you were . . ." She touched his side gingerly, carefully skirting the stitches she'd made. "I had to come back."

The heels of his hands inched down the sides of her neck. "You're soaking wet."

"It's raining. Listen," she whispered, leaning so close that the sound of his breathing poured directly into her ear, displacing the rainfall. She lifted her hand to his shoulder and discovered damp skin and wet hair that smelled of Ivory soap and fresh rain.

"I just took a shower," he explained. "I should have waited for you."

"You have a *shower*?"

He moved her a few steps until a cool draft washed over her face, proclaiming a breach in the tunnel wall. "Feel that? I have an aqueduct and a natural shower stall. I can shower here when it rains. But I think you've had enough of the rain, Angela." She didn't realize how cold her hands were until they were enclosed in his. His gentle gesture and the music of water peppering rocks sent a quicksilver shiver through her body. "You're chilled."

"And you still feel warm." She lifted her head, heat-seeking in the dark, and her cheek brushed his. "Do you think your fever's worse? I should have picked up a thermometer."

"My body's always on the warm side." He chuckled. Such a rich and welcome sound. "Same as your little dog's. Do you sleep with her?"

"No."

"You slept with me," he whispered, brushing his lips across her forehead.

"Yes," she admitted. "For a while, just as you asked."

"And if I ask again?"

He couldn't know how much she cherished the prospect of being asked. "I'll cross that bridge when I come to it."

"I'll take you there."

He retrieved her belongings for her and led her through the tunnel. Deep in his den he lit a candle, draped her slicker over the back of the willow chair, and told her with a look that the next move was hers. She knelt beside him, and he handed her the flashlight so that she could examine the wound in his side.

It looked good, for an amateur job. She applied more antiseptic, a homemade salve he provided, and a bandage. "If this starts to fester..."

"I'll know what to do." He drew her into his arms. "Do you know how hungry I am?"

"All I know is that I had to come back because I knew—" Her voice went hoarse. Her throat ached and tingled, all at once. "Because you're here."

He lowered his head and kissed the corner of her mouth. "Does that bother you? Finding me in a place like this?"

"It bothers me that you're hurt." She wound her arms around his neck. "Not finding you at all would have bothered me."

He slid his hands down her body, molding her to him. "And finding me so hungry for you that I can hardly..."

"That bothers me." She traced the ridge of his collarbone with the tip of her nose. His virile scent made her quiver inside. "I want to feed you," she whispered. "How shall I feed you?"

"I'll want to gorge myself, but you mustn't let me," he said, rubbing his chin over the smooth plane of her forehead. "Small, tender bites only, in my weakened state." He kissed his way down the side of her face, making her tip her head back to give him access. "Come cross the bridge with me," he whispered when his lips reached her ear.

"I . . . stopped at the store this morning."

She could feel the smile his lips sketched against her cheek as he asked, "Protective gloves?"

"I just thought . . ."

"Caution is good." He looked into her eyes. She saw no misgivings in his. Only the shadows of cares and caring. "Caution is wise, Angela. Feeding the wolf is probably not wise."

"Have a small bite, anyway," she said, returning his kisses now. "Just a taste . . ."

But a taste was not enough for either of them. Small kisses gave way in one quick, fierce, tremulous breath, mouths sinking into each other like two on the verge of starvation. She savored the taste of his lips, his tongue, but she devoured the tangy heat inside his mouth until he took it away, turned his head, and dove back for his share.

He took her to his rustic bed and removed her damp clothing, piece by piece, worshipping with warm breath, warm lips, and warm tongue every inch of her skin as he uncovered it. He touched her and suckled her until she was full to the brim, unable to contain the voice of her pleasure. His groans echoed hers, and he prodded her for more by finding her small, shy, desperately needy places and coaxing them to vibrate with ecstasy. She reached for him, caressed him, sought his eyes in the shadows as she drew him deep inside her. Their joining became the vortex of a slow, sensuous spin. Pleasure washed over her, wave after wave. She burst like a seed pod, broadcasting bits of herself, which the heat of his shuddering climax blasted into infinity.

"Oh, my," she whispered as the after-shivers rippled through her. He sank against her slowly, like the lush, damp silk of a collapsing parachute sliding over her sensitized skin and off to one side. She cradled his head to her breast and stroked his long, heavy hair. "My wolf," she said with a surfeit sigh. "How beautiful you are."

He nuzzled her breast, stroked her hip, and gave a pleasured sound that might just as well have been made by a wolf as by a man.

Her breasts rose on a deep breath. He gave another contented sound, and she smiled. "I should feed you some real food."

"Are you hungry for real food?" She laughed. "Neither am I."

He nuzzled some more. She petted his hair some more. Their glistening, tingling, replete bodies were smiling.

"I've missed your night visits," she whispered.

"Have you?" She answered *Yes* with only a wistful moan. "But you have the boy now," he protested gently. "You have friends. You're getting involved in things, feeling more secure. That's all very good."

"So you slip back into your cave, like Puff?"

"Something like that." His hand slid over her belly. "But now you've found the beast's cave."

"I would uncover more of his secrets, too," she said. "If I tell you about my demon, will you tell me of yours?"

"What makes you think I have one?" He rose over her, candlelight glinting in his eyes, a smile toying with his lips. "What? You question my choice of residence?"

"I'm enchanted by it, actually. And you."

He smiled and covered her with the wolf pelt, putting the soft hair against her skin. Then he settled on his back and drew her against his good side, pillowing her head on his powerful chest. "Then tell me about this demon."

"I was enchanted by him, too."

He groaned. "So I can't indulge my ego in your flattery."

"You have nothing in common with him." The observation made him laugh. "No, that is a compliment. He's a very public man, visible, high profile, and he enjoys every minute of it. In private he demands complete . . ." She drew a deep breath, reluctant to recall her humiliation at the hands of another man, to reveal her shame. But his fingers moved over her arm in a subtle, comforting caress, and she uttered the ugliness in a small voice. "Complete submission. So the enchantment soon wore off, and I tried to go my own way. He started seeing someone else, being seen with her, which was all well and good.

"Except that he would not leave me alone. Privately, his attentions to me became obsessive. There were phone calls, unwelcome visits, not-so-subtle messages. But I couldn't prove anything. He made sure of that. I tried to deal with him quietly, privately, and, of course, that didn't work. I confronted him in public—once when he'd been following me. Everywhere I turned, he was there, but he was so . . . so damned clever about it. I finally tried to get someone to help me. He managed to make it look as though I was just imagining things. Or making things up. Or even harassing him. But then he'd show up again. And he would . . ." She squeezed her eyes shut tight. "Oh, God, he would make his demands."

She heard him swallow hard. She waited for him to ask for the ugly details, which would shame her more, she thought, but she would tell him if he asked. She would give him the details to make him believe, if details were what interested him.

They were not. "He hurt you," he said quietly. "He had no right to go near you, and he should have been stopped. You tried the police?"

"Oh, yes. They came once and actually caught him at my place." She gave a humorless laugh, remembering. "He said that I'd called him."

"And they believed him?"

"Why wouldn't they? He's their boss."

He turned his head toward her. "The chief of police?"

"Worse. The commissioner. And I'm just some woman who went a little berserk when he gently but firmly broke off our relationship." She sighed as she drew the wolf skin up to her breasts. "I was forced to take a leave of absence from my job because I made an utter fool of myself right there in front of kids, co-workers, everyone. It happened one morning when he stopped in at school to speak to one of the classes, to play the esteemed police commissioner right after he had been harassing me the night before. I mean, the man was as brassy as he was contemptible.

"Anyway, I was tired, and I was . . ." She found the nerve to lift her head and look into his eyes. "Maybe I *was* a little crazy by then. But he scared me, and I acted—" She closed her eyes, and she felt a tensing of muscle in the arm that held her. "All right, yes, like a crazy person, right there in the hallway at school. He even had my friends thinking I'd totally lost it."

"You're a teacher," he mused.

"I was." She nodded firmly. "And I will be again. But they do a background check when you apply for a teaching credential in this state, so as soon as I do that, he'll know. He swore he'd never let me get away." She paused, then announced quietly, "I'm thinking of buying a gun."

He studied her for a moment, as though he were sizing her up for a new hat. "What if you'd had a gun the night that guy came bangin' on your door? Would you have shot him?"

"If he'd gotten in, yes. I think I would have."

"But I'm the one who got in," he reminded her. "You would have shot me."

"If I had a gun, I wouldn't get so panicky. I wouldn't just . . ." He was looking at her solemnly, unconvinced. "I need to be able to protect myself and my . . . and Tommy T."

"Do you want to see him carrying a gun?"

"No, of course not. I'm not talking about carrying one or even shooting one. Just *having* one."

"Ah."

"You said yourself he should have been stopped. I don't know if I would have shot him, but I could have scared him with it at least."

"The scum who hurt you, the cop?"

She nodded.

"People point guns at cops all the time," he said. "Maybe you'd think the threat was enough. It would show in your eyes, Angela. A cop would know. He'd see you hesitating right off, and he'd go for the gun. But there's another side to this particular cop, a cold-blooded, cruel side. You're one of the few people who ever saw that side. Maybe he would have turned your gun on you." He peeled her hand from the fur pelt and placed it on his bandaged side. "This is what happens, Angela. This is what handguns are used for."

"I know." She laid her head on his shoulder and inhaled the sexy musk of him. "I just want to feel safe. You make me feel very safe, but you can't always be there."

For a long while he stroked her hair in silence, and when he spoke, he sounded distant. "I don't have a gun. I used to, but I don't anymore."

"Tommy T says you don't need one. You have other power."

"Other power," he reflected, stretching the word out as if it were something sticky. "There have been times when I've thought, If I only had a gun. Not for safety, but for peace. For stopping pain. The pain has been hard to bear, and there were times when I wished . . ."

"W-wished . . ." Her throat suddenly prickled with dread, and she slid her ear closer to his heart, just to hear its steady beat.

He put his hand to his head. "My demon lives in here, Angela. It's cold-blooded, and it's cruel, and it's always there, waiting." There was no pain in his voice. There was no passion. "There are times when I don't want anyone around me, when I can't stand the light."

"Migraines?" she whispered fearfully, even though she knew the malady only by reputation.

"That's been suggested. So has some kind of stress-related condition. So has insanity. Mental illness. Whatever the polite term is these days."

"Do you take medication?"

His quick gesture indicated the table, the baskets of herbs, the sweet burning scent drifting from the coffee can. "I use the medicine you've seen here."

"Does it help?"

"More and more I believe it has helped. At times it was all that kept me from following through on a fool's wish. It's best if I keep to myself, and I've tried." He stroked her bare arm. "But then the boy came along. And now you. And in the dark like this, I can almost . . ." He spoke almost reverently, and in such hushed tones that she had to hold her breath so it wouldn't compete. "I'm better off with the dark. I'm not afraid of it. I see better, think better, handle the pain better. When the light's in my face, sometimes I can't . . . function just right."

She closed her eyes and held him tight. "Tommy T doesn't really know who Jesse Brown Wolf is, does he?"

"Jesse Brown Wolf is Jesse Brown Wolf. There's not much to him. The shell of a turtle."

She drew back, scowling. "No, I disagree."

He gave a cool-eyed smile. "And just what do you know?"

"I *believe*"—she stressed the word and waited until he invited more with a nod—"that there are two sides to the man, both equally—"

"Angela, Angela . . ." He turned his face from her. "You must beware of two-sided men."

Her sails suddenly limp, she tried a different tack. "Tommy T thinks Jesse might be working for the police."

He gave a skeptical hoot. "Look out! Everybody run for cover."

"Because of the sketch Jesse asked him to make," she explained. "Of the man who tried to break into my apartment and the boy who's been causing so much trouble. There were two sketches. Tommy T's brother took the first one away from him, so he made a second one."

"Shit." He groaned. "Clowns have no right to play cop."

"Clowns?" She thumped him on the chest. "What, you and Jesse? Are you going to tell me something outrageous, like you're Jesse's twin brother or something?"

He scowled at her, rubbing his chest. "Not hardly."

She scowled right back, and it made him smile. "Identical cousin? I think maybe I've seen this movie."

That made him laugh. He looked away, but the notion kept right on tickling him, and when he looked again, she was still scowling. Which made him laugh until he had to grab his side to keep from splitting it open. "Ouch. Hurts. But I guess . . . I had it coming," he sputtered, groaning. "Do you know how long it's been since I've laughed until it hurt?"

She shook her head. "How long has it been?"

He cupped her cheek in his hand, and his eyes smiled for hers. "How long since you made love, before today?"

"I don't remember much of anything before today," she said.

"You've lost track, too?"

"I've lost track," she whispered with a saucy smile. She threw her leg over him, and taunted him with her thigh. It didn't take much to arouse him. He groaned when she straddled him like a recklessly naked bull rider, took him in hand, and handled him with painstaking care. "Let's lose track again."

19

Tommy T was stretched out on the floor with a big pillow stuffed under his chest, his new sketch pad spread open, and several small characters marching across the page. He was experimenting with a new set of colored pencils, but he wasn't sure he liked the effect he was getting. The TV was still on, but he hadn't paid much attention to it after *Gargoyles* was over. The voices of the local newspeople were keeping him company while Stevie hung out in the kitchen, chowing down on dry kibbles. He was thinking it would be nice when Angela got to switch to the early shift like Deacon Peale kept promising her.

"... discovered in Anoka County, apparently the victim of a hit-and-run driver . . . still unidentified . . ."

Tommy T glanced up at the TV. A photograph filled the left side of the screen, with the words "Can you identify this woman?" Some statistics and a phone number completed the picture. He stared. The glow from the screen seared his face. His tongue thickened, throat clotted, stomach felt queasy, but he kept staring. The voices sank into an unintelligible buzz, bothering around his head like a fly. Eyes glued to the screen, he pushed himself off the floor, went to the phone, and dialed the number.

"I know that woman they showed on the news. Where is she?" The voice on the line started in with questions. What was his name? Where was he calling from? What did he know about the woman? "Where is she?" he asked again. "Just tell me where she is."

"Can you give me her name, please?"

He tried to swallow. The news show was on to something else, but somehow that image had been etched on his eyeballs. It was an awful picture of her. Her eyes were closed. Her hair wasn't right. Too straight. Too flat, like she'd been sleeping on it for a week. She was always fluffing her hair up whenever anybody took a picture of her, which nobody had in a long time. Not in a very long time.

"Did you witness the accident?" the female voice on the phone asked.

Accident? Somebody ran her over and left her, like a dog or a deer. *Roadkill.* He closed his eyes as a strange shudder rippled through him, shoulders to toes. "Is she—" He had to clear his throat and start over. "Is she in a hospital somewhere?"

The woman took her time responding. "We really need her name first." Another pause, then, gently, "How old are you?"

"Old enough to use the goddamn phone," Tommy T snapped. Anger felt good. It felt real. "Will you just tell me where she is?"

"I will if you'll just tell me *who* she is."

"Her name is Ricki Little Warrior," he said huskily after a pause. "She's my mother."

When Tommy T failed to show up at the café and nobody answered the phone at home, Angela told herself not to worry. The boy had some worries of his own, and he hadn't gotten used to explaining his comings and goings yet. It was a problem they'd have to work on. She would make clear to him that it wasn't a matter of not trusting him or not respecting his maturity. It was a matter of safety for himself and consideration for someone who cared about him.

She reached for the phone as the speech was forming in her head. It was a speech she wouldn't have any right to deliver without first making one long-overdue phone call.

"Roxanne? It's Angela."

"Angela! Angie, my God, where are you? We've all been worried sick!"

"I know." It was good to hear her sister's voice. Honest, artless contrition stung her, and she spoke softly, steadily. "I'm sorry. I've wanted to call you so many times. I had to leave, Roxanne; there was no other way. But I'm—"

"No other way for what, Angela? It's unfair to treat the people who care about you this way. I mean, seriously, where are you?"

"I'm living in . . ." The first concern sank in slowly. *Seriously, Angela, you've been unfair to me.* She backed up and regrouped. "I'm living in a comfortable place, in a nice Midwestern city. I have a job, and I've made—"

"You've made us all crazy with worry, Angie. I suppose you need money to get home."

Angela sighed. "I don't need money."

"You sure? When are you coming home?"

"I've moved, Roxanne." She smiled. She suddenly liked the sound of what she was saying. "I'm fine where I am."

"Which is . . . ?"

"Roxanne, I know this sounds crazy, but Matt Culver made my life—"

"Matt Culver has a new girlfriend," Roxanne reported. "Another new one, not the same one he was going with when you left. Of course, he still asks about you. I mean, he continues to be quite concerned, wondering if I've heard anything."

"I'm sure."

"He's mounted quite a search. We weren't sure . . ." There was a sigh at the other end of the line. Unusual for Roxanne. She actually sounded distraught. "You weren't yourself, Angela. I couldn't imagine . . . I mean, I just wasn't sure what you might . . . do."

"I'm very much myself, Roxanne. The fact is that Matt Culver abused and harassed me." She paused to allow for some reaction, but there was none. "I know you find that hard to believe, but it's true. I'm not putting up with that anymore. I don't want him to know where I am, because I don't want him bothering me. For right now, I think it's better if you can say you don't know where I am. Because you don't. So just . . ."

"I swear I won't tell anyone, Angie. You know me."

Angela nodded. "I'll keep in touch with you, okay? Because you *are* my sister, and I do love you."

"I . . . I love you, too. Please, just tell me where you are. What state, what—"

"Not tonight," Angela said, "but I will keep in touch." The long, hollow pause made her feel removed from everything, not just her sister and her former life, as if she were sitting on the moon holding a seashell up to her ear. "Are *you* okay?" she asked finally.

"I told you, I'm sick with worry."

Angela laughed. "This call and a good night's rest should solve that problem. I'm really doing fine on my own, Roxanne. But I miss you."

"I miss you, too, Angie."

She stared at the phone for a long time after she hung up. The distant whine of a police siren made her shiver. She fixed herself a cup of chamomile tea and took it to bed with a slim volume of poetry, contemplating Dickinson and Swinburne as she listened for the sound of a key slipping into her new lock. *And time remembered is grief forgotten.* She could go for that. The steaming tea and Swinburne's melodic verse lulled her to the edge of sleep, where she drifted, half listening, half dreaming.

She was all set to deliver a scolding the next morning, but there was no one sleeping on the sofa but Stevie. Now it was her turn to feel a little sick, and it did no good to tell herself not to worry. She boarded the next bus for Riverside Avenue and made tracks for the river bluffs.

There was no one lurking around Middle Earth except the cat. By this time Angela was feeling fairly foolish and substantially let down. She swallowed her pride and stopped in at Darlene's to ask Tony whether he'd seen Tommy T in school the previous day. No help there. He had to be out on the streets searching for his delinquent brother, Angela concluded angrily.

It was Mr. Bird who gave her the news about Tommy T's mother. The boy had turned to the old man when he'd needed heavy-duty help from an adult. This he had done, Angela realized, to protect her, to spare her. In his mind, she was a "wuss." In her own mind, she was, for the moment at least, a washout as a friend. But she was determined to change that.

Her head was in such a spin over the whole dreadful situation that all it took to send her flying out of her skin was a knock on the door. She fumbled with the security chain. "Tommy T?"

"It's . . . Jesse."

He'd come to her with a name, a face free of shadows, and a guarded look in his eyes. She wanted him to reach out to her, to take her in his arms, but he seemed glued to the floor, his arms hanging at his sides like tools suspended from hooks on a wall. "I heard about the boy. About his mother," was all he said.

"Did he tell you himself? Did he go to your . . ."

Jesse shook his head. "The old man told me."

"Mr. Bird? He gave me the news, too." Her recollection of the old man's report, coupled with the vacant look in Jesse's eyes, made her feel hollow inside. She backed away, dazed.

He crossed the threshold and shut the door behind him, sparing Stevie a quick head-scratching when the pup tried to climb up his pant leg. A soft-spoken word from him settled her down.

"Mr. Bird was the one Tommy T asked for," Angela said. "He was with him when he identified her. I should have been there, but I guess he didn't think I would want to get involved with the police." She wrapped her arms around her own middle. "I'm afraid I've earned my reputation as a coward."

"I haven't heard. Must not be too big of a reputation."

"What scares me now is him being gone, just gone. I didn't even get to see him. He'd run away before I got there. I went to your, um . . ." She gestured for lack of a word, shrugged for lack of a direct way to reach him. She really wanted to reach him. "But no one was there." Her eyes sought his. "You're okay?"

He ignored the question. "The boy doesn't have any close relatives around except his brother, who's disappeared. And, like you say, he probably wanted to keep you out of it. The old man said there was talk about social services and placement. He figures that's why the boy took off. He's been down that road enough times before."

"They could place him with me, couldn't they?"

He stared at the hardwood floor. "That might get complicated."

"Everything gets complicated, no matter how hard you try to keep it simple." She looked to him plaintively, searching for some hint of a gleam in his dark, adamantine eyes. "I thought maybe he'd come to one of us. You or me or . . ."

"I've got a pretty good idea where he'll turn up," he said quietly, and she questioned him with a look. "They're sending his mother's body home. He'll find a way to get there."

"I would have taken him. All he had to do was ask. Why didn't he?" He stared at her, his eyes hinting of some brittle knowledge. They drew her to him, and she laid a hand on his arm. "Jesse, we ought to be there with him. He needs us."

"He needs you, maybe."

"I've never been to an Indian reservation. I wouldn't know where I was going or how to find him."

"You'll be okay. All you need is a good map." His voice dropped nearly to a whisper. "It's hard for me to . . . hard to . . . get there without a car."

"I'll rent one," she said. "Just come with me."

He shook his head tightly. "I've got things to take care of here."

"Like finding Stoner? Like—"

"Like fixing toilets," he snapped, stepping away from her. "I get mixed up in stuff like this, I'm just askin' for trouble."

"What kind of trouble?" she demanded, dogging him step for step. She laid her hand gently over his wounded side. "Worse trouble than this?"

"Much worse." His arms hung at his sides, fists clenching and unclenching. "You need a hero, you gotta wait till nightfall."

"And then?"

"And then," he repeated deliberately, sardonically. He closed his eyes and shook his head, as though he'd been thoroughly routed. "And then all you gotta do is ask."

Angela had sold her car months ago, so she had to dip into her cash reserves to rent one for the trip. She couldn't pull off an eight-hour drive on no sleep, but she decided that leaving town in the wee morning hours wasn't such a bad idea. At 4 A.M. she would miss all the traffic and still have plenty of daylight to maneuver in when she got there. With luck she would not be maneuvering alone. She followed East Franklin nearly all the way to the river, just as she'd been instructed, then turned north, skirting his park.

His park. It was dark and deserted, and she chuckled to think that a year ago she would have avoided such a place even in broad daylight. She would have avoided the entire neighborhood, especially at 4 A.M. She certainly would have avoided the man who emerged suddenly, rising from the riverside slope. He wore a denim jacket, boots, and blue jeans, a slouch hat pulled over his face, but she knew him immediately. And she was more than glad to see him.

She reached across the seat to unlock the door for him, regretting her choice of a compact car as soon as he got in and shoved the passenger seat back as far as it would go. His legs would still be cramped. She apologized, explained, berated herself for not thinking. He said nothing. His eyes were hidden beneath the brim of the hat.

"Are you okay?" she asked timidly.

With a quick jerk of his chin he drew her attention to a road sign. "Take Ninety-four to Three-ninety-four west to Four-ninety-four north. Then west. Got it?"

"Got it," she said, inhaling deeply of his scent—crisp night air and autumn woods—which had filled the little car the moment he'd gotten in. "Thank you for coming. Are you . . . *okay*?"

"You wanna pull over and check me out?" His lips twitched a little, as if he almost wanted to smile. "Wait till we cross over into North Dakota. Anyplace west of Fargo, I'll submit to a complete exam. Before sunrise, that is."

She smiled for him. "My hero."

"Not for long," he muttered as he turned to glance out the window.

On the way out of the city they rode together in silence. Except for one distant siren's howl, the six-lane trail was softly lit, nearly deserted, peaceful. It took them through the western suburbs, past shopping centers and industrial parks, all sleeping. Once they'd left Hennepin County behind, they were "out in the country." The change was more abrupt, more marked than metropolitan areas Angela had known in the East. The terrain was flatter, and the road seemed straighter. But she was more interested in the roadside than the road itself. She caught herself veering off to the right a couple of times.

Jesse suddenly sat up, pushed his hat back, and gave her a quizzical look.

"Sorry," she said, quickly straightening their course. "I guess I was . . . I thought you were asleep."

"I thought you were awake."

"Sightseeing," Angela said with a shrug. Then she confided, "I keep thinking we might see him. I know it's crazy, but I keep looking for him along the road. I can't help hoping. Wondering where he is right now and just . . . hoping."

"People don't stop much along the Interstate, but sometimes you can get picked up near a ramp. Did he have any money?" She shook her head. He swept his hat off with one hand and raked his mostly tied-back hair with the other. "Anything he could sell? Did you notice anything missing?"

"I didn't look." He was staring at her as though she'd discounted the obvious. "Well, he's never taken anything from me. Why would I?"

"His mother's dead. He's trying to get home. He'll do what he has to do." He stared straight ahead, into the path forged by the headlights. "It would help to know if he had any money."

"Does he think of it as going home?" She refused to think so. She'd finally begun to think of her apartment as home and—even though she kept telling herself not to count on anything—of Tommy T as family. "Did you know his mother?"

He shook his head. "But I think she was a shirttail relative of mine. According to Art Bird, her family went on relocation back in the fifties or sixties." He glanced at her to make sure that an explanation was in order. "It was a government program to get Indians to leave the reservation, move to a city, get some kind of vocational training, maybe a job. It was part of the 'Termination' policy, when the plan was to terminate the reservations. They did it with some, actually abolished them, but mostly it was just another failed social experiment. A lot of people moved, though. That's why there are so many Indians living in your neighborhood."

"*My* neighborhood?" She smiled. "I'm the new girl on the block."

"Just passing through?"

"That's what I thought. That's what I'd planned." But she hadn't planned, not really. She had simply moved. She had gotten off dead center and vacated. She'd done the right thing. She was certain of that now, as certain as she'd ever been of anything in her life. "I'm thinking of applying for a job at the school," she told him. "Just do it, and let the chips fall where they may."

"Gutsy."

"I like working there. I like teaching. I'm a good teacher," she recited, building her case. "I shouldn't have to give that up. I should be teaching." She was working to convince herself. When the second thoughts formed, she voiced them, too. "If they'll have me. If he doesn't interfere. If he doesn't butt in and try to convince them I'm a nutcase."

"You're a missing person," he reminded her, the hint of a smile in his voice.

"Not really. I simply walked away." She glanced at him. "Okay, I *ran* away."

"And went into hiding."

"The voice of experience speaks?"

"The nutcase who knows." He tipped his head back on the neck rest. "You're right. I shouldn't talk. I generally don't."

"How often do you get them?" she asked, as if he'd been confiding symptoms to her. But he hadn't, and he ignored the question. "The headaches," she insisted. "Are they predictable at all? I mean, what should I do if you have one?"

"Nothing. Just leave me alone." He closed his eyes, as though he would withdraw from her now, then gave a chuckle. "I don't grow fangs when the moon is full."

"But you change." She waited for him to deny the supposition, but he said nothing. "Sometimes, right? Sometimes you change."

Still no comment. Ah, God, where was the man who had held her in his arms, the man whom she'd held deep within her body? He couldn't keep that man from her now. She wouldn't permit him to. Not now.

"Do you—or *does he* come to me only when he's . . . hurting? Or do you know?" Then, softly, because she had to know, "You do . . . remember?"

"I remember," he said, eyes still closed.

Her throat burned with the threat of unwanted tears, but she held them back.

And he could feel them. Without opening his eyes or touching her or hearing them in her voice, he could feel the heat of her unshed tears. She'd trusted him. She'd come to him and with him. He'd been with her and inside her, and he remembered every move, every nuance, and it was his turn to squirm. He didn't want to do this to her. He could feel morning breaking all around him, sky lightening, certitude sinking, and he did not want to do this to her.

Give her something, he told himself. But he had so little, and he was using what he had to hold himself together. He couldn't tell her how scared he was. He couldn't tell her what going home meant for him, what sorrow dwelled in the stark hills, what memories were carried on the night wind.

He reached mechanically for a knob on the dash. "Does the radio work?" *The radio, for crissake.* Big concession. A rich male radio voice predicted sunshine, then slid away with Jesse's impatient spin of the dial. *Say something.* "You like rock music or what? I used to be a country fan myself."

"What do you like now?" *Anything,* her eyes pleaded. *Give me even the smallest piece of you.*

Small pieces were the only kind he had. Small, scattered shards. He felt sick. He felt stupid. If the car died, he'd know what to do. Let him help out. Let him fix something. But ask him to name something he liked, some ordinary thing he found enjoyable while they were barreling down the road, heading due west?

Jesus, due west, where the unremitting light from on high would surely fry his raw flesh right before her pretty eyes.

"Quiet."

Tiresome as hell, but it was the only answer he had for her. He flicked the radio off and settled back, stubbornly retreating from her.

Quiet. He liked it, yes, needed it desperately at times, but not now. It was hardly what he wanted to share with her now.

Of course he remembered. He carried the taste of her on his tongue, the smell of her in his nostrils. He remembered how it felt to hold her body against his. He remembered every sweet sound she'd made, every loving word she'd said. He'd been her lover, her happiness, her hero.

But not for long.

Find the boy for her, he told himself. That's what she wants. That's what Jesse Brown Wolf has to offer. He could have asked Arthur Bird to go with her. That would have been the smart way, the easy way, with no deposit and no damn return. But it would not have been Coyote's way. The fool's errand, that was Coyote's way. And so he was barreling down the Interstate, headed due west, where Coyote was bound to be skinned, filleted, and fried in the Dakota sun.

Which was exactly what he deserved.

He pretended to sleep, but he knew the moment they'd crossed the state line into North Dakota. He could hear the wind. He could feel the cloudless sky. They'd put Fargo behind them, and he could sense the isolation, without and within. He lifted his hat off his face, tossed it on the backseat, and instead of breaking the silence himself, he challenged her with a look.

"It must be pretty quiet here most of the time," she said, picking up on the one word he'd given her miles back, before he'd retracted into his shell. "I haven't seen too many noisemakers since we crossed the state line." She spared a glance and smiled at him. "Do you miss it?"

"What? Mile after mile of grass?"

"It's peaceful, isn't it?"

"It can be, I guess." He turned his face to the window and watched the brown-and-yellow grass roll by. "Time was when I couldn't stand to be closed in. I wanted big sky, lots of fresh air and sunshine, plenty of elbow room." Time was, he thought. He remembered the wanting. Not so much what he had done with it, but how it felt. "If you're not peaceful on the inside, all this

266

peacefulness on the outside doesn't do you a damn bit of good. Quiet is one thing. Peace is something else."

"Peace is a sleeping child," she mused. "Assuming he's been fed and he has a safe place to sleep. Safe and warm, with someone watching over him."

"Or her," he said, letting his mind wander where it would on the sound of her voice. "And she wouldn't have to be a child."

"It's a gift, then. Are you more peaceful on the inside when you're providing for someone else's peace? A child, say?" She slid him another glance. "Or a woman?"

"Oh, sure." He gave a dry laugh. "You get somebody's toilet workin' right, it's pure bliss for the soul."

She acknowledged his self-deprecating joke with nothing more than her wise-woman smile. He watched more miles pass. The more miles that passed, the more chaotic his stomach became, but when she suggested a stop for food, he pounced on it like a pup on a toad. Any delay was just fine with him. A truck stop wasn't much, but it was a stop. And it presented a telephone opportunity, which was necessary for his plan. Even as he contemplated sticking his head in a vise and cranking it down as tight as it would go, he congratulated himself for coming up with at least a half-assed plan.

He made his call, then joined her at the small corner table tucked behind the cigarette machine. "Listen, I called a buddy of mine who's a cop. I called him yesterday and told him about the boy, and I just called him again." He rapped his knuckles on the table, his hands bracketing the paper plate with the sandwich he'd ordered but couldn't eat. "He's there."

"Tommy T? Where? He's okay? Where is he?"

No breaks for answers, but he had a solemn nod for each of her bubbling questions. "He's with this cop I'm telling you about. Pete Singer. He's with Pete. He rode in on a gravel truck."

"Tommy T did?"

"Yeah." He nodded again, staring at his dusky, unadorned hands. "So he made it all right. Burial's tomorrow morning."

"He's at the police station, then? That's where we're going first?"

"That's where we're going." He cleared his throat. Might as well tell her now. Still couldn't quite look her in the eye, but he was on a roll, started by good news, and he needed the momentum to prepare the way. "I used to be a cop. I haven't been back in a long time, but they know me there."

He could feel her incredulous stare drilling into the top of his head.

"A . . . *cop?*"

"Yeah." Finally he lifted his eyes to meet hers. They were big with amazement. He shrugged. "Just an ordinary Indian cop. No chief, nothing like that."

"Tommy T thought you might be an undercover cop. A special agent or something."

"Kid's got an imagination that won't quit." He glanced out the plate-glass window. Alfalfa stubble surrounded the white house across the road. "About like this countryside."

"You're pretty creative yourself." He looked at her quizzically. She gave him one of those looks that said *Get real.* "I keep remembering that Missing poster."

"If I'd been tracking you down, whoever wanted you would have had you by now." She looked at him closely, as though studying him anew. He studied her right back. "Right? You believe that?"

"What about the sketch you got from Tommy T? Weren't you doing a little police work with that?"

"I still get the urge sometimes. I catch myself thinking like a cop." Absently he watched a woman pull up to the Ethanol pump outside, lining the back bumper of her Blazer up with the hose. "I'll watch a cop stop the traffic so a bunch of people can get across the street safely, and I'll feel like . . ." He turned away from the Blazer with a sigh. "It was a stupid idea, stupid move, getting him to make that sketch. I should have kept my nose out of it." He smiled, remembering. "It was a damn good sketch, though."

"It was."

"I'd like to see Mike Richards put together the right combination, break up Chopper's little gang, take Gayla's ex-boyfriend out of circulation."

"Keith." He questioned the name with a look. "Gayla's ex-boyfriend," she explained. "His name is Keith."

He shrugged, shoving the paper plate aside. "Keith is Mike Richards's problem. Keith and his boss, who's the one they really want."

She nodded, and they both stared in silence at the unwanted sandwich.

"We'll be able to take Tommy T home, won't we?" she finally ventured. "After his mother's funeral?"

He shoved his chair back from the table. "That'll be up to him, I guess. You wanted to go and find him, and I'm just showing you the way."

20

Despite her continuing involvement with lawmen and ex-lawmen, Angela hadn't had enough real experience with police stations to define "usual," but the one in Fort Yates seemed unusually quiet. Three young men stood outside smoking, indifferent in their T-shirts and jeans to the crisp autumn wind. Each one in turn acknowledged Jesse with a quick nod. She couldn't tell whether any of them actually knew each other. But once inside, he was recognized. Surprise registered subtly on the face of a uniformed cop here, an office employee there. Jesse led her quickly through the reception area and down a corridor, confirming his identity wordlessly, meeting each disbelieving look with a curt nod. Angela didn't see any prisoners. No suspicious characters in handcuffs. No one looking uncomfortable or out of place except the two of them.

It was a relief when a smiling, barrel-chested cop met them at an office door and offered a welcoming handshake. "Hey, Wolf. How's it goin'?"

Jesse introduced Angela to Pete Singer. The name actually did make her heart sing. This was the man who had found Tommy T. "Is he—"

"Where the hell you been, man?" Pete demanded as he delivered a genial punch to Jesse's arm. "Damn, it's been . . . how many years since you quit? Four? Five? Jeez, looked like the ground opened and swallowed you up."

Jesse smiled almost sheepishly. "I ended up in the Cities."

"Big-city guy now, huh?" Pete pushed the door open wide and stepped back, permitting them a peek into the small, starkly appointed room containing two desks, several cabinets, and one blessedly familiar face. "Been lookin' out for your boy."

Reluctantly, Tommy T rose from the vinyl-cushioned chair, his face stony, his eyes flinty with caution. Angela moved toward him slowly. She didn't want to embarrass him. She blinked furiously, but she couldn't stop the burning tears from gathering in her eyes. "I'm really glad to see you."

"Glad to see you, too," he allowed quietly. "You're missing work."

She laid a trembling hand on his springy hair, and when she was sure it was okay, she pressed closer, smiling through her tears. "You know my schedule better than I do."

He stood firm, collected, looking up at her with a growing glow in his eyes. "Somebody's gotta keep track so you don't lose your job. Had a hard enough time finding one."

"I lost my mother too soon, too," she said, stroking his hair. "Any time is too soon, but I was nineteen. I felt so lost. So empty."

"I don't feel nothin'. What was she doing out on the road like that? She was always doing something stupid, like she didn't give a shit what happened to her." He hung his head. "I just had to see to it she got buried, you know? Make sure she wasn't left—" A quick, unsteady gesture expressed his disgust. "Left laying around somewhere like . . . like some ol' piece of trash."

"I understand," she said softly. He nodded, suffering her hands to claim his small shoulders. "I'm so sorry."

"They didn't even know who she was when they found her."

He swallowed, blinking hard, glancing aside quickly. "I was the only one who knew who she was."

And he had claimed her. "You're a good boy, Tommy T," she said, and then she thought, What a wretched understatement. He had done a man's job. He had identified his mother's battered body. "A good son," she amended. "Nobody could ask for better."

"She keeps on leaving. She just keeps on . . . leaving." He looked up at her again, fiercely. "Now she's gone for good, and I don't have to keep lookin' for her to come back. This time she ain't comin' back. She ain't never comin' back." His voice finally cracked on the last phrase.

"No." She tried to pull him into her arms. "But . . . I'm here."

"Yeah, well, I don't need no mother." And to prove it, he backed away with only a slight sniffle. "I get done here, I'm goin' lookin' for my brother."

"I'll help." Angela took a quick swipe at her cheek as she turned to the men, who stood in the periphery, waiting for safe containment of the moment's overflow. She managed a damp but confident smile. "Jesse wants to help, too."

"Jesse's a cop," Tommy T snapped, sparing the man a hot, defiant stare.

"Used to be," Jesse said. "Not anymore."

"I had you figured for a cop. That sketch you made me do, that's what got Chopper thinkin' Stoner narked on him. But it was me. You turned me into a damn narc and nearly got my brother killed." The boy was pulling away, retreating behind the flimsy chair he'd vacated as his dark eyes rained darts on the adults surrounding him. "Cops don't do nothin' about guys like Chopper. They pick 'em up and let 'em go." He turned to Angela, his closest ally. "Dark Dog should've killed that damn punk. He should've just snapped his fat neck."

"Dark Dog doesn't kill children," Angela said.

"Chopper ain't no *child*." He dropped into the chair with a weary sigh. "And neither am I. I don't know if I ever was."

"Have you had supper?" Hot, nourishing, solid food was all she could think of to comfort him with.

He hung his head again. "Ain't hungry."

"I think I am. I think *we* are." She looked at Jesse.

Jesse turned to Pete. "Can we take him?"

Incensed, the boy sprang away from his chair. "What do you mean, can you take me? I go where I please and do what I please. I came here on my own. Then this guy"—he waved a menacing fist at Pete, who stood back, unfazed—"picks me up for no god-damn reason, and we gotta talk to some judge who says he's gotta talk to some relatives I'm supposed to have. I had a grandma, but she died. I ain't got no damn relatives except Stoner, and I ain't stayin' here after tomorrow."

"We'll go get us something to eat," Jesse said. "Then we can—"

"I don't wanna eat with you," Tommy T spat, his eyes glittering. "I'll eat with her, but I don't wanna eat with you."

"Jesse and I came together," Angela said quietly.

"It's okay," Jesse told her.

"No, it isn't," she said. Then, to the boy, "No, it isn't. Jesse may have saved your life in that playground, Tommy T. He helped me get here, and we came because we care about you. And we're going to eat together. Tomorrow we'll go to your mother's funeral together." She put her hands on his shoulders again. He tried to shrug away, but she would have none of it, and finally his trembling little body acquiesced to her hands' comforting. "And then, if you're willing, we'll drive home together."

"You're gonna have to talk to the judge, Jess." Pete cleared his throat and added quietly, "It's, uh . . . it's Robert Takes The Gun. He's the one you'll have to talk to."

Jesse turned, and the two men exchanged loaded looks. "He's a judge now?"

"Yeah. But he's got nothing against you, man. I mean, you know, him and Lila, they're doin' good. And your daughter's doin' good, too. You seen her lately?" Jesse gave a subtle headshake. Pete gave a chin jerk Tommy T's way. "She's gettin' close to his age."

"I know." Jesse sighed. "I know."

"You doin' okay?" Pete asked, scrutinizing his friend as if he thought he might be hiding something. "You're lookin' a helluva lot better than you were the last time I saw you."

"I quit..." The announcement drifted, as did Jesse's gaze, his thoughts drifting away from all specifics, all memories. Finally he shrugged. "I quit a lot of things. So I'm, uh..." He shook his head, swallowed, sought Angela's eyes. He found them. She hoped he saw the support he was looking for in them. He gave a quick nod. "I gotta find these guys a place to stay."

"The boy's enrolled with the tribe," Pete said. "He's technically in tribal custody now. You'll have to talk to the judge, Jess."

"Shit," Jesse hissed, suddenly glaring at the policeman. "I asked you to look out for him for me. That's all I asked you to do." He pointed his chin at Angela. "She's going to get him something to eat, and after that..." He glanced at Tommy T. "Well, he's not staying here tonight, that's for damn sure."

"We're hunting him up some relations," Pete said quietly.

"Right now he's got Angela." He gave Pete a deal-maker's look. "I'll be back to talk to the judge, how's that?"

Pete looked at the boy, standing shoulder to shoulder now with Angela, then indulged them all with a quick nod. "I tried to feed him twice, but he hasn't eaten much."

They rented two rooms in the quiet riverside town's only motel, then paid a visit to the single eat-in café. Jesse exchanged polite greetings with the people who recognized him, but they kept looking at him as if they thought he might be masking something and they were just trying to get a glimpse of what it was. Angela wondered whether it was Dark Dog, but she didn't ask, for she knew Jesse could not tell her. But maybe her phantom could.

Tommy T kept saying he wasn't hungry, but when the food came, he ate. And when they returned to the motel and got him to lie down, he slept. The cares fell away from his young face and peaceful sleep settled in.

Jesse reminded Angela that he'd promised to check in with Judge Takes The Gun. "You can come with me if you want, but I might as well tell you up front—" His brief glance seemed apologetic. "This gets complicated. He's married to my ex-wife."

"So I gathered," she said, following him out the door. "Does that mean he'll give us problems with Tommy T?"

"Your guess is as good as mine right about now," he said, holding out his hand for the car keys.

"You don't have a license."

He responded with a thin, empty smile. "This is the rez." She wasn't sure what that had to do with anything, but she dropped the keys into his palm. He bounced them a couple of times, his eyes challenging hers. "Besides, nobody's gonna touch me here. Haven't you noticed? They look at me like I might drop down on all fours any minute and bite their leg."

"And will you?"

His smile warmed up a little. "Maybe later."

They caught up with Judge Takes The Gun just as he was about to leave his office for the day. "Robert," Jesse greeted the portly, middle-aged man who was dressed more like a cowboy than a judge. "This is Angela Prescott. We came about Tommy Little Warrior."

The judge shook Angela's hand, eyeing her dispassionately. "What's your connection with him?"

"I guess you could say we've sort of informally adopted each other," she said.

"Informally, huh?" The big man turned to Jesse. "What about your connection? You into informal adoptions these days?"

Jesse shook his head. "I've been doing some work at the school the boy attends. Minneapolis. I've been living there."

"That's what we figured." Takes The Gun folded his arms over his chest, shelving them on his paunch. "Monica doesn't need the money you've been sending. We're keeping it for her, though. It's in the bank."

"That's good." Jesse glanced away, nodded quickly, the words forming on his lips again without a sound. Then he cleared his throat. "Anyhow, Tommy T's been staying with Angela most of the time since school started. Otherwise, he'd still be living on the streets. His mother pretty much deserted him."

The judge nodded sadly. "She always was a wild one, from what I've heard. Where's his father?"

"Dead, according to what she told the boys," Jesse said, falling into filing his report, a routine he'd established in this very building, this office or one just like it, but in another life, another time. "He's got a brother, about fifteen. Mixed up in some gang trouble. Disappeared about a week ago. Could be dead, too, but there's no way that kid's gonna stay here not knowing what happened to his brother. You try to place him with somebody else, he'll just take off."

"You're asking me to place him with . . ." Takes The Gun looked at Angela.

"Me, yes." She squared her shoulders. She wasn't sure why he was scrutinizing her so suspiciously. She might have been a missing person, but, heck, she was no criminal. "As I said, Tommy T adopted me. He's very resourceful. He wants a home, and he wants to go to school. He's doing well in school, and he really shouldn't be—"

"What about his brother?" The judge reached back and claimed a handful of papers off his desk. He scanned the top page. "Stony Burke Little Warrior."

"Stony Burke Little . . ." Stoner, Angela thought. It was easier to think of him as a pure and simple menace when he was just *Stoner*. "Well, he's . . ."

"We don't know where he is," Jesse said. "There was some gang trouble, and, well, Stony . . ."

Takes The Gun scowled. "The older brother's mixed up in that gang trouble? What about Tommy?"

"No," they said in unison, glanced at each other quickly; then Angela looked back at the judge. "No, he really isn't. Not Tommy . . . T."

The judge studied the pair before him. "You two together?"

"No."

"We're friends."

"Friends of Tommy Little Warrior, alias Tommy T." Takes The Gun seated himself on the corner of his desk, putting him at eye level with Angela. "You're non-Indian."

"I'm . . . not Indian, no."

"You're not black either, and the boy's half and half. That makes it tough." He tossed the papers atop a folder lying open on the desk, then asked quietly, "Why don't you ask for custody, Jesse?"

The suggestion seemed to draw the walls in close around them. All eyes were fixed on the desk. No one spoke. Angela wasn't sure anyone even breathed.

Finally the judge tapped the front of the desk with his boot-heel. "You going over to the burial tomorrow?" he asked. Jesse assented with a grunt. "Won't be much of a funeral. Maybe I'll pass the word. Get some bodies over there so it don't look too bad to the boy."

"Bodies?" Jesse looked up, almost smiling. "Jeez, that one. That's really bad, Robert."

Takes The Gun shrugged, smiling a little, too. "Would you like to see your daughter?"

Jesse stiffened, swallowing audibly. His response was husky. "I promised Lila I'd stay away, and I have."

"That's right, you have," the judge allowed gently, as though he were speaking to the child rather than the father. "Monica still remembers it all, Jesse. She was five years old, but she still remembers. She still has nightmares about it."

"So do I."

"She feels to blame." He rose from the desk, arms folded judiciously once again. "You lose a child the way you and Lila did, it does a lot of damage. It's no surprise you two split up. But my wife needs to stop blaming you, and our daughter needs to stop blaming herself." He gestured, touching Jesse's arm in supplication. "She's just a little girl."

Jesse nodded. "And you're a good father to her. I figured you would be."

After a long silence, Takes The Gun ventured, "If I thought *the two of you* were asking for the boy . . ."

"It's not like that." Jesse stepped back, his eyes wary. "Angela's been good to him. I'm not . . ." He shook his head, exempting himself while he pleaded her case with the judge. "You don't have to worry about me being involved."

The judge continued to study Jesse. "Are you working steady?"

"Yes."

"Do you have a place to live?"

"Yes."

"Have you quit doing all the crazy stuff you were doing before?" A wounded look came into Jesse's eyes, and the judge smiled, seemingly satisfied. "You must have. You're not dead. You still get those headaches?"

"I'm not asking to take the boy myself, Robert. I'm telling you, Angela's been good to him. You put him with someone else, try to keep him here, he'll run."

"If a kid that age is gonna run, it's pretty hard to stop him."

"He loves this woman, Robert. She took him on his own terms, made no judgments, and he . . ." He looked at Angela, and for a moment she thought he might be speaking for himself when he said solemnly, "He loves her for that."

"I asked him. He says he wants custody of himself." Takes The Gun turned to Angela. "It's not that I have anything against you for being white. It's just that we have this long history of white people taking over on Indian kids, and we'd rather raise them ourselves." He lifted one hand, as if staving off a protest. "I know you couldn't prove it by the boy's mother, but we don't have to worry about proving anything by her now, do we?" He turned back to Jesse. "You're making this hard for me, Jesse. Why don't you come over and see Monica tonight? She's really gotten big since you—"

"You gotta be outta your mind," Jesse ground out. Like a trapped animal, he eyed the door. "I shouldn't even be here. I shouldn't be anywhere *near* here. I'm a lot better off just keeping to myself." Head bowed, he began rubbing his temples with the heels of hands. "I've gotta get outta here . . . now."

"Jesse, are you—" Angela touched his shoulder. "Are you okay?"

He glowered at her. "You comin' or not?"

"I want to talk with the boy tomorrow," Takes The Gun said. "Don't try to pull anything, Jess. If you take him, I'll be down on you pretty quick to get him back."

"We'll be there with him at his mother's funeral," Angela told the judge.

She hurried to catch up with Jesse as he flung the glass doors open. It was dusk. The air was cold and crisp. Early stars were beginning to dot the darkening sky. He strode to the car, took the driver's side, took the wheel again, but he took the wrong street— not that there were many choices—the wrong direction.

"Where are we going?" Angela demanded, thinking of Tommy T sleeping peacefully in the motel bed. When they got home, she'd get him a bed. He ought to have his own room and his own bed.

Jesse turned to her, his eyes glittering like black gold. "You wanna know what that was all about, don't you? I'm gonna show you. I want you to see."

Night fell like a soft shroud over the desolate graveyard. The motley collection of markers was nearly overgrown by prairie grass, dry and spent for the season and warped by the everlasting wind. Sundown had settled the wind, but the secluded place still felt cold and bleak.

They left the car parked on the side of the gravel road, and Jesse led the way on foot across a dry, grassy field. When Angela threatened to stray from his side, he reined her in, pointing to a yawning hole that stood ready to receive. She pressed close against his side. "How did you see that?" she whispered, and he chuckled cheerlessly. "Night vision, huh?"

"No need to whisper," he said. "They know we're here."

"Who?"

"The *wanagi*. Ghosts."

"Oh, dear." She held fast to his belt on the far side of his waist as they swished through the grass. "What if I don't believe in them?"

"I think their feelings are past being hurt."

"Do you believe in them?" she asked in a small voice.

"Does it matter?"

"I think so, yes." She gripped his belt tighter. A full, misty white moon hovered low on the dark and distant horizon. "Don't try to scare me, okay?"

"Okay."

But his steps had slowed, and she was very much afraid they'd come to the piece of ground he wanted to show her. She could tell that it was the grave of an infant. A nursery for eternity, everything in miniature. He lowered one cracking knee to the ground beside the small stone. "My son lies here," he told her.

She stood stock-still. *You lose a child* . . . the judge had said. Jesse was going to tell her something terrible, and he was going to do it in this disturbing place so that she would know the full import of it. And she was very much afraid, for herself and for him, because this was what haunted him.

"My son was three years old," he began, his voice as deep and steady and gentle as she'd ever heard it. "My little girl was almost six. We lived kinda out in the country, so they used to play together a lot, even though Monica was getting to be pretty big for her little britches. She was good with him, though. She liked to dress him up and playact all kinds of games. That night she had him dressed in a white pillowcase and little cowboy boots."

"A pillowcase?"

"She cut armholes in it and a hole for his head. She was wearing this top of her mother's that had beads and sequins sewn on." He spread his hand over his zipped jacket, patting his own chest to show her where the decorations had been. "I don't know what they were playing dressed like that. I guess I never asked. Anyway, Lila was gone. Since I was home for a change, she said I could watch the kids while she went to the store. Get to know my kids, she said. I was gone a lot. I pulled extra shifts, real busy being a hotshot cop, and I was getting noticed. There was even talk of . . ." His deep sigh sounded like the night wind in a deserted canyon. "But I knew my kids. I used to get up at night with them when they were babies, feed them, change their pants, all that. Hell, I knew my kids."

She wasn't quite sure whether he was talking to her or to the small white marker. "We named him Ira," he said, stroking the carved letters on the stone with his fingers. "It was my grandfather's name, plus Lila had a brother named Ira. Isn't that funny, for such an unusual name to be on both sides of the family?"

"It's a nice name," she said solemnly.

"I shouldn't be sayin' it out loud, especially not here. The *wanagi* . . ." His quick laugh sounded distant, hollow. "Spirits. Ghosts. A baby ghost. Great big eyes, like Casper. Another cartoon. Damn, I'm such a fool. Such a goddamn . . ."

"Jesse, what happened to the baby?" she coaxed. "What happened to Ira?"

"I'd shot a snake earlier. A rattler. Impressed the hell out of the kids. One shot. Blew the head right off. I'm quite a marksman, or at least I was last time I checked. Been around guns all my life. I had an uncle, used to take me hunting. Then I did a hitch in the Army. And, of course, I was a cop. I was hell on wheels when I was a cop." He dropped his hand to his bent knee. "I left the gun in the patrol car. It was a .357 magnum, a double-action revolver. Big gun for a big man. Not the kind you'd want, right?" He glanced up at her. "What kind were you thinking about?"

"I . . . don't know. I haven't . . ."

"Well, you got all kinds of choices. You gotta consider—"

"You'd shot a snake," she reminded him gently.

"Yeah." He nodded, staring into the deepening darkness. "The snake. I didn't wanna just throw it in the brush, because I didn't want the dog to get hold of it. With the kids watching every move I made, I put the damn gun on the dash, took the snake, and headed for the, uh . . . the . . ." His whole body jerked as though startled, but he went right on staring, his voice, his story streaming into the night like a black ribbon, quietly, steadily. "I heard the shot. I heard my little girl scream. But my baby didn't make a sound. Not a sound."

"Oh, my God." Angela's own mind's eye painted a scarlet-and-white picture for her, complete with a small face that resembled his father's. "Oh, Jesse."

"He was lying there on the front seat, that pillowcase all covered with blood. And he had no pulse. His little face"—his hand covered the side of his own—"half gone. My little girl holding the gun in her small hand and looking right down the baby-fucking barrel."

"So . . . she . . ."

"No. I did it. I was the fool who . . ." He breathed deeply, filling his lungs with cold night air. "I put Monica in the backseat. We took him to the clinic. I blasted the siren loud enough to wake the dead, let 'em know he was comin'. God, how he loved that damn siren."

"It was an accident."

" 'Guns don't kill people,' " he recited tonelessly. " 'People kill people.' "

"That's a slogan. Sound-bite philosophy. It's bullshit."

"And I was the best bullshit artist around. Cocky as hell." He chuckled derisively. "Coyote."

"Coyote sets things right," she whispered.

"Coyote is a fool. An embarrassment at best, and at worst . . ." With a groan he dropped his head into his hands and clutched at his hair.

She moved behind him, curling around him like a protective shell, her arms around his shoulders. He closed his eyes, tipped his head back, pillowing it between her breasts. She laid her hand on the side of his head, and he turned his face to it, parting his lips over the heel of her palm, which his teeth claimed as he drew a slow, shaky breath. His skin felt cool but clammy, as though he'd been running on a cold night. His pain was a living, breathing, mind-twisting thing.

"How can I help?" she asked.

"You've done enough. You brought me here." He squeezed her hand. "Now go back to the room. Please."

"Come with me."

"I need some time alone."

"Did you bring any . . . medication?"

"I have medicine." He gripped the small gravestone and used it like an old man would, levering himself off the ground with great difficulty. "Coyote medicine," he said with a sigh. "If I end up howlin' at the moon, I'd just as soon not have an audience."

She reached for him, touched his hair. He caught her hand, flattened it to his temple, and held it there.

"J-Jesse?" Different, maybe, but not so different. She wasn't sure who this was, friend or lover. "Are you . . . still with me?"

"Still here, still hangin' on." He laughed, rubbing her hand over his cheek. He touched a finger to his lips. "Very still. Still and quiet."

"I'm not leaving you."

"Yes, you are," he insisted, but she held fast to his hand. "Yes," he repeated patiently. "Go see to the boy. His mother died, and she had no sister to become his mother. You are a woman. You can be that sister."

"If the judge says—"

"I say." With his hand beneath her chin, he tipped her head, looked into her eyes. "Coyote sets things right. Weren't you just saying that?"

In the moonlight his eyes glittered with pain, surely, but with something more. Something both terrible and beautiful, some-thing that drew her inescapably. "Jesse?"

"Let me be alone here for a while." Gently but firmly, he set her away from him. "It's necessary, Angela. Right now, tonight, it's necessary."

She did as he asked, making her way across the moon-washed tundra with careful steps. She felt no fear, and she knew it was because he watched after her. She returned to find Tommy T still sleeping soundly, peacefully, like a child who'd been fed by his mother and tucked into bed. Exhausted, Angela crawled into the other bed and drifted on the edge of dreams.

He met her there, on the edge of dreams. Like a dark phantom, he came to her during the night, through the door that connected their rooms. He took her to his room, and they made love, touching each other with exquisite tenderness, eager to give pleasure and take away pain, solicitous of shared beauty and sorrow. Their coupling augmented the beauty and subdued the sorrow. Awash in moonlight and serenity, the loving continued long after the mating as they lay in each other's arms. For a while they spoke only of the moment, of how remarkable their bodies were and how well they fit together, of what felt good and what would feel even better.

But after a while they spoke of how they had come to this place, this moment, and of what tomorrow might bring.

"Did you mean what you said about Tommy T?" she asked. "Do you really think he . . . *loves* me?"

"Do you really doubt it?" He sighed, shifting her in his arms so that he could tuck her close to his side. "But Takes The Gun would turn the boy over to his wife's first husband, who is a menace to children."

"I don't believe that for a minute," she said, fiercely determined to defend him against himself. "His wife's . . . *Jesse* . . . Jesse Brown Wolf is a good man. We have children living in the streets, in the empty rooms of condemned buildings, and while most people look the other way, Jesse . . . Jesse, *you* take their part." Soberly she added, "Dark Dog doesn't turn his back on the children who need him."

His abrupt laugh echoed deep in his chest, beneath her ear. "Dark Dog is a myth. He's a costume put together by a boy with a head full of imaginary heroes."

"Then who's Jesse Brown Wolf?"

He pressed a kiss into her hair and whispered, "A man who has all he can do to get through until morning."

"I think . . . if you could put that terrible night behind you . . ."

"Have you put your fears behind you?"

"Not entirely. But I was alone when I ran away. I had no one to look out for but myself. I'm not alone anymore." She lifted her head and rested her chin on his chest. "Like it or not, neither are you."

"Like it or not? I tried not to like it too much, but I'm afraid I do." He brushed her hair back from her face, cherishing with a touch, a look. "God help me, Angela, I do."

"I suspect that's the way God intends it, that we not be alone." And she didn't want to be, would not be, not anymore. "I was alone with Matt. That's the way he wanted it. He wanted nothing in my life but him, and that left me so cut off that I was as vulnerable as a single tree in a thunderstorm." She smiled wistfully. "Someone pointed out to me that it helps to get to know your neighbors. Someone was right."

"I'm not exactly your neighbor."

"Oh, yes, you are. You are the Good Samaritan." He cut her off with a groan, but she scooted up to meet his protest, nose to nose. "You *are*. You live in the womb of the earth, and you are—"

"Stop." He touched a finger to her lips and whispered, "Stop. Don't do this, Angela. Don't tell me who I am."

Feeling saucy and secure, she kissed his warning finger. "Then let me tell you how I feel about you."

"Don't do that, either. Show me," he said, rolling over and tucking her beneath him. "Show me now."

The sun was too bright and warm for a funeral, the mourners too few, the service too short. The son of the deceased stood too straight and tall and revealed too little of what Angela knew he felt. He held his head high, but his eyes remained downcast for the most part. When he looked up, no anger, no sorrow, no affection registered in his flinty gaze. Steadfastly, he did what he said he would do. He saw that his mother was properly buried. Her grave was marked with a small metal placard, supplied by the funeral home, enough to name her and date her brief presence. It would soon be overgrown, Angela thought. The prairie would soon claim Ricki Little Warrior for its own.

Jesse explained the boy's options to him as he walked them to the car. Judge Takes The Gun was willing to give Jesse temporary custody of Tommy T. If he didn't like that idea, he could stay on the reservation with a great-aunt, whom he'd only just met, but who was also willing to take him in if that was what he chose.

"I ain't stayin' here." Turning his back on Jesse, Tommy T jerked a thumb over his shoulder as he squinted up at Angela. "And I ain't goin' nowhere in his custody. I can take charge of myself. I wanna go back to my own school. I need to find my brother, who's hidin' out because this guy . . ." He turned an accusatory stare on Jesse. "You're workin' for the cops, aren't you? You didn't *used to be* a cop. You *are* a cop."

Jesse folded his arms and stood his ground. "I'm your ticket back to the Cities."

"I don't get it. How come that judge is willing to let me go with you and not her?"

"Because I cut him a deal." Jesse shrugged. "You and me, we're related, Tommy T. Your mother was my cousin. Second cousin, third cousin, it doesn't matter. We're related."

"I ain't related to no cop. If Stoner finds out they stuck me with a damn cop . . ."

"I'm not a cop, and you won't be getting stuck with me. You'll be getting Angela. Just between us, she'll be getting you." He exchanged glances with her, then looked back at the boy. "That's *if* you cooperate."

"Yeah, but if you get custody, I'm supposed to live with you. That's how it works."

"This is a special arrangement so you can go to school. I won't interfere unless you give Angela trouble. Which you won't." He laid a hand on the boy's shoulder and would not be shrugged away. "Right, Tom Terrific?" he said quietly.

Tommy T's jaw dropped. He stood staring up at the man, the mask between them having rudely fallen away.

Jesse mindfully met the boy's astonished gaze and gave a quick nod, confirming Tommy T's worst fears. "I won't be going back right away," he told Angela. "I need a couple more days here."

"We can wait."

He shook his head. "The boy should be in school. You have things to do. I have things to do." He opened the door on the driver's side and invited her with a gesture to take a seat. "There's always someone headed that way. I'll catch a ride."

"What about my brother?" Tommy T demanded, his glare growing more heated. "Now there's nobody to help me find my brother."

"There is." Jesse turned to the boy again, pleading his credibility with a steady look. "There still is, as long as you hang in there with him. You know what I'm saying?" The boy stared, unflinching, apparently unimpressed. "It's up to you," Jesse said. "You started it all. You can't quit on your creation now."

"A cop," Tommy T muttered, still staring. "A damn cop."

"Maybe that's not as bad as you think. Is that possible?" The question seemed posed for his own consideration as much as for the boy's, but the prospect clearly titillated him as nothing else had in some time. "What do you think, Angela? Is it so bad?"

"You turning out to be an ex-cop?" She smiled. "I don't think it's so bad."

"How about you, Tom Terrific?"

"Don't call me that," Tommy T ground out. "You got no right."

"Okay." Jesse shoved his hands in his jacket pockets, his smile fading as he backed away. "Okay. Drive safely."

The drive back to Minneapolis seemed eternal. Angela respected Tommy T's reticence, but as the miles dragged on she kept hoping he would open up. He didn't. He kept it all inside and watched those miles drag their everlasting tails along the side of the road.

An unusually agitated Darlene greeted them with passing relief, dovetailing condolences with more grief. "We are in deep trouble, girl. We gotta find ourselves another place to live."

Angela glanced into the living room, where Tommy T had settled with pencils and sketch pad in front of the TV, then shooed Darlene into the kitchen. When they were beyond the boy's earshot, she posed the question "Why?"

"The new tenants in that little apartment in back?" Angela offered a quizzical look. "Name's Mickels or something like that. They took off for the weekend and let a couple of boys from Detroit use the place." Darlene paused, obviously expecting something more than Angela's puzzled look. "Well, you know what that means," she insisted impatiently.

"What does it mean?"

"Weekend dealers. They pay the tenants to disappear for the weekend, set up a temporary shop to try out the location, pretty soon they're permanent neighbors."

"Oh, dear." Dealers. Darlene wasn't talking about cards. *Drug* dealers. "Did you call the police?" Darlene shook her head. "Why not?" With lips pressed together, the head kept wagging. "Darlene, you of all people, you *never* back down from—"

Darlene signaled for a halt. "These dudes are different. We're talkin' evil now. The police would just be a little inconvenience for them. Just enough to shake their tree a little. They get a little shook, they shoot people, no problem."

"Oh, dear." Angela sighed. There ought to be some way to stop this. Law-abiding people shouldn't have to move out of their homes to make room for criminals. "Maybe we should complain to the landlord."

Darlene braced her arm on the edge of the counter and planted her other fist on her hip. "First news flash, honey, we got no proof."

"But you're *sure*. Drug dealers from Detroit."

"Sure as I'm standing here, but complain to the landlord, girl? You can't get to Hickey except through Morrison, and you know how worthless he is." Darlene wagged her head slowly. "Uh-uh. Those boys move in, we either move out or hide under the bed at night."

Angela scowled. "But we already live here. We were here first, and we have the children to think of. We can't just let them drive us out, and we certainly can't let them set up shop."

"They'll be back. If not next weekend, then it'll be the one after that. That's the way they operate."

Jesse was unavailable, which meant Angela's guardian phantom was missing, too. She glanced toward the living room. Maybe Tommy T could invent them an interim hero. "We'll talk to Sergeant Richards."

"Who has to turn it over to Narcotics, who sets up some kind of a bust right here in our building."

"Which is better than having somebody set up a drug shop," Angela said.

"That's easy to say, but when they wake you up in the middle of the night and the bullets start flyin'..." Darlene punctuated her lesson by drilling the center of her palm with her index finger. "The way it works is, they take them by surprise. Which means we get surprised, too."

"Unless we go undercover and help set up the bust."

"Undercover!" Angela gave a "hush" signal. Darlene leaned closer. "I'm keepin' my ass undercover, girl, and I suggest you—"

"What are our choices, Darlene? Where can we go? We've signed leases, and there's no boys-from-Detroit release clause that I know of. And if we just let these drug dealers move in, we'll have bullets flying anyway."

"Okay," Darlene said, singsonging the word with a sigh. "We reel our scrawny rubber chicken necks way out there, we have a quiet little talk with Mike Richards." Darlene folded her arms tightly under her bosom. End of discussion. "How's Jesse?"

"He seems to be healing pretty well. From the bullet wound, anyway." Angela glanced away. "He didn't come back with us."

"He'll be along soon."

"He made some kind of an arrangement with the tribal court for Tommy T." She laid a hand on her friend's arm. "Oh, Darlene, a few weeks ago I was afraid to get involved with this boy. Now I want desperately to be involved. Now my greatest fear is that I could lose him"—she snapped her fingers—"just like that."

"But that fear ain't gonna stop you." Darlene smiled knowingly. "From loving him. From taking him into your heart and home."

"No, it isn't. It can't." Angela returned the smile. "And the love is so much stronger than the fear. Isn't that amazing?"

Darlene nodded. "Amazing."

A ngela was surprised the day Matt Culver showed up.

His appearance itself didn't surprise her. Matt prided himself on making good on his threats. What surprised her was that the sight of his bulb-tanned face at the top of the stairs didn't scare her much. In fact, she was relieved to find that the black Lincoln with the rental plates had been illegally parked next to the curb in front of the house by someone other than a visitor from Detroit. It was just Matt Culver. Big deal. She looked up, stared him right in the eye, and told herself that whatever he was after, he wasn't getting it from her.

She climbed the steps without hesitation. This was her home, her territory, and she would not even think of running. She was cool, *way* cool, and Matt Culver was no longer at the top of her list of concerns. He was not a jittery-stomach deal. Not a heart-pounding deal. Just a distasteful, disgusting, big smelly deal.

And it was a new smell, she realized as she approached the landing where he stood waiting, looking quite pleased, quite smug. He'd changed his cologne, traded one designer scent for another. *Big smelly deal.* He stood up there—the words "you've been naughty" dancing in his gray eyes—watching her like Big Daddy, thinking he was about to mete out the consequences of his choosing.

But there would be no consequences. She had her hatpin. She had her pepper spray. She felt pretty smug herself, knowing that she didn't have to let him into her apartment. The man was not welcome here. She didn't want him stinking the place up, she didn't want his glossy shoes treading on her floor, and she didn't have to make any excuses.

She didn't even have to greet him civilly.

"What are you doing here?"

"You took the words right out of my mouth. Angela, what in God's name are you doing in this"—he surveyed the shabby hall-way—"rat hole?"

"There were no rats here," she assured him as she stood before him at the top of the stairs. "Not until today."

"You don't mean that, Angie." His smile was as fixed as his stance, deliberately blocking the door to her apartment. "I've been worried about you. Searching everywhere, worried sick."

"I believe the sick part." She mimicked his smile.

The hiding was now officially over. A wondrous sense of relief settled over her like the answer to a prayer. It didn't matter whether her call to Roxanne had led Matt here. Angela wasn't going to worry about whether her sister had "narked her over," as Tommy T would say. Roxanne was stuck in her own limita-tions, and Angela had decided to accept that. Her sister was her sister—no more, no less. But Angela had been made over, re-created, and she felt, she *knew*, she was stronger than she had ever been. At this moment she was as ready to assert herself as she would ever be.

"What do you propose to do now that you've found me?"

"I propose to take you home. It's the least I can do." He stepped closer, menacing her with his size, his deportment, his obnoxious dapperness. "I've found you, as I told you I would. I'll find you again. And again. You might as well stop running."

"I have stopped running." Her hand hovered over the head of her hatpin, which was woven into the side seam of the skirt of her uniform. She'd gladly use it on him if she had to, and she wouldn't be the least bit squeamish about sticking it to him good. Her smile was just as self-assured as his. "What are you going to do now, Matt? I'm not running. It's hard to chase someone who's not running."

"I don't chase women. I don't have to." He ran his narcissistic fingers through the gray hair at his temples. She wanted to laugh him right out of his illusion, but she suppressed the urge. He arched a brow. "But I do find people who go astray. That's part of my job, and I do it very well. You went astray, Angela."

"I went *away*. You wouldn't, so I did, and I'm glad I did. All right, so you've found me. I repeat." Her eyes narrowed. "What are you going to do now?"

"Whatever pleases me." The smiling villain idly adjusted the front of his open topcoat. "I can, you know."

"No, you can't. It pleases you to intimidate me, but I'm not willing to be intimidated anymore. So you can't do whatever pleases you."

"Don't be ridiculous."

"I'm not ridiculous," she said breezily. "And I won't be reduced to behaving in a ridiculous manner. Never again."

"Is that so?" He gestured expansively. "You can say that with a straight face, living like this?"

"Absolutely." She nodded toward her door. "Get out of my way. I'm not playing games with you anymore."

"I don't play games, Angie. You know that." He folded his arms, taking a territorial stance. "You know as well as anyone that I have a long reach. Did I ever happen to mention that I went to school with the Minneapolis chief of police?"

"I'm impressed."

"My concern for you, my judgment, my word, would not be questioned."

"I'm due at—"

The front door flew open at the bottom of the stairs, and kids flooded the foyer like bubbling water on the rise. Tommy T came bounding up the steps.

"Hi, sweetie! How was your day?"

"Pretty good. Mrs. Garrett signed me up for a special program, so I might be getting a mentor in art." He eyed Culver suspiciously as he cleared the landing. "Who's this guy?"

Angela reached for the boy, deftly maneuvering him away from her pin hand as she invited him to her side. "He's someone I used to know from where I used to live."

Tommy T wrinkled his nose. "Whew! Who spilled the perfume?" But he had a nose for more than the obvious. "You're a cop, right?"

Culver glanced from one to the other, clearly puzzled. "Angela told you about me?"

"Nope. I can just tell. What do you want with Angela?"

"I'd like to take her home where she belongs, but, like you, I'm just paying her a visit."

"I ain't visiting. I live here." He stepped in front of Angela and gave the man a hooded, formidable, thoroughly male stare. "My mom died, and now I live with Angela. You ain't takin' her nowhere."

"I'm not surprised to find you with another man, Angela. I would have expected him to be taller." Culver dismissed the boy with a rude snicker. "I'm glad somebody's looking out for you, though. Especially in a place like this. Anything bad that can happen most certainly will happen in a neighborhood like this."

"Bad things happen everywhere, but the worst of it is—" Angela grabbed Tommy T by the shoulders and pulled him back to her side. "The worst of it is to go along with the bad stuff because you think you have no choice. You think you have to tolerate the bad stuff or you'll lose everything. But that's not true. I'm here . . ." She pointed to the floor with a poker finger. "I'm *here* to tell you that's not true. I think I could go back now, Matt. I could go back and live my own life and not be bothered by you. But I'm making new plans. I like them a lot better than the old ones." She smiled. "I'm making them myself."

"The new woman?" He smiled, too, giving her waitress's uniform a pointed once-over. "Poverty becomes you, Angela. It must be the hunger in the belly that kindles that fire in your eye."

"I really don't have time for this." She waved him aside. To her surprise, he moved. "We have nothing to talk about, and I have things to do."

"We'll stay in touch," he said, watching her shove her key into the door. "What are your qualifications for foster-mothering a child, by the way? With your history of emotional instability—"

"You're wasting your time with this, Matt." She pushed the door open, ushered Tommy T into their home, and gave Culver a dismissive glance. "I really thought you were smarter than that."

With a sigh, she closed the door and pressed her back against it as though she half expected the man to try to force his way in. "He doesn't scare me," she told herself, then nodded at Tommy T, who stood close by, assessing her defensive position, probably considering one of his own. "Don't let him scare you, either. He's got no leverage here. He's just blowing hot air."

The boy shrugged. "I ain't scared of him. Just an old guy dressed up in fancy clothes."

"Poverty becomes me," she mimicked as she tossed her thick sweater jacket into the closet. "I called my sister to let her know I was okay, and then I applied for a Minnesota teaching license. I'll bet that's how he found out where I was. Can you believe he'd go to all that trouble? Just to prove his power, well . . ."

She snatched an envelope off the telephone table and waved it before Tommy T's big, appreciative eyes. "The point is that he doesn't have the power to stop me. See this?" The boy nodded dutifully. "I'm very well qualified, and now I'm licensed. See these?" She snatched up some papers. "I'm applying for a teaching job. Maybe I'll have to start out as an aide, but I will work my way in, because I'm a good teacher."

"That guy did bad stuff to you, didn't he?" Tommy T asked gently.

"Some people live to push other people around. They don't care where they push them. You let them push you over here, pretty soon they want to push you there. You think they'll be satisfied if you make a concession, but they won't. There's no end to it. It's the pushing they enjoy." She laid the papers aside. "People like Chopper."

"Chopper's a punk. That guy's a cop. But they both did bad stuff to you, so I don't see any difference." He dropped into the lone living room chair, his face furrowing into a scowl. "I hate being small."

"We're not small," Angela insisted. "And we're not letting people do bad stuff to us anymore, and we're not letting anyone sell drugs in our building." He looked up at her quizzically. It was a problem she hadn't discussed with him, but she realized that it was time to. "Some bad boys from out of town are trying to use our building for their candy store." She sat down on the arm of the chair, pleased with how hip she sounded. "What we have to do is figure out who we can trust. Let's make a list."

"A list?"

"People we trust. People we *mostly* trust. Nobody's perfect, and we have to remember that, but who can we mostly trust?" She laid her hand on his shoulder. "I trust you, Tommy T."

"Same here. I trust you. And Stoner. Except when he's high. Or when he's lookin' to get high, which is . . ." He shrugged. "I just know he'd never screw me over . . . on purpose."

"Neither would my sister." Angela mirrored his shrug. "She likes that guy who was just here. She likes his fancy clothes and his fancy reputation. She doesn't think I know what's good for me, and she doesn't think getting pushed around is all that bad. We just simply don't see eye to eye, my sister and I."

"I don't think I'd like your sister too much if she'd tell you to stay with that dude."

"I don't have to listen to her." She smiled. "She's my sister, and I love her, but I don't have to listen to her. Or trust her, for that matter."

"Stoner wouldn't give me up to no cop. I mean, I trust him that much."

"You love him." He looked up at her and shrugged again. "That's all you can really give him right now, isn't it? You have to be honest with yourself about what's in his head and what's going on with him. You can't count on him."

"He thought he could count on me."

"Let's think of some other people we trust. Darlene?" Tommy T nodded. "Mr. Bird?" Another nod. "Mrs. Garrett? Gayla?" More nods. "Gayla's still trying to figure things out, but basically—"

Tommy T's face brightened. He had news. "She's getting into that alternative school program, she decided."

"So she's using her head to make a choice. That's a good sign. I'm glad." Angela tipped her chin up. "How about Sergeant Richards?"

"He's a cop."

"I know. He helps with the Neighborhood Watch."

The boy wagged his head. "You can't trust a cop. You can't tell anything to a cop. The next guy he picks up, he tells it right to him. Tells him you told. Then he lets the guy go, and you're screwed." He gave another boyish shrug. "You can trust Richards if you wanna, but you gotta be real careful what you tell him."

"What about Jesse?" It was the first time she'd mentioned him since they'd been to North Dakota a couple of weeks back. She'd been afraid to say his name aloud, afraid it might tip some delicately balanced boat that was simply floating on faith. She was almost afraid he didn't exist anymore, that Puff had drifted away in a prairie mist.

Tommy T glanced away.

"Have you seen him?"

He shook his head stiffly, but finally, when he turned to her again, he let her read her own misgivings in his eyes. "Have you?" he asked quietly.

She shook her head. With shared looks they acknowledged mutual disappointment, silent wishes. He lowered his eyes, studied the stubby brown fingers in his lap. "I used to trust . . . Dark Dog. But I just made him up. I know there's no such thing as a superhero. How could there be?" He looked up, bobbed his shoulders again. "Flesh and blood is all, just like you and me."

"What about someone who puts flesh and blood on the line for you and me?"

He swallowed hard and glanced away.

"That was Jesse," she persisted. "Not Dark Dog. Maybe he's got problems, too, just like us ordinary people, but in spite of that he still comes through for us. What about somebody like that?"

"What problems has he got?"

"Flesh-and-blood problems that he keeps to himself and tries not to bother anyone else with. Have you . . . checked to see whether he's there?"

He shook his head, pulling a frown. "What do you mean, *there*?"

"He's helped me, too, Tommy T. Remember?"

He heaved himself out of the chair and headed for the window. "Why didn't he come back with us?" he asked as he surveyed the street below.

"He has some pieces to put together. Flesh-and-blood pieces."

"I guess he needs Fox, then." He turned to her. She could see the alternating impulses in his eyes. The artist and the realist, the believer and the betrayed, the boy and the man. But at last a hopeful luminescence prevailed. "I mean, Dark Dog does. Or Coyote. I don't know about . . ." He dismissed other possibilities with a quick gesture. "See, in the stories, as long as there's even one piece of Coyote left after he's gotten himself blown all to hell, Fox can make him whole again."

"Would that be okay with you? I mean, if he were really whole. If he gave up the secret life and became just—" Her gesture invited the possibilities for another review. "A man."

"As long as he wasn't a cop. *Ever*."

"Well, what if that's who he is? What if that's who he really is?"

"No way. Dark Dog can't be a cop. That guy that was just here is a cop, and you said yourself . . ."

"I'm not talking about him." She eyed the boy pointedly. They shared a precious secret. "You know who I'm talking about. It seems to me that the only way Fox can restore him is by putting the pieces back where they really belong."

He considered the charge for a moment. "How am I supposed to know where they really belong?"

"If you're Fox, you'll know." She gave him an all-knowing look. "If he's Dark Dog, he'll show you."

Angela had a point. The link between Jesse Brown Wolf and Dark Dog had bothered Tommy T until he'd been just about ready to pitch his sketch pad into the river. Then he got to thinking about all the other superheroes and how dorky their public identities were, and he figured, why not an ex-cop? After all, Coyote had his stupid cheesehead side, which could easily lead to real assholey-ness, like maybe trying to bust kids just minding their own business for picky stuff like curfew violations when there was some jerk holding up a store right around the corner. Which was probably why Dark Dog, or Jesse, was an *ex*-cop, trying to redeem himself by helping kids out.

It worked. It made perfect comic-book sense. He loved it!

Having come around to a new way of thinking, Tommy T paid a nighttime visit to The Den. "Are you there?" he inquired in his best stage whisper through the hidden hole in the river bluff. "Dark . . . or, whoever . . . are you there?"

"*Whoever?*" The voice was not disguised, and the chuckle seemed almost joyful. "Where've you been, Fox?"

"Where've *you* been?"

"Here and there. I had things to take care of, promises to tend to." After a pause: "People to find."

"Stoner?" Tommy T surged toward the hole, holding up just short of falling in. "You found Stoner?"

"He says his name's really Stony. Says your grandma named him after a TV cowboy."

"That's what they used to say." Jesus God, what a relief! Tommy T could hardly breathe, he was so glad. Thanks be to God and all the superpowers, his brother wasn't—the prospect he'd repeatedly x-ed out of his mind with a giant black mental marker—lying in a drawer in the morgue with a tag declaring him unknown, unloved, and unmissed. "Where'd you find him? Where is he?"

"He's okay. He's around."

"I wanna see him. Is he back—"

"No, but he's safe, and right now that's what counts. For now, you'll just have to take my word for it. You've got a place to stay, and he's got a place to stay. Which is good, Tommy T. Winter's comin' on."

He hugged himself, literally hugged himself to keep from jumping up and down. Plus, like Dark Dog said, it was getting cold. The breeze off the river felt almost frosty. "What about you?"

"What about me?"

"Doesn't it get cold down there?"

"I have the very best winter coat."

"Angela's been wondering, you know, if you're okay." No response. Above his head the night wind rattled the few leaves that were left on the trees. It was a lonely kind of a sound.

Tommy T cleared his throat. "A guy came lookin' for her. You know how scared she used to be? No cops, no hospitals, she said that first time. Well, this guy showed up, acting like he was hot shit, you know, he was gonna take her back with him, back to where she used to live before she came to us. I mean, you know . . . before she came *here*. But she stood right up to him, told him no way."

"Did he hurt her in any way?"

Whoa, Tommy T thought; sounded like that news had Dark Dog bristling some. "He didn't touch her. I'da ripped his face off if he tried."

"It's a good thing you were there, Little Fox."

"There's something else. She said we're not letting any drug dealers take over our building. She was talkin' like, who do we trust, trusting cops, maybe we could talk to Sergeant Richards and all like that. I don't know what's goin' on exactly, something about bad boys from out of town, but Angela's gotten to be pretty nervy lately. I don't want her stickin' her neck out too far. She still doesn't really understand about . . . that there are some guys around here who can just do innocent people without givin' a shit, you know?"

"Yeah, I know. So what did she say about trusting cops?"

"She thinks there's maybe one or two you might be able to trust, like, sometimes," he reported reluctantly. "But she's gotta say stuff like that to a kid. Did you know she was a teacher before she came here?"

"Do you trust teachers?"

"Sometimes. I trust Angela. She's gonna stay around here. She's gonna get a job teaching. Try to, anyway."

"That's good." There was a long silence. "Do you want to come down here and see where I live, Little Fox?"

Yo! Had he heard right? "Could I?" He had his feet through the hole before Dark Dog could change his mind. "Bit-chiin."

Tommy T dropped into The Den and stood up slowly, trying to get his eyes to adjust. When a warm hand claimed his, he realized there was going to be no light for his eyes to adjust to. "How do you see?" he asked as he stumbled along behind his hero like a beagle on a leash.

"You have to ask me that? I thought you knew."

"Well . . . sure."

"Good." His guide's chuckle echoed in the earthen passage. "I'm glad somebody does."

"Trouble is, I've been keeping, like, regular human hours lately. Lost my night vision."

A match flared, its light bobbing before his eyes. The flame doubled, then tripled. Dark Dog lit at least a dozen candles while Tommy T turned full circle, taking tiny, shuffling steps in the straw, examining every amazing detail of the mystical chamber that housed a superhero. It was perfect. He could not have dreamed it up any better. "This is so cool," he rhapsodized, wide-eyed. "This is *so cool*."

"You see me here, Little Fox. You know who I am, what I am. Just a simple man with a complicated problem." The big man offered him a hand-hewn stool. "Complicated, like most problems." He chuckled. "Simple, like most men."

"But I've seen you do stuff like . . ." Tommy T seated himself and looked at Dark Dog—in this place he was nobody else but Dark Dog, damn it—full in the face. No hat, no wolf pelt, no face paint. But the shadows helped. Okay, so maybe he did look a lot like Jesse Brown Wolf. "How do you explain the dogs?"

"I don't. Some things can't be explained, I guess."

"I guess." The boy spotted the wolf pelt lying on the bed and remembered the way he'd bargained with Grandpa Bird. He liked seeing it there on the bed, where Dark Dog slept. He liked the way the place smelled. Sage and sweet grass. He did a quarter turn on the stool and noted the willow chair, the cool wall hangings, the rocky shelves. "So who's in charge of me? You or Angela?"

"The judge didn't want to take you out of school. He could see that you were being fed and cared for. I've known him for a long time. He thought you and me might be good for each other." He folded his arms across his chest, took a real Batman pose. "So I took a cue from a fox I know and gave Angela's address as my own."

Tommy T grinned. "She's kinda gotten stuck with me, hasn't she?"

"I have a feeling if I actually tried to take you, she'd fight me for you."

The boy nodded consideringly, then grinned again. Jesse remembered the way he'd stood tall and presided over his mother's burial. A son to be proud of, and Jesse hoped somewhere, somehow, Ricki Little Warrior realized that. Some parents reaped what they'd sown with their kids. Others didn't have a clue what they'd been blessed with until it was too damn late. Or almost too late.

"You're in charge of yourself, Little Fox," Jesse said. "The judge knows it, I know it, and Angela knows it. If you wanted to go your brother's way, we couldn't stop you."

"You have to be with somebody. I mean, everybody does. Stoner hangs with his friends so he don't get pushed around, but still . . ."

"Still he's on the run."

Tommy T hung his head. "Maybe that's my fault."

"I don't think so."

"I don't wanna get pushed around, either. I don't like being scared. I don't like being cold and hungry. And I especially don't like it when somebody goes off and, like . . ." He bit his lip, bit off the accusation, then shook it off for good measure. "My mom was really trying to get it together this time. Somebody had to stick with her, just so she'd keep trying." He sighed and peered at Jesse, candle-flame shadows bobbing on his small face. "She must have been lost, you know? Out there on that road. She kept on losing her way."

Jesse nodded. "Happens to a lot of us."

"Yeah, well . . ." He sat up straight and looked Jesse in the eye. "You know what? It ain't gonna happen to me."

Not long ago, Jesse would have sneered automatically, but the boy had taken the edge off his cynicism, exposed it as a shroud for failure. It pricked him to be in the presence of a strong believer. It shamed him, remembering that he had been such a one himself once. It stirred him, too, in a way that he resented being stirred.

For if the damnable agitation kept up, it promised to move him just as surely as the pain did.

He came to her once again on the murky plain of dreams. She'd heard nothing, of course. As always, he made no sound. He had not come to her this way in some time, not to her home, her bedroom. He greeted her with a kiss, and she put her arms around his neck and kissed him back, trying to draw herself up to him or draw him down to her, but he hovered there, his arms braced on either side of her, blissfully trading kiss for kiss with her.

"I've missed you," she whispered as she unzipped his jacket and snuggled inside, inhaling the cold-night-air smell of him that she loved so well.

"You know where I live. You could have found me there."

"Who would I find?" She took his face in her hands, her fingertips prizing its cold, chiseled contours. "I haven't seen Jesse, either. Nobody has, and I've missed him, too."

"Jesse," he said as he harrowed her hair with friendly fingers. "Jesse saw his daughter for the first time in years, told her he loved her. Saw his ex-wife, made his feeble apologies. Not that he hadn't done all that before, but it didn't mean much before, coming from a man who was incapable of feeling any of it."

"And now he's capable?"

"He wants to be."

"And you?" She sighed when he laid his cool forehead against hers, and she wondered whether his head hurt and he sought balm, or whether it was simply tired and he sought rest. "I seem to be in love with two men," she said sadly.

"And you're a one-man woman." He touched his open lips to hers and fed her of the breath his body had warmed.

"That's right," she whispered into his mouth.

He leaned back, his hands rubbing her shoulders. "Pick one."

"I don't think it'll work that way. I need both." The last thing she wanted to do was drive him away. She swallowed hard, rackingly loud. "I need both at the same time."

His hands stilled. "One lives in the dark, the other in the light."

"I need all of you, all the time, day and night." She slid her hands over the backs of his and held them tight. "Don't come to me without Jesse. I'm a greedy woman, and I want all of you, *all of you*. Complete and whole."

23

This wasn't the first time Jesse had been offered more pay for less work, but it had been years since he had allowed himself to sample so damn much bait. Lately he couldn't seem to say no. This time it wasn't Angela asking him, at least not directly, but he had to do something to keep her from sticking her neck out any further than she already had. If he didn't take the bait, or become the bait himself, from what Tommy T had told him, he figured sooner or later Angela would.

What Tommy T didn't know was that with help from Police Sergeant Mike Richards, who was obviously looking for some kind of medal, Angela and Darlene had cooked up a scheme supposedly guaranteed to rid their building of "drug-dealing vermin," as the two women had dubbed the team of suppliers who had set up their little candy store on two occasions now. Richards had told them that the whole building could be confiscated by the city if it was being used for drug trafficking. And he'd told them that the city had been known to make residential property available for purchase for special projects like the one they had in mind—a shelter for homeless kids.

That was all those two needed to hear. Richards knew it, and he'd laid it on pretty thick with Jesse. He could just see them buying into some Hollywood notion that it was their duty as good citizens to play undercover cops. Darlene's sister, another bait sampler who must have earned her kid back several times over by now, was on deck again to make a drug buy, and it had been hinted that Angela and Darlene might be part of some sting-operation batting order, too, if they wanted to inject a little excitement into their lives.

Jesse didn't like any of it, and he'd let Richards know exactly what he thought of letting the women—and, by extension, their children—get involved in anything so blatantly risky. Naturally, Richards had nailed him with, "You sure talk big for somebody's who's bowed out and gone under."

So Jesse had been goaded, good and proper. He was ripe for it after the trip back home. He'd gone knocking at Lila's door expecting nothing but trouble, but he'd gone with his hat in hand and his head held high. He figured the latter to be the part that surprised her. The last time she'd seen him, he could barely lift his head. He'd never told her much about his headaches. The worst of his behavior, all the drinking and brawling and howling he'd stooped to, was not as disgusting to him then as the paralyzing pain he'd been trying to mask.

Not that he'd been any too successful. Pain? she'd quipped. Did he think he was the only one who hurt? She'd show him pain. The last time he'd seen her, she'd laid into him with a stick of firewood. Between the two of them, they'd sustained more agony than one household could accommodate. Something, someone, had had to go. Jesse had hit the road.

And then there was Monica. The last time he'd seen his daughter, he'd found it impossible to look her in the eye. The pain had worked its way deeper, from his head to his heart. He'd been afraid to touch her. He'd had no words. As a father, he was a complete washout. There had been nothing he could do to dispel the nightmares, for they'd owned him then, too. But even though his throat burned terribly, this time his tongue was not too thick to allow him to speak to her from his heart. This time when he took her in his arms and wept with her, he was not blind drunk. This time he actually saw her tears, and he was not ashamed of his own.

And so he was ready to do a little volunteer police work. No badge, no gun. He was acting on a hint from his sometime employer, property manager Don Morrison. A hint, a hunch, and a prayer.

Like Jesse Brown Wolf, Don Morrison worked in one world, lived in another, and took pains to keep the two completely separate from each other. Each man had carved out a river-bluff hideaway. Jesse had used his hands. Morrison had used only a small part of his considerable fortune to build his half-million-dollar house overlooking the Mississippi River. Few outsiders had visited either place, for both hideaways harbored secrets.

Unlike Jesse, Morrison really wanted to show his place off more, but he generally resisted the temptation. He welcomed the opportunity to make an exception when Jesse showed up at the door. Jesse had been there before, but he'd never been invited inside. Morrison had thrown a lot of work his way in the past several years. Jesse did the job efficiently, thoroughly, and always made sure he got paid. He was no pushover, and Morrison respected that, along with his resourcefulness, and he'd said as much. He'd told Jesse that he could come up with more lucrative work for an efficient, resourceful, reserved employee like himself. All he had to do was say the word.

"You said your family would be gone this weekend," Jesse reminded Morrison when he stepped inside the door. "I figured this would be a good time to start on that wall you were talking about taking out." He surveyed the clean lines of the soft-contemporary-style home's spacious, sunlit foyer, lifted his brow appreciatively. "And maybe talk about a job that pays a little more than what I've been pullin' in."

Morrison's black eyes brightened in the way of an angler feeling the first sign of a tug on his line. "Looking to better yourself, Jesse?" With a grand gesture he directed Jesse though a pair of French doors, which took him into an impressive office, all done up in oak and hunter green, richly scented with cedar and leather. The duck and bird-dog prints, the gun case, and the cherry-wood humidor proclaimed the room's masculinity. Jesse made no bones about getting an eyeful, and Morrison fairly glowed with satisfaction.

"I'd like to own a house, a car, maybe a few acres of land," Jesse said.

"You won't get that as a handyman." Morrison lifted the humidor lid, but Jesse shrugged off the offer of a cigar. "Or even as a property manager," he said as he closed the box. "Certainly not if you're working for somebody as cheap as Ed Hickey. But the thing is, Hickey owns the kind of property worth managing."

He opened the cabinet behind the desk and pulled out two cut crystal glasses. "You've heard the expression 'Location, location, location'? That's what makes a piece of real estate valuable. If you want to be a man of property, you've gotta know those things. Now, you and I would not want to live in one of Hickey's buildings."

With a raised palm Jesse declined the offer of a drink from any of the bottles on display in the cabinet. Morrison made a selection for himself. "What's the matter? You don't see your brand?"

Jesse chuckled and shook his head. "Nobody purposely stocks my brand, which is why I decided to just kick the habit altogether."

"There's a lot to be said for clear thinking." Morrison poured himself two fingers of bourbon. "Where do you live, by the way?"

"Near the river," Jesse said. "It's nothing like this, of course, but it's near the river."

Morrison took visible pleasure in showing Jesse his own riv-
erfront property. The wall he was planning to remove was in the
lower walk-out level. Jesse instinctively took account of the fact
that it was not a load-bearing wall and wondered how the studs
were anchored. He glanced at Morrison, who seemed to be
amused. Amusement turned to amazement when he introduced a
pair of Dobermans in the kennel just beyond the sliding door. A
few quiet words from Jesse, and they were as docile as lapdogs.

"Is that some kind of Indian trick?"

Jesse smiled.

Morrison led the way to the four-car garage and showed off
the BMW that would spend the winter stored in his garage, away
from Minneapolis's heavily salted streets. He could afford a hotter
car, he told Jesse, but he didn't want to be too conspicuous a
consumer. He was, after all, only a property manager. An honest,
hard-working yuppie, proud owner of a symbol of yuppie
achievement.

They returned to the office. Jesse peered into the gun case,
affording Morrison the excuse to snap the interior light on. The
other trappings of his success obviously gratified the man, but
here, clearly, was his passion. Morrison had a weapon for every
form of prey. Carbines and rifles, handsome oiled stocks, custom-
ized actions, elephant-stopping calibers.

"I don't know how conspicuous this is. Most people don't
know much about the value of guns, you know? They think, Yeah,
firepower, cool. Or they think, Dangerous, don't touch. Either
way, most people don't appreciate the beauty." He opened the
unlocked case and removed a highly polished, well-used antique.
"Look at this. Is this a beauty?"

It was a turn-of-the-century, military-issue Springfield rifle.
Jesse recognized it because his uncle had hunted with one he'd
inherited from *his* uncle. Morrison generously offered to let him
hold it. He shook his head. "How old are your kids?" Jesse wondered offhandedly.

"I know what you're getting at. I've taught both my kids how to handle a gun, how to protect themselves. My wife, too. You never know. Some of the people I deal with..." He shook his head as he put the rifle back in its place and reached for a nondescript A-bolt rifle. "You just don't know these days. Now, here's one that has a history. This gun has killed three people. One accidental shooting, one suicide, and one actual intruder."

"Guns don't kill people," Jesse recited with an empty smile. "People kill people."

"Yeah, right. Guns don't speak, either." Morrison rubbed the stock affectionately. "This one does. I mean, think about it. Three notches. See, I put the notches on it myself, even though the kills weren't mine." He fingered the three grooves in the stock. "I'm just fascinated by the history of the thing. You hold it in your hand, and you can feel the history. The story this thing has to tell. Think fast, boy!" He tossed the weapon. Jesse made a reflexive catch. "Can you feel it? That life-and-death history. One minute they're breathing and talking, just like you and me; the next, they're history."

"Yeah." *Play the man's game,* Jesse told himself as he automatically checked the magazine for ammunition. *He's just blowing hot air. He doesn't know history from the price of a loaf of bread.* He managed a distant tone. "Yeah, I can."

"You know guns. There's nothing timid about the way you handle them."

"I was in the Army." Jesse glanced up. The man had checked him out. The satisfaction of his advantage burned in his eyes. "I was also a cop."

Morrison nodded. "Why did you quit?"

"I think you know that I quit being a cop to become a drunk. What you don't know is why I quit being a drunk." Morrison lifted a brow, inviting the explanation. "Because I didn't like cheap booze, and I couldn't afford the good stuff."

"Fair enough." Morrison continued to scrutinize him, as though what Jesse said interested him less than the way he said it. "You'd like to have money for the good stuff?"

"The good life," Jesse said, surveying his surroundings appreciatively for good measure while Morrison poured himself another drink. "The house, the car, the land. Seems like hard work can only pull a guy up so far, only get him so much." He lifted one shoulder as he moved closer to the display of photographs on the credenza. "I ain't greedy, but I am lookin' for a little more than what I got."

"And you should have it."

Jesse surveyed the family pictures, exhibited in leather frames. A boy and a girl at various stages of childhood, both smiling, both innocent, both seemingly happy. How was that possible for the progeny of a drug dealer? His wife was attractive, but she was no glamorous babe. Did she know what her husband really did for a living? Were the diamond earrings and pendant a gift he'd bought her with crack money? Jesse remembered what it felt like to put a man in handcuffs in front of his wife and kids. *Don't be home that day*, he silently told the photographs.

A rumpled pencil sketch lay beside a group portrait of the Morrison family. Jesse's gut clenched at the sight of the white paper. "Nice family," he said casually. "Who's the artist? One of the kids?"

"My kids are musicians, both of them. My daughter plays piano and sings like a pro. She'll be onstage at the Ordway one of these days. But neither one of them goes in for drawing." Morrison tapped a finger on the paper. "This kid is quite an artist."

This kid. Tommy T's face flashed in Jesse's brain, and his heart thudded wildly. *Quite an artist* was an understatement. Quite a fox, quite a fixer, quite a friend.

How close are you? How much do you know about him? "Your kids' friend?"

"No way. My kids don't even live in the same world." Morrison chortled into his glass, sipped, then shook his head. "No, but that's actually a very good likeness of two guys who work for me. I'm thinking about replacing this one." He pointed to Gayla's ex-boyfriend, Keith. "The other one's just some street kid. Somebody I wouldn't even know except for this little gem. They took this sketch off some kid. Then they lost the kid, whose friends are telling us now that he's not the artist. It's his younger brother. Whoever it is, it's just a matter of time, you know. They love to ice snitches. It's the best part of their game."

"Kids' games just ain't what they used to be," Jesse said, collecting himself, holding himself on a tight rein.

"You use these kids only as long as they're useful. When their time is up, you sic one bunch on the other. They shoot it out. When the smoke clears, you see who's left standing, you got your new runners." Morrison drained his glass, set it down next to the sketch, and smiled. "Works like a charm."

"You want me to replace this guy?" Jesse singled out Keith in the drawing.

"He's a junkie. He's not dependable." The man looked at Jesse as though he were sizing him up for some kind of fit. "You've been working for me for a long time. You mind your own business, do your job, and make damn sure you get what's coming to you. A guy like you, with your ambitions and where you're located, you're going to waste."

"And I'm tired of being wasted."

"Then let's do something about it." Morrison sat on the front edge of his desk, arms folded, looking for all the world like the benevolent patron he fancied himself. "How would you like to supervise your own territory?"

Jesse smiled. "I like to piss on a fire hydrant as much as the next guy."

"You still got something going with one of the tenants in the apartment house on Eighteenth?"

Jesse's heart tripped into overdrive. How could Morrison know about him and Angela? Nobody knew. Not even him and Angela.

"The one you paid the rent for to keep her from getting evicted," Morrison recalled with a man-to-man smile. "Being an enterprising man, you either had something going with her or you got your money back in trade on that deal. Am I right?"

A deep chuckle was Jesse's only response.

"The thing is, you want to be very careful what kind of deals you make for yourself. You know what I'm saying? You do the kind of work that gives you a reason to walk into a school, hospital, rental property, you name it. Places where my business thrives. You're like an independent contractor, which is perfect," Morrison allowed smoothly. "But independence doesn't pay well. I pay well." His eyes were full of dark but glittery promises. "Are you interested?"

"That's why I'm here."

"Good." Morrison extended his hand.

Jesse steeled himself against his aversion to touching snakes and shook it.

"Now, we've got a couple of tenants in the Eighteenth Street house we want to encourage to move on, and that woman with all the kids we're talking about is one of them." Morrison gave him a sly look. "Any of them yours?"

"Hell, no."

"Not that you know of, right?" Morrison laughed. "Anyway, I hope you won't miss her too much. Neighborhood activists call too much attention to the property. We don't want that. So I've got plans to relocate her. I expect the one upstairs to clear out on her own, soon as she wakes up and smells the coffee. You know her, too, don't you?"

"I've done some work up there," Jesse said evenly. "You know that."

"You looked after her pretty well, too, as I recall. Fixed everything up just right at her place." Morrison grinned. "How was she?"

"Hell, I ain't *that* damned enterprising."

"That's what I like about you people. So modest and humble." Morrison laughed and slapped him on the back. "Which is exactly what I'm looking for. Somebody who's practically invisible. You handle the money and the merchandise and keep the kids in line."

"When do I start?" Receipt of the goods was crucial.

"I'll be in touch. I'm gonna have to personally introduce you to my supplier. Trouble is . . ." Morrison squeezed his shoulder and rocked him back and forth as though they were trading locker room gags. "All I've got for Jesse Brown Wolf on my Rolodex is a P.O. box. You got a car, right?" Jesse nodded. He had access to a car, courtesy of the Minneapolis Police Department. "You're gonna need a phone."

Jesse nodded again and smiled as he spoke into the tiny microphone embedded in one of the buttons on his shirt. "I was thinkin' cellular."

Jesse met Mike Richards at a marina in Brooklyn Park. It was after dark, and the place was closed for the season. There was no one else around. The two men leaned against the hood of Mike's Toyota, suburban lights winking at them from the far shore as the waters of the Mississippi rolled past them into the night.

"What's the verdict on the tape?" Jesse asked.

"It's a good start." Mike lit a cigarette, turning to Jesse after he'd expelled the first lungful of smoke. "You're gonna see it through, aren't you?"

As long as Richards stuck to his end of the deal. "What about Angela and the boy? What kind of protection are you offering for them?"

"I've picked Chopper up twice in a week. Haven't been able to hold him. You need to keep Tommy T off the streets, especially at night." Richards glanced away, dragging his jacket zipper up to his chin against the late-autumn chill. "Maybe you should send him back to the rez for a while, just to be on the safe side."

"The kid's trying to go to school, Mike. He's got a place to live now. He's trying to live like a normal twelve-year-old. Who knows how long it's gonna take you to get this mess cleared up?" The thought of sending the boy away made him lock his jaw for a moment while he glared at the policeman. "Huh? When will he be safe?"

"You know the answer to that."

"You damn well better tell me when they're gonna bust that house," Jesse said quietly.

"That operation is completely independent of what we've got goin' here, Jesse. You don't—"

"I wanna know when it's goin' down so I can be sure they're out of the way. I strapped on that wire for you guys. Now you gotta give me at least that much."

"Narcotics has its own timetable." Richards stretched his hands out in front of him. The night swallowed up everything but the cigarette and his wedding band. "They like to spread that net out just right, jerk it in when they're ready, and make the evening news with a nice, big haul." He made a clucking sound in his cheek as he demonstrated the motion. Then he took a quick drag on his smoke and spat it out with a sigh. "Look here, I'm just a cop on the street. They don't tell me nothin'. You'll probably know before I do."

"That house is full of kids."

Richards gestured, frustrated. "Hell, they all are."

"You guys, you set this stuff up, you don't care who—"

"What do you mean, *you guys?*" He tapped Jesse's chest with the back of his hand. "It's *us* guys, Jesse. You're back in it now, with both feet. Not that you haven't had one foot in it all along, looking out for the kids the way you do."

"If you're stepping in shit, ain't gonna matter much whether it's one boot or two," Jesse said wearily.

"You got that right." Richards gave a short laugh.

Jesse wasn't amused. "I want to get those women and kids out of that house before that deal goes down. They won't know what's going on. They won't be tippin' anybody off."

Richards puffed on his cigarette. He was a man who didn't like to promise anything he couldn't deliver. "I'll see what I can find out."

*   *   *

319

Angela came awake slowly. She could feel his presence in the room, smell his woodsy scent. She curtailed her own breathing and listened hard for the sound of his. It was a challenge, pitting her senses against his silence. Finally she gave up on the game and turned over. He was a shadow heaped in the chair near her bed like a pile of laundry, just waiting for her to notice, to remember.

"Jesse?"

"He's comin' along," he whispered, his voice drifting closer. The bedsprings squeaked as he seated himself next to her. "He's comin' along."

"What's that supposed to mean?" She scooted toward him. "He seems to have disappeared."

"No, he hasn't." He reached for her and drew her into his lap. "I love you, Angela."

The words washed over her like a desperately needed warm shower. Every muscle in her body came alive, aching, at once stretching out and threatening to snap back. She groaned. "Who loves me?"

His laugh was a deep, sensuous tickle in her ear. "Who loves you, baby?" he teased in a passable impersonation of Telly Savalas.

"Be serious."

"I've *been* serious. I've been down-to-earth dead serious for so damn . . ." With unsteady fingers he raked the bramble of her hair back from her face. "I love you, Angela."

Oh, how she wanted to believe he could truly be whole enough to love. Lovingly she touched his temple. "How are the headaches?"

"What headaches?"

"They're gone?"

"No, but they're not as bad." He drew her hand to his lips and kissed the tips of her fingers. "I can deal with them. They don't scare me as bad as they used to. They don't . . ." He sighed. "Hell, I don't have to live and die by the pain in my head, do I?"

"I hope not, because . . . I love you, too." And love was an emotion to be acted on. She slipped her arms around him and held him close. "What are we going to do?"

"Move in together?" He rubbed one hand over her back in big, soothing circles and gave a mischievous chuckle. "Your place or mine?"

"Mine's about to be taken over by drug dealers unless we do something pretty quick. I've been trying to tell Mike Richards—"

His hand stilled. "Let Mike do his job, Angela."

"I could at least try to find out when our new neighbors are going away again. If they were planning on going away for a weekend, that would be a sure tip-off, wouldn't it?"

"Yes, it would," he said quietly, running his hands slowly up her back. "It would put your name at the top of the bad guys' list. And then, no choice, you'd have to move in with me."

"It must be getting pretty cold in your—"

"I'll keep you warm."

"I knew you'd say that."

"You know I'd do it, too." He leaned back, taking her face in his warm, callused hands. "Don't try to play cop, Angela. It's too dangerous. The important thing for you to do right now is to look out for Tommy T. He can't be wandering around on the streets, not even during the day. Not until they get Chopper out of circulation."

"I need another bedroom," she told him, purposely, stubbornly, changing the subject. "For the kids. For Tommy T, and for who knows who else I might take in."

"Do you take in stray dogs?"

"I take them straight in for their shots first." She pinched his thigh through his jeans.

"Hey, I like that." He nipped the side of her neck. "Was that rabies or distemper?"

"That's the new one for fleas. Now, if you've got temper problems, that cure goes . . ." She slid her hand into his back pocket.

"Oh, yeah, better give me the complete treatment if you want to domesticate me."

"I do," she said, shifting on his lap, straddling him as she reached around him to slip her other hand into his other pocket. "I've got all kinds of plans for you. Breeding you, for example, gifted stud that you are."

He chuckled. "Are we talking offspring by the litter now?"

"I'm talking family. Lots of family." She sighed wishfully. "I wonder if I could get Jesse to knock out a wall for me."

"You could get Jesse to do anything for you. He feels the same way I do, but he has a hard time showing it." He kissed her gently, his lips eagerly teasing hers. "I've got all the charm."

She smiled against his mouth. "You told me once that you had no feelings."

"That was when I was just a dream."

"Who are you now?" she demanded, even though the only answer she really wanted was a physical one, a response to the bittersweet ache deep between her legs.

"You want to go on dreaming, Angela?" He nuzzled her neck, then licked her like an affectionate pup. She shivered when he whispered against the damp spot he'd made. "Dream me loving you again."

"I've been dreaming of you loving me as Jesse," she said. "Together in this bed on a lazy afternoon. No hurrying, no worrying. Doesn't that sound dreamy?"

"Dreamy." He lifted his head, squaring his shoulders on a deep sigh. "Like I said, Jesse's comin' along. Gettin' it together, piece by piece."

"Tommy T says it's Fox's job to put the pieces back together."

"So the story goes. I think love is the glue." He brushed her hair back and touched his lips to her forehead. "Don't do anything crazy, Angela."

"I can't," she said, giggling. "You're sitting on my hands."

"Mmm, so I am." He brushed his mouth over her eyebrow and whispered, "Trust me, okay? Believe in me. I'm pretty damn sure love is the glue."

"Don't bark, okay? Do not make a sound." Tommy T clutched Stevie under one arm, using his hand as a moderately effective muzzle. The dog wiggled and whined softly. "Damn, I wish Dark Dog was here. He'd make you be quiet. 'Course, if he was here, we wouldn't be hiding."

He peered cautiously over the back of the old sofa that served as porch furniture for a neighbor on the next block, who didn't appear to be home. The house was as dark and quiet as the street. Chopper and one of his flunkies were heading across the street, just passing through a pool of streetlamp light. "Okay, okay, they're gone now. Ready to run like hell?"

The dog was ready. As soon as Tommy T relaxed his arm, she leaped to the porch, pulling her leash taut. Together they hopped off the side of the porch and took to the shadows, bounding from yard to yard. Nearing home, they took a roundabout approach, heading for the side door.

But someone else had gotten there first. Two strange men. The late-model Explorer parked in the alley had to be theirs. It didn't belong to anyone Tommy T knew. What was more surprising, they used a key to get into the house. *His* house, the one he shared with Angela and Darlene, the kids, the old folks down the hall. *His house.*

Tommy T watched the entire proceedings from his position behind the backyard retaining wall. "Look at that. That ain't the Mickels, is it? No way." Stevie was back under his armpit, squirming and muzzled. "It's those guys Angela was talkin' about. They're ba-ack," Tommy T sang softly. Not that this was a singing matter. It was just that it was predictable. It was the way things seemed to go. Just when you thought it was safe to make a mad dash home, and you made it, and you thought you were home free . . .

"Okay, so what do we do? Go get Dark Dog? We might not make it, Stevie. Chopper's lookin' to roast my ass, and he'd probably make dog jerky out of you." Stevie whimpered. "So we just tell Angela when she gets home, right?" The dog's back legs churned against his jacket like an eggbeater. "Then she sticks her neck way out there and tries to blow that whistle she wears around her neck, huh? That's not good. Maybe not *really* blow the whistle, but, like, go down there, go to the door, and . . ." And what? "And try to do something, and all hell would bust loose, probably."

And probably explode in the faces of innocent people, he decided as he watched another stranger approach the side door to his home. *His* home, damn it, the first real home he'd had in a long time. He wasn't about to give it over to a bunch of punks dealing drugs. There was a light on in the Dexters' window, but they were just old guys. Leave them out of it. The windows at Darlene's place were dark. No help there.

"Who the hell are those . . ." Two young women were trotting up behind the man, who'd reached the side door. "I don't like this, Stevie. If Angela sees this . . ." Actually, he wasn't quite sure what she'd do, but she'd for sure do something. Call the cops, probably. Get herself hurt, possibly. He'd rather have Dark Dog on the case than the cops. "We gotta pick her up, get her home, take her through the front door, hustle her upstairs, and then . . ." Then what? "Get her watching TV with us. Soon as she falls asleep, we get Dark Dog."

Jesse had two plans to follow—Morrison's and Lieutenant Breyer's. He'd been skeptical about both from the outset, and Breyer's had already failed. Breyer was a poker-up-his-ass nar- cotics officer whose plan was to put a tail on Jesse's car, but the tail was either very good or very lost. Jesse was betting on the latter.

Morrison's plan was to lead Jesse down the garden path— actually a network of river roads—meet up with a nameless some- body who would be Jesse's contact, and get him started in his new job. His function would be to transport the two things Mor- rison did not want to be caught with—cash and crack. This was to be the critical meeting, the introduction of a new man, a new contact for the supplier. As the new man, Jesse had not been told where the meeting would take place, so he had to follow Morri- son's car. He had yet to prove himself. It was takeoff time, the moment of greatest uncertainty in any flight. This would be the one and only time the three links in the supply chain would ever meet face-to-face.

This was the time to catch the key players with the goods.

They met at a public campground that was closed for the win- ter season. It didn't surprise Jesse that Morrison had a key to the gate. He had contacts in every corner of the city's woodwork.

There were no wires this time. No radio, no telephone calls en route. Too risky. They were operating in a complete blackout, so that nothing could be traced. They emerged from their separate cars, Jesse ostensibly taking his cues from Don Morrison, whose sleek black Dobermans piled out of his car behind him. "My in- surance policy," he told Jesse as he wrapped the double-lead chain around his gloved hand. "Everybody agrees no guns, but you know they're packin' something somewhere. Thing is, they don't like dogs. They'll act like it's nothing, but they've got a healthy respect for dogs."

Jesse approached the big, lean dogs confidently. Each in turn stretched its neck to take a sniff of his palm. Satisfied, each in its turn permitted him to pet the top of its head. A sign of complete submission. Coyote was the alpha male, the one who dominated.

"Actually, the dogs seem to have quite a healthy respect for you," Morrison said. The acknowledgment pleased Jesse, since Morrison didn't know the half of it. "I've never seen them act like that before. They generally don't let anybody come near them except me and the trainer I got them from."

Jesse leaned over and spoke to the dogs quietly. They lay down immediately, looking to him for approval. "That's amazing," Morrison said, a hint of uncertainty creeping into his voice.

Jesse jammed his hands into his jacket pockets and shrugged. "I like dogs. They can always tell."

"Must be an Indian thing." Morrison was studying him curiously. "Some primitive sensitivity to the, uh . . . what language was that you used?"

Jesse glanced up, gave a brief smile. "Primitive gibberish, brother to brother. You're right, it's an Indian thing."

"Ever thought about becoming a dog handler? You know what I paid to have these guys trained for . . ." He eyed the dogs in their prone positions. "Christ, you'd never know they were trained to kill. But one word from me and they'd have you on the ground."

"Really." A set of headlights swung around the last curve, illuminating the ground fog that drifted over the numbered campsites. "Here comes your friend," Jesse said, turning his face from the light until it blinked off. Both car doors slammed. "Two friends."

"Let's see you handle them the way you handled those dogs."

"It all works on the same principle," Jesse muttered as he watched the two amble over as though they were out for a stroll.

"Hey, man." The taller of the two stopped short when the dogs suddenly popped up like slices of toast. The shorter one, who was carrying a gym bag, piled into his buddy from behind. In the dark, Jesse couldn't tell much about either face. "What's up, man? You takin' your dogs for a walk?"

"I don't like dogs," the shorter man grumbled. "Tell him to put those dogs back in the car."

"No problem," Jesse said, taking the leash from Morrison. "I'll put them in my car." A quiet word and a subtle hand signal gained their full attention. "Come on, guys, get in the back." He shooed them through the open door. He leaned in after them, taking a moment to roll the window down a couple of inches and speak to them, brother to brothers, while in the darkness his hand worked subtly to unhook the leash.

"Jesus," Morrison muttered. Then he turned to the pair he'd come to do business with, who were clearly relieved when they heard the car door close. "Jesse's got a way with dogs. You see why he's the new man. I've had my eye on him for years. Very quiet, very careful, does what he's told. Jesse, this is Fred and BJ. They've got something for you."

Fred was the bagman, and BJ was the tall dude. There would be no last names. Jesse wasn't particularly eager to let these two get a look at his face, but he knew that was part of the procedure. He had the home-court advantage. They had a vast network of people who owed one another some kind of debt, people who were closer than blood relations. It was loyalty based on cold-sweat fear. Everywhere these guys went, they had backup.

"I sent Keith over to Eighteenth Street," Morrison told BJ as he handed Jesse his car keys. "He thinks he's gonna be in on that setup. You got somebody waiting for him?"

"Keith's a dead man." BJ signaled for Fred to hand him the gym bag and follow Jesse to Morrison's car. "You'll be one boy short before the night's over."

Jesse returned with the zippered cash bag Morrison had

tucked under the front seat of the car. BJ satisfied himself that the feel of the cash was right, then transferred the gym bag to Morrison, who handed it off to Jesse like a hot potato.

"They gonna do him there at the house?" Morrison asked as casually as he might inquire about a plan to fix Keith up with somebody's sister.

"They'll probably handle it like a drive-by so it looks like local retaliation. No connection to anybody we know."

"Kinda makes it bad for that location on Eighteenth, if you wanna keep using it," Jesse said, a plan forming in his mind. He couldn't count on anybody finding him at this point.

"Using it for a little distraction right now," Morrison said. "Give the cops something to occupy themselves with while we teach you the ropes."

"Let's see if I've got it right so far." Jesse took the gym bag to his car, where he was supposed to stash it in the wheel housing. Through the cracked window he spoke quietly to the dogs, who acknowledged him with acquiescent whines. Then he opened the back door.

"Fuck, don't let those dogs—"

Morrison tried every command in the book, but the dogs already had their orders. Three dogs to three humans. From Jesse's perspective, the odds were excellent. Canine tenacity predated human sin.

The tall man made the mistake of trying to run. One of the Dobermans flew at his back, knocked him to the ground, and began shredding his down jacket. White fluff billowed like milk froth.

"Get him off me! Get him off!"

Fred froze in his tracks, gaping in horror.

"He likes the taste of you," Jesse told BJ. "Tell you what, I'm gonna open up the trunk of Don's car, and you can—" Dog number two interrupted Jesse's plan with a vicious snarl at his former master. "Don't move, Don," Jesse warned. "That dog is trained to kill."

"Not me, you sonuvabitch," Morrison shouted. The dog snapped at Morrison's flailing hand, pulled off his leather glove, and flung it into the air.

"That language is not particularly offensive to him, Don. Just don't move. You move and he'll go for—" Jesse wheeled when he sensed movement. "You!"

Fred was trying to slip his hand behind his back. Jesse signaled the dog that was busy ripping his shrieking buddy apart. Instantly the Doberman was in Fred's face.

"No! No! Down!"

Jesse moved in to disarm the bagman. With a whistle he signaled the dogs to back off. "I thought we were having a friendly get-acquainted meeting here," he said, feigning shock as he palmed Fred's pistol. "Is this any way to meet and greet an unarmed man?"

"You're a dead man, Morrison." BJ pushed himself up to his hands and knees. Blood and drool drained into the grass. "Where'd you get this crazy—"

"He's the one who's a dead man," Morrison said, still pinned against his car by his own dog.

"You gentlemen get such a charge out of pronouncing people dead, you oughta become coroners. Now nobody's dead yet, but these dogs . . ." Jesse chuckled as he shoved Morrison's key into the lock and opened the trunk. "I'm telling you, a dog attack is not the way I'd personally choose to go. They're carnivores, you know. You'll be safe in the trunk." He pointed the pistol at the man on the ground, who moved a little faster when the slavering Doberman snarled again. Jesse waved the pistol at cowering Fred. "You, too."

Fred eyed the dog as he shuffled past, stupidly jerking his arms up in response to snapping teeth. "I hate dogs."

"The feeling's mutual," Jesse assured him. The two men wadded themselves up and crammed themselves into the trunk of Morrison's car. "Here, if you folks need a little diversion in here, feel free to indulge," Jesse said as he dropped the gym bag between them. "The hit's on Don. He's already paid the bill."

Another growl accompanied more gnashing of canine teeth. "Told you not to move, Don," Jesse said as he slammed the trunk shut.

"What do you want?" Morrison's pleading felt like a sweet tickle in Jesse's side. "Take the cash. Don't leave it on them, hey. It's all yours, my compliments. Just put it in your pocket and disappear."

"I could if I wanted to, couldn't I? But the problem is—" Jesse was on the move, but now that he had the upper hand, he found himself enjoying the chit-chat. "I told you a little white lie, Don. Fact is, money doesn't mean much to me."

He reached for the fancy phone in the well-used car the Department had provided and punched in the numbers. "Yeah, this is Brown Wolf." He was feeling downright cocky, and he couldn't help smiling. "My tail seems to have lost me."

"They didn't want to get too close, and they blew it," Breyer admitted at the other end of the line.

Jesse gave the narcotics officer his location. "I've got two boys and their goods in the trunk of a Chrysler LeBaron. Nice-size trunk, but they're big boys, and I doubt if they're leaving each other much air." He glanced at Morrison. "And then I've got my boss here, squatting next to the car with two dogs salivating over him."

"What dogs?"

"His own dogs. He must not treat 'em right, 'cause they're ready to rip into his belly and chew on his bowels. And I've gotta be someplace else right now, so I suggest you get your people over here."

"You stay right there, Brown Wolf," Breyer shouted in his ear. "You stay there and hold—"

"These dogs ain't lettin' him go anywhere anytime soon." He smiled again as the mere shifting of Morrison's foot set the dogs off. Morrison wailed. They'd drawn blood from his ankle. "Maybe never."

But Jesse spoke to the dogs once again before he took off, just to make sure.

Angela could tell that something was up. Tommy T was early. He stood outside the café, shivering, because he couldn't bring Stevie inside, but he wasn't budging from the premises without her. She told Deacon that she couldn't stay until closing. He wasn't happy, but he knew she'd been looking for another job, and he was going to be even less happy about losing her. To his surprise, she'd turned out to be "one damn good little waitress."

"This is the last time I'm covering this shift," she told Tommy T as they walked away from the café. "Absolutely the last time."

He nodded, glancing up at her, then down at Stevie trotting ahead of them. Obviously he had a problem, and he wasn't sure how to broach it. They walked briskly, their misty puffs of breath coming faster after a couple of blocks. Tommy T kept stealing furtive glances over his shoulder, around every seemingly quiet corner, behind every denuded bush.

"Is someone—"

"Maybe we should go to a movie tonight, huh?"

"A movie?" She gave him a *Get real* glance. "It's pretty late for a movie. Besides, I'm beat."

"Well . . . when we get home, let's make some popcorn right away and watch that Jim Carrey movie again on the new VCR," he proposed eagerly.

"Okay." She cut him a glance. She knew there was more.

He offered a tight smile. "How did your interview with the schoolboard people go?"

"Very, *very* well. Mrs. Garrett was telling me that there are two teachers who say they're leaving at semester time. First and third grades. I've taught both those grades, plus I have a major in French, which would qualify me for the French immersion program if a spot opens up there. Mrs. Garrett thinks I have an excellent chance. Oh, I'm so excited," she chirped, hooking her arm around Tommy T's neck for a quick squeeze as they walked.

Stevie growled.

"Oh, yes, you get one, too," she said, reaching for the dog. Tommy T started to hand her the leash.

But Stevie wasn't looking for affection. The dog jerked the leash mid-handoff, dragging it behind her as she went bobbing down the sidewalk and darted out of sight.

"Stevie!"

Tommy T raced after her. Angela picked up her pace, determined to keep him in sight. He turned a corner and disappeared behind a yard fence. She caught up with him in a dark driveway. His shoulders were heaving from his run as he assumed a high-noon stance, facing down some threat that lurked in the shadows. Stevie yapped her head off. Angela moved in, and the shadows separated.

Chopper was standing on the dog's leash. "Too bad I got rid of Hog. He liked these little fluffy ones. Especially—"

"Give me my dog," Angela said. Loose gravel scraped against the pitted driveway beneath her shoes. She stood shoulder to shoulder with Tommy T, *her* Tommy T. Purposefully she peered through the shadows at the big moon face. This was not just a kid. "I'm not about to play games with you, Chopper. Move your foot."

"How'd you know my name? This fuckin' little narc tell you?"

"Everyone in the neighborhood knows who you are. No one likes you, but we all know your name. So if it's a reputation you're after, you've got one." She gave a short, deceptively easy laugh. "For being an absolute horse's ass."

"Angela—"

The shadow near the fence moved just as Chopper lunged.

"Protect the right flank, Mr. T!" Angela shouted, but she, too, was moving. She'd visualized her maneuver, start to finish, and she was ready to execute it. She dodged the full force of the weight her attacker threw against her. With Stevie yapping to spur her on, she drew out her hatpin and buried it in Chopper's pudgy groin. He yowled. She stuck her whistle in her mouth and blew for all she was worth as she doused him with pepper spray. He yowled again.

She pivoted toward Tommy T. "Catch!"

The spray can arced across the driveway.

Tommy T had one elbow in the shadow's neck. He snatched the atomizer out of the air, turned his face away, and let the punk have it. Another howl erupted as the acrid smell filled the air.

"Damn, I wish I had my beeper," Angela said, feeling pretty powerful when she saw that what she had was a teary kid, rubbing his eyes and rolling on the ground at her feet. He crooked one leg gingerly away from his body, like a freshly neutered dog trying to figure out how to pee.

Light filled an upstairs window. A window on the ground floor lit up, and the overflow of light defined the shapes in the driveway.

Tommy T had the other boy's arm bent behind his back. The boy was bigger, but Tommy T was pumped with triumph. "I wish I had my stun gun."

"*What* stun gun?"

"The one I gave Fox in my last strip."

"What's goin' on out here?" A porch light flooded the front step, but the man wasn't about to stick his head out. He shouted through the door. "This here's private property. I don't need . . . Angela, is that you?" A gray head of hair risked an appearance.

She recognized John Gleason from the Neighborhood Watch meetings. "Yes, John, it's me and Tommy T. We were ambushed by these two punks. Would you call the police for me, please?"

Jesse knew he couldn't outrun the screaming squad car, so he pulled over. The suburban cop strolled up to the window and flashed his light in Jesse's face. *Christ*, there wasn't time for this.

"I'll tell you right now . . . I don't have a driver's license"— *shit, Brown Wolf, come up with something*—"with me."

"Where is it?"

Jesse sighed *most* dramatically. "Somebody stole my billfold.

Today's been a real bitch, and if I don't get movin' here, it's gonna get worse. I've got a kid—"

"Home alone?"

"Right." That was good. Might even be true. "I'm really runnin' late."

"Registration?"

He turned on the dome light and pulled it out of the glove compartment, glancing at it quickly as he handed it over. His name, a fake address. The police department had provided the car, complete with registration and proof of insurance, but he hadn't had time to get a driver's license. He decided, right then and there, that he wanted a driver's license with his name on it and an address. A real address.

"Sorry to add to your troubles," the cop said as he handed him the citation. "You gotta slow down. Your kid needs you to get there in one piece, wouldn't you say?"

Yes, he *would* say. Moreover, Jesse needed Keith, and he needed him in one piece. He needed him under the gun first, quivering, cowering, as he looked down the barrel at certain and imminent death, but still in one piece and able to sing. And if the cops didn't scoop up the ball back there with Morrison and get him under lock and key, this would be the last time Jesse would play on their team.

On his way again, he smiled as he reached for the packets of clay paint he'd mixed earlier. The traditional white with black stripes. He'd thrown the makings of his wolf face into the car at the last moment. He hadn't been quite sure how it was going to figure in, but he'd had a hunch there would be one last hurrah for Dark Dog before he faded into the mists of legend.

The boy would love this. With any luck he wouldn't be a witness, so Jesse could even embellish it a little when he told him the story. He imagined himself looking over the boy's shoulder, making sure he got all the details of his face just so.

*   *   *

Keith was obviously feeling no pain and completely trusting of the man who accompanied him into the backyard. The two of them were laughing about something that had been going on inside. Keith lit a cigarette, puffed on it hungrily, adjusted his red-and-green baseball cap, and shuffled his feet. Higher than the price of gas, Jesse observed from his perch on the roof.

The beefy assassin lit a cigarette of his own. "Your boss says you've outlived your usefulness, Keith," he announced casually on the tail of a stream of smoke.

"What are you talking about?"

"The way he had it planned, you wouldn't know what hit you," the big man explained. "But that wouldn't be much fun. What I was thinking was, with all the snow you've eaten tonight, how 'bout a little dessert?" He unzipped his jacket and pulled out a pistol. "How 'bout this, huh? How 'bout you eat this? Quick and painless, and you're in control for once, for the final moment of your dumb-ass existence."

Jesse watched as the man forced the gun into Keith's hand. Sputtering some unintelligible sounds of protest, Keith dropped his cigarette. It was a game, Jesse realized. A game this guy had cooked up for a kid who was out of it. Totally out of it. The gun wouldn't be loaded. Either that or the first chamber was empty. But there would be another weapon somewhere, maybe two. Maybe ten.

The wolf pelt blocked the wind, but Jesse was chilled to the marrow. He felt numb, distant, as though his body were receding into the night and disappearing, but he made himself stay, made himself witness the icy spectacle of a young man looking down the barrel of a handgun. He saw Monica. He saw Ira. He saw Tommy T and Stoner and a thousand other young faces, untried lives, unsung songs.

"Do it, Keith," the big man said. "Do yourself a favor and"—he chuckled—"do yourself."

Predictably, Keith turned the pistol on his tormentor and pulled the trigger. The hollow click was predictable, too. The big man laughed maniacally as he reached behind his back.

Dark Dog dropped from the roof, fur pelt billowing like a cape. "What the hell . . ."

He bowled the big man off his feet, wrestled the gun away, then placed the barrel squarely in the middle of his back. "Don't make a sound." His voice rose only slightly above the sound of his pulse pounding in his head. Not pain. Just a simple blast of adrenaline.

Close by, a siren pierced the night's deceptive peace.

Welcome home, Jesse thought. *Let 'em know you're coming so they can welcome you home.*

He lifted his painted face and let the young sleeze he'd just saved get a good look at his unlikely rescuer. Let him think this was a trip to end all trips, and maybe, if the kid had anything resembling a brain in his head, it really would.

"Listen, Keith, if you want to live to see another sunrise, you'll lay that piece on the ground."

"Who the—*what* the hell are you?"

Dark Dog grinned. "What do I look like?"

"Some kinda . . . coyote man or something."

"Now, you see," he said to the man whose face he had planted firmly in the ground. "Keith's not such a dumb-ass. He knows a coyote from a murdering sonuvabitch, and what he's gonna do is . . . get over here, Keith." He motioned with the pistol. Blue lights were suddenly spinning all around the yard. The side door of the house flew open and the first of the rats scurried down the plank. "We're getting out of the way, just in case."

"Oh, Jesus . . ." Keith swayed, looking a little dizzy. He couldn't decide which way to jump, but he finally opted for his deliverer's side of the yard as dealers and hopheads spewed from the back door of the house and into the waiting arms of the police.

"Good idea. You just stand here quietly and pray." Jesse signaled one of the wide-eyed young uniforms now storming the yard as if it were a beachhead. "Hey! Bring me some cuffs."

The cop did a double take. "Who the hell are you?"

"See, you don't have to feel bad, Keith. Everyone asks the same question. Guess they can't believe they're really seeing me in the flesh." He grinned at the cop. Not a shot had been fired. Not a drop of blood had been shed. He didn't care how he looked or what anybody thought, because, *damn*, he was flying high. He laughed. "Hell, that's why I carry American Express."

"That's real funny," the cop said as he tossed a set of handcuffs. "Are they making a movie around here, or should I call Animal Control?"

"You should probably not insult Dark Dog when he's holding a gun."

"Dark who?"

"Dark Dog!" It was Tommy T, popping through the lilac bushes, eyes bugging out like a kid's at Christmas. "I knew you'd come. I just knew you'd smell trouble and come running."

"You gotta be kidding," said the cop who'd provided the handcuffs, watching the boy wrap his arms around his hero's waist.

"He's not kidding." Mike Richards appeared, beaming at the two of them like a talk-show host presiding over a gushy reunion he'd set up for TV. He gestured expansively. Besides Keith and his would-be executioner, the police had eight people in custody. "Does this look like a joke to you?"

"But Halloween's over."

Turning to Jesse, Mike ignored the rookie's remark. "We got the bundle you left in the trunk. You forgot to tell us what the magic word is for calling off the dogs. We had one hell of a time keeping them from separating Morrison from his balls."

Jesse ruffled Tommy T's hair. "No magic. You gotta be part dog."

"This guy's undercover, right?" The rookie had both men laughing. "I don't get it. He's an Indian, right? It's some kind of an Indian thing."

"Damn right it's an Indian thing, but it's got nothing to do with any movie. They never get it right in the movies." Tommy

337

T looked up at his hero. "And you should've seen how Angela and me took care of Chopper."

"Where is Angela?"

"She was right . . ." He turned toward the gate that led to the front yard. She was standing on the other side of the fence, trying to persuade the cop to let her through. "There she is. We were just turning Chopper over to the cops, and here comes more cops, so we didn't know if everybody was . . ."

Mike signaled the officer on gate duty to let her through. She strode through the yard as though she, too, were fully in charge. The costume didn't appear to surprise her, nor did the array of cops and criminals in her backyard. She only had eyes for her phantom and his sidekick, and they for her. It was a love feast of the eyes as she approached. Tommy T surrendered his position, instinctively recognizing the need for private words when she stepped up close to Dark Dog.

Jesse reached for her hands, clasped them in his, next to his thighs. "You okay?"

She nodded, her head bumping his chin. "You?"

"Sure, for somebody who looks like a fool, I'm—"

"You don't look like any such thing." She nodded over her shoulder, then glanced up. The paint made him look beautifully fierce. The look in his eyes was fiercely tender. She smiled. "Just ask the expert."

"For my final trick, I'm about to disappear into the night." The wolf snout was like the bill of a cap, his jewel eyes glittering beneath it just for her. He pointed with his lips. "For his sake."

She could hear Tommy T chattering with Mike. "For his sake . . . what?"

Dark Dog was backing away. Angela followed, tracing his steps, clutching his hands.

He gave a quick headshake. "You gotta let me go now. Otherwise, their next move is to unmask me." He took her by the shoulders, turned her around, and drew her back to him, planting a hasty kiss on the crown of her head. "And you can't watch. He can't see, even though you both . . ." Through the padding of her jacket she felt a firm squeeze. "Trust me, Angela. I love you." She stole a peek over her shoulder, and he smiled, his jewel eyes glittering. "Me. Jesse Brown Wolf. I love you."

She did as he asked. She turned away. She didn't hear a sound, but she felt his absence, and she knew the instant he was gone.

"Hey," Tommy T called out, his voice resonant with winning jubilation. "Where's Dark Dog?"

"He disappeared into the night," Angela quoted.

He grinned. "Bit-chiin."

She smiled. "Way cool."

She trusted him to come back to her, and when he didn't, she went looking for him. She went to The Den, and all she found was an empty hole. Everything was gone—the bed they'd made love in, the colorful wall hangings, the willow chair, the candlelight. Her flashlight illuminated nothing but dirt and rock. She didn't say anything to Tommy T. She was sure he knew.

She continued to tutor at Many Nations Elementary School, but she'd been looking forward to the holiday break. Deacon Peale had asked her to stay on at the café between Christmas and New Year's, but her waitressing days were over. After Christmas she would replace the third-grade teacher who had given notice that he would be moving on. She would be able to afford a bigger apartment with a bedroom for Tommy T. Together they had made a list of requirements, and he bought the newspaper himself every Sunday and combed through the rental section, marking "possibles" with a yellow highlighter.

She didn't have to worry about breaking her lease. On the heels of the spectacular drug bust in their backyard, the house on

Eighteenth—which, as it turned out, Morrison himself actually owned—had been claimed by the city, just as Mike Richards had promised. With the help of the Block Club and one of its sister associations, Homes 4 Us, Darlene had started the paperwork to make her dream of a shelter for homeless teens become a reality.

Christmas was a time for quiet celebration. The gifts were modest and practical, but the enthusiasm for the celebration and for each other was unrestrained. Everybody had a job to do to help get Christmas dinner on the tables that had been set up in Darlene's living room.

But Tommy T kept looking out the window, watching the sidewalk he and Tony had cleared of snow. He had a feeling he was getting something else for Christmas. He wasn't sure where the feeling came from, but it was burning so strong in his blood, he didn't question it. Something else was coming, something really good. And when it appeared—when *they* appeared—he realized that what he was getting wasn't just for him. The best part was going to be the sharing. The *really* best part was how happy she was going to be.

"Angela!" He collided with her in the kitchen doorway, took the mashed potatoes out of her hands, and set the dish on the nearest card table. Boy, he was going to bust for sure. "Angela, look who's—no, no, close your eyes. Gayla, give me that scarf." He pointed to the red muffler that Gayla—who looked like she was *really* going to bust for sure—was about to drape over a shelf for some kind of decoration. She'd been putting red-and-green junk up all over the place, but she parted with the scarf without debate.

"What in the world . . ." But Angela humored him, bending at his signal to come down to his level.

Gayla was closest when the knock sounded at the door.

"Tell them to keep their shirts on for a minute, okay?"

"Them?" Angela asked, smiling now, for she'd had an inkling, a strong Christmas feeling . . .

"Them there ey-y-es," Tommy T sang merrily as he tied the

blindfold in place, and then improvised. *"I've* got 'em cov-ered up, *I've* got 'em cov-ered up, them there ey-y-es."

Angela giggled. "That's a song you didn't pick up off the radio."

"How do you know? I listen to all kinds of stuff, especially when I'm drawing. Helps me get the feel of ... okay, now, open the door and bring in Angela's—" By this time all heads had popped out and up, all eyes on the door as Gayla opened it with the flourish Tommy T's gesture called for. There were a couple of squeals and a gasp or two, Gayla's included. *"Surprise!* that she's been pining away for ever since ..."

Angela's mysterious Christmas kiss was warm and wet, tasted like wintergreen, and smelled like winter in a man's hair. Her heart raced wildly as she put her arms around his neck and kissed him back, much to the delight of the room they were playing to. "Who is it?" she asked. "In the dark, I could swear it's ..."

"Okay, try this one." He changed the angle and kissed her again, eliciting applause this time.

"May I touch your face?" His cheeks were cold beneath her palms, his ears downright icy.

"You can look at my face." He pushed the blindfold over her head and greeted her with a loving smile. "And you can touch anything you want."

The hoots and cheers made her blush, but the invitation made her hug him eagerly. "Jesse, oh, Jesse, where have you been?"

"Tying up some loose ends. Here's one of them, right here." He turned to the guest he'd brought with him, who stood just inside the door with an arm draped around his brother's shoulders. "Stony Burke Little Warrior. Got himself a holiday pass."

"Pass for what?" Tommy T asked.

Stony beamed. "Jesse got me into a drug treatment program. Now I'm in a halfway house."

"Doing real good, too," Jesse said, slipping the boy an approving wink. "Both of us."

"You're in a program, too?" Angela asked.

"They're experimenting on me over at the university medical school." He laughed. "I'm one old dog who can actually sign a consent form."

Her eyes widened in horror. "*Experimenting* on you!"

"They're studying holistic alternatives to drugs for my headaches. It's helped a lot." He gave her an affectionate squeeze. "You've helped a lot, you and—" He smiled at Tommy T. "You and the Fox here."

"I should have been there with you when Mom died," Stony told his brother. "I'm sorry, I . . ." He shook his head, glanced at Gayla, and gave a tight smile. She was standing there awkwardly, obviously pleased to see him and unsure exactly how she ought to show it.

"Wasn't much for us to do except say good-bye," Tommy T said. "That's all we could do. That and try to stop bein' mad at her, which I'm workin' on. She couldn't help it, you know. She was just . . ."

Tommy T looked up at his brother, whose face had filled out and whose eyes were clear and sober and bright with gathering tears. The two hugged each other hard and fast, and the whole room vibrated with emotion when they emerged from the embrace, both furiously blinking back tears.

"We brought a turkey," Jesse announced, giving Stony the cue to raise the plastic grocery bag aloft. "Isn't that what the Indians brought to that pilgrim pot luck? A turkey?"

"That was Thanksgiving," little Billy informed him. "This is *Christmas*."

"Heck, the turkey's almost done already," Poppy announced.

"Wolf, you *are* a turkey." From the kitchen Darlene pointed an imperious finger at him. "Makin' this poor woman sit around and wonder would she ever see your big muzzle again. You had to know we had plans for you."

"What kind of plans?" He took off his jacket and signaled Stony to do the same.

"Work plans," Darlene said. "We had a work plan for you.

Rearranging walls, patching up holes, fixing plumbing, turning this place into a shelter for kids who don't want to spend the winter on the streets."

"That's a big job. Christmas, huh? You sure?" He greeted Billy by hauling him into his arms. "Those kids aren't always easy to handle."

"You wanna tell me all about it, Wolf? Like I don't know what it's like to ride herd on kids."

"I'm willing to help you out whenever I'm not working." He glanced at Angela, who couldn't stop watching his every move, couldn't stop smiling, could hardly believe he was actually there. "After I get through some extra training. I'll be working with kids myself." With some hesitation he turned to Tommy T. "As a cop."

Angela's eyes widened. "Really?"

Tommy T's narrowed. "A *cop*?"

Stony laid a hand on his brother's shoulder. "No, he's right. We need good cops. Black cops, white cops, red cops, yellow cops . . ."

Tommy T scowled back. "What have you been doin' out at that halfway house? Watchin' *Sesame Street*?"

"I was hidin' out from Chopper before you and Angela stuck it to him good."

"That was Angela stuck it to him," Tony supplied. "Don't nobody wanna mess with Angela's hatpin."

"Anyway, I was hidin' out. Ajax wasn't no help to me, couldn't hardly remember my name or nothin'. I didn't have no place to go, and I thought I was a dead man." He turned an affectionate grin Jesse's way. "And then this bloodhound tracked me down."

"Wrong breed," Jesse said with a laugh.

"Whatever." Stony went right on grinning. "He saved my life. Twice. And look at him. I don't care what he wears, he's got 'cop' written all over his face. So I figure he might as well get paid for it."

"Tell you what, Mike Richards has been hounding me on that

score, too." The boys groaned in unison, and Jesse laughed again. "Well, maybe I'm not the only dogface around, huh? Anyway, Mike's been *reminding* me that the police force should be part of the community, not an army of occupation. So he's right, there aren't enough Indian cops around here." He looked up at Angela as he set Billy down. "Did I ever tell you I used to be a pretty good cop?"

"You may have mentioned it."

He shrugged boyishly. "It might be a while before I'm willing to carry a gun. I might never be."

"All you need is a dog," Tommy T said. "I guess that might be pretty cool. Canine officer."

"Well, that's been suggested, too." He slipped his arm around Angela. "I hear you've got a new job."

"Very soon." She hugged his waist. "I'm so glad to see you."

"And I am . . ." He inhaled deeply. "*Real-ly* hungry for that turkey. Man, that smells good."

Dinner was a boisterously joyous affair with plates passed from table to table, kids up and down, laughter and stories in generous supply. Anyone who hadn't cooked was on cleanup detail. The scent of fresh-brewed coffee filled the rooms as the December sunlight dissolved in the windows. Jesse delivered two cups to the table where Angela and Darlene sat, relaxing, enjoying the after-dinner serenity. Half the kids were upstairs watching a movie, supervised by Gayla, willingly assisted by Stony. The rest were sleeping.

All but Tommy T, who had been waiting for the right moment to show Jesse his artwork. Jesse took his coffee and joined him on the sofa, where Tommy T opened his sketch pad and spread it across both their laps. The panel cartoons told the story of an unarmed hero smashing a drug ring to smithereens. "See, this is where Dark Dog leaps off the roof and onto—"

"That's a pretty tall building there." Jesse disputed this aspect with a skeptical look and a smile.

Tommy T shrugged. "He climbed out this window here. Here's Fox, see."

"Nice outfit. Pretty incredible detail." Jesse glanced away. The women were headed for the kitchen again, something about heating up the pies. He couldn't get over how sweet Angela looked in a simple sweater and slacks. Couldn't get over the way she'd greeted him, the way she kept looking at him, the way the gleam in her eyes made his blood rush . . .

Tommy T was staring at him.

He smiled. "So they've got you in a program for smart kids."

"I've got a mentor in art. He's a cartoonist for the *Star Tribune*. He's pretty good himself, but he does political stuff. The best part is . . ." He slapped his work proudly with the back of his hand. "This is gonna get published as a real comic book."

"No kidding?" Jesse was truly impressed. "I probably won't be able to afford you anymore."

"I'm gettin' a lot more than five bucks a pop, I'll tell you that." Tommy T studied him intently, unabashedly. "You still have custody of me? Like . . . as if you was my dad or something?"

Jesse returned a steady look. "How would you feel about that?"

"Well, I tell you . . ." The boy's eyes strayed toward the kitchen. The voices of the women drifted back to them, a timeless, boundless comfort. "Angela's kinda like my mom now. So if you wanna be my dad . . ." He turned to Jesse again, expectancy in his eyes, his young jaw set. "You're gonna have to marry my mom. Because that's the way it's supposed to be. I really believe that's the right way to do things."

Jesse's heart swelled like a helium balloon. "You do, huh?"

"So if you wanna do right by my mom, I'd feel just fine about that. How would you feel about having a son?"

"Blessed," he said quietly, his throat tight. "Like crawlin' out of a hole, Tommy T. Like I'd been given a second chance."

Tommy T turned a page in his sketchbook. "I've been to The Den," he said reverently, and they both looked at his rendition of the place on paper, the profusion of candles, the baskets of dried herbs, the cat sitting on a rocky ledge, and the face of a wolf in the shadows.

"I don't live there anymore," Jesse said.

"It was a cool place."

"Yeah, it was. But it was a place to hide. I'm done hiding." He swallowed hard. "You helped me put the pieces back together, Little Fox."

"I hate to lose Dark Dog," Tommy T said sadly.

"You've got him right here," Jesse said, tapping a finger on the sketch pad. Then he touched the geometric design in the middle of the boy's school T-shirt. "Right here, too, Tommy T. That's where you mended him. You took him to your heart."

The boy looked up at him with his face so full of guileless wonder that it made Jesse want to weep for joy. *A second chance.* He managed a smile. "Hey, if I'm gonna be somebody's dad, I have to earn a living, and the hero business didn't pay very well."

"It's gonna pay me. Can you imagine getting *paid* for making up heroes?"

Jesse laughed and shook his head, but it really wasn't that big of a stretch. Not for his boy. Not for Tommy T.

"And guess what. I'm getting an eagle feather from Grandpa Bird. After that night when, you know, we busted all those creeps and punks and all-around sons of bitches, Grandpa Bird said I'd counted coups and earned a feather. So I'm going to a *yuipi* ceremony, and I'm gonna learn some songs, and then I'm getting a feather." He gave Jesse's arm a shoulder bump. "You wanna go with me?"

Jesse bumped back. "Wouldn't miss it for the world."

The *yuipi* was held in the backyard sweat lodge of one of the teachers from Many Nations Elementary School. An assembly of men, young and old, came together to pray in the traditional way, with hot rocks and purifying steam, sage and song. Arthur Bird tied an eagle feather in Tommy T's hair, made curlier than usual by the steam, and one in Jesse's long, straight hair, left unbound for the occasion.

Later, Jesse joined the old man for a private moment at the edge of a small frozen pond. He hunched his shoulders against the chill wind blowing off the ice, the eagle feather fluttering next to his face. The old man waited. Finally Jesse asked, "Am I still Coyote?"

The old man took his time, too. "What do you think?"

"Some days, yeah."

"Can't do without Coyote. He sets things—"

"I know, I know, he sets things right." Jesse sighed. "That's a wolf pelt you gave me, not a coyote pelt."

The old man shrugged. "It's what we had. It's what the boy traded me for. We urban Indians, we make adjustments."

Jesse blew a puff of mist and watched it dissipate over the pond. "So how long do I have to keep the pelt?"

"Until you find a successor." Arthur Bird cackled. "Took me a hell of a long time."

"Yeah. Thanks a bunch."

"My grandfather told me that boys start looking like men long before they really get to be men. In the old days the men would take the boys and show them, test them, make them prove themselves.

"And then the old days were gone. Things started to change, and the men stopped doing these things we're doing today—making the sweat, sharing the pipe, teaching the songs. And the boys, you know, they didn't know what to do with themselves. A lot of them just stayed boys in men's bodies. Coyote's like that sometimes." He gave Jesse an appraising once-over. "Looks like the men might be growing up faster these days."

"You think so?"

"I was gray-headed when I finally got the message." The old

man punched him in the shoulder. "At least you're not gray-headed."

"I still get the headaches sometimes."

"Yeah, well, I got arthritis." Arthur Bird's eyes glittered like jewels in the cold winter sun. "It's always something, ain't it?"

Epilogue

Spring had been slow in coming. After all the excitement in the winter months, what with Angela's new job, the wedding in February, and the baby coming, then one adoption after another and the new apartment on Lake Street, it was a lot for a guy to get used to all at once. Top it off with being cooped up with a crying baby and all that snow in March, man! Tommy T was glad to see the first buds on the trees, the yellow-green grass, and the tiny purple flowers springing up amid last year's fallen leaves. He was glad to see the river flowing ice-free.

And he was glad to find that The Den was still there, still undiscovered, as far as he could tell, like some small island in a huge urban sea, invisible, unchanged, undisturbed. Still a magic place.

It was late afternoon, and he was feeling a little weird, which was the way he'd felt a lot lately. He didn't know how to describe it, exactly. He thought of it as being itchy inside. Mad at everybody and nobody in particular. Bored, even though he had plenty to do. Unsettled, even though he was more settled than he ever had been. Ever since he'd turned thirteen last month, his skin had felt tight all over his body. It was . . . weird.

He squatted in front of the entrance to The Den. He heard footsteps, and he hunkered down even though he knew who it was. He knew there was no use hiding. He was glad about that in a way. In another way he was mad as hell. It was . . . weird.

"I thought I might find you here." He refused to look up when Jesse squatted beside him. "Checkin' out the old digs, huh?"

"You come back here by yourself sometimes," Tommy T said, hating himself for pouting like a kid. "I know you do."

"You're right. I do." Jesse snapped a twig in half. "Especially when things aren't going just right."

"You think about running away, moving back?"

There was a long pause. Together they watched the river flow, let it wash through their minds, settle the grit. "Is that what you're thinking about?" Jesse asked finally.

"I was only a couple of hours late getting back from my art class. I saw some guys I used to know." He stopped to adjust the tone of his voice. Damn, he hated that whining kid voice, and he especially hated it when he caught himself trying it on Jesse. It never got him anywhere. He cleared his throat. "I was just show-ing them some of my drawings."

"Ajax?"

"He always liked my drawings."

"I know. I've been trying to get Ajax off the streets, back into school. It's tough. He says he's too old to change." Jesse snapped another twig and tossed it toward the river bluff. "Kid's nineteen. If he doesn't change, he may not see twenty."

"Maybe I could . . ."

"Not if it means hangin' out on the streets, Tommy T. We're lookin' for you to come home at a certain time; you don't show up, we go lookin'. We need to know you're okay." He chuckled. "Angela was ready to call out the National Guard."

"Shit."

Another long pause. Just like old times, Tommy T thought.

Just the two of them, talking without staring each other down, without getting in each other's face.

"Getting used to having a baby around hasn't been easy, has it?"

Bingo. Yeah, he had a few things to say about that. "You guys coulda had your own baby, you know, later on. You didn't have to take Gayla's baby."

"She asked us to. And we all three talked about it, and we agreed."

"I . . . didn't know the kid was gonna cry so much."

"You didn't know she was going to take so much of Angela's time."

"Did you?"

Jesse chuckled. "No, I guess I didn't . . . remember."

"Well, I don't care about that part of it. I got my own stuff to do. I'm around Angela at school. Hell, I can't do nothin' without her finding out."

"Sure you can. You're in charge of yourself, Tommy T."

He looked over at Jesse. He'd kind of gotten to like the way Jesse looked in his blue jacket with the police patch on it. But he couldn't help remembering how cool he'd looked with his face painted for war. No weapons, nothing. Just his wits and his traditional ways.

His father. Damn, that was hard to believe.

"'Member when I used to come here, and we used to talk?"

Jesse smiled. "*You* used to talk."

"Yeah, but you listened. I always knew you was listening." He stood up, his eyes on the river, the ripples glistening in the sunlight. "I felt like I wasn't alone then, you know? Plus, we had our freedom."

Jesse stood, too. He shoved his hands in his pants pockets and looked across the river, side by side with Tommy T, watching the cars catch pieces of sunlight as they trickled slowly across the bridge. "You remember what it was like the rest of the time, being alone?"

"Yeah." Cold, mostly, even in the summer. It always came back to that, when he started thinking about it. Feeling cold. Being hungry, being tired and not being able to sleep, being scared. Maybe freedom wasn't quite the right word.

"That was before we had Angela."

"Yeah." *Angela.* He had to smile, remembering the first time he'd seen her getting that white squirrel to take food from her hand.

"Now we've got—" Jesse laid a hand on his shoulder and rocked him, like they were buds. "Hell, Fox, you and me, we've got a family. We've got ourselves a whole damn tribe."

"Yeah." Tommy T nodded. It was true, they had a lot to take care of, and mostly that was cool. They still spent a lot of time at the house on Eighteenth; Jesse was teaching him how to do carpentry, plumbing, masonry. When he got his own place, he was going to be able to fix things himself.

Jesse tapped a small rock with the toe of his boot and sent it rolling down the embankment. Trying to raise a boy who was used to raising himself was a major challenge. He faced similar challenges on the job. Similar, but not the same. Tommy T was his son, and there were special things a guy wanted to give his son. Special powers, superpowers, like wisdom and courage. It took a lot of courage to pick up the pieces, to change what needed to be changed, to move on.

The glue, as he'd once told his gutsy angel, thinking he'd made some big discovery, was love. News to Angela? Hardly. The key, she'd taught him, was acceptance. Acceptance and respect. He'd started with himself, with Coyote, and worked his way up from there.

"I come here sometimes when things aren't goin' just right," Jesse confessed, "and I remember what it was like, living alone down there. Maybe it was what I needed then. 'Cause I felt like shit most of the time, so I really felt like I belonged in a hole." Tommy T looked up at him. Jesse saw an old man's empathy in

354

a young man's eyes, and he confided, "What I need now is my family."

Tommy T nodded. "Your daughter's comin' out sometime this summer, right?"

"Her mom's bringin' her out to see the Mall of America, Valley Fair, and me. Monica wants to ride the Wild Thing out at Valley Fair." He sighed and shook his head. "I think you might have to stand in for me on that one, partner. I've never ridden a roller coaster."

"No kidding?"

Jesse shook his head again, and it was Tommy T's turn to confide, "Neither have I."

"Okay, okay, we take the whole damn tribe, and we all pile on." He shivered, envisioning himself on the ride he'd only seen in TV advertisements. "Jeez, that thing looks mean, though. I don't know . . .'"

"Somebody has to stay with the baby," Tommy T said, and then each one pointed to himself, and they both laughed.

"You know what else I've never done?" Tommy T ventured. "I've never built a tree house."

"A tree house?" Jesse gave a mock scowl. "You workin' on a bird hero or something?"

Grinning now, Tommy T shrugged. "We did the underground thing. Do you think we're too old for a tree house?"

Jesse considered the face of his son and thought about Arthur Bird's crazy riddles, something about a man in a boy's body, a boy in a man's body. Wisdom and courage were all well and good, but what about childhood? Here was a boy who was about to become a man before he'd had much of a chance to be a boy.

"Actually, I think I'm due for some high livin'." Jesse tipped his head back and scanned the treetops. "Yessir, Little Fox, with your imagination and my ingenuity, I think you and me could put together one hell of a good tree house."